Guyana Betrayal

Norma DeHaarte

GUYANA BETRAYAL

Norma De Haarte

Sister Vision
Black Women and Women of Colour Press

ISBN 0-920813-80-1

Canadian Cataloguing in Publication Data

De Haarte, Norma 1933-
Guyana Betrayal

ISBN 0-920813-80-1

I. Title.

PS8557.E483G89 1991   C813'.54   C91-093700-1
PR9199.3.D443G89 1991

Editor: Nan Peacocke
Copy Editor: Hazelle Palmer
Cover Painting: Rachel Henriques
Cover & Book Design: Stephanie Martin
Typesetting: HINDSight
Printed and bound in Canada by union labour

Published by   Sister Vision Press
               P.O. Box 217
               Station E
               Toronto, Ontario
               Canada M6H 4E2

Dedication:

To Joy and to all my children and grandchildren

Acknowledgement

My thanks to Stephanie Martin and Makeda Silvera for believing in the project and for their enthusiasm, support and constructive criticism.

Nan Peacocke for the long periods spent together during the editorial work and her care and respect for the manuscript.

My friend Charisse De Freitas who said to me - 'go for it, it have great potential'.

Tamai Kobayashi, of Sister Vision Press for all her work on the manuscript.

The existing generation is master of both the training and the entire circumstances of the generations to come; it cannot indeed make them perfectly wise and good, because it is itself so lamentably deficient in goodness and wisdom; and its best efforts are not always, in individual cases, its most successful ones, but it is perfectly well able to make the rising generation, as a whole as good as, and a little better than itself. If society lets any considerable number of its members grow up mere children, incapable of being acted on by rational considerations of distant motives, society has itself to blame for the consequences.

John Stuart Mill
Utilitarian, On Liberty and Considerations
on Representative Government.

Guyana...thank you for your most sweet voices.
Norma De Haarte

Prologue 1973

When Phyllis Barnes finally decided to get out of bed, it was five-thirty in the morning. She had been lying there, trying to go back to sleep for the longest while. She did not know what had awakened her, but there she was, tossing and turning from side to side. Changing positions did not help. She even tried to lie on her stomach, but that was worse.

Phyllis' thoughts wandered on to the unrest in the city. New Town was suddenly restless. Too many people were on the streets in heated political discussions about the government's policy and what they were actually doing for their people. There were few jobs for adults and fewer still for young people. There was angry talk about the need for training programmes. At the height of all this was the promised retrenchment. Worst of all, the police were using rough methods to break up groups of youths who lingered idly around the city. The people's problems, however, were not personal enough to cause her alarm and the discomfort she felt. She sat up then, pulling on her slippers, thinking about things close to home. Right at this moment things were going alright, the children were doing well at school and settling down for exams. "Well!" she sighed, "everyone except Alex."

Phyllis thought about her conversation with Tom several days ago when she had hinted at Alex's restlessness.

"Stop worrying about the boy, he's okay. Just like a young boy growing up," her husband suggested. "He's going to be fine, you know.

Alexander is a great name and a great man too," he said, laughing lightly, not wanting to be serious.

"That's the same thing," she retorted. "That name! Why can't you say Alex like everyone else? I think that name is too much of a burden and responsibility for..."

"Women!" he cut in. "Always discontented with something or the other. The real reason you don't like the name, is because it's my grandfather's name. Why don't you say so? But he was a colourful old chap in his day," Tom added.

"Hm hmph," Phyllis tried to stifle a comment but failed. "Colourful indeed!" she countered; this was a sore point, but she didn't want to get into any more arguments about the name.

"Colourful, yes," Tom insisted, "after all, what would you call a man who sowed a few wild oats? Remember it was he who set down the family business, our good fortune today." Tom would not let up. "Sure he went away to the bush for a while, but he brought back gold." He paused, "Money!"

"Hmph hmph," Phyllis responded again and of course failed in her attempt not to be critical. "If you call abandoning the family for years, with not a word about your whereabouts 'colourful'." She paused, "I can only say that your idea and my idea of colour is not the same... But, we do have the store," she conceded.

Tom was sobered by his wife's remarks. He had sensed Alexander's restlessness during the past week, so he said soothingly, "Don't worry too much dear, after all he's our son and he will be okay." Then to himself more than to Phyllis, he continued. "We'll keep an eye on him and do the best we can. He's just a boy and you know what boys are like. I think we should give him some serious responsibilities right now, since we want him to run the business later. That ought to keep him busy. What do you think about that?" Just then the telephone rang and Tom got up to take the call.

Phyllis felt relieved for the moment. There were things she did not tell Tom. She had been waiting for the right opportunity to do so. Alex did not like the store. He was always in a hurry to leave, not like his younger brother Eric who was fourteen years old, the image of his father, strong, not too handsome, but very enthusiastic about the store. After school in the afternoons he would hurry there to help. On Saturdays he would be up early, taking a quick breakfast so that he could leave with his father and be the first to stand behind the counter in the patent medicine section. Eric liked being there, he was quite different from Alex.

Phyllis remembered too well Alex's anger last Saturday when she asked him to help Paul Ben, who worked in the hardware section. "Alex!" she had called out to him, having seen him make a few trips to the entrance and back. "Today is a busy day," she said, trying to encourage him. "Customers are waiting. Go and give Paul a hand and stop marching backwards and forwards."

"Look Ma," Alex answered sullenly, "you know I can't stand this place! I ain't able to get my hands dirty with paint oil and putty and dem things."

"Look boy, don't waste time talking. Get the customers what they want," she encouraged.

"Why not ask smarty over there to give a hand?" countered Alex, pointing to Eric, "he ain't doing nothing now, just standing there as if he own the place."

"Don't stand there and argue," his mother scolded, trying to control her rising temper. "I don't want any argument! We'll straighten this out later."

Phyllis had sensed Alex's growing resentment whenever he was asked to help out. She decided it was time for a showdown and a serious talk, but not in front of the customers. She hoped that he would stay for a while at least and was perturbed when she called later across the aisle for Alex, only to hear Paul say wearily, "Miss Phyllis, Alex lef' as soon as your back turn."

So he had openly defied her. However, worse than Alex's behaviour last Saturday, was the encounter she had with him downtown, during school hours. She was very angry. How long had this been going on and with his 'O' Level exams only two months away in June.

Alex was just as surprised to see her. But what shocked her most was his companions, Kevin Marshall, Vida Das and another boy. They were all far older than Alex, in their mid-twenties. More alarming was the fact that Marshall, known as "Cat", and Das, known as "Dealer" were young men well known to the public and the police alike. She knew nothing about the other youth who stood in the background. Her heart skipped a beat. My God! she thought, Alex with these young criminals! She panicked and scolded loudly. "Alex, what the devil you doing out of school at this time and with these boys?"

3

Hearing this was enough, Alex was embarrassed by his mother's loud scolding. "I ain't doing nothing," he said, his anger rising. "What you see me doing?" he asked insolently, "I only standing here talking to my friends."

"Friends!" she cried out, visibly shaken, frowning at the youths. "I didn't know that, that..." she stammered.

"Well they are," Alex said wilfully, "even if you don't like it."

"Alex," she said with authority, "you're coming with me right now."

"I will come, when I finish talking to my friends," Alex said to complete the finale.

To her annoyance, passersby were becoming interested in the little scene. She tried to save face. "Listen, I'm going to the bank at Main and Murray Street," she said. "Meet me there in half an hour."

As she walked away, she tried to calm her nerves, her rising fears about Alex's odd behaviour. Seeing him now with the boys, she said a silent prayer he would obey her instruction to meet her at the bank.

That was yesterday. Alex had not met her at the bank.

As she quickly prepared breakfast, she pondered how she was going to put it over to Tom, whose hopes were for Alex to manage the store, that all was not right with their eldest son. Why couldn't Alex be like the others? He was only one year younger than his sister Daphne, the eldest. Daphne was nineteen, self-possessed and a fine looking young lady. She was an excellent accountant and she would surely become a manager at the city bank where she worked. There was Eric who knew what he wanted. He was going to be a pharmacist. She was proud of him.

"Morning Ma," Daphne called in a hushed voice as she came into the kitchen, yawning. "What you doing up so early. I hear the noise and get up to see who's moving about," she said, looking closely at her mother.

"Morning girl," Phyllis greeted her, "hope you sleep good, 'cause I scarcely had a wink last night."

"Why?" Daphne asked, laughing lightly. "You and Daddy had a row? It must have been after I fall asleep, 'cause I didn't hear a thing. I'll fix the table," she offered, waiting for her mother's reply.

"Girl, you know your father. He doesn't quarrel with nobody. He just say what he got to say and he's finished," Phyllis said. "No girl, I worried about Alex. Lately, you see how he's behaving in the house, getting on everybody nerves. Then yesterday guess who I see that boy with downtown and during school hours? Cat and Dealer! Them two criminals." She took a breath, "Child, I nearly get a heart attack, I really worried."

"Look Ma, don't worry with that boy," Daphne comforted, conscious of her distress. "Sometimes I think all he want is two hard cuffs and that should settle him down..." Then giving the matter a little more thought, she added, "But you know Daddy, he let that brother of mine get away with a lot of things and he now feeling big before his time. Alexander the Great!" she scoffed. "His problem is that he got a swell head. Ma, you just leave him to Daddy and don't worry yourself too much." As far as she was concerned, there was one simple way of solving the whole thing and settling down her problem brother. She surveyed the breakfast table, added the final touches and left the kitchen to get ready for work.

Phyllis was still thinking of a way to tell Tom about Alex when the family finally sat down to breakfast. As the memory of Alex and his companions flashed through her mind she felt an urgent need to get the situation out in the open but she waited calmly until everyone was finished and had left the table. Then very casually she said, "Tom, let's take a few minutes and talk about Alex."

Tom, who felt he had given the matter the attention it deserved, and that Phyllis was overreacting, said with impatience, "Look Phyl, the last time we talked about Alexander, I thought the matter was settled. You only worrying uselessly."

"Well, you don't have to behave so cranky, I can't help worrying. And if you think giving him something special to do at the store is the answer, go right ahead," she said, irritated. However, she knew he had a lot on his mind and decided that for the present, it was better not to say anything about Alex's companions.

Tom, regretting his outburst, tried to ease the tension. "Girl, you know I very busy this morning, 'cause I got to go down to the wharf and get them goods that come in. You know the boys that work down at that waterfront," he said with emphasis. "And you know if I don't hurry down there fast and get them crates off today, you know what's going to happen and we can't afford it. So I got to move fast if we want to make a profit off this shipment."

He paused. Phyl said nothing.

"And don't forget the work we got to do, after we get those crates to the shop," he said. Then seeing her frown he sighed and added, "Look, I'm promising now that we'll thrash the matter out on Sunday." He got up and left the table deep in thought but Phyl knew Alex was distant from his mind when he drove off with Daphne and Eric.

"Well, I'll just have to wait," Phyl spoke her thoughts out loud. However, she made up her mind to use every opportunity to keep an eye on Alex.

"Alex," she called out. She knew he always lingered in the mornings and that gave her an idea.

"Alex, Alex," she called, "wait for me and let's leave together."

"But Ma, you'll only make me late," Alex said, grumbling, as he entered the sitting room to find Phyl latching the windows.

"Help me lock the others and check the other rooms quickly, then we'll leave right away," she said, ignoring Alex's sullen expression. They closed the house quickly and left.

They lived on the outskirts of New Town in a beautiful bungalow, lately renovated and comfortably furnished. There was a well kept kitchen garden which supported the family's needs and well placed coconut and other fruit trees surrounding the property. Phyl and Daphne were working relentlessly on the front garden, which presented a splash of suburban elegance.

Transportation was always a problem and today it proved to be no different. However, they took a taxi, and it took only a few minutes to get downtown.

Phyl stopped the taxi a couple of blocks from Alex's school. They continued on foot. "Look Ma, you can't come to school with me," he said with resentment. "What my friends would think?"

"Friends! Don't use that word to me at all," Phyl scolded, remembering the boys she saw with him. "I don't know how you get in company with those crimin... wild boys." She hesitated to use the word to describe his companions. She could not come to terms with it and might further increase his resentment.

"I'm not going to the school gate with you, but as soon as I get to the store, I'll call your teacher to find out if you're at school. And mind you, I'll call again after lunch time," she persisted.

"You can't do that Ma," Alex protested. "When my friends find out, they will laugh at me, especially now they see you following me."

"I have no intention following you around. But I'm making sure you do what's expected of you," she said sternly.

"Ma! You said you're not going to the school gate, now look where we reach already," Alex said with such irritation that she felt guilty,

6

because they were now opposite the school, only a few yards from the entrance.

"Alright," she said and stopped. "Don't forget. I'll call your principal as soon as I reach the store," she added as she hurried away, crossing the road to get to her destination.

Alex turned away angry and frowning. He hated the idea. Treating me like a child! he thought bitterly.

As she left, Phyl saw Alex was still frowning and she smiled secretly. She was not going to call the principal, not yet. However, she realised she had touched a sensitive nerve and knew that he was not going to leave the school compound today nor tomorrow for that matter. She was going to take the situation in hand bit by bit, a day at a time and hopefully she'd have a good plan in mind by Friday.

Phyl had become aware over the past few days that the tensions in the city had heightened, moving steadily towards a calamity. It was not the arguments that disturbed her. Those lively heated discussions had suddenly changed and people were swearing vengeance as an outlet for their pent up hostilities. Patience was slowly ebbing, as somehow the past seemed to interfere and become a hindrance to the present, which appeared not to provide the promised rewards and satisfaction that would lessen frustration, humiliation, hurt and anger. There was no doubt the mood of the entire city was changing and she knew sooner or later, every man, woman and child would be affected.

Friday dawned bright and sunny. There was not a cloud in the sky. It was going to be a beautiful day. The morning bore no signs of the approaching storm.

At breakfast, everyone was more than surprised to hear Alex ask his father if he wanted him to help at the store. He explained he had nothing to do at school that day since the other classes were doing exams in his classroom. Tom questioned him about his exams and after satisfying himself Alex was not shirking his class work, agreed he could help. Tom explained what he had in mind to do with the new goods that had arrived. As Tom talked with Alex, he glanced across the table at Phyl, who could not help but notice the look of triumph on his face. Didn't he tell her that Alexander was going to be alright?

Phyl pondered her son's sudden enthusiasm, but she was relieved and shrugged off her disbelief with a sigh. She knew it would be busy. With the pressures brought on by unloading the crates, no one, not even

Alex, would have time to complain. Things were working out fine — Alex had provided his own solution for Friday.

After breakfast, Tom drove the family downtown. He let Eric off at the entrance of his school and Daphne at the bank.

The store opened at nine-thirty on Fridays, and just as Phyl had predicted, there was no time to spare.

Tom, Phyl, Alex and another store hand, worked in the back while Paul and the cashier minded the store. Everyone was involved, caught up in a traffic of checking, counting, unpacking and stacking. The morning passed quickly.

Near lunch time, Phyl with her arms laden was moving towards the front of the store, when she saw Paul coming towards her, talking excitedly.

"Listen! Listen to this, Miss Phyllis," he said, pointing to the portable radio he carried. "Like all hell break loose, they got trouble downtown! It just come over the radio that everybody on strike. Teachers walk off the job; water works and sewage workers follow them too. The civil servants and even stevedores walk off," Paul spoke rapidly, paused, took a breath then went on. "Thank God Tom worked fast and get them crates off the wharf yesterday!" During this recital Paul went with Phyl who signalled she couldn't hear a word from the radio, deposited her load, arranged the items quickly on a shelf, then moved towards the back-store, Paul following with the radio so everyone could listen to the news. By the time they got to Tom, the news was being repeated once again. This time Paul remained silent, gesturing to them to listen.

"Thank God Alex in the store today," Phyl sighed to herself, glancing at him in relief.

The announcer was saying, "It seems that a large number of government workers have taken to the streets, bearing placards. Right now we are trying to estimate the number and groups of workers on strike, as well as the unions representing these workers. Our reporters are at work getting these facts and figures for your information; the situation looks grave. As soon as these figures are available we will immediately report them to you. Thank you, and now back to some light music." He concluded his report.

However, no music came on as they all waited, listening, tense and expectant. It was the announcer's voice that broke the silence.

"Ladies and gentlemen. We have another news flash. Fires and looting have been reported downtown. There has been no report of injury so far and the police are already on the scene. We ask you to cooperate by staying in your homes. There is no cause for alarm. Therefore, we implore you to keep off the streets and stay calm. Everything is under control. Thank you." He said as he terminated the report, "we will be keeping you informed."

Paul ventured a comment in the silence that followed the report. "Lord! The country come apart. The people tired with pushing around, man! Poor wages, poor working conditions, no work for the majority of people and nobody listening."

The others stood in a daze, too stunned to comment. It was unbelievable that such events had actually happened and in such a short time. Phyl instinctively turned to look for Alex. "Tom!" she cried out, "Alex gone."

Everyone stared at the spot where Alex had been standing only a moment ago, but he was nowhere to be seen.

Tom moved towards Phyl and held her, "Man, pull yourself together. Why you taking on and carrying on so?" he said scowling. "After all, he is a boy and you know boys like to go to those things. He had to sneak out, he couldn't ask you to go."

"But Tom," Phyl said, feeling slightly embarrassed at her reaction. "You hear the police out there and you know that means there will be shooting. You hear they pleading with people to stay home." She stifled a sob and looked at Tom for understanding. She couldn't explain this premonition of disaster. So she said, "You know with the police and the situation down there anything could happen. Just anything could happen and Alex out there."

Tom decided to close the store. Phyl and the other employees except for the watchman were sent home. It took some doing but he was finally able to convince Phyl it was better for her to go home.

"Stop worrying about the boy," he said, trying to calm her fears. "If I hadn't the store to secure, I too might have gone to see what's happening and I'm sure when you get home, Alex will be there or get there shortly after."

Tom tried to control himself, he was exasperated by Phyl's behaviour during the past few days. He felt she was making a big fuss around nothing, after all, boys will be boys. He knew that well. He couldn't understand why she carried on as she did just now, she surprised him. He was very angry but did not want to show his irritation when his employees were around. He made up his mind to thrash the matter out once and for all on Sunday.

After Phyl and the others left, Tom and the watchman worked quickly to board and bar the windows and doors. His attempts to secure the store were modest, but he had no intention of making things easy for looters.

As usual, Eric stopped at the store. There he found only his father and the watchman, working speedily at the task of securing the building. Tom insisted Eric leave immediately for home. Eric, not one to be easily thwarted, proceeded to give his version of the teachers walkout, as well as other incidents he had witnessed on his way to the store.

"Dad! If you see people on the streets," he said excitedly, "either they going to the fire or they coming from the fire with things in they hands."

"Oh yes. And what were you doing there sir?" Tom asked somewhat annoyed.

"Well..." Eric hesitated, a little embarrassed. "I wasn't exactly at the fire. I was in a side street across from the fire and the looting," he said as he tried to allay his father's suspicions, explaining quickly, then before any other interruptions added, "I saw a man fetching a king size spring-filled mattress on his head, he alone. And another short man carrying a refrigerator on his back and..."

"A refrigerator?" Tom asked sharply, "Boy you making fun."

"Yes Dad, a refrigerator," Eric said, nodding his head. "One big like the one we got here in the store."

"Good Christ!" Tom said loudly, looking upwards, "people gone crazy or something?"

"And Dad," Eric continued, "this lady come down the streets with one of them lunch baskets hanging on the handle bar of her bicycle, if you see shoes. All kinds of shoes, but the joke was, the lady wearing only oneside shoes."

"That was no lady," Tom snorted in disgust, his anxiety rising. "Look son, we can't do anything about what going on atall. All I can do is try to protect this store the best I can. You try run along home now."

As Eric turned to go Tom asked, "You see Alexander anywhere by the fire?"

"No Dad... but if he gone there he ain't going home just now. Ah going Dad," he added, going through the doorway when Tom called out. "Go straight home, no more side street viewing for you. Go straight home," he repeated as Eric went out the door, nodding his head.

It was already 9:00 p.m. Phyl had been home for hours with Daphne and Eric, who had already given their versions of what they had witnessed and what they heard about the upheaval downtown. There was no sign of Alex and Phyl couldn't shake off the feeling something was wrong.

She paced backwards and forwards, staring out of the window, down the street in the direction which Alex must come but there was still no sign of him.

Tom got home at 11:00 o'clock. He entered the house calling for Alex but it was Phyl, her face lined with worry, who explained Alex was not there. What the hell is this! thought Tom, now fully understanding the misery Phyl was going through as he too became worried.

"Look, I..." he said, hesitating. He had decided he would go downtown and search for Alexander. But just as he was about to leave, they heard footsteps on the stairs.

"Ha, you see you like to worry too much," he chided Phyl, trying to hide his true feelings, laughing lightly. "Hear the boy coming up the steps now," he said and rushed to open the door, only to see a policeman standing on the threshold. Tom was startled, he was so shaken he was barely able to talk to the tall, dark officer towering over him.

"Are you Thomas Barnes?" the policeman asked. Tom nodded his head, a sinking sensation in his stomach.

"Do you know anyone named Alexander Barnes?" the policeman went on. Tom stuttered as he identified the name as his son's.

"Sir," continued the policeman, "we would like you to come down to the station, your son was caught looting... Ah... he was shot..."

"Oh God, no!" Phyl cried out, horrified.

"Nothing serious, just a slight leg wound." The officer's voice was calm. "Your son was held... and he is to be charged along with one Kevin Marshall and Vida Das for the murder of Sue Choy, owner of Choy's Supermarket on Broad Street."

A horrible silence followed, marked by Phyl's accelerated breathing, then a loud moan. Tom turned in time to see her falling to the floor and grabbed her.

"Get the smelling salts quick," he said to Daphne as he and Eric tried to get Phyl to the settee. Daphne was back in a flash and Tom, holding the phial to Phyl's nostrils, revived her. As she opened her eyes and tried to sit up, Tom asked, "You okay now? Don't try to get up, lie still for a while," he coaxed. It was only then he remembered the policeman, who

11

had been standing at the threshold, but came in to help. "I'll be with you in a moment," he said.

"Tom, I have to go with you," Phyl said, "I can't stay here and worry about what's happening."

"Well, if you feel strong enough," Tom conceded. "We'll both go down to the station."

Phyl's mind was in a turmoil as she dressed hurriedly. She looked at the frightened faces of Daphne and Eric and told them not to wait up, everything was going to be alright, repeating over and over, "That's not Alex. We know him well. There's got to be a mistake!" She knew it was useless but what could she say to them to ease their distress, even her own. Where had she and Tom gone wrong? They had tried so hard to be good parents. Had she been over-reacting in her zeal to do what was right and had been too firm, even hostile or unkind to Alex? How did all this start anyway?

The Beginning 1947

"I say, old chap, I've seen you some place before. Bill Kelly, Cambridge... This is my friend and colleague, Courtnay Stokes. We are on our way to British Guiana," said the tall, slim young man, his hand extended in friendship.

The stranger greeted Hoffman as he moved down the aisle looking for his seat.

"Hoffman. Lucius Hoffman, Gray's Inn, also bound for British Guiana, my homeland. Happy to make your acquaintance," he said and shook hands.

"That's it," Kelly said, pleased. "I never forget a face. Quite a stirring address you made at that student rally last April. Admirable, I dare say. Colonialism is abominable."

"You two should get together later and give it a bash," the equally tall and well-built Stokes said with emphasis, clearing his throat. Both men understood he was in no mood for serious conversation. They chatted for a while as the other passengers were settling in and made acquaintance, talking about their destination and purpose.

Kelly and Stokes were engineers. There were a few Irish teachers, an architect, a botanist, two missionaries and several civil servants, all bound for Guiana, as well as two whom Hoffman thought were adventurers. The younger had openly declared that England was the last place on earth any sensible person would want to be at the moment, considering all the destruction and hardship caused by the war. They had heard about Guiana, and that's where they had made up their minds to go.

"Just about died here. What with the bombs, the rationing and this filthy weather an' me waiting for a break to soak up the beautiful tropical sunshine. Me lungs 'ad it, enough is enough. It's the fresh air for me," the middle-aged, clean-shaven and jovial traveller said, as if urged to make a confession while Hoffman and the others chuckled heartily.

"You think it's funny, eh? Not at my age. It's the sun for me an' sipping your rum under the cool shade of a tree." He directed this remark to Hoffman who listened, smiling. He could imagine the man sprawled out, glass in hand. Then his companion said in a conspiratorial tone, "Afterwards it's the Maz...runu, how do you say it?" he asked. Hoffman obliged. "That's it. We'd be off to the Mazaruni to make a fortune in gold," the older one said, sniffing the air, while rubbing his hands in glee as if Eldorado was just waiting.

That was before they left Heathrow. Hoffman, now reflecting, sat in a half reclining position, seat belt unbuckled with a magazine in hand, trying to read. Time after time he glanced at his fellow West Indian passengers, who sat quietly with serious faces.

They had exchanged small pleasantries and greeted each other cordially, but had refrained from the lively, spontaneous conversation which was so natural to them. He pondered this uncharacteristic behaviour and assumed they were preoccupied with the thought of going home or were just worried about travelling by plane. Air travel was relatively costly and new, not to mention, somewhat frightening. However, he doubted fear could be the main reason for their reticence, because the men about him were experienced soldiers as anyone could see from their decorations and uniforms. Nevertheless, knowing his fellow West Indian must never be hurried, he waited.

His patience was rewarded when the plane reached Jamaica, the first Caribbean stop. He saw the ice breaking as the men began to relax and converse with ease. The talk centred mostly on the war and their experiences fighting on enemy territory, the British withdrawal, the bombing of Britain and so on, until a soldier said, "See this." He lifted his left hand. "I lost two fingers and there's still a piece of shrapnel in my right leg," he announced with a superior air, touching his leg, hesitated a moment, then went on in his acquired British accent. "I'm proud to know I fought for the mother country."

The soldier next to him took the medal, examined it and said without enthusiasm, "Well, I got hit on my shoulder, nothing serious, but man, it's a good feeling to know I was there. I was actually in the lines."

Hoffman, pretending to read the magazine, was listening in rapt attention. As the medal was passed his way, he took it, glanced at it, then directed a question to the owner.

"Excuse me," he remarked as an opening gambit to gain attention, coughing slightly. "What did you say your name was and where are you from?"

"British Guiana and my name is George Steele," the soldier replied, then repeated, "Steele."

"Pardon me," Hoffman answered, "I thought you said Dickens, Falworth or something like that."

The soldier, a simple man, looked puzzled by Hoffman's remark. He repeated his name, stressing it so that there would be no doubt about what he said.

"I thought you heard me," Steele regarded Hoffman, feeling slightly embarrassed, but now looking intently at the stranger with large, dark compelling eyes, features smooth and handsome, with lips parted in a mocking grin, exposing beautiful teeth. He couldn't understand what the man was thinking but he made him feel silly about his name being Steele and not Dickens and the other name he called.

"A thousand pardons my good man," Hoffman said suavely to Steele's remark. He knew exactly how the soldier felt but he didn't want to hurt the man. Poor chap. He looked so confused, but he must finish what he started. So he ventured again with a bright smile on his face.

"Are you from Georgetown, New Town?" Hoffman asked.

"I'm from neither. I grew up in Berbice and I'm proud to be a Berbician," the soldier said.

"Ah ha," Hoffman said with mock amazement, as if he had made a discovery, though inwardly amused as he watched the soldier's reaction.

"Let me see if I have it right," he persisted, "you are from Guiana, you were born and grew up in Berbice." The soldier nodded his head in agreement, trying hard not to be unfriendly, but he was becoming wary of Hoffman's persistence.

"Married?" Hoffman continued and the soldier shook his head. "Ah ha," Hoffman said, his voice sweet and light, now he knew what he wanted to do all along. This smug talk of patriotism made his mind up. It gave him the opportunity to begin his work. He knew how to deal with

15

this kind of attitude. He would probe their doubts with the sole purpose of making these soldiers and others think. He had to break the bonds that bound them, worse than the chains of slavery that had bound his ancestors. He didn't want to hurt the man, but he had to tear the scales from his eyes, starting now.

"So you are not of European birth or heritage," he said smiling, "just as none of us here are. Only a short while ago your ancestors and mine were slaves to these same Europeans, who possess many of our plantations today, that they got off the backs of our people." He paused for a moment, observing their reaction, then continued.

"I would appreciate it very much if you would illuminate my ignorance as to why you feel proud and honoured to give your life and limb in battle for your master's cause: the Europeans' cause, the same Europeans who, to this day, continue to exploit our country and our people."

This speech was followed by complete silence. Soldier Steele, who had provided the spring-board for the refined verbal attack, was uncomfortable as were the others within hearing. Like them, he threw sidelong glances at the other passengers nearby, wondering if they too had heard. They were all caught off guard and were totally unprepared for the turn the conversation took. So they sat with expressionless faces.

Most ordinary people spoke about Europeans in whispers, especially in their midst. But this young man was different. He had the audacity to sit on a plane owned by Europeans and with Europeans all around, proceed to condemn them for exploitation. Whoever he was, he was a brave man, and more than that, he spoke with a lot of authority. You had to appreciate what he said.

Hoffman observed the men around him. He knew exactly what they were thinking. He had done it. He had seized a slight opportunity, then assailed their doubts with pinpricks which shocked more than lengthy arguments. He could have patted himself on the back, but suppressed the elation, realizing there was more work to be done. This was just the beginning. Then without a second thought, he interrupted their reverie with a hearty chuckle, merely to put them at ease.

"I'll bet you gentlemen will get a small pension for your discomforts," he said, winking at them knowingly. Steele nodded. He decided after the exposé, it was better not to say anything that might get Hoffman going again.

16

Hoffman was aware they were embarrassed by his outspoken manner, being familiar with their fears, for he too shared their experiences and history. His intention was not to upset them further, but to calm their anxieties. However, he meant to complete what he had provoked.

"Gentlemen, do not feel embarrassed for my sake or yours," he remarked in a conciliatory manner. "Remember England, our England, our mother country...," he laid emphasis on 'mother country', "... is a democratic country and each and every subject and citizen has the democratic right to speak out."

He paused to see the effect his words had produced. As he glanced at Steele, it seemed that his eyes shone with a new glow as realization hit him. He sat upright instinctively, nodding his head and a semblance of a smile lightened his whole countenance which a few moments ago was creased with worry. Hoffman felt relieved. If he had been successful with Steele, he was certain the others were experiencing the same sensations. He did not want to alienate them, but to alter their way of thinking. As he appraised the effects of his remarks his spirits rose, encouraging him to maintain his purpose. There was renewed vigour in his words as he continued to assert his opinions.

"If you are proud to be part of that country, proud to bare wounds for your mother country, be proud to enjoy democracy. You and I are subjects, therefore we have the democratic right to speak out," he said with gravity and passion, pausing for a moment to let it sink in and was pleased to note they were now well relaxed. Then in a little more than a whisper, he added for their benefit: "I'm a Barrister-at-Law, Gray's Inn, on my way home to make some small contribution to my people and country."

The soldiers now understood Hoffman's persistence and authority. They gazed at him in admiration and relief, elated to be in his company. The tension lifted.

This incident took place before they landed at Piarco Airport, Trinidad. During the time they were in transit, they all got together for a drink, talking and gossiping about home, the cricket games they hoped to play, comparing West Indian heroes in Test Cricket with great English and Australian players. The conversation remained on light topics. However, never one to allow an opportunity to slip by, Hoffman suggested as they returned to the plane for the final stretch to Atkinson Airport, as a final gesture of camaraderie, they should keep in touch.

17

"I'll be in New Town. It should be easy to find the place, everybody in the area knows my family," he said as they exchanged addresses. "I plan to open my office downtown immediately on Lawyer's Row, so come and see me anytime. I'll be looking forward to your visits."

Satisfied, he sat gazing through the window on his left, trying to determine their position. Soon the Pakaraima Mountain Peaks in the distance caught his eye, causing him to sit up and his heart to pound as excitement rose in his breast. He was now truly on his way home and it was for this moment he had harrassed the stewardess for a window seat. He had been away for only a couple of years, but it seemed like a lifetime.

They were flying over the boundless and inescapable region of the Essequibo, when the plane gradually began its descent. He sat up, alert, drinking in the magnificent scene before him. As the majestic mountains in the distance grew clearer, he could see the peaks, clouded in swirling mists, bathed in beautiful sunshine radiating from a clear blue sky, so native to the tropics. Even the clouds appeared to sail merrily by, none lingered; it was as if they too danced to the beat of the tune he felt in his heart. He felt a sudden impulse, a wild abandon to jump up and dance and announce, "Home, I'm home!" but restrained himself, pressing closer to the window, until he could feel the cool metal through the white cotton shirt he wore under his jacket, as he looked downwards, observing the lush verdant forest below, stretching away endlessly in the distance. It was June, the heart of the rainy season and he could swear that the smell of the dank forest below pervaded his senses.

"This is beauty!" he muttered inaudibly, feasting his eagle eyes on the virgin territory expanding beyond. This living carpet, woven in every hue and tone of green, luxuriant and alive, has a pulse for only those who can feel it, thriving, increasing, and surviving. Like my people, I will most certainly continue with our struggle to be free, he thought with conviction.

His mind flew back to the year he was a freshman and a student had asked him if he planned returning to the jungle when he completed his studies. His retort was dim in his memory, but the chap had kept clear of him. They never stopped trying to impose their myth of superiority. Jungle indeed! For them it is forest, for us it is jungle. He knew only too well where the jungle was. It was back there in their awful cold, damp, dark and dismal cities. Here the air is always fresh with abundant

18

sunshine, pure nourishment to feed the determination to survive. And I belong here in this paradise, he reflected with passion and pride.

The plane made another descent. He felt warmer and eased off his jacket, still looking out. A few houses appeared here and there, then more grouped together in small communities dotting the river banks. He saw large fields, some still rich with the ripe golden rice being harvested and others with herds of cattle, toy-like, probably munching on the long, sweet grass as they wandered along. Then out of the corner of his eye, he saw the gleam of a huge body of water. He followed its winding trail upriver. Hundreds of tiny islands huddled together, inundated by the river; the treacherous current sweeping and distorting their banks, rushing on to join scores of tributaries.

This is the majestic Essequibo and her tributaries, bounded by lands rich in soil for farming and a wealth of forests. The Porkknockers, in their endless search for the gold hidden in the highlands and mountain regions, for diamonds in the creek-beds, make this their home. There is no other place like it, he mused. This abundance of wealth is our heritage and our birthright, paid for with the blood of our ancestors through vile slavery.

He pondered the many protest marches and demonstrations in which he had been involved as a student, his hostility against colonialism and its ruthless exploitation and oppression. He was overwhelmed with pride as he remembered the ovations he received for his public addresses while representing the West Indian student body. He knew he was well equipped, and determined now more than ever to use every opportunity to arouse consciousness and continue the struggle with his own people.

In this mood he left the plane at Atkinson. In the tiny lounge a tumultuous welcome awaited him and the other passengers. There were representatives from the military, family, friends and well-wishers decked out in gay colours who kept arriving in hired motor cars and open trucks, decorated with banners and streamers. Photographers vied with each other, squeezing in and out of the throng. Laughter filled the air. He was greeted and garlanded. His heart swelled with pride. He had not expected to see so many faces, especially after the prolonged delay through customs. "It is a day I will remember all my life!" he declared.

As the motorcade headed by the Kaiteur Steel Band drove down the narrow dusty road into the Garden City of Georgetown, he barely saw the faces of the inhabitants who ran out of their doorways to wave, but he heard their noisy chattering and cheering. He saw the plush grass alive

with yellow daisies, fields of red-green pineapple, jamoon trees laden
with purple fruit, groves of sweet-scented oranges and limes, the winding
Demerara River and its irrigation kokers, the flaming yet elegant hibis-
cus, the flamboyant prickly rose, and fern. He inhaled the smell of guava,
eucalyptus and burnt cane permeating the air and his senses, invigorat-
ing his tired, tense body. He marvelled at the beauty of his surroundings
and he knew that he would fight the world and stop at nothing to secure
this paradise.

Chapter 2

"Pat, Pat!" Phyllis called, not too loudly — to avoid attracting the attention of Pat's mother. She was worried Mrs. Sandiford would look out the window and see her standing in the yard. Pat would really get it! Her mother's hostility did not escape any of Pat's friends when they visited and Phyllis didn't want to get her cross with Pat by calling out that early in the morning. Phyllis was tense as she waited. She and Pat were good friends, and would continue to be so, in spite of Mrs. Sandiford's behaviour. There was such a noticeable difference between the two that everybody wondered how it was that a woman with a plain face, harsh lips and square chin could have mothered such a beautiful child. Except for Phyllis' mother, no one in the neighbourhood knew Pat's father. Her mother had told her when she was younger that Pat's father was very handsome, a real show-boy, the life of every party and that he had disappeared long before Pat was born.

Pat's complexion was a smooth sapodilla brown. There was only one thing she inherited from her mother: the thick long black hair that framed her face. Her eyebrows were naturally curved and rich black lashes heightened her brown eyes. She had a button nose, below which pearly teeth glistened through perfectly shaped lips. As she thought about this Phyl sighed, content with her reflections, wishing she had her friend's beauty, but not her mother. She was about to call for the last time, when Pat appeared at the window, her finger on her lips, gesturing her to go

21

around to the window overlooking the sitting room. Phyllis skipped around to the window and waited. She knew Pat was checking to make sure her mother was in the kitchen or some place where she couldn't disturb them too quickly. Then she heard Pat hissing and looked up to see her leaning out the window.

"Hey Phyl girl. Don't tell me you're ready for school already," Pat said, whispering, "I can't even get to the bathroom yet, still got the breakfast things to wash up."

"No girl, not yet. I really come to give you the news."

"News! Talk fast," Pat said, glancing over her shoulder, "Mom's in the kitchen."

"Remember that lawyer Hoffman who keeps those big meetings in the Green," Phyl said excitedly. "Remember he visited the school day before yesterday, when you weren't there? Guess what?" she went on hurriedly, "He's actually going from house to house talking to people and last night, Ma said he's coming to our yard eight-thirty this morning."

"This morning?" Pat said, surprised, "girl, I want to see him, but I have so much work to do this morning. I sorry I couldn't see him that day and now, shucks, I don't know..." she said with disappointment.

"But that's why I decide to come and tell you now," Phyl cut in. "If you hurry up now and do the work, you could finish in time, come and pick me up and then we'll wait for him. Though I saw him before, I don't mind seeing him again atall. Then we could go to school after, even if we're a bit late." Phyl spoke with urgency. Pat nodded her head at Phyl's suggestion. She was excited at the thought of seeing Hoffman, whom all the girls at school thought to be very handsome. As she considered the situation, she doubted she could contrive any last minute plan without making her mother suspicious. She knew if she hurried her mother would want to know what the rush was all about and the worst thing would be to leave the breakfast things for Lillian, her younger sister to do. Thinking about this only irritated her. She dare not let her mother know she wanted to leave early to see Hoffman, her mother was so easily upset.

She hoped the remainder of the week ran smoothly, because she didn't want to give her any excuses which could be used to prevent her from attending her school friend's birthday party on Saturday night.

Knowing there was nothing she could do about all these things, she said to Phyl, "Look. Wait for me until 8:15 and if I don't come by then I can't make it and we'll meet and talk at school."

"Okay girl," Phyl said, then asked, "still going to the party?"

"So far so good," Pat whispered. "What about you, though I shouldn't ask." She smiled.

"Well you know that party would be no party without me," Phyl quite perkily informed her.

"Girl, if it's the literature book you want, can't get it now. But I'll bring it to school," Pat cut in. Phyl was astonished. What literature book was Pat talking about? She didn't ask for any book. Then noting Pat's eyes were blinking rapidly, it clicked; Pat must have heard her mother coming and was giving her a hint.

What a fool I've been to think Mrs. Sandiford wouldn't catch us, Phyl thought, annoyed with herself and outraged by Mrs. Sandiford. She never gives us a moment of privacy, always sneaking around, waiting for the opportunity to literally pounce on Pat and her friends, then berate us for talking idly and wasting Pat's time. Poor Pat could never get a minute to spare. Always doing some work in the house. Mrs. Sandiford is not going to scare me away like the other girls. I'm not going to run away one bit, I'm going to stay. Phyl made a solemn promise and put on a bright smile as she waited for Mrs. Sandiford to appear.

"But is who and you talking at me window so early in the morning before bird's wife wake?" Phyl heard Mrs. Sandiford say sharply.

"Oh is Phyl. We're talking about something she's got to learn for Friday," Pat said, trying to act normal and praying she didn't hear them going on about the party. Knowing if she showed too much interest in the event, her mother would definitely decide her excitement was enough cause for suspicion and that would be the end of the party.

As Mrs. Sandiford stared angrily out of the window nearby, Phyl with a bright smile greeted her appropriately, then said to Pat, "Alright girl, if you can't get it now, bring it to school," paused and said politely, "Going Mrs. Sandiford... Pat, see you later." But her smile vanished when she turned away.

Phyl remembered the Saturday morning she had noticed Pat for the first time in Vieira's "Salt Goods Shop". She was awe-struck as Pat's cat's eyes rolled and coloured, while Vieira and his wife pounced at each other in their usual early morning cussing out. The more they carried on the more Pat giggled and her eyes glistened behind her shopping bag. Then she met Pat again at Enterprise High at the beginning of the school year. She and Pat were twelve at the time and were both placed in the Second Form. Now sixteen, they were still very close.

23

Phyl was a happy and spirited young woman, the eldest of four children. Phyl, Donna and Elaine were born two years apart, and Barbara, the youngest was now two. Louise Martin loved her children and was especially devoted to Phyl, who looked like her father and carried the same birth mark, a black mole on her left cheek just below her lips. Like her mother, she was warmhearted, humorous and endowed with a vitality which was partly inherited and partly due to youth. She sparkled with confidence and happiness.

Mrs. Martin loved to see the two girls together and often told Pat she was just like one of her daughters. Mrs. Martin had counselled Phyl when she told her how Pat's mother behaved: "Look chile. You an' Pat is good friends, so don't bother with her. When you go there, you make sure you tell her mornin' an' howdy. Always be polite. Some parents too stupid an' they always goin' to remain so," she said. She silently reflected on Beryl Sandiford: stupid indeed. She get herself mixed up with a man who was a known butterfly. He was too busy flying from flower to flower to be serious an' Beryl was too blind. She shut her eyes to all the talk about the other women an' the children they get for him. She asked for trouble an' now she just won't grow up. Pat is such a sweet child, good looking like the father. She an' Phyl suit each other.

"And what the devil you two talking about so quiet?" Mrs Sandiford said as soon as Phyl left, "With you hanging half-way out the window. I thought you in the bedroom doing your work." She had expected to see Pat tidying up and suspected something was going on when she heard the giggling and whispering. "This girl is always a problem from the time she born," she muttered under her breath.

Pat often heard her express her displeasure in many ways. "God knows it hard bringing up a girl child without any support from the father." Or it was, "Boys better than girls any day". Once the fire of her mother's hatred was kindled Pat was at her mercy. That was why she was afraid to ask her about her father. "He was a scoundrel, a trickster who took advantage of innocent women. He was nothing but a good time dandy," her mother would say.

Mrs. Sandiford had never forgiven him for leaving her pregnant and without support. Her bitterness knew no bounds. She had persuaded herself with self pity and tears that it was his fault she got pregnant, he had destroyed her career. "Look at my condition! If it wasn't for that man!" she had cried and grieved secretly. She had been so shapely and tall, very fair with masses of long, good hair.

When she first came to the city, everybody gazed at her figure and her hair. The day she went into the manager's office at Bookers store, she knew she had the job, even before they discussed her application. Pat's father had talked about marriage when she told him she was pregnant but the scamp upped and disappeared. She never set eyes on him again. She finally had to give up the job when she could no longer hide her appearance. He had ruined everything, even her chances of marrying a good man and she would hate him until the day she died.

Then she met dark and homely Roy Sandiford. He was head over heels in love with her. She had thought she could never marry an ordinary man like him. He was deeply infatuated with her and was a mechanic and held a good job. He had offered to marry her even though he knew she was pregnant and she agreed. She felt no affection for Pat when she was born, discouraging any closeness between them. During this time she had borne four more children, Lillian, followed by three sons. "No girl child is ever going to upset my life again!" she railed. As far back as Pat could remember, it seemed that no matter how hard she tried to please her, she lived in an atmosphere of constant belittlement, blows and censure.

Pat wished her mother would treat her differently. She was old enough to understand and accept the fact that her father had abandoned them, but hated the way her mother kept reminding her about it. She often wondered what her mother's life had been like when she was growing up. She knew her mother was the elder of two sisters. She had met Aunt Thelma, who lived on the West Bank. The two of them never seemed to get along well. Presently, they were not on speaking terms and she hadn't a clue why this was so. A few years ago her grandmother and grandfather died, one following the other. They all went over the river to attend the funeral. Even then the atmosphere between her mother and aunt was tense. Consequently, visits among the family were rare.

Again, she searched her mind for an explanation for her mother's attitude. No matter how hard she tried, the unpleasantness would continue to exist for reasons she could not fathom. Maybe as she grew older she would understand. But for the present, she had to make the best of a difficult situation. In spite of her anger, it was in her best interest to assume a cheerful air. She made up her mind nothing was going to prevent her from attending the party on Saturday night; so disguising her annoyance with a bright smile, which she hoped would still her mother's suspicious nature, she said, "Phyl was just telling me about that

25

lawyer Hoffman, who make those big speeches in the Green that everybody talking about."

Her mother said nothing, and she continued in a pleasant manner, "He's going to their yard today, visiting from house to house to talk to everybody about joining a new organization he's started."

"Eh hm," her mother replied without enthusiasm. "So he visiting from house to house now. I wonder what tricks he got up his sleeve," she said with sarcasm.

"You think he'll come by our house this afternoon?" Pat asked, trying to keep up the conversation as she moved about doing her chores.

"I know it was something had you all whispering so," Mrs. Sandiford said reproachfully. "Anyhow, don't bother to waste time rushing home to see that man. And if he come here anytime at all when I not at home, you lock this door and talk to him through the front window." Pat, shocked by this instruction, stood staring speechless.

"I hope you listening good to what I'm saying and don't stand there looking at me as if you stupid and you have no understanding," Mrs. Sandiford said harshly. "I hear the man fresh, so you do what I tell you and keep out of his way."

Chapter 3

Pat finally left the house around eight twenty-five that morning, still looking down the block to see if Phyl was anywhere in sight, though she knew it was already late. Having told her mother what she and Phyl were discussing, she didn't doubt her mother would be watching from the window to see if she'd stop at Phyl's house. But she had no such intention.

Eager to reach the school gate in time, she increased her pace, until she was nearly out of breath. She had to talk to Phyl before the school bell rang for classes and pass on the news about Hoffman. Phyl was her friend, the only friend she ever had. She could talk to Phyl about her troubles without fear of ridicule. Phyl never tried to joke or make light of her problems, she was kind and understanding. She was a prankster alright, she would never miss a chance to skylark, but would never knowingly hurt anyone. She was a cinch at impersonating people's antics, sending everyone into fits of laughter. Phyl had a flair for doing the most ridiculous things and it was really useless trying to thwart her. Pat laughed out loud as she remembered the times Phyl "ambushed" love notes, then wrote in her own funny words of rhymes. She would tie shoe laces of two unsuspecting people sitting together, creating an uproar when they got up. She tied and untied hair ribbons, and pinned people together with finesse. There was never a dull moment with Phyl, something exciting was bound to happen. Of course some people say she's a menace, she's too bold, Pat thought, I know she gets on my mother's nerves. Anyhow, Phyl knows this and my mother's just wasting her time getting worked up trying to get rid of Phyl, trying to break up our friendship. Her thoughts returned to her mother's comment about Hoffman. It was very disturbing. She hated gossip and she had to be very careful, but she must get to the bottom of this whole situation. Her mother had a passion for criticising everybody without knowing the facts. This was a good chance to show her how wrong and unfair she was. The idea that a man like Hoffman... a public figure too. The whole thing is too absurd.

She reached school late in spite of her efforts, rushed though the school gate and barely got into class on time. It was one of those days when everything moved at such a pace, she never got a chance to talk to Phyl alone. At recess she had time only to whisper to Phyl she had something important to discuss, before both of them rushed off to committee meetings for the coming inter-high sports. She was very glad when the lunch bell rang so she and Phyl could be alone together on their way home.

They moved along at a leisurely pace, deliberately remaining behind the press of students hurrying through the school gate, into the flow of the midday traffic. It was then Pat related in detail the conversation she had with her mother.

"Girl, it really shocked me what she said this morning after you left."

"Don't worry to get shocked, you should know her by now," Phyl said in jest. "Ain't you know, you could be as white as snow, that lady will find something wrong with you."

"If she stands at the gate of heaven, I sure not one soul will get pass her, not even me, especially me," Pat said and both girls giggled uncontrollably. "After all the man is a well-known lawyer."

"But you know our people. Now is the time they will say all kinds of things about the man because he's doing something big and important, forming his own organization," Phyl said, considering.

"Then again, you and the girls say he's got everything, charm, brains, handsome and got people rushing to meet him. A man like that could do no wrong in some people's eyes... after all, he got what it takes..." Pat said with sudden maturity.

"You're right," Phyl said, nodding her head, "he surely got everything."

"And the more I think about it... because of his position he might very well get away with anything, people might just let him. Come to think of it, which other big shot ever go to talk to people in their yard and make them feel important? Not one! You won't see another lawyer or judge doing that, not even the mayor who grow up poor like everybody. All of them like to get people running to them."

"You hit something there," Phyl said. "Only the police, the bailiff and the dead-runner visit poor people regularly. And you know that yard next to us, only a slight drizzle and it flooding up to your knees, always muddy and slushy. Just think, eh, he actually went in there to talk to people," Phyl spoke in awe.

"Then don't forget, he will most decidedly shake a few hands and after that everybody on his side, who could judge him?" Pat said.

"Well we know who," Phyl said laughing and Pat couldn't help joining in. "Anyhow my mother is bound to hear something or other about his visits during the past two days."

"Well, what you think about those lectures the principal planning for us on Mondays and Fridays?" Pat changed the subject, "I mean nobody ever talk about sex openly. I'm wondering if something happen and he found out." Pat spoke with some apprehension, "I just don't feel like going."

"Not a thing happen," Phyl said in her usual jocular manner, "That man just likes to talk and his brains always ticking away searching for something new so he could keep us under scrutiny." Then she added, "Don't think is you alone, I just don't feel like going neither. But you know you could only absent yourself with a doctor's certificate or death."

By this time they reached Phyl's gate. "Look, see you later and I'm sure to bring you some news," she added as they parted for lunch.

Phyl rushed into the classroom after lunch. She was late and Pat was relieved to see her. As their eyes met, Phyl signalled she had some news. "Hot juicy news! Brace yourself for a session after dismissal." Pat was distracted for the rest of the afternoon.

"Come on man, spill it quick," Pat urged Phyl. "I can't take this suspense any longer."

"Girl, what my mother tell me is really going to knock you out." Phyl spoke with relish. "It appear that when Hoffman was visiting from house to house the day before, he met this girl Mavis in the yard next to ours. He introduced himself and asked the girl where he could find her mother, then started to chat up the girl. Well this Mavis is thirteen, big for her age and is the hot, saucy type. So when Hoffman asked her how old she was and complimented her for being so attractive, she just tell him to get lost and mind his own business. But he laughed, embraced the girl and said he like girls with spirit. But would you believe, it was the same time her mother went searching for her and come upon them. 'What the hell you hand doin' round my daughter mister! Who the hell is you?'"

"Shucks girl, that must have been something to see!" Pat cut in. "I wouldn't like to be in his shoes. They had a big row, eh?"

"No man, didn't we say the man got brains. He calmly introduced himself to the lady and told her about the organization, inviting her to join, but not before he said her daughter was just about to take him to meet her. Then he complimented the lady for doing a good job bringing up Mavis, of course a crowd gather round... Actually he sweet talk the lady so much she cool down and didn't know what to believe about what she saw. And he, knowing fully well he had her in the palm of his hand, told her it was a great pleasure meeting her and he was sure one day she was going to be very proud of Mavis. 'Madam, let me tell you a secret, Guiana will soon need all the fine young women like your daughter and young men too, to accomplish the bright future that is just around the corner.'"

"Well. I could guess how she beaming," Pat said laughing, "'Cause nobody never call her Madam before and he a distinguished lawyer at that. And don't forget the hand shakes."

"I think she was on cloud nine," Phyl declared, laughing too.

"So what happened after?" Pat asked.

"Not a thing then," Phyl said and Pat groaned, "other than more people gather around to listen, while he asked her about her family, where the husband worked and so on. Then he told the gathering they were all living in bondage, worse than their foreparents who were slaves. How his organization was prepared to fight for poor people's rights and so it went on."

"I wonder if it was my mother, how it would end?" Pat asked, shaking her head. "So everything ended peacefully?"

"That was until her husband asked about Hoffman's visit and wanted to know how she come to be the centre of the gathering. Then the whole thing come out. He is a loudmouthed man. So he asked her at the top of his voice what she so pleased about and give her a good tongue lashing. 'Lawyer or not, the man damn fresh! How dare he put his hands 'pon my girl child, I know his type. He's neither family nor friend and you allow the man to get away with it. You got a lot o' big mouth in this house, yet you let this man excite you with he big fancy talk!'" Phyl spoke with emphasis, then added, "And Mavis mother didn't say a word in defence. I guess she was embarrassed by his loud scoldings 'cause the neighbours always listening."

"How did he know about Hoffman's visit?"

"I'm sure one of the same neighbours tell him everything before his wife tell him," Phyl replied.

"What a mess," Pat said with sympathy. "You and I know how news travels in this neighbourhood. So that is how my mother found out."

"You're right. Who was there and who wasn't, everybody talking about it now, so that's the story," Phyl said, then added after a thoughtful silence. "Personally, I think he's right about the terrible situation in the country. So in spite of everything I want to go and hear what he has to say at one of his meetings in the Green. I hear the crowds getting bigger. You think your mother will let you go? We could go together."

"Well not after that story you just tell me. My mother will get a heart attack," Pat remarked and both giggled. The party was three long days away and she was determined to be there.

For the rest of the week Pat was careful not to do the slightest thing to upset her mother. By Friday, Pat thought things were going smoothly, she kept her fingers crossed. She and Phyl had already decided what they would wear for the occasion but Pat did not mention a word. She was cautious to keep her excitement bottled up, but the moment her mother was safely out of sight, she practised special dance "shots", twirled and spun around in restrained delight. Then the blow fell. Mrs. Sandiford brusquely announced she would take Pat to the party though she had agreed in the beginning that Phyl's mother would take them. Now Phyl was vexed and Pat, though embarrassed, dared not try to get her mother to change her mind.

"Don't tell me you young people will let Beryl prevent you all from having a good time when you get to the party," Mrs. Martin coaxed Phyl, when she angrily explained the situation. Phyl considered this and agreed that her mother was right. Later, when she met with Pat she put on a bright face and reassured her. "Girl, the main thing is that you get to go. She could only dampen our spirits before the party, afterwards we'd be too tired to care." Both girls burst into laughter and prepared for the party.

31

Most of the students agreed Fridays were the best at Enterprise High School. The girls, neatly dressed in white cotton blouses and navy blue skirts sharply pleated, hair tied with shiny ribbons; and the boys, in well seamed khaki pants, white shirts carefully buttoned up to the collars and down to the cuffs and adorned with the blue school ties, streaked with red and gold, marched briskly into Assembly Hall to the strains of a smart, zippy tune played by Bill Stephen at the piano.

As Bill vamped away, nearly everybody tried to prevent themselves from tripping openly, for should the principal catch anyone in the act, this blunder was punished by suspension. To miss this treat, this most agreeable diversion, was out of the question. So many students, boys no less than girls, learned with artistry, to include a few sly steps on their own while marching. Of course those who persisted in this feat kept their eyes peeled for the principal.

"Is why you don't watch what you doin' atall?" A tall, heavy set, moon-faced boy of sixteen, with beady eyes, hair cropped close to the skull, impeccably dressed, snapped at Phyl.

They had collided.

"And is why you don't keep you' two lef' feet together Albert Edwards?" was Phyl's stinging retort. Her eyes watered in pain as she bent over cautiously touching her wounded toes. "You mash me toes with you' big, fat, stone crusher heel... you big, clumsy boob..." She hopped aside for the jerking line to move along. Removing her shoe with the other foot, she inspected her toes, wiggling them, trying to suppress the pain. Albert went with her too.

"Is who you calling clumsy... girl?" Albert angry, his beady eyes practically closed, began to castigate her. Then seeing the pain in her eyes he softened. "Girl... you ever see me on the dance floor yet... I'm a cool, smooth mover... smooth, smooth... I could teach you a thing or two..."

Phyl knew Albert was a boaster and he thought he was "it". He believed he was suave, handsome and with money to burn, always rubbing it in that his father "is a police inspector." As he mingled with the girls, he felt they couldn't resist his "charms". But there was a flaw in Albert's character, which a few girls found out too late. He would brag about these exploits to his buddies. When the news got back to his victims, they flushed as they reported about Albert's sweaty "paws".

Phyl suspected she was one of the girls Albert marked out as a recipient of his "charms" and benevolent gestures. But try as he might, "posting" several notes she was not persuaded.

"Let me tell you something..." Exasperated, she wrote back, "Just keep your little beady eyes off me... yeh, or I'll take these notes and run you in to the principal!" she replied with deadly seriousness. Then watched smiling as Albert read the note, biting his lips in embarrassment.

"Girl... I'm one of those big guys who move light and smooth, look... I'm sorry, really sorry... It was an accident." Albert spoke with deference, his eyes drooping appealingly, his manner seemingly expressing regret for his short comings.

Phyl made a little laugh, indicating forgiveness.

"Look after dismissal, I'm inviting you... I mean you and your friend to Growler's for cherry drinks... whatever you girls want... I won't mention anything to a soul... on my word of honour!"

Albert sounded earnest and Phyl's eyes lit up with interest. They moved back into the tail-end of the line.

"I'll let you know later," Phyl answered with spontaniety, letting her words hang out, her spirit beginning to soar.

Reaching the Assembly Hall, Albert went across to stand in the regular place with the boys, while Phyl joined the girls, her eyes shining, her mind racing.

"Girl, you can't mean you want to be seen going into Growler's Cake Shop with that sickening Albert Edwards!" Pat, her curiousity roused, asked eagerly, later that morning while working with the group assigned to costumes and props. She was reading the note Phyl wrote in response to Albert's offer. "Four o'clock," Pat added sceptically, "We gone home then... at least I got to get home before then."

"Seen with Albert!" Phyl feigned an injured look "You know me better than that... girl, you crazy or what? I want to fix that scamp good good."

"But you say here, you an' me..." Pat began reading the note, "going down to Regent Street to get some material. If we don't see you outside when we pass back, we gone... I didn't know we're going shopping?" She was beginning to take a keen and vigorous interest in the affair.

"Oh," Pat said, light dawning in her eyes, "You devil..." She giggled beaming at Phyl was was aglow with anticipation. "You devil... I love it, love it!" she squealed. They shook with quiet laughter and excitement.

"Poor Albert," Pat whispered, "He tangled with... I mean tangoed with the wrong girl... I'd love to see you and he in a tango across a dance floor."

"Tango... with that big flat foot boob!"

Their imagination running riot they whooped and chortled again and again.

"... is what with the two of them now...?" The group around them pondered and speculated, listening to their squeals and laughter as they observed them in awe. "They up to something."

After the school hymn was sung and prayers said, the principal announced the date for the August Inter-High Athletic Championship, the names of house captains and the colours selected for each house. As the captains stood up, they were acknowledged with loud cheers. Next he informed them shields and trophies for the events would be on display in the auditorium from the beginning of the following week and that the information about practice sessions would be on the notice board, adding those students whose names were not on the notice board and who were interested in taking part should see their house captains. Each student had been automatically placed in a house on admission.

The principal, a dramatist at heart and a keen observer of his students at work and play, selected a student to perform at assembly. Thus assembly gradually became the forum for exposing potential talent. The performer today was none other than Phyl, and most of her classmates were apprehensive. Pieces were often long and difficult and their success depended upon the performer's ability and wit.

Phyl, smiling as usual, stepped quickly on the platform and a ripple went through the audience. She announced her piece, and a stillness fell. She began quietly, looking down into the rows of anxious, pensive, cool, familiar faces gazing up at her. Her eyes shone, her voice rose and she commanded their attention; she was "Rosalind".

As she postured and proposed her views of the behaviour of women and men during courtship, the audience broke into fits of laughter, it was difficult keeping a straight face. However, she affected the appropriate sentiments with a degree of maturity and as the piece ended, the hall resounded with whoops, whistles, cheers and vigorous thumps.

"Well done," the principal said, shaking her hand.

Phyl received resounding applause from her classmates who cheered the loudest as a gesture of identification, pride and triumph.

After Phyl's presentation, the principal returned to the stage. By this time the students had simmered down and awaited a certain announcement... the date of the graduation ceremony referred to as "Speech Night". It was a gala affair held annually. It had become a tradition, each year the celebration became more spectacular.

"I know that you have been awaiting this particular announcement," the principal said, "So I have great pleasure in declaring the last Friday in July, as the day for our Speech Night to take place at the Town Hall." He gave the date, then raised his hand as the students were about to cheer and continued, "The staff also decided, the second weekend in August would be appropriate for the celebration to take place at the Town Hall in New Amsterdam." The presentation of the graduation programme in the principal's home-town was anticipated. However, in a joyous outburst of chorusing and whooping students from that region overwhelmed the others.

When the cheers had died down he continued with his announcements.

"This year, there is a change in evening wear for the young ladies in the choir! In the past, all gowns worn by the ladies were the same colours, pale blue or white. However, after consulting with the female members of staff, it was decided colours be allocated according to choral parts." The girls now began cheering wildly, then he held up his hand. "Hear me out," he pleaded. "The design also has been changed, no more long sleeves," he cried out and the girls let out a wild yell. When they quietened down he continued. "There will be two layers of frills along the neckline, which will also be lowered a little. Patterns will be distributed before you leave school at the end of the day." He paused, aware he could contain them no longer and the cheering and yelling were louder than before. Then he remembered the high-heeled slippers and waved them to silence. He gave permission for them to be worn and they cheered to their hearts' content.

"The formal wear for boys will be the same serge suits, white shirts and bow-ties of course. Shoes will be the same black patent leather." It was now the boys' turn to cheer. Men's clothing was very expensive so they were relieved no significant change was made in their attire. This did not prevent the girls from hissing, "Same old things!"

The principal paused for a while in order to give his excited listeners a chance to let off steam, meanwhile he consulted with a teacher or two, then continued:

"The play for this year's graduation ceremony will be *The Feast of Ortolan*. The teachers have just assured me all parts have been stencilled.

We need volunteers, although we have already selected students for the lead parts. We are counting on you to make it as outstanding a presentation as all the others have been. I promise you, it will be a feast indeed for all the senses. So please come forward, we need your help." After a few more encouraging remarks he added that volunteers should talk with the Senior Master.

"Girl, you were great," Pat said, grasping Phyl by the arm, as they left the assembly. "Those lines suit you down to your toes."

"Thanks girl, but I knew all along I could do it," Phyl said with utmost confidence.

"But girl, I was worried you might forget your lines. I know a few girls well who would feel glad if you did, you know who I mean. I was praying and mouthing them, just in case you did and looked in my direction." They giggled heartily.

"Nah, I wasn't worried one bit," Phyl said, remembering the exhilaration she felt from the experience. "All I have to do is get up on that stage and I'm raring to go!" Then inspired by their successful performance she added, "Let's sign up for parts as pages or jesters in our Speech Night play."

"Cripes girl, not me. I would faint from stage fright," Pat said in alarm, letting go of Phyl's arm. "Girls as pages or jesters. I sure the principal would never do that, not he."

"Want to bet?" Phyl asked with such determination and daring that Pat gazed at her, knowing full well the range of her unconquerable nature.

"I ought to know you better and could just imagine you! What I'll bet anybody is... you will be the first girl in an all boy's play. That's bound to make some of our dear friends envious," she said, nodding her head in sudden wisdom.

Chapter 4

As the date for graduation exercises drew nearer, Pat and Phyl like all the other students, were caught up in a whirlwind of preparations for the celebrations. As yearly examinations were completed, students were freed from the strain of classwork. They forgot their books for a while and indulged. Students in the upper forms, who had taken the Cambridge overseas examinations, were more than overjoyed. They had devoted hundreds of hours to study. Now they hoped their efforts would be fruitful, earning for them the certificates which were valuable passports to innumerable careers. Until the results were released, a temporary break devoted to preparations for Speech Night was most welcome.

These preparations started soon after the principal made the announcements. By the middle of July, the whole school was engaged in a variety of activities. Every member of staff, every student was obliged to take part. This resulted in a constant buzz of activity, a constant stream of movement inside and outside the school building.

In the main hall *The Feast of Ortolan* was rehearsed every day. Gradually, this became the main attraction, drawing crowds of students who thoroughly enjoyed every moment.

Phyl had accomplished her aim. At first the principal was astonished at the suggestion but after the idea took root, it appealed to him greatly, so Phyl and another girl were added to the cast, much to the envy of some, who after hearing how it came about said, "They always knew those same two were too aggressive and pushy!"

The regular programme consisted of works from Bach, Beethoven, Brahms and a variety of Negro spirituals. This year the school's top soprano, Vera Black was to perform the solo from Handel's Messiah. However, the high point of the choir's contribution would be the rendition of songs in foreign languages. The girls were hard at work polishing their French and Spanish pronunciation.

In the small auditorium, the choir under the distinguished guidance of Madam had been practising twice weekly; now practices were scheduled for every afternoon in the week.

As a rule, all prize-winning events were the foundation for the celebration. Students who were successful at the Overseas Examinations and had performed with distinction were formally presented with their certificates. Aside from academic qualifications, those who displayed distinguishing qualities and a high standard of conduct were also presented with awards.

Sports played a very important role on the school's curriculum. The cricketers who excelled in competition would be presented with cups and shields on Speech Night. It was an established fact that the school's athletic team was a force to reckon with, male and female alike, winning awards and trophies for the school and prizes for themselves.

Decorations and props were made on the first and third floors, there was scarcely a quiet spot or corner to be found in. As the day of the celebration drew nearer, activities increased and tensions heightened as grand rehearsal approached. Grand rehearsal was arranged to take place at City Hall two days before Speech Night, in order to guarantee a day of rest before the formal event.

Friday night was Speech Night. Long before 8:00 p.m. the time the celebration was due to begin, small crowds began to gather to observe the arrival of invitees and students. The celebration was the talk of the town; besides, word of the new gowns had circulated and this was a sight onlookers were certainly not going to miss. They assembled along the entrance of the City Hall. It was just as well, because parents, well-wishers and invitees also began arriving early to secure the best seating.

It was a glorious and memorable sight. The girls decked out in varying shades of pink, blue, green and yellow, greeted each other with little screams of delight as they made their way up the curved and highly polished stairway. Their countenances fresh, youthful, smiling from ear to ear, their hair shiny, beautifully curled and arranged. In their long gowns, they presented striking contrast with the boys in midnight black suits, dazzling white shirts, black bow ties and shoes that shone like glass. In the gala atmosphere of the foyer, girls selling programmes for the proceedings, floated to the entrance and back, simply as an excuse to show off their gowns. Tonight was their night.

At eight precisely, the principal got on stage, welcomed the audience, the chairman and other invitees responsible for the presentation of awards and prizes.

The Chairman, an eminent member of the bar, well-known for the way he delighted his audiences with his wit, greeted the audience befittingly and introduced the programme.

With Madame at the piano, the choir set a lively pace with a medley. The audience was tense with the anticipation of an excellent evening. As the choir completed the songs, they burst into rapturous applause. The Chairman was charming, he knew how everyone felt about the first item; but due to the length of the programme there could be no encores. The best was still to come!

In this atmosphere, student after student, group after group, walked on stage outwardly cool but a little nervous. Spurred on by the audience, they responded creditably.

It was time for the presentation of awards and certificates. Students filed out, accepting the honour with traditional deference. Pat stood among the students who were waiting to return to the stage when a young man standing near her looked at her admiringly and whispered, "You're really a beautiful girl. Why so serious? Smile for me please." He stared at her in open admiration.

Pat looked up swiftly into his eyes, cool and penetrating, observing her. She felt suddenly embarrassed and confused, but somehow managed a smile. My gosh, he's handsome! Pat thought as she averted her eyes, keeping in mind the principal's warnings at grand rehearsal that inattentiveness would delay the process. She listened, alert for her name, then moved off to receive her prize.

She was back in the line again and as the other students joined in, she found herself moving gradually towards the stranger again.

"You deserve every prize," the young man whispered. "I'll be waiting right here," he said as she moved off.

Now Pat wished she didn't have to go back to the stage again. She would have to return to the same place as before and she was very uncomfortable, so she stood hesitating. What on earth is the matter with me? she pondered. Why is he staring at me so? She felt a delightful sensation, yet she felt strained and confused. She was relieved when the line stopped a few paces away from the admiring stranger, but she felt his gaze on her.

As Pat moved away to receive the final award she vowed she would not look in his direction again. "I'm not going to look into those eyes again, never," she muttered. But when she sat down and tried not to glance in the direction of the stranger, it was no use. She found herself looking straight into the eyes of the young man as if she were drawn by a magnet.

Pat rose with the choir, moved towards the stage and took her place immediately behind Phyl, as both sang the same choral parts. Whispering, she quickly recounted what had taken place, directing Phyl's gaze where the young man stood.

"Hey girl, that's Ken Masterson from Washington High," Phyl said, looking at him in admiration. "Don't you remember him?"

"I remember something vaguely," Pat said, trying to remember.

"You forget he was their cricket captain last year. Remember the match they played against us, when he put the first two balls straight in the pavilion and not a man moved."

"Oh yes, you're right, it's now coming back, and we cheered and went on crazy, shouting and screaming how handsome he was! Gosh I knew there was something about him," Pat said and they continued whispering, while the choir was settling down into position.

"Didn't he get a scholarship or something to study abroad?" Pat asked.

"Right," Phyl said, nodding her head.

"We'll talk later," Pat said, seeing all the girls were in place and the choir was ready. Then Madam touched the warning key, which prevented further conversation.

When the choir began Pat realized she was standing diagonally to Ken Masterson. She could not help looking straight in his direction and she could not change her position since any movement would upset the closely defined choral arrangement. He continued to gaze at her. She remembered what he said and felt a rush of excitement, then a wave of confusion as she tried hard to concentrate on the song.

The choir began with 'Si me vers avez', followed by 'Gai Papillon'. Pat prayed she would not betray all the long hours of hard work spent in perfecting pronunciation and the careful deliberation which went into each composition. She stared glassily ahead and managed to get through 'Connais-tu le pais'. She breathed easier when they began 'Chante Chante Toujour', this was her favourite French song. As the choir reached the climax of the last phrase and held the final note without a pause for breath, the audience burst into enthusiastic cheers. Pat muttered a thankful prayer, knowing the worst was over and the delightful Spanish songs were yet to be sung.

When the noise died down, the choir began with the melancholic 'Estralita', next a brisk, spirited 'Cabalito'. Then Madam played the introduction to the rhythmic and seductive 'La Paloma'. As the choir sang to the pulsating beat, the audience could barely restrain its impulse to join in. By the time the piece ended, the audience were already on their feet cheering wildly. The foreign language presentation was clearly a triumph with 'La Paloma' the *piece de resistance*. The chairman was left with no alternative but to bow to the demand for a repeat performance. So 'La Paloma' was sung once more to a grateful audience.

Madame struck the chord to introduce the Negro Spirituals, the final rendition. As the choir sang 'Steal Away' Pat was relieved the evening had finally come to an end and the celebration had moved without a hitch. She knew from the excitement in the air everyone, parents especially, had thoroughly enjoyed the occasion. However, since Ken Masterson had talked to her, she had not been herself. His remarks really moved her. She had become aware of him only tonight, but there was no doubt in her mind she was attracted to him as much as he was to her. She felt heady, sort of dizzy and excited for one moment, then confused the next. She hoped she'd see him again, but not tonight, she needed time to think. Besides she didn't want him to get in touch with her when her mother was around.

The celebration finally came to an end. Parents, well-wishers, students, and teachers all glowed with the satisfaction that everything had turned out well. As for the principal, the evening's success was an example of his students' high standard of performance. He nodded his head with pride as he shook hands with parents, reminiscing on the vivid images of beauty, colour, and grace the girls especially presented.

As the audience made their exit, Ken Masterson hung back. He had seen Pat talking to a lady he presumed was her mother, so he took his time, staying behind in order to introduce himself as they moved towards the exit. However, as they drew nearer he seemed to lose his nerve. He

41

was puzzled by his sudden lack of initiative but as they passed him, he nodded respectfully at the older woman and smiled at Pat.

"Who is that fresh young man who nodded at me and making eyes with you?" Mrs. Sandiford asked sharply, and Pat, utterly destroyed, was unable to speak.

"These young people nowadays too brash and upstarted. I know good what's going on. Is one of your school friends, eh?" Mrs. Sandiford fretted while Pat remained silent with embarrassment.

Not even the entertainment could have softened her, Pat thought bitterly. She had known all along that should Ken Masterson try to get in touch when her mother was around, things were bound to go wrong. Now she dared not say a word, not even to sigh, since anything would be interpreted wrongly. On the other hand she was saved from saying things that might plunge her in a web of future problems.

Pat sat silent next to her mother in the taxi on the way home. She fumed inwardly. Tonight of all nights! She was very happy until her mother chose to make those crabby remarks about Ken Masterson. She exhibited her acid temper and narrowmindedness for all to see. Now to a complete stranger... It was unforgivable.

As they had driven off she had glanced back and Ken Masterson was still standing where they had left him. Although his expression was puzzled he waved to her. Well, she was fed up with her mother's attitude to all her friends. She was seventeen and old enough to choose her own friends. She always tried to please her mother yet she could not escape her bad temper, cruelties or harsh criticism. Her attitude remained the same regardless and tonight was the last straw, Pat vowed.

Still very angry when she got home, she went straight to bed thinking about Ken Masterson until she fell asleep and dreamed about him. She dreamed about the tall, dark, handsome stranger with dark penetrating eyes. He called her by name, as if they had known each other before. He held her fingers to his lips, kissing each one slowly, as he clasped her to him, whispering he wanted to hold her there forever and ever. He kissed her neck, her cheeks, her lips and she lingered in his warm embrace, thinking she too wanted to stay there forever and ever. But a sharp voice startled her out of her dream. It was her mother calling. Was it morning already? She tried to concentrate on the dream but it was useless, the voice snapped through the doorway to jerk her wide awake.

"You not getting up this morning? Today is Saturday and you got a lot of work to do. Last night pass and gone long time, today going already." Pat tensed as she sat up, her lips tightened as she tried to control the anger swelling inside her. She had a will of her own and today she was going to block her mother out. She had things to think about other than housework. She got up then, looking at the clock on the dresser. She had overslept a lousy few minutes! She frowned at Lillian, who shared the bed, still lying fast asleep. Neither thunder nor lightening could rouse her, much less her mother's sharp, shrill voice. Then she made a decision. She, from this day forward, was not going to rush around to get things done in this house. She was going to take her time. Nevertheless she completed breakfast as usual and called the rest of the family, as she set the tea on the table. She was the last to sit down. But try as she might, she found it difficult to control her temper as she stared at Lillian who sat around idly, after everyone left the table.

"The least you could do is put the cups and plates in the sink and tidy the table," she hissed at Lillian.

"Me? Mom say is your work to wash up, is not me to do that," Lillian said with typical guile.

"You playing deaf eh, you playing the fool!" Pat's voice was bitingly cold.

"Since you know I stupid, I going to tell Mom. You vex 'cause you got to wash up and you want me to do it. I.."

"What's going on in there? What's all the arguing about in there?" Mrs. Sandiford yelled, "Pat, you don't have time to waste! You have to hurry and get to the shop. Lillian, you get out and let Pat get on with her work." Lillian, making mocking gestures, left with a smile of triumph. At that moment Pat felt like striking her. She thought of the consequences and shrugged her shoulders in irritation. She seemed to be annoyed about everything today. Her mother, the housework, Lillian for lazing around doing nothing. She would push them all from her mind and think about Ken Masterson, the stranger who had come into her dream. That would help her to forget. She relaxed then, completed her tasks, collected the shopping list, basket and money, bade her mother goodbye and rushed out the house. She knew Phyl would be waiting for them to go to Vieira's Shop together.

"Girl, I just wake up and now getting ready," Phyl said when Pat arrived at her house. "I was so tired after all the excitement, I could scarcely open my eyes this morning. It will only take me a few minutes, come in."

So while Phyl got ready they all talked about the celebration.

43

"I waited 'til you come to say, youall look real stunning last night..." Mrs. Martin said, "Last night when we were coming home I was telling Phyl there was not one person present who didn't make a good comment. Everybody was talking that the singing was tops. As for the dresses they really made a hit and everything should be in the papers today. The papers man pass through yet?" She spoke with pride and enthusiasm.

"Ma, how many times you going to ask the same question?" Phyl said laughing. "Girl, Ma more excited than we to see what the pictures look like in the papers!" she remarked to Pat. "But Ma, suppose they don't mention a word in the papers, much less put a picture, what you going to do?"

"What? They can't do that child. Not after dem reporters with they cameras flashing all the time hurting people eyes, jumping from place to place blocking people view taking a whole set a pictures. What they going to do with them?" Mrs. Martin said as if she personally would be injured if such a situation occurred.

"Ma, you know they can do what they want. Is their papers and is not a big shot school like Queen's College for big shot children. It's a school for poor people children," Phyl said unabashed, shrugging her shoulders, while Pat listened, smiling, thinking she didn't dare backtalk her mother. She would surely collect a blow for her efforts.

"Pat, you really look beautiful last night," Mrs. Martin's voice brought her out of her reverie. "You look stunning." She heaped praises on Pat while the girls giggled in appreciation.

"Thank you Mrs. Martin," Pat said, feeling a surge of happiness for the genuine praise.

"I sure there had to be some young men in that town hall last night, admiring you all the time," Mrs. Martin went on, placing special emphasis on the last phrase. Pat and Phyl burst into uncontrollable giggles.

"Ma, like you're a fortune teller?" Phyl said, winking slyly at Pat as they continued giggling.

"Like I say something to tickle youall?" Mrs. Martin said chuckling.

Knowing the truth about the situation, Phyl was now eager to get out of the house, so she and Pat could give full reign to the enchanting meeting with Ken Masterson.

"Girl, how come you meet a guy like Ken Masterson last night of all nights?" Phyl asked in an intimate, eager manner as they made their way to the grocery. "That boy is really good looking eh, and he got an eye for spotting good looks too," She winked at Pat and they began laughing all over again.

"Well, it wasn't really a meeting," Pat said, trying to act cool and in control of the emotion she felt as she thought about Ken Masterson whispering to her in the aisle and her dream of him. "I was standing in the aisle with other others waiting to get back on stage, when someone said..." She repeated what had taken place.

"Girl, I know lots of girls would give their eye teeth, just to talk to that guy and kill themselves if he spot them!" Phyl said emphasising her remarks with sighs and swoons of delight. "They would die if they had your experience."

"Phyl, you're a real ham. You're always clowning and joking," Pat said laughing at Phyl's antics.

"Clowning, joking! I wish it was me. But girl, suppose he called at your house and run straight into your mother? That would be the worst thing to happen," Phyl said soberly.

"See, you joking again," Pat said, but this time she wasn't smiling.

"Joke, this is no joke! You know she would spoil the whole thing," Phyl said, her former ardour deflated.

"Well she spoil it already, since last night," Pat said frowning as she explained about the run-in and rebuff Masterson got, as he waited near the exit.

"Pat, I don't understand how your mother could act so heartless. If he should pay you a visit, what you going to do girl?" Phyl said, concerned.

Pat remained silent, trying not to let the moodiness she experienced earlier swamp her.

"You know, I think we rushing the whole thing. How could he do such a thing? He doesn't even know my name and remember I didn't talk to him 'cause I was too embarrassed by this guy's boldness and attention. The way his eyes kept following me around, honestly Phyl, I don't know how I didn't fall over myself. The whole thing was truly one-sided, remember," she said and her spirits lightened, as she remembered her confusion the night before.

"Well, I would bet you, he listened especially to hear your name so he knows that already. Girl, watch out and don't fool yourself. I sure last night was not the end, mark my words," Phyl expressed her firm opinion. "And if it was me, I'd be walking on air, dreaming and hoping to see him again."

45

Pat appreciated the comments but at the moment she didn't feel like talking about it anymore. She wasn't sure about the way she felt and what to think. She tried to minimize the situation.

"Girl, I'm sure he's got lots of girl friends besides he looks older than you and me."

"Of course he's older, but who cares? Age got nothing to do with this," Phyl said stubbornly. "Besides he's popular and I hear he teaches at his old school."

"Well girl, if he's so popular, I'm just small fry," Pat said coolly. "You were telling me last night about a scholarship," she said, still taken in by the handsome stranger in her dreams, doubting he could ever be interested in her.

"I hear he's got a scholarship to study in England, but he has to take care of the boarding and lodging expenses. So he's teaching and his family is pitching in to help. I think he's leaving early next year or sometime then."

"Well, that's it," Pat said with finality, "He's going abroad."

"Hey girl! What's wrong with you. This guy ain't married nor engaged to anybody yet," Phyl burst out, causing them both to giggle and become light-hearted again.

They had reached the entrance of the shop where they would make their purchases.

"Let's forget the whole thing, besides it would be difficult to continue with that noise in there." Pat held back awhile, pointing to the traffic of customers inside the shop. "Then we're not sure who's listening."

"Girl, suppose you bump into Ken Masterson when you going home? What would you do eh?" Phyl whispered as they entered, determined to have the last say, her eyes winking mischievously.

"You're a devil Phyl," Pat said laughing nervously, "I should know you won't let it rest. I would just walk by coolly, face serious as if I didn't recognize him."

"Eh heh! You'd have a serious face, but your heart would be racing and bumping and your knees knocking," Phyl said brazenly and both laughed. Once inside the shop they talked about the celebrations, the trip out of town to New Amsterdam and the plans their parents had made to send them to commercial school during the August vacation. Both thinking this time their school holidays were going to be very different from the past.

46

Chapter 5
1949

"Friends, fellow countrymen, lend me your ears. We are gathered here tonight... to bury the Caesars of our world, not to praise them." His voice rose in crescendo.

"Ah, ah! You hear the man, Christ Man! Listen how he slapping dem down with their own words," said a listener standing in the crowd.

"A learned man! Besides boy, they don't dare touch he when he get down to talking. Notice all the horse guards standing outside the Green? They don't dare put a foot inside!" the second listener replied.

"But is what's wrong with you," another listener interrupted in a scornful tone, "This Green was left to poor people and their children by some rich Dutchman... I trying to remember his name..." He paused, trying to remember, but the name eluded his memory so he continued, "This is we poor people ground and we free to come here an' air we views without harassment an' interference from the police."

"Man, like you memory short," the first speaker countered. "Only the other day the horse-guards rush some people an' the police arrest a few when that Indian doctor Chandra Ram Jattan an' his white wife had a meeting right here to protest the harsh conditions the sugar workers suffer on the estates."

"But is the same thing ah keep trying to tell you, all the time," the second speaker said with great contempt for their lack of insight. "They ain't going to touch he though, they don't dare. Look around." He gestured, "You can count dem people in this Green? It full to running over with people, besides, the man is a lawyer. He got all the cards," he snapped at them in defiance.

Then Hoffman began to speak again, after the noise died down.

"They have climbed and trampled on the backs of our people for too long! They have built palaces and castles for themselves and their heirs on the sweat and blood of our forefathers. While you my brothers and sisters are left with nothing... nothing but hunger and rags for yourself and your children." He paused again, looking intently at the rows of work worn faces of the enraptured men and women gazing up at him in tense concentration, then said, "That is what you and your children will inherit, nothing but hunger and thread-bare rags." He paused again, then cried out. "But is that what you labour for? Then you will agree with me that it's time this confounded nonsense stop." And the crowd thumped like thunder.

When the noise died down, someone shouted for all to hear, "O Moses, Moses, lead us, lead us on to victory!"

"Amen, amen," the crowd said in harmony. Hoffman, now fired by the agitated shouts of approval from the thousands packed in the small square, responded with gravity.

"Let my people go!" he cried out loudly, "let my people go!" And the crowd moaned and murmured to his biblical call for liberty. When the murmurs died down he went on.

"My brothers and sisters, you and only you, are the ones to assuage this utterly barbaric situation. You have the power and that power gives you the authority to make an investment in your future; therefore commit yourself wholeheartedly to fight for what is yours and not give in until you have known victory."

The crowds were literally hanging on to his words, barely breathing, waiting and he urged them on.

"Therefore you must stand firm, stand together, until these infidels and pirates who live upon your blood and sweat know your purpose."

"Hear, hear, hear," the crowd shouted their approval.

"This land is our land! This land is overflowing with wealth, our wealth, but not for the likes of kings and princesses!" he said with resentment, then asked, "What do you get for your blood and sweat?"

"Crumbs or bullets," a voice willingly obliged and the crowds broke into laughter. So the tension lifted.

"My brothers and sisters," he continued, "the only way you could achieve your aims is to organise before you vote. For too long we have been unorganised," he said with disappointment. "But we must organise into one strong band, a band with one purpose in mind and that is to free our land, our country from these usurpers, who continue to pillage our wealth, your wealth, your children's wealth."

"Hear, hear, hear!" The roar that went up from the crowds was deafening.

"Then to this cause, add your name to the growing list, a steadily increasing band of supporters..." he encouraged them.

Hats were passed around for a collection and during this interval, he pleaded with the huge gathering.

"My brothers and sisters, I've noticed that you have been spreading out into the roadway. I'm beseeching you now to find a place in the Green, because you and I know the powers that be. No names! No warrant!" He spoke with mockery and sarcasm, "Are you listening to every word said here tonight and I don't want you to come to any harm. However, we want them to know that it is your sweat, and taxes that build all these public roads and streets. So when their hired lackeys..." he paused, but when he spoke again there was no mockery in his tone, only raw anger and resentment.

"You and I know, one of our own join with the other side since he's promoted to Chief and gives the police orders to brutalize you all, his own people and you and I know who we talking about." He paused again and the crowds shouted courageously, "No name! No warrant!"

"Alright," he added quickly, "We're on the same wavelength, but it's another matter when these lackeys rushing you, to injure and maim you. Because whether they want to admit it or not, they too are involved. We are all involved." His voice rang out with the outrage he felt. As the crowds roared their solemn approval, he took the opportunity to direct the flow of the collection which was brought and placed near his feet.

"Eh heh!" a voice rang out, "You all hear what the man say. After all is we road 'cause we pay for it. So why the hell can't we use it now?" And the crowds around him guffawed. "You all ain't see how these people bare-faced? We have rights there and even that they want to deny us. I tell you all, this man is a real power with words."

"You too right. He's a real power with words," a young woman near to him said. "You ever hear him when court in session? Man, you all try and make time to go, even if is one time only. I telling you it's an experience you'll never forget." She slapped her chest persuasively.

"Is true," another young man said. "I could tell you 'cause I go regularly to the courts to listen to the man and you all right, he's a real power with words. Hear how he addressed the judge in a murder case, 'Your honour, this is highly preposterous. You are one of our great thinkers'..." He placed extra emphasis on his words for the benefit of his listeners. However, before he could finish, a woman asked, amazed.

"You mean he tell the judge he was talking nonsense? Man, that is something to hear and see for your own self. That man ain't frighten of nobody atall. I got to go one day at least."

"And what else you think he mean?" the young woman asked, vexed by the interruptions, impatient to share what she knew. "Look, Hoffman getting so much cases, he can't even take off the crop and don't bother think is freeness either. He does let you know straight away that good lawyers don't come cheap, so you have to pay him the full fee, before he appear in court for you." Noting her audience was now firmly in her grip she continued.

"My brother-in-law get charged for larceny and went to Hoffman. Hoffman listen to the story good, then tell he that the police ain't got a case. He could get him off, but he want his money first. Now my brother-in-law still got a small balance for him, but you know Hoffman could fix things 'cause the case keep putting off and putting off, but he paying Hoffman off this weekend, thank God! And he say an expensive lawyer better than jail any day," she spoke with finality.

"She right you know," another by-stander promptly agreed. "My next door neighbour got a son always in some trouble or the other, this boy is a real problem, I tell you! The other day he beat up another boy so bad that the police just lock up the brute for wounding."

"The young people nowadays got too much passion and they can't control it," another voice interrupted with a timely explanation. The speaker continued. "So the mother went to Hoffman crying. Well he get the boy out on bail, but it was the fee! Man ah hear when he first slap the fee 'pon she, she cry out louder than before! Anyhow, he tell she flat that she didn't supervise the boy properly and because of that she in big

50

trouble now, 'cause this time he heading straight for the jail. Look, I tell you, she rush and get that money so fast, I don't know where she get it from in this hard guava season, but she pay off Hoffman the three hundred dollars fast, fast."

"But the man tell her the truth, he didn't lie to her," was another response to which everyone nodded and murmured in agreement. By this time the collection with the hats was completed. Meanwhile another speaker addressed the crowds, but no one paid any particular attention to him because their appetites were well whetted by Hoffman. So they suffered the oration in polite boredom. Then as soon as the speech came to the end, they began to cheer and chant.

"We want Hoffman! We want Hoffman! We want Hoffman!" all the while clapping to a rhythmic beat. Hoffman was not about to let the crowds depart without the memory of the rich, smooth flow of his voice. So he came forward slowly as the chanting reached a climax. He thanked them for being there, then announced an approximate but large sum collected, still urging them to give more, quickly listing a number of tasks the money would help to accomplish, promising to present a financial statement at the next meeting.

As the crowds prepared to leave, satisfied, he sounded a final warning. "Now go straight home. Do not stand in the roadway, or you will obstruct the free and orderly flow of traffic. You may stay and talk if you want, but once you leave the Green, keep moving. Don't forget the enemy is lurking out there at the street corners, so don't give them the slightest chance to get at you. My brothers and sisters, au revoir and adieu."

The huge crowd drifted off slowly down the road. However, hundreds remained to continue the arguments, discussions and gossip which normally followed.

"What was them foreign words Hoffman used just now?" an old timer who remained in the Green asked a young man next to him. He guessed the young man to be either a civil servant or a teacher, from the way he had spoken earlier, and might be the right person with whom to strike up a conversation. Then, unwilling to appear dull, he added, "That was Latin or Greek?"

"Oh no father," the young man answered with deference, "that was French," he said, repeating the phrase as he explained, "he meant to say, see you again and goodbye."

"Oh ho. Thank you," the old-timer said, warming to the young man, who didn't know him but addressed him with respect. "What do you think 'bout what the lawyer said tonight?"

"The man is the greatest," the young man declared. "He is the only man I feel could lead the people out of this servitude these white people stubbornly maintain, just to rob us of our wealth. This land and all its wealth belong to us, that is a fact. My great grandmother came here and suffer indignities, beatings and rape for their cause. It's our time now to strike back! Slaves like Acabre, Quamina, Cuffy and many others toiled, sweated, then were brutally quartered by these same people so that we could inherit some semblance of freedom today. Now, we have to pick up where they left off and continue the fight. The time is ripe, the man is right! We must not sit still and allow these pirates to take our sugar, bauxite and tobacco and give us chaff. We are still in another kind of slavery, because our minds and our country are exploited without any resistance from us. We must retaliate and take what rightfully belongs to us and our children." He spoke so fiercely that by the time he was finished his anger was well roused.

The old-timer nodded his head as the young man spoke, but refrained from interrupting, awaiting his turn.

"You're right," he said, when the young man was finished. "Hoffman talks with a lot of power and he's bold, but I ain't so sure he's the only one or the right one to represent us. Man, that Union Leader is just as bold and fearless and he's doing a great job too. Then that East Indian doctor, Ram Jattan, from Corentyne and his white wife, they first rouse the people into action, demanding they get their rights now. Remember Hoffman first join with them, now he split up from them. Man, a lot of important people coming forward to fight this colonial government for the same cause. I is an old man and I didn't get much schooling, but I always used to hear my father say to watch out for them people who likes to talk big because they does always let you down, when they get what they want."

A few more bystanders had drawn nearer, attracted by the interesting interchange between the two. Then the old-timer, sensing an audience, continued, "I see many of them come and many of them go. They always fighting for poor people but remember what the Bible say, 'We have the poor always,' and that's true. It can never change."

The young man, riled by the old-timer's quotation, blurted out, "That's another thing," then checked his anger. "They continue to use the

Bible to educate us and our children just to clog up our heads with stories that are out of place in these times. For instance, the Bible says 'The meek will inherit the earth' so we continue to be meek while they continue to make huge profits from our raw material and labour. Now, you tell me who will inherit the earth?" He paused to allow his statement to sink in, then went on. "Of course they and their children will inherit everything. That is most logical, it's happening all the time. But I'm saying the time for talking is finished, we must organise and fight them now."

"But that is what I'm saying all the time. Other people fighting too," the old man insisted. "The other day that Union man marched with the stevedores to the manager's office. They stop the work from going on and was fighting for higher wages."

"Ha. Yes and they won," the young man quickly pointed out, "they were a force to reckon with and won higher wages."

"I can't say that they really win," the old man spoke with scorn.

"What do you mean? Didn't they get higher wages?" the young man said, as if he couldn't believe his ears.

"I am an old man," the speaker reminded him, "but I look at it this way. The workers get a few dollars more, but they pay dearly for it. Then the bosses up and hit back. Now the men can only get a few days work, in the long run the pay envelope shorter and some of them get beat up badly by the police. You call that winning?"

"You win some, you lose some," was the quick, terse reply. "The men won time to do other things, find other jobs, find time for their families and most of all find ways to squeeze the bosses. They got time to think about what to do with the gains and no time to think of the losses." The murmurs and nodding heads around them were positive signs the others in the group agreed with him.

"Don't worry with de old man," one listener said. "He old already and his skin get soft. He had his day already, but we can't be complacent any longer. We young and we got to fight for what we think is right for our generation."

"Ah!" the civil servant said, greatly encouraged, "The fight is not only for better wages, poor people have a right to vote in order to get better representation. In this day and age, in all this so-called freedom, people can't vote. Therefore it is up to us to force them by sheer numbers to give us that right and this is what Hoffman meant."

"But the law say only people with property and money got that right. We ain't got property and we can't change the law," another listener said.

"You may not have property, but you are taxed for every article you buy. It's all included in the food, clothing, household articles, school books and every single thing you buy. Therefore you are tax payers, just like the people who own property," the young man attempted to explain the facts simply.

"Now look at that. I didn't know that. If I wasn't at this meeting tonight, I would never understand that. You see, if you don't stop to listen sometimes, you never learn anything," the listener responded. "We got to organise in truth, Hoffman is right." They all agreed with murmurs and nodding heads.

"Every man, woman and youth must organise and force them to give us our rights to vote. It's not going to be easy, but with that right to vote, we will pressure them to make the necessary changes to improve our country. As for me, Hoffman is the man for leader." The civil servant continued to hold his audience. "So when we get that voting right we use it. Then we will have them by their tails." He spoke with confidence and authority.

"Have who by their tails?" the old-timer repeated, appalled. "You people young and you hot blooded and Hoffman putting wild dreams in you all head. But the powers that be is not going to give in. They got everything in their favour, money, the police, everything. Mark my words, you all keep a tally. People like Hoffman with their fancy talk always promise things they can't deliver. Then as soon as they gets what they wants they forgets you," he said without rancour as if his knowledge made him safe. Then he added, "Look me old bones tired and it late. Ah feeling cold. Stan' well and good night to all you young people." With that he drifted off and a deep silence followed his departure.

Now the young man, who only a few moments felt satisfied his opinions were well received by those around, was thoroughly peeved by the old-timer's attitude and his hopeless remarks. "Like a prophet of doom," he said, frowning, trying not to lose his temper.

"Hoffman won't get anywhere with these old-timers. They are too old and set in their ways to change now. The development of this country rests with young people and people with young minds; not with those who are not willing to fight. Then this Bible situation..." he blurted out, just about to criticise the old-timer's belief in the Bible, paused, considering the pensive faces around him. It occurred to him the majority of his listeners were also brought up to regard these teachings literally, therefore he might alienate them. So he decided discretion was better than valour.

Another group, slowly winding their way home was also loud in their praises for Hoffman.

"I hear from the time he start to talk in court, you could hear a pin drop, everybody just hanging on to every word he say," a young woman paid tribute to the lawyer. "My cousin is a court orderly and he tell me that one time when Hoffman make his address to the jury, the spectators up and cheer loudly." Everyone laughed heartily at this astonishing disclosure.

"Wha' happen?" someone asked after the laughter died down.

"What you expect?" the young woman's reply was quick and terse, "Everybody know you can't clap in court."

"I know that. You think ah stupid? I just want to know what happen after the clapping take place."

"Well," the young woman said, less severely, "the judge banged loud on table and threatened to throw everyone out if he hear a pin drop after that."

"I sure that did it 'cause nobody wanted to get thrown out," a sober voice said. "So you won't hear a pin drop after that."

"I hear the man he was defending win the case," the young woman began talking again.

"Well after all, what you expect when he defending you," another voice promptly cut in.

"I wasn't finished speaking," the young woman said, her temper rising again. She wanted to get on with her story but these constant interruptions provoked her. "I was going to say that the man who win the case have his farm near the sugar estate and the estate owners use to deliberately flood his lands everytime the man crop growing."

"Man, I tell you, dem people is wicked people. They too bad yeh."

"They just want to make sure the man and his family perish," another interrupted.

"I hear the farmer so happy," the young woman continued without losing her temper this time, "he take a fat gold tillary and the best fruits and vegetables to give Hoffman," she said pompously.

"That was to show his appreciation," another interrupted.

"Exactly," she calmly agreed. "I hear the poor man was suffering for years and not a lawyer would take his case."

"Man, not everybody bold enough to fight dem sugar people. Sugar is money and power, don't forget dem people own this country."

"Hoffman refuse the gifts at first, he said he did what he set out to do. But the farmer said if he take the gifts back his wife would be vexed, so Hoffman had to take them," the young woman said.

"I would do the same thing if was me," someone voiced his approval then thoughtfully added, "Man, he probably get hundreds of gifts from people 'cause I hear he does win them cases hands down."

"And don't think he does get them from only the people he represent. I hear when he visit people in the town or country, if he only mention he like something, they give it to him right away." Another favourable opinion.

"I think he is really a lucky man," someone commented.

"You call that luck. Well I call that greediness," Mavis mother said, she was with the group all the while but had remained silent, waiting for the right moment to say her piece. She had decided after her run-in with Hoffman and her daughter, nobody, not another big shot, was going to pull the wool over her eyes again! "Look, this man you all talking about is a big shot lawyer. He got a seat in the Town Council already and now running for a seat in the House of Assembly. Then remember, only people with property and money could get in. He got so much already, what the devil he want with gifts from people who struggling like hell for a living. He get paid for his service. Good God man!" She spoke with disgust.

An ominous silence engulfed the group. Then a new voice said, "You know the saying, 'Thems that got always gets more.'"

"Like you all grudge the man," the young woman stormed at them. "What you all want the man to do? He work hard for it and use his brains. So what you all expect him to do?"

"You too right to say he use his brains," Mavis mother said with sarcasm, remembering her own experience. "Look how he always sweet talking the women and got them flocking 'round he when he selling the pamphlets. Then if they say they don't have money to pay for it, he always searching them to get it. That is right for an upstanding lawyer to do? I don't care what nobody say, I see for myself and I think he greedy and covetous," she said in a matter-of-fact manner.

"Eh eh!" a male voice said, chuckling, breaking the deep silence which hung over the group of mostly women. "If the women like it, that is their business, as long as he don't try that with my wife 'cause I know she would fix he up good and proper," he paused a while and continued. "Man, you can say what you like. But everybody know right now Hoffman is the most popular man in the city and all over the country, no matter who bad talking he. Look at that crowd in the Green tonight. That Green was ram packed with people and people packed all round the market square. So he got to be doing something right."

Hoffman was popular. People knew him well, because he talked with them in the market, the cake shop, salt goods shop and at the trench corner. He visited them in their poor run down houses and tenement rooms which he reached after negotiating a pass through muddy and slushy yards. He chatted with them at the 'gate mouth', even by the stan' pipe, never refusing to take a drink, a smoke or specially prepared delicacies. He won their greatest admiration because he never forgot a face, calling everyone he encountered by first name, encouraging them to join in the cause. As for the women, they thought it a privilege as well as a pleasure to be singled out and recognised by someone as prestigious. Tall, stately and handsome, he was frank in his admiration for them. So they warmed to his vivid compliments by turning up at his meetings in huge crowds, bringing in tow their lovers, husbands, fathers and brothers to witness and listen to a tru' tru' son of Guiana, a real man! He got the makings of a born prophet. This is we God! Some claimed passionately and dared anyone to reason otherwise.

Chapter 6

Phyl felt a kindred spirit with Hoffman. She listened when he held everyone spell-bound, some willing to risk combat with the police in order to maintain their democratic right.

"People always blame poverty for all their misfortune in life. Know that you are master of your own fate, when you choose to think." The principal's words came back to her. He always spoke with a burning passion. Many times he would halt the class he was teaching to break into a discussion, spurred by some current issue. Boy, was he deep! She soon joined Hoffman's Peoples' Democratic Party. This eagerness to become involved was more than the curiosity of youth or the pride of walking in the shadow of an eminent lawyer. It was a consciousness, gradually becoming apparent, spreading among adult and youth alike. Lack of work, bad working conditions, inadequate education, insufficient training, and a lack of recreational and cultural facilities: they were all bound by these and were fed up with being patient, passive and "lesser". Hoffman now roused them into an active and determined force. Their spirit of purpose was now kindled.

Phyl began distributing leaflets and talking to people who lived around her neighbourhood. Before the year was over, she volunteered her typing skills.

"Girl, it was by chance I was at Headquarters one afternoon, when Mr. Hoffman came in. He wanted some information typed quickly, but his regular typist had already left, so he asked me if I could type and I said yes." Phyl told Pat, still enthusiastic and pleased by the encounter.

"Girl, you get to talk to him face to face. What did he say? Did he let you type it?" Pat said all in one breath.

"He doesn't take your word so easily," Phyl said laughing. "He asked when last I typed and how fast I think I could type."

"He sure wasn't taking any chances," Pat said, chuckling.

"Well, I typed a few lines for him to see, then he gave me the thing to do. When I was finished, he told me the information was highly private and I must on no account repeat anything I read while typing."

"Girl, he surely wasn't taking any chances," Pat repeated.

"Girl, that got me so mad. I just tell him if he didn't trust me, why he let me type it in the first place. He stared at me, with his eyes opening wide, then burst out laughing and asked if I would like to work for him full time. I told him I couldn't but if he had any work to do in the afternoons, I would be glad to help. That's how I come to be there nearly every afternoon."

"But that's getting you in deeper with Hoffman. How could you manage his typing in the afternoon, after working so hard at school all day?" Pat asked.

"That's not hard to do. When I get home in the afternoon, I have nothing much to do. I feel excited about doing all those private letters and things for him. It's like I'm doing my bit for the country, I feel important." Phyl spoke quietly, without the usual animated gestures but as one devoted to a cause. "Pat why don't you come and get involved too? We're organising a rally for young people and I'm on the planning committee. We can work together. It would be fun. Why not ask your mother? I'm sure if she knows what we're doing, she'll allow you to come," she urged.

"What kind of rally and when would it be?" Pat asked, thrilled by the invitation. "But you know my mother," she said, doubt creeping into her voice. "You know how she thinks already. She doesn't trust young people alone together and you know what she'd think about Hoffman and a bunch of young girls alone together."

"Girl, I know your mother long enough, but if you want to come I'm sure I can fix her good. And I'll bet she'll agree to send you," Phyl said trying to persuade her. "I'm not working with Hoffman without learning a few things, I tell you."

"Okay," said Pat sceptically, "I won't mind going but you got to come this afternoon before six o'clock, don't come later when it's dark. Because she already say, your mother got you galivanting around the town too much."

"Look man, don't worry with her," Phyl said, laughing heartily. "That's the talk to scare you, but when I finish laying it on she'll send you. She's going to be so easy." She was in high spirits.

"I hope you're right," Pat said, uncertain.

"Don't worry about a thing," Phyl countered.

"What about the L.C.P. Fair," Pat asked, as they were about to part, "Still going?"

"Course. It's only once a year and I won't miss it for anything."

"I don't want to miss it either, but you know I have to play it safe," Pat said with a burst of confidence.

Arriving at Phyl's gate they stopped and chatted for a while. When they parted, Pat reflected on her friend's good fortune. Phyl had secured a teaching post for the following academic year in a school outside the city. Mrs. Martin was so proud. She even relieved Phyl of many accustomed chores. She encouraged her daughter's independence. Pat recalled her own mother's reaction when she told her she was going to apply for a teaching position in a rural area.

"Why you in such a haste to work so far out in the country? I mind you all these long years without a father, what's the big rush now? You just stay in school 'til the right job come along," Mrs. Sandiford said coldly.

"But you don't understand," Pat said, trying to reason with her, "Jobs harder to get in town and it's getting harder every year with more students leaving school. I'm sure I could get a job just like Phyl 'cause I have my certificate and I got a letter from Father Francis already. All it means is I'll have to travel everyday. I'm already accustomed to getting up early."

"What!" Mrs. Sandiford cut her off sharply, "You went behind my back to the minister already? Well! It's the same thing I talking about. You start already to act like a woman in here and you ain't working any place. When you get a job then I won't be able to talk to you at all."

"Mom, all my classmates leaving school and getting teaching jobs in the country." Pat ignored her angry remarks and tried to reason. "Soon I'll be the only one in the group left in school." She considered the outcome with dread. "And the oldest student hanging around, when the new students begin school."

"I don't want to hear anymore of this stupid talk and until you can mind yourself, you obey my orders!" Mrs. Sandiford closed the conversation and abruptly turned away, leaving Pat feeling wretched.

Hurt by her mother's attitude and angered by her false reasons for not wanting her to work, Pat stood in shock, staring, unseeing. Was she to be deprived of the satisfaction of finding a job and making a career for herself? All her friends were doing just that and with the situation in the city, suppose she never got a job? She suspected her mother would find other excuses if she made any effort to get a job. She had gone along with Phyl and got the recommendation from the Minister, thinking her mother would be pleased. Why did she send me to school, if she doesn't want me to think for myself? If she thinks she's going to control me all my life because my father walked out on her, she's making a sad mistake, let her wait and see. She raged inwardly, tears of frustration running down her cheeks.

It was six o'clock when Pat opened the door to Phyl's knock and signalled her mother was in her room.

"Pat is your mother home?" Phyl asked brightly, going in and seating herself comfortably in the morris settee.

"She's in her room, let me call her," Pat tried to act natural. "Mom, Phyl's come to see you," she called down the hallway.

"Good evening Mrs. Sandiford," Phyl called out loudly while Pat went and tapped on her door.

"What's all the big fuss about," Mrs Sandiford shouted back. "I hear youall, tell her to sit down and wait, I'm coming."

She had heard us very well, Pat said to herself as she went towards Phyl, shrugging her shoulders. But Phyl was not a bit put off, so while she waited she chattered away. Wisely, no mention was made of Ken Masterson, a topic which heightened their enthusiasm whenever they met.

"Girl, you lucky," Phyl had declared the last time Pat told her Ken wanted to walk her home. "Man, he's so handsome." Phyl rolled her eyes dreamily, clasping her arms in ecstasy, "Anyhow I'm too busy with Hoffman's organisation right now to think of anything else, but if it was anybody like Ken Masterson, well... hm hm," she sighed.

She was the lucky one Pat thought. Lucky to have an understanding mother who backed her up and never treats her like a child or a fool. "It's you who got luck, not me. Thank God for the mother you have," she had said to Phyl.

After a while Mrs. Sandiford sidled into the sitting room, without a word of greeting.

Listening as usual, Phyl thought. "How are you, Mrs. Sandiford, hope I didn't disturb you from your rest," Phyl said brightly, smiling and was amazed to see her smile returned.

"Child, what you want to see me for?" Mrs. Sandiford said in a superior manner. Phyl suppressed her irritation and she kept on smiling.

"I'm sure Pat told you about my volunteer work with Mr. Hoffman."

"Pat tell me something or other, I didn't pay too much attention," Mrs. Sandiford said dryly.

"Pat, I thought you explained to your mother, the kinds of things I help to do at the organisation headquarters." Phyl's surprise was so real, Pat too was nearly taken in by it though she said nothing. She was even more surprised when Phyl went into incredible detail about the work she did and how important it was to the organisation. She paid glowing tribute to Hoffman. Despite the rumour, she insisted he was a great man and without doubt, a great leader. Mrs. Sandiford listened as she held forth.

"I'm on a special committee and we planned a big youth rally, which begins next Saturday, ending Sunday afternoon. Mr. Hoffman asked me to invite three people I know well. So I'm extending one of the invitations to you."

"Invite me?" Mrs. Sandiford said, truly surprised.

"Yes, Mrs. Sandiford. Mr. Hoffman wants parents who would be good chaperons and observers to keep an eye on things and see that everything is in a smooth running order." She noted Mrs. Sandiford was pleased about the idea. "The rally is mainly for young people, but you know when they get together, there's bound to be some confusion. Mr. Hoffman wants parents who are firm and can handle the situation without panicking. I recommended you, my mother and god-mother. Mr. Hoffman expects the mothers to bring along their eldest, especially for the Sunday rally."

"Tell Mr. Hoffman it's very nice of him to invite me and he could depend on me." Mrs. Sandiford paused a moment and said, "And thank you for recommending me to him."

It was now Phyl's turn to be amazed by Mrs. Sandiford. She had been prepared for a barrage of questions, which she was well armed to face. Now Mrs. Sandiford's ready acceptance floored her and set her thinking. Mrs. Sandiford's attitude was well known. The neighbourhood classified her as sour and unfriendly. Perhaps she's aware of this and tired of being left out, Phyl thought. Perhaps she's making an effort to change. If that's the case, it would be a pleasure to keep her involved for Pat's sake. Phyl was elated.

"You didn't mention what time the rally begin next Saturday," Mrs. Sandiford's voice brought her back from her schemes.

"First, please let me thank you for accepting the invitation on behalf of Mr. Hoffman, I know he will be very pleased. Ah, according to plans made by the committee, the programme starts at ten-thirty Saturday morning. But you and the other parents are asked to be there as early as nine-thirty, so you can be briefed." She gave Mrs. Sandiford a small leaflet.

"I'm sure I can be there," Mrs. Sandiford said, glancing at it. "And thanks again. Well, I know you young people always got something to talk about, so let me leave you alone." Though the girls tried not to show it, they were amazed. Mrs. Sandiford got up.

"I hope is not too much dressing up though," she hesitated, "I don't..."

"No, Mrs. Sandiford," Phyl quickly cut in, "It's just a simple function, Pat can help you select something. I got to go now." Phyl got up, bade Mrs. Sandiford and Pat goodbye and left.

It was incredible Pat thought. Her mother actually sat down and conversed with Phyl, then agreed to attend Hoffman's rally. It was incredible! Her mother who rarely left the house, other than for church, was actually going to meet other people and it was all Phyl's doing. Phyl had indeed learnt a few things from Hoffman, how to sweet talk difficult people.

After that day, her mother always spoke of Phyl in glowing terms. Phyl's got a head on her shoulders. That girl is bright. She had suddenly recognized Phyl's worth and elevated her into the realms of higher intellect and ability. With her mother in this present and rather unusual mood, Pat was glad to go along with her to the rally, noting how much her mother enjoyed her new role, proud to be involved. The function was such a success, she even offered to be available for any other occasion. There were plans for follow up rallies in various areas outside the city. Phyl thanked her for the offer, very determined to keep her busy.

It gradually dawned on Pat, her mother's attitude was changing, even her familiar short temper was easing. The tension between them lightened. It was now easier for friends to visit and to get out socially, as long as Phyl was included in these plans. The two were now inseparable and Mrs. Sandiford began to relax her vigil.

It was during this time Pat met Ken Masterson again. He casually dropped by her school one afternoon after dismissal. It wasn't as casual as it appeared to Pat. Afterwards he had laughingly explained to her how he had ridden at breakneck speed from his school so he wouldn't miss her. From that day on he walked with her a roundabout route to her house. Ken was puzzled the first afternoon when she asked him to leave her a short distance away, but he went along with the idea. She was excited at Ken's attention, pleased he liked her so much, he wanted to walk her home. But she forestalled him instinctively. Even though her mood was mellowing she was not prepared to risk a meeting between Ken and her mother. She remembered her anger and the hurt over the job, something she had set her hopes on. She enjoyed Ken's company, the interests they shared and she wanted things to remain that way.

One afternoon, Ken insisted he'd take her to her gate. She explained her mother would violently oppose the friendship or make things difficult for them. As they both planned going to the L.C.P. Fair, afterwards she would decide on what to do.

Ken was not satisfied with the way things were going. He disliked the roundabout way he walked Pat home, leaving her at odd points in the neighbourhood. He knew he was attracted to Pat on the night of the celebration, now he was falling in love with her. She was very different from all the other girls he had met, a real paradox. Quiet, without any airs and absolutely beautiful. She was not a flirt, she was free from guile.

He secretly enjoyed the admiring glances they got from old and young men alike. Considering Pat's explanation why he shouldn't take her home, he remembered the snub, the cold hard glare he got when he tried to talk to her mother on Pat's Speech Night and partly understood Pat's reasons. But he wasn't fully convinced and was against meeting her in secret. From the beginning, he knew instinctively Pat was the girl with whom he wanted to share his life and his feelings for her could no more be dismissed than her mother's opposition. It was something they must both face. Hide and seek was out of the question. It would have been a great pleasure to escort Pat from her home, rather than meet her in the gardens, but seeing how upset she was when they talked about it, he would leave things as they were for the while. But the matter had to be settled.

The bandstand in the centre of the Promenade Gardens was decorated with huge pots of palm fronds and gaily coloured neon lights strung around the circular roof, which bobbed up and down in the cool breeze. The Militia Band had played during the afternoon to entertain the children who were accompanied by grandmothers, mothers, aunts and older sisters. Now the band was packed and ready to depart at eight o'clock, in order to make way for the Syncopators Orchestra to entertain other adults who began converging in large numbers around the bandstand.

Young couples strolled arm in arm or stood around holding hands, waiting for the tired grandmothers and their charges to vacate the seats and depart. The seats were arranged in a deep circle away from the stand, making cosy accommodations near the tall rose bushes which perfumed the air. Interspersed, huge trees filled with forbidden fruit stood like giants, filling the air with a sickly sweet smell, while the shorter blueberry, like great fans, wafted in the breeze.

A few small boys were standing on tip-toe at the ornate fountain, at the entrance of the path which led to the stand, squirting water at each other. The constable, tired of chasing them away from this alluring game, left them to their pranks. Couples floated by unaware of the boys, until the mischief makers accidentally squirted water on them. Couples, engrossed, shrugged it off or chased the boys away, quickly forgetting the incident. This was their night, the night they waited and made all sorts of plans for. Free from adult condemnation they walked arm in arm. The beauty of the garden, the arcaded paths, the smell of the flowers, everything was perfect and nothing could break the spell.

Ken arrived early and waited for Pat, just at the head of the path, right in front of the bandstand. He stood aloof, observant, listening to the music, the laughter, the chatter. Then he became bored and restless, wondering why Pat was taking so long. After a while he moved down the path and stood away from the crowds at the entrance, wanting to see her when she arrived. He stood staring into space, thinking about his feelings for her. She was simple and innocent, yet he saw the woman in her quiet smile and the shy way she looked at him.

"Hello Ken. Have you been waiting long?" she called out as she came towards him accompanied by Phyl. Surprised, he smiled at them, but his eyes saw only Pat. She looked so lovely, he gazed at her entranced.

Pat wore a simple dress of pale green organdie, gathered at the waist with three quarter length sleeves trimmed with lace. Everything about her held him spellbound and it was difficult to take his eyes away from her.

"Hello Pat, Phyl. I was here most of the time waiting... Ah," he groped for words, "ah... I didn't see you girls."

"Listen, I'll see you two later, yeh," Phyl rushed to his rescue. "I'm off to the dancing rink," she said hurrying off, before he could make a reluctant attempt to persuade her to stay.

"Pat, you're more beautiful tonight than ever." He looked down into her eyes studying her face as he took her hand in his. "I don't know if it's the colour of the dress, but everything matches you perfectly. Where would you like to go first?"

She shrugged her shoulders.

"Let's walk around the booths with the handicrafts at the further end, then work our way back," he decided. "Let me know as soon as you're tired."

They strolled along holding hands, overwhelmed by the emotion between them, silent, but in tune with each other.

Soon they were touring the booths, food stalls and viewing the local talent. Mid-way through the tour Ken left, then returned with Phyl, insisting she stay with them a while. He stood by urging them on as the girls played games of chance, matching their wits at anagrams, tossing hoops and pulling strings to win the desired prizes, thoroughly enjoying themselves. Phyl, determined to get back to her favourite pastime, left promising to return in time for them to leave together.

"Pat, I'm sure if I handle the matter correctly, your mother will permit me to visit you," Ken said as they sat in an arcade awaiting Phyl's return. "The truth is, I hate the way we see each other... you know. It's just as though we're doing something wrong."

"I feel the same way, but I couldn't tell you the truth. There's no way my mother is going to allow you to visit. No way! My mother isn't easy to live with and it's difficult to admit that even to you," Pat said, laughing nervously.

"But she allowed you to be here tonight, so she couldn't be all that difficult," he said trying to calm her. He could feel her trembling.

"That's all Phyl's doing," she said and explained about her mother's sudden admiration for Phyl.

"She's changing I'm sure of that," Ken saw the situation differently and tried to reassure her.

"Changing!" Pat said, anger sparkling in her. "I know she can't change and I know why she's hard as nails to me. I'm a living memory of her past and many times I feel like leaving, but I have no relatives I know, no place to go. So I stay and burn and hope."

"Please Pat, we're going to face it together. Trust me," he pleaded.

"I know what you want to do is right, but I also know what I experience. Can a leopard change its spots?" she asked, grim faced and Ken sensed her hopelessness. They were quiet for a while, then she asked reluctantly, "When do you want to come? No matter what I say, I know we can't go on seeing each other this way either. She's bound to find out and I don't know which is worse."

"I'm glad you're deciding to get it over with, please let me take you to see my parents. They'll love you Pat. Wait and see. Would next Sunday be okay?" He was enthusiastic.

"Sure, next Sunday would be okay, it will give me a few days to break the news to her. But please let's cross one hurdle at a time. I just want time to think about this alone. It may seem as if I'm exaggerating, but you won't understand until you see for yourself."

"Don't worry, my sweet, everything is going to turn out right for us, you'll see." He caught her in his arms and kissed her.

Nearly a week went by since the night they talked and Pat still could not break the news to her mother. Fearing it would destroy her present pleasant mood, she kept putting off the event. On Friday afternoon when she got home she racked her brains, searching for a simple way to put it over, then changed her mind thinking it would be better if Ken called and she acted surprised. But she gave up the idea when she thought what her mother would do to Ken and plucked up the courage to talk.

"Mom, do you remember the boy who nodded at us as we left the Town Hall on Speech Night?" She spoke as if it didn't matter.

"Which boy? I don't know what boy you talking about," Mrs. Sandiford answered as if she wasn't a bit interested.

"Remember you said he was fresh and asked if he was my school friend?" Pat was dusting the living room when her mother entered, so she seized the opportunity to talk before her courage left her.

"I think so, so what happen he's sick or dead?"

"No, nothing like that," Pat hastened to explain, trying to overcome her nervousness, sure her mother remembered the incident. "He's a friend of mine and he's coming to see me on Sunday afternoon," she finally forced the dreaded words out.

"Coming here? Like I wasting my time, spending money to send you to high school." She glared at Pat and left the room without another word.

Pat felt as though a weight was lifted off her head. She had worked herself up to such a state of anxiety about her mother's reaction, expecting a torrent of abuse. But in spite of her unpleasant attitude, it seemed that Ken was right, she had anticipated the worse. She didn't know whether to laugh or cry as she sat down and tried to calm her nerves.

But after that sparse conversation, not a word passed her mother's lips as she stalked the house, a forbidding figure, her mouth set in a grim line. Pat sensed a deadly seriousness, a growing tension in her worse than she'd ever experienced. She spent the next two days disturbed and edgy, praying for Sunday to come.

On Sunday afternoon, when she heard Ken's knock and hurried to open the door, Ken was startled by her grave appearance.

"Take it easy, we aren't doing anything wrong," he said, taking her hands in his, squeezing them, thinking they were as cold as ice.

"Ken's here Mom," she called out as she showed Ken to the morris settee. He, watching her closely, trying to read her mind and she, not knowing what to say, silently praying, hoping, forcing a smile to hide her growing uneasiness. She was disturbed when her mother sent Lillian and the boys to the country to spend the day with their uncle. Now she was glad they had gone. Embarrassed that her mother was deliberately delaying, and wanting to put an end to the strain, she went to her door and knocked, repeating Ken had come. When there was no reply, she walked away feeling suddenly calm and prepared for a crisis.

"Mom will be out in a while," she said and sat down next to Ken. Then she heard her mother's footsteps. "Ken this is my mother." She introduced him as her mother came nearer. Mrs Sandiford nodded her head at the introduction, but kept her arms folded across her chest.

"Well young man, what can I do for you?" she asked crisply. Ken looked straight into her eyes and was shocked. There was no warmth, no welcome, only a cold expressionless stare. Pat had warned him, yet he didn't expect this cold hostility. He glanced at Pat and she smiled back. Somehow her anxiety seemed to vanish.

"I hope you can remember me. I nodded to you and tried to get your attention on Pat's Speech Night." Ken tried to check his own confusion as thoughts raced through his head while he forced himself to think of something appropriate to say. "I'm happy to have this opportunity..."

"So Pat tell me!" she cut him off.

"I met Pat and I would like to visit her, with your permission of course." Ken was standing while they talked as Mrs. Sandiford did not invite him to sit nor did she.

"You mean to tell me you meeting my daughter behind my back and carrying on?" she lashed out at him.

"Mrs. Sandiford..." Ken tried again, but was cut off.

"I didn't sent Pat to school for that. It's a long time before she start thinking about any man. She's a school girl, young man! And school is school."

Ken was confounded. He looked at the cold eyes staring at him unblinking and was appalled by the vicious remarks. What private hell did Pat live in. She tried to warn him but he never believed such behaviour was possible.

"Pat and I have done nothing wrong," his tone was serious. "I like her."

"You like Pat. Or you come to my house to give me and Pat trouble and worries. Where you working?" She assailed him bitterly.

Ken's anger was rising. He wanted to wound this woman, to attack her, to shock her and stop her crude insensitive remarks but he forced himself to remain calm and patient. "I'm a teacher and I plan to study abroad..."

"So you planning to put my child in trouble," she leapt at him again, "then run out the country and leave us. Well, let me tell you something young man, that is the last straw. Pat and I had enough of that already. I had enough of it bringing Pat up without a father. Permit you to visit Pat, never!" Her eyes sparkled with hostility.

"I'm not here to bring trouble. I'm here to do what is right, to get your consent." Ken spoke coolly, thinking she was beside herself with anxiety for Pat, but wasn't thinking logically. She was very unreasonable.

"Pat is too young. I'll give no consent. Pat is still in school and she has to obey my orders."

"Mom be reasonable. All Ken wants is to..."

"You shut up. I know good what he wants to do."

"I won't shut up and I'll see Ken whether you like it or not!"

"Oh yes! Well you listen good to what I'm saying. Either you obey my orders or you have plans to live somewhere else. You hear me, you hear me good." She turned on her heels and left.

A shocked silence followed her abrupt departure. Ken and Pat were speechless, each thinking their own thoughts. Waves of anger and shame coursed through Pat while Ken could not comprehend the blind rage vented on him.

"Ken, I mean it," Pat whispered, "I don't care a hoot what she said. I will see you," she declared and he, dumbfounded by the collision, did not reply. So they sat, quiet communicating with their eyes when Mrs. Sandiford reappeared.

"Young man, I think it's time to leave." She fixed her eyes hard on him. "It's getting late and decent young men don't stay late in other people's houses uninvited." She stood waiting as Pat and Ken exchanged glances, silent but determined. Ken bade them both goodbye and left utterly deflated.

Ken found himself sitting on his own front steps. He could not remember the streets he walked to get home. He was so terribly unhappy and weighed down by the situation. He reflected on the absurdity of Mrs. Sandiford's behaviour. He had assumed that by making his intentions known to her he would be permitted to visit Pat openly. Now all his hopes were dashed to the ground.

But he was not going to be dictated to by Mrs. Sandiford. Why should he feel he was doing something evil? The woman actually said as much. He was not going to drown his feelings for Pat to satisfy Mrs. Sandiford. He loved Pat and felt a protective urge whenever she was with him. He knew it would be sometime before he could discuss any concrete plans for their future.

He had fought hard to keep his temper under control, he truly felt like shouting her down and giving her a good piece of his mind, but he controlled himself when he thought about Pat and what she might have to face after he left. He stifled any remark that could lead to violence. Yes, he had felt the violence. The woman had insulted, threatened him and terminated the discussion abruptly. Though he hated meeting Pat in secret, the eruption tonight had forced a challenge. He was going to see Pat and no one could stop him.

He thought about his parents and the way he was brought up to be open and honest. His parents never treated him cruelly nor unkindly. They always talked things out. They were firm and he never got his own way. He remembered when he was eight years old, his mother and aunt were not on speaking terms for a long while because of him. Aunt Vera had struck him across his back because he had done something wrong. He remembered his mother sending him outside but he heard them quarrelling through the jalousie. She exploded and told Vera she could break her own children's back but keep her hands off him and never, never do it again. Then Vera said his mother was bringing him up like a damn sissy and that did it. They really had it out, then Vera left in a huff. He didn't see her for over a year and was very glad, because she always terrorized him. But after the row his mother did give him a good scolding.

Tonight his blood boiled at the viciousness he encountered. Pat was right from the beginning and he was so set on doing the right thing and getting Pat all to himself he hadn't listened. Now he feared what could happen to her because of him.

The following Friday around mid-morning, Pat heard a brisk knocking and opened the door. "What you doing home at this time of day?" she asked, surprised to see Phyl.

"I should ask you the same thing," Phyl said as she moved into the sitting room and dropped herself down into the settee.

"Well there's a meeting at school this morning, so we got the day off," Pat explained. "The principal and the teachers got some problem about salary increases, they weren't satisfied with what they got and there was big rowing going on. I hope they will be able to iron the situation out today."

"I hope they don't end up ironing each other out," Phyl laughed. "Anyhow, in my situation Mr. Hoffman got quite a lot of work to do. So with a little encouragement from him, I took a day's special leave to help him out. Anyhow, I see it as a break from the classroom and the noisy school." Then lowering her voice, she spoke rapidly, "Ken wants to see you tonight, I know you at home so I told him I'll fix it. He'll meet you at our office."

"I'll be working late tonight," her voice rose normally.

"Girl, I know it was something special bring you here this morning!" she laughed uneasily, her eyes revealing her anxiety at the suddenness of the request.

"I have something special for your mother from Mr. Hoffman." Phyl's eyes twinkled with excitement as she nudged Pat to compose herself. "I hope your mother will be able to help out."

"Let me go and tell Mom you've come to see her, she's in her room." Pat moved to get up.

"Oh my gosh," Phyl said in mock alarm, ready with her drama. "Good morning Mrs. Sandiford, I forgot my manners." She winked at Pat, both knew she could be listening.

"Hello Phyl, not at work today?" Mrs. Sandiford said with a little concern as she entered the room.

"Sorry to disturb you this morning," Phyl sighed, she was surprised by Mrs. Sandiford's promptness.

"No, it's good to see you. You're not bothering me atall," she ignored Pat.

"Well, Mr. Hoffman said I should talk to you. I'm on special leave and starting tonight I have a lot of work to do. You know the organisation is working hard to get every last person of voting age on the list. So I have a lot of typing concerning that and I've come to ask you to allow Pat to help out tonight. I'll be there from six, but I have to work through the whole weekend."

"I don't mind Pat helping out, but what time you all will be finished?"

"Shouldn't be later than nine o'clock."

"It's a bit late, but as Pat with you it's okay." She was thoughtful, then added, "Be back here by nine-thirty," she addressed Pat frostily.

"Thank you very much Mrs. Sandiford. I knew you'd agree," Phyl said and got up satisfied.

"Anything else?" Mrs. Sandiford urged.

"Oh yes," Phyl said, a bit overcome, thinking Mrs. Sandiford had been listening to them. "Mr. Hoffman asked me to give you this invitation." She gave her the printed card, noting her smiles.

"Oh." Mrs. Sandiford perused the invitation.

"As you can see, this time the function will be held over the West Bank, so I hope you can make it. I have to let him know early what's your decision."

"It's going to be alright, tell him it would be a pleasure to be there."

"Well, I got to run along now, I have so much to do I don't know where I'll begin. See you later Pat." Then bidding Mrs. Sandiford good-bye, Phyl hurried off.

Pat spent the rest of the day wondering why Ken wanted to see her urgently. Since the row, he had not met her after school. She was worried that her mother's behaviour had frightened him away. Now he probably meant to break the whole thing off. It couldn't be anything else because he'd already told her he planned to leave for England in September. But she told him she would meet him regardless of what her mother said. Well, tonight she would find out what it was all about.

The girls met at six o'clock.

"Ken came around to our house last night. Girl, he was all worked up." Phyl explained as soon as they left the house. "He wanted to talk to you and said he didn't see you for the whole week because he didn't want to get you into anymore trouble with your mother. He was actually going to your house and hang around 'til he got a chance to see you. Girl, I had a hell of a job trying to talk him out of it. I told him that would get you into worse trouble than before, he doesn't know your mother well. Suppose she looked out the window and saw him. Well that straightened him out a bit. Then I remembered the invitation, I was going to take to her next week. Thank God for that. So he and me made up the other stuff about you helping, to get you out."

"I thought he broke off the whole thing because my mother terrorized him. As much as I like him a lot, there was nothing I could do. I don't know how to thank you Phyl."

"Broke off! That boy's crazy about you and he's not going to give up atall. I prove that last night. After he left I told Ma how your mother behave and Ma said your mother doesn't think straight atall 'cause young people can always find ways. Ma is right 'cause you mother only forcing you and Ken together. Ordinarily you and he would go along cool but now I don't know."

Pat was only half listening, her mind was on the meeting and the risks. Ken had done his best but there seem to be no other way out. She

73

had always been uneasy about meeting Ken after school but now she was not going to stop seeing him secretly, if that was the only way she could see him. She was sick of her mother's domination.

Ken waited uneasily, remembering the cold, hard, merciless stare in Pat's mother's eyes. He worried for Pat and was relieved when she appeared with Phyl. The three chatted a few minutes then he and Pat left after agreeing to return for Phyl before nine.

Hand in hand they strolled along, talking lightly at first, until they entered into Camp street and crossed into the shady avenue with its dimmed street lights. There was little traffic at this hour on the street which ran on both sides of the avenue. Here, set on large properties, were the luxurious homes of influential lawyers, doctors and businessmen. Sprawling bungalows and two and three storied family mansions boasting countless glass windows and jalousies. They walked past the splendid neighbouring gardens where the sweet odour of the dank earth, plush grass and flowers followed the length of the avenue, in spite of the strong salt air, blowing in from the Atlantic.

As they passed London Theatre where eager patrons were already buying tickets for the next show, gales of laughter broke the silence of the neighbourhood. Fire flies danced madly overhead under the flamboyant trees. A train hooted in the distance and gates clanged shut across the junction at Lamaha Street. A boy and a girl about ten riding on a gent's bike, the girl pedalling furiously, passed them going the wrong way. They screamed and laughed as the bike screeched, creaked and vibrated. Yet they hardly noticed these diversions as Ken, now desperate to know what happened after he left on Sunday, pressed Pat for answers, until he was satisfied nothing worse had occurred.

The train had gone past by the time they reached the gates but a cloud of smoke, dust and grit still lingered in the air. As they reached the old Dutch Koker that spanned the canal, Ken saw the clay brick embankment was deserted, and guided Pat along the ridge.

"I can't stand the suspense any more. What did you want to see me so urgently about?" Pat said as they sat down. Ken, deep in thought, did not reply. He drew Pat closer and pressed her tightly to him. How was he going to break the news to her, he didn't know where to begin.

"Did you miss me Pat?" he said, kissing her on the forehead. "I missed you so much, I know it will be worse later." He rained kisses on her face and neck and she responded, sighed heavily and pushed him away. He held her firmly.

"Look at me Pat. You haven't answered my question. I love you and won't do anything to hurt you, you mean too much to me." He sensed her frustration and understanding swept over him. "These secretive meetings are maddening, forcing us together and whenever I..." He paused, "I'm sorry Pat, I shouldn't have pressured you."

"Hush Ken, I love you too." She put a finger to his lips and touched his cheeks. "I missed you too, when I didn't see you where I usually waited, I thought my mother frightened you away and I wouldn't see you again. I pushed you away just now 'cause I was afraid and ashamed of myself. I know it's stupid to think everything we do is wrong." They remained quietly absorbed in each other's embrace until she said, "What going to happen to us Ken?" Then Ken remembered what he wanted to tell her.

"I got a letter today from my uncle, the one I told you lives in England. He wants me to spend the summer with him, so I can learn my way around before I start med school. That means I could only delay leaving until around the second week in August.

Pat said nothing.

"Right now I have mixed emotions about going, though I've been waiting for this opportunity."

"I understand how you feel, but it's what you always wanted. So it's now or never for you. I'm sure things will work out okay," Pat said seriously.

"Pat, I want you to meet my parents and if it would help, I'll come and try to persuade your mother again," Ken said without warning.

"Oh God no!" Pat said in alarm. "That's out of the question. I'm sure I could manage it if it's planned for the same day Mom goes over the river to the rally. But you're sure your parents want to see me... after the way my mother went on with you? You're their only child and I mean..."

"Well, I told them everything about you, except the way your mother behaved, that's our business. They want to see you and I know they'll love you as I do." He kissed her again and again, then with arms around each other they started for Phyl's workplace.

The city was changing. It was the mode of greeting which revealed the motive power in the people's lives.

"How're you?" or "How do you do?" was met with, "Man, girl ah dey hey waiting 'pon God's mercy" or "He takes care of the birds of the air! So we got to thank God for the little he provides." Or "What we goin' to do? The scriptures say, 'look at the lilies of the field, they toil not neither..'" followed by hard luck stories.

Conditions were bad in the city. Few people had jobs and were barely able to eke out an existence from the pittances they received as wages. But they felt powerless to find solutions to improve living and working conditions, so they bore their frustrations in a subdued silence. But gradually, people with influence in the community and with new political ideas began to defy the system which stifled native opinion, achievement and development. Union leaders, workers, doctors, lawyers, poets, writers, religious leaders and others spoke out. Together they injected a new mood and way of thinking and the people's consciousness rose. There was no doubt the people became aware of the possibilities for there was a marked change in their responses.

"Man, girl, God ain't no Bajan! He sends the rain on the just and the unjust and we got to fight for our own."

"The scriptures say, you only got to ask and you shall receive. Seek and you shall find, Knock..."

"Who God bless! Let no man curse. Ah busy busy fighting with life."

They no longer felt helpless or isolated and their religious zeal and social convictions were a powerful influence on their attitude. They used every available means to express themselves. Slowly, they began to acquire little niceties. After all we're all God's children and these are small comforts in a harsh existence. So floor polish and linoleum. Window blinds and maiden hair fern, towels and teacups, bicycle and radio ain't exclusive to these big shots, they declared with emphasis. Native property owners in the city with seats in the Town Council, had continued to harangue the old guard colonists. Now bombarded from all quarters, they had to make concessions. Gradually they began to lose their grasp. So the ripple widened as they grappled with the problem of housing in the community. Run down and neglected dwellings, houses and other buildings were demolished or renovated and replaced with comfortable and pleasing structures. Slushy tenement yard lots were filled and levelled, and cement pathways were laid, making clean, easy access to dwellings, ending the misery of poor tenants. Then came the installation of piped water and electricity.

Public thoroughfares were considered nightmares, overwhelmed with pot holes, dark and mysterious in rainy weather, pitfalls and traps for bruises and sprained joints in dry season, a frightening experience for pedestrians as well as vehicular traffic. This situation slowly began to disappear. Roads were repaired, asphalted surfaces and paved sidewalks were laid, while well constructed cement gutters drained the streets, more appropriately than trenches which retained the black slime and the stench of rotting garbage.

The changes of the city were demonstrated by the incessant traffic. The flow of bicycles was ever increasing, along with a growing number of cars, motorcycles and buses, which vied with each other for the right of passing. The result was a hue and cry for traffic regulations which led to the imposition of stop signs for which many a fool paid the high price of injury, even death, before the lessons were learnt and the rules accepted.

Changes were painful and slow, but the people had seen the light. Hope and purpose had motivated these strivings. These were the modifying forces acting for the present and the future. The people were done with being molded. They had broken the frame and gradually began to shape their own destiny.

Chapter 7

Time eventually caught up with Pat and Ken, who was just three weeks away from leaving for his studies abroad. Pat had gradually smuggled out of the house items of clothing which she hid at Phyl's. There she dressed, then left to meet Ken who took her to his parents.

"Do come in. After hearing so much about you, I'm pleased to meet you, and from what I see, Ken is right!" Donald Masterson, in his forties, greying, tall and as handsome as Ken, clasped Pat's hands warmly, drew her close and kissed her. Pat immediately liked him and felt safe. "Vi, Vi!" he called out, "The young people're here. Where're you girl?"

Pat finally met Violet Masterson.

"Ken talks so much about you," Ken's mother spoke politely and Pat sensed her efforts to make much of her. Later, when they were alone his mother said, "You're so much younger than Ken and very attractive, but you know Ken will be away studying for a long, long time. Meanwhile you might meet somebody else you like more than Ken." She went on talking about Ken and never gave her a chance to reply. Ken was the centre of the conversation and it was obvious that she adored him. She was the essence of tact, quite unlike Pat's mother.

"You girls don't know how happy I am, now I have my two best girls together," Ken said, elated. He held them on his arms, kissing them both, while his mother smiling proudly, benevolently, contentedly, never betraying her true feelings. Pat was glad she met Ken's mother, regardless of the cost.

They planned the last meeting together as Pat's school would be closed at the end of the week. She welcomed the end of school but she was aware her secret walks with Ken would also come to an end. Everything was going wrong. She had no job. When all her friends were working or making efforts to do so, she dared not attempt it. Ken would soon be going out of her life and everything looked dull; she was miserable! Suddenly she realized it wasn't the end of the world. She had a right to do something about her own future, regardless of the oppressive authority hanging over her like a sword.

Consequently she and Ken made plans for their last meeting and it was Phyl as usual who helped bring it off. They both left together for a party where Ken was waiting, then they slipped away. Hand in hand they toured the main shopping area downtown, now quiet and almost deserted, save for a few couples and a family or two window shopping. As they walked along the shady avenue on High Street, Ken talked about his plans for the future, when he would return home and make his contribution. Pat knew his goal was to become a pediatrician. He had selected that field of study because he felt there was too much sickness and suffering among the children and the infant death rate was too high for such a small population. Then he talked about the plans his parents had made for his departure, wishing there was some way that Pat could accompany him to the airport.

They reached the head of Camp Road, yet Pat scarcely spoke, as arm in arm they stood for a while observing the deserted Sea Wall stretching away to the east, as far as the eye could see. At intervals, boisterous, gusty waves rushing in from the Atlantic, billowed over the wall breaking the peace and quiet of the sparsely wooded areas and parks _ a haven for lovers.

"You've been very quiet Pat. But I know how you feel. I'm going to miss you very much." Ken spoke softly as they sat on a shady mound. Pat felt her heart would break and averted her eyes, but he turned her face to his. "You're on my mind all the time and I know things are going to be alright in the end. I just know it. Until I met you I was never serious about any other girl in my life. Will you wait for me? I know it's not going to be easy." He drew her closer, hugging her. "You haven't answered my question."

"You know I will. But right now I feel so left out and alone, but I'm happy for you," she whispered, attempting to be cheerful.

"I shouldn't have brought you here, God knows how I love you. It's going to be sheer hell not seeing you. How beautiful you are." He looked at her adoringly. "Let's go." He spoke suddenly as he shuffled to his feet.

"No, Ken, no, I don't want to go, let's sit for a while, please." She drew him back and he, trembling, kissed her softly on the mouth.

"I love you," he moaned as he reached into his pocket. "This is my going away gift." He placed a ring on her finger and was pleased by the surprise in her eyes, as she gazed at the simple gold band with an unusual twist of two exquisitely crafted hearts, delicately initialled with the letters P and K.

"Ken, Ken, you're forgetting! It will be impossible...." she cried out. Understanding and disappointment washed over him.

"Please." He enveloped her with hugs and kisses. "Look Pat, we've got to leave now," he whispered huskily.

"No, I want to be with you and nothing else matters." She clung to him, all their pent up desires exploded as they responded instinctively. Moaning softly, he restrained his wild impulses as he removed her clothes. Her eyes filmed with tears and pain as her body trembled and vibrated to her first encounter.

"Are you okay?" he whispered, kissing her over and over again. Breathless, they looked at each other wishing their world would never end. He planted tender kisses on her face and lips while she held him in a tight embrace, her arms entwined around him.

"I'm okay... I'll be alright." She shivered as an unfamiliar thrill coursed through her body and he was surprised at how calm she was.

"Pat, if anything goes wrong..."

"Please don't talk about that now. You said you love me and I love you too, that's all that matters."

"I'll never forget tonight and I'll be always thinking of you. My future is yours." He made a solemn promise.

But time had moved too quickly.

"Oh God, it's late! Let's go." Pat spoke anxiously as she looked at the eerie darkness with concern. So they made a hurried departure. And just as they suspected, when they got back the party was over, but Phyl was still waiting at the gate.

"Gees man, you all had me worried," Phyl attempted to control her anger. "The party finished a long time ago."

"Hello Phyl... sorry to keep you waiting, but the time just raced by." Ken was apologetic and Phyl noticed he was distracted. She glanced at

Pat and was astonished by the difference. Pat, in high spirits, her eyes shining, was holding on tightly to Ken.

"I hope you understand; it's our last time together." No one said anything for a moment. "I'll walk you girls home," Ken stated, breaking the awkward silence.

"Dear Lord!" Phyl said looking upwards, exasperated. "Not tonight, it's too late and I sure sure Mrs. Sandiford waiting and watching from every window. Look Pat, you try talk to Ken yeh. I can't understand the two of you atall tonight."

"Look Ken, if you want to take us home, you do it." Pat ignored Phyl.

Phyl could not believe her ears. What had come over Pat tonight? She ought to know her mother better than either Ken or I do, she thought, yet she doesn't seem to care! Ken is another one, after the messing up he get. But all two of them, like they gone mad tonight. Neither one of them thinking straight. Something wrong because Pat walking right into jeopardy and she ain't even aware of it!

They took Phyl home, then hand in hand they went the rest of the way, whispering and embracing. As they neared Pat's house they saw all the lights on.

"I'll come with you," Ken whispered, suddenly feeling nervous. "There's someone at the window."

"No, no, I'll go alone." Pat attempted to compose herself, suddenly helpless and afraid. "Go Ken, quick!" She pushed him. He, unnerved, yet wanting to shield her, stood rooted to the spot. In a split second he made up his mind to go, when Mrs. Sandiford rushed out the door, whip in hand and rained blows on Pat as she dragged her towards the house.

"Please let me explain Mrs. Sandiford..." Ken held on to the short, tough bamboo cane, but she let go and began cuffing and kicking Pat.

"Ken go, for God's sake!" she screamed as she ran into the house with Mrs. Sandiford right behind her.

Ken, boiling with anger, clenched his fist tightly as he struggled to control himself. Then it struck him the terrible thing in his mind he wanted to do. For the first time in his life he was about to explode and do something really violent. Then the door crashed shut and the outrageousness of the situation overwhelmed him and he burst into tears of frustration and anger.

"Oh God make me suffer if I ever forget tonight and Pat! But I know my heart will never let me forget," he cried softly, his eyes blinded with tears.

Chapter 8

"Did you see this morning's papers?" Phyl asked Pat.

"No girl, I ain't had the time to even look at papers."

"This came yesterday, after you left," Phyl whispered, tucking a letter into Pat's blouse. She had agreed that Ken use her address. "Child like you going out?" She went into the living room, appraising Pat as she made herself comfortable, thinking of the terrible night before Ken went away to England, remembering what Pat had told her afterwards. She had known something like that was going to happen. She could always tell when disaster was going to strike. Pat looked different these past few weeks; she looked more mature now, self-confident, even if she was acting somewhat indifferent.

Mrs. Sandiford had given her a good ticking off as well, not that it bothered her one bit. The only thing that bothered her was poor Pat, she couldn't even go to the shop without Mrs. Sandiford threatening her. She had laughed, when Pat said she told her mother Ken had left and she didn't care what happened.

"I'm trying to get out for the appointment with Father Trim. I got to reach in time for ten o'clock... Almost sure to get the job," Pat lowering her voice, cooly explained, "But I hate the way the old coot keep eyeing me up."

Phyl knew Pat made several applications for assistant teaching positions in the city, as well as in areas just outside.

"I can't afford to mind you all my life. You old enough and is time you start looking for a job." Mrs. Sandiford dropped the bombshell a few days after she found out Ken had left. She was full of surprises. Pat didn't wait for another urging.

"What's this thing in the papers you telling me about? Hm... you walk with your own copy girl?" Pat commented as Phyl spread the papers on the coffee table.

"Listen to this headline girl. 'Old nanny and farm labourer inherit estate worth millions'," Phyl read.

"What, who?" Pat said, drawing nearer.

"Listen man, 'Wealthy sugar cane planter and landed gentry dies leaving estate worth millions to his nanny and trusted farm hand.' How you like that girl, fantastic eh! 'These honest, trustworthy, hard working employees, faithfully served the family all their lives. Now over sixty-five years, both were in their teens when they began working for the late owner who was just a small boy of six.'"

"They lucky girl! Wish it was me... I could do with some of that money, especially for what I have in mind," Pat said.

"Listen... it says not only the plantation but all the money and family jewelry are to be divided according to the terms and provisions in the will."

"Well, I happy for them but I can't see why you so excited... you know them?"

"No. Here're their names... Josiah Brown and Beatrice Bishop. But guess who representing them? Hoffman! And they're bound to win the case."

"Wait, wait, what case you talking about?" Pat asked, puzzled, "You just read to me the estate is to be shared according to the will."

"Well, it seemed the estate owner, John Halpenny had a nephew twice removed. He in England, and he's challenging the will on the grounds that the old man was mentally unsound."

"Oh, oh! I now understand. But like you said, Hoffman's the best lawyer. Still, you never know. For their sake I hope they win or that would be a terrible thing for them... Well I ready. Just let me get this envelope with these references." Pat darted inside and was back in a flash, so they left the house.

"I'm going to work for Hoffman full time," Phyl said eagerly.

"You're joking! You can't be serious," Pat responded, "I ain't hearing good."

"Course I'm serious, dead serious. I already give Hoffman my word. You're forgetting your friend is a first class organiser and he knows this too. He said we got to get at the young people in order to change the old people's attitudes. It's very important for all of us, we have no power in this country. That's why Hoffman and all the local politicians fighting strong for adult suffrage now... and the government bound to change the laws and make it imperative people twenty-one and over vote," Phyl explained.

"But Phyl," Pat sighed disappointed, still surprised, "What happen to all our plans to go to Training College together, your career? Hoffman can't pay you."

"Don't worry about that," Phyl cut in, "Hoffman promise to pay me twice what I'm getting as an untrained assistant... You know how teacher's salary small already... I know we agreed about Training College but you see the big fighting up to get in... besides I'm fed up with teaching right now, I think I need a break. Hoffman has a lot of confidence in me, you could never guess the important documents I see and all the important people I meet who fighting behind the scenes for a change of government. Lucie says I'm his right hand, he doesn't know what he'd do without me..."

"Who's this Lucy?"

"You forget Hoffman's name is Lucius, I call him Lucie."

"Hold it right there girl, don't tell me you falling for that man. He's more than twice your age and you know he's married."

"Ha, ha, is what's wrong with you, you making me laugh yeh. I admire the man but he's not my type, so don't bother to get excited. Girl, you know I won't get involved in them things. He's a true lady's man, you should see..." Phyl in high spirits, her eyes a study of mischief, paused, noticing the worried expression on Pat's face.

"Take care Phyl, 'cause the more I think about Hoffman the more I feel he's not so good for you to be around. I don't know how he get you to throw your whole career overboard for his job with no future in it. You know you out in the cold if he doesn't win the election coming up, while he's still a well known lawyer with a knack to get people to follow him."

"Don't worry. I telling you everything going to be okay. Hoffman's bound to win the election, he can't lose. You know what adult suffrage means? Then look at the thousands and thousands who support him. Everything is well planned. Politics is a game of tricks and he already got a few up his sleeve mark my words. We'll talk later."

"What did your mother say?"

"She said it was up to me, 'However I make my bed I must lie on it'. You know how she like to use parables. She didn't fuss. If that's what I want, she isn't going to force me to change my mind. I start at the end of the week, before school close... It's a fresh start with Lucie, so wish me good luck."

"Well good luck girl. I hope you know what you doing this time. See you later." So they parted.

Pat was thoughtful as she hurried for her appointment. She sensed Phyl's enthusiasm, but she was disturbed by the whole thing. Hoffman was just exploiting her admiration for him. After all, he had his profession to turn to, regardless. He was selfish, encouraging Phyl to give up her career. Suppose the election flopped? Where would Phyl be? He only wanted to use her for his own ends. He couldn't do without her. She's his right hand. Hm, hm, Pat frowned. He was so full of tricks. She was irritated, but said a silent prayer Phyl would see through him before it was too late. Then pushing these thoughts aside she prepared for her interview.

"I got the job," Pat said to her mother when she got home. "And this is the letter I got from the manager, Father Trim... I have to take it to the headmaster the week before school reopen in September." She handed the letter to her mother without any show of emotion.

"You should be laughing and happy you get a job so near in town, besides all your friends getting ahead, while you still behind. You better try and catch up with them before it's too late."

Pat was angry and deeply hurt by her comments. Why was it so difficult to talk to her? Did she dare tell her about the interview with that lecherous Father Trim? She vividly remembered the weight of his hands on her shoulders. His clammy hands stroking hers and the weird look in his eyes as he gazed down at her, while she sat at his desk. She was angry with herself for saying nothing because she wanted the job so badly. But she must watch out for him and take care not to be alone whenever he came around to the school. She couldn't tell her mother. God knew it might provoke her anger and suspicion. Well, if she took a shower now, which she needed that too might provoke a number of questions. She decided to bear her troubles in silence, reflecting Phyl was the only one she could talk with. Phyl! She remembered Hoffman, he and Father Trim were both lecherous men, there was no doubt about that. She must tell Phyl about it. "God give me courage," she muttered.

In the new school term Pat went off to work and discovered she liked teaching, even though she had so much to learn. With the encouragement she got from the senior staff, along with the challenges, she felt much lighter in mind than she could remember. She chuckled to herself when she thought how she outwitted Father Trim. He visited the school fairly regularly. The first time he called her into a make-shift office, which was used as a storeroom for teacher's materials and records. But that day was a bad one; the regular traffic in and out the room made it difficult for him to pursue his intentions. He inquired about her progress and said she got a good report from the Headmaster. But though his eyes still devoured her and his hands caressed hers, whenever they shook hands, she felt it wasn't worth making a scene. She made sure he could get no further and always acknowledged him formally. She knew her position depended on the manager's and Headmaster's assessment and she meant to hold on to her job at St. Christopher's Anglican School.

As the school term drew slowly to an end, Pat was certain she was pregnant. But she dared not confide in anyone especially at school for she would be fired immediately. She made up her mind that telling her mother was out of the question. She worried she would begin to show and the other teachers might suspect. However, as the present fashion of full skirts and dresses kept her condition well hidden she decided she would arrive at a solution after the Christmas vacation.

Phyl paid her usual visit during the week before Christmas in order to bring her up to date with her new situation.

"Phyl you look tired," Pat said, regarding her closely. They were standing on the platform outside the front door.

"Girl, we're working late every night and I have so much to do, I don't get home until after seven at nights... Lucie an' me working on that voting list thing I tell you about. We got to make sure every man who is to vote for us, vote our way!" Phyl declared, smiling at the idea.

"How can you all make sure?" Pat said, astonished such a strategy could be devised. "I mean it's the whole country involved, then what about the other parties, they expect certain people to vote too."

"It's very simple. You set up things in such a way that the people you expect to vote for you, vote in your favour, whether they're sick or whether they want to go out on polling day or not. Hoffman..."

"I still can't see how it could be fixed... it's such a tremendous task." Pat spoke with disbelief.

"Ah girl! We set up our own little system, a smooth system like the proxy..."

"Matching votes to names, but that's crooked!" Pat said, alarmed.

"Look Pat! These people beat our foreparents with bull whips, chop off their necks, quarter them, burn them, flay them alive and you shocked and frightened about being crooked over pieces of paper. This is what you have to do to get them out for good."

"You still ain't understand we're not dealing with the same people alone. What about the opposing parties and what about yourself, you're involved girl." Pat spoke with more than a little concern.

"I'm not worried 'cause Hoffman got everything well covered. He'll be working it all out and he's got to win."

"That wasn't you talking just now, that was Hoffman! And I'm not concerned for him, I'm thinking about you. What will happen if some government official find out, or the opposing parties. I read all the election notices as fast as they put them them in the papers and it says people could be jailed for voting without consent. Don't tell me you feel good knowing you could be involved. And bum names too."

"Look, stop fretting yourself," Phyl made a little nervous laugh. "Everything is well covered I tell you and it will give me the greatest pleasure to do something like this in revenge for the past. It's our time now from here on... Don't forget Lucie's a lawyer... we're not committing any crime, we're only making sure we get what is ours. Can't tell you more..."

Pat sighed but remained silent. She was sure Hoffman was putting all these thoughts in Phyl's head and she prayed she wouldn't get into trouble. But the more she thought about it, she knew sooner or later Phyl would come to her senses. She wouldn't pressure her. But that man Hoffman surely got a knack for converting people to his way of thinking and didn't care whom he used to further his cause.

"Phyl girl, I think I'm pregnant," Pat said, breaking the silence between them.

"Pregnant!" Phyl echoed, "Oh God!" She held her hand over her mouth as if to silence her outburst. "I thought you were putting on weight. Your mother know? Jesus!" she said in alarm as Pat shook her head.

"Is that I struggle to send you to high school for?" Mrs. Sandiford darted out and grabbed Pat, pounding her in a wild frenzy. "All we trying with you, you're nothing but a disgrace to this family, tramp, slut... ah going to knock it out of you." She pounded Pat who put out her hands to avoid the blows.

"Don't hit her Mrs. Sandiford!" Phyl cried out, "I'm going for my mother." But she was too afraid to leave, alarmed by what Mrs. Sandiford said she would do. As Mrs. Sandiford tried to drag Pat inside, the girl suddenly lost her balance; too late Phyl tried to grab her as she fell down the steps, striking her head as she hit the bottom, then lapsed into unconsciousness.

"She look bad. She's dead, Mrs. Sandiford. We got to get her to the hospital quickly." Phyl knelt down besides Pat touching her forehead and feeling her pulse, appealing to Mrs. Sandiford who stood in the doorway and wouldn't budge.

"We got to get her to hospital. Pat, Pat, try to get up," she called urgently and Pat stirred slightly, moaning.

"Mrs. Sandiford you mean you going..."

"You and she is good friends, so you take her," Mrs. Sandiford said without emotion and closed the door.

Pat tried struggling to her feet. "Don't rush, take time," Phyl cautioned. Pat pulled herself into a sitting position helped by eager hands. She pressed a hand to her forehead, her eyes hurt, her side ached. She was battered and bruised but wanted to get up, most of all to cry but no tears came.

"How you feeling you getting any pains? You could stay by yourself till I run an' get Ma?"

"Don't leave me Phyl, I'm frightened. Wait a little bit, I might be able to walk to the hospital."

"I'm frightened too, you ain't feeling any pains yet," Phyl said wiping her tears away.

"Look call that boy passing and ask him to help," Pat motioned to Phyl. She was beginning to feel numb but she couldn't tell Phyl. She had heard about this kind of thing and was dead scared the worse might happen, before she could get medical help, so any stranger would do. Phyl quickly called out to the young man. Curious, he came willingly, took a look at Pat sitting on the cold earth, bruised face and dishevelled clothing and offered to help get her to the hospital.

Chapter 9
1952

"Come on Pat! You've got to pull yourself together, " Mrs. Martin said, "Stop being down-spirited and feeling sorry for yourself. The party would be good for you and Phyl. New Year's is the right time for young people to meet and have a nice time... You don't think so Phyl?"

"Sure and Maltinoes or Chinese Sports Club would be the best place to go. What you say to that Pat?"

"I still don't feel so good."

"Child I know. But you got to get out and move around to build up your strength." Mrs. Martin, smiling, spoke with great concern, "Remember, school opening next week, so you got to move around more or else you body will tire quickly."

"Look Ma, you don't worry, I'll get her to chance it." Phyl was undaunted by Pat's despondence. "Pat, man, you don't have to dance. We could sit around and enjoy the music. You know Washboards, your favourite band is playing at Maltinoes Sports Club; we could go there and really enjoy weself. Like Ma said, the party will do both of us good."

Pat didn't know how to refuse under such affectionate and kind pressure. Tears sprang to her eyes as she thought how much they had done for her and their genuine concern for her welfare. "I don't have anything suitable to wear. You know my mother wouldn't give you any of my good dresses." She dabbed her eyes as she made an effort to control her tears.

"No excuses, you remember that lamé dress you like so much? Well you wear that and I'll find something else, so we'll both be wearing old dresses." Phyl spoke with such emphasis that they both giggled.

"Girl, stop laughing and go and get the dresses so we can check them out," Pat, now lighthearted, said. Phyl clowning, jumped up in delight.

"Ma listen to this, Pat going. Ain't I tell you she'll change her mind," Phyl called out to Mrs. Martin who was in the kitchen.

Pat sat back thinking about the changes that had taken place in her life. It was a struggle to blot out the sufferings she had experienced during the time she spent in hospital. Her grief at the loss of the child, then the pain and shame of knowing how she came to be there. She could never live to endure such cruelties again. How she prayed she would die and told Phyl so. But it was Phyl and Mrs. Martin, faithful and constant visitors, who forced her to eat, combed her hair and insisted she was worthy. You can't do that! I sure that young man would go mad with worry, if he only hear what you saying. He won't be able to study one bit! Mrs. Martin reminded her about Ken. She had completely forgotten him and thinking about him helped to lift her out of her despair. At that moment she made the decision that Ken must never know about her ordeal. Then she got Phyl to promise to keep it a secret from Ken and help her to find a place to stay. She couldn't live in the same house with her mother again.

She would always remember the afternoon, two days before she was discharged from the hospital.

"Pat, my house is small but me and all the girls agree, so if you want, you can stay with us for as long as you like," Mrs. Martin had opened her doors to her and she was overwhelmed with gratitude. She burst into tears.

"Oh Miss Martin, you're a real mother to me. You always stand by me. I have no father and now I have no mother atall." She cried so much that afternoon, she thought she didn't have any tears left.

"You and Phyl like sisters already. Whenever I miss her she at your house and one more girl can't make any difference." Mrs. Martin smiling, made light of the situation, "So you all will now have all the time in the world to talk." Pat knew she understood.

"Well," Phyl said, returning with the dresses on her arm, "you take yours. How you think this would look tonight?" She held the other one up to her. "And we still got to decide whether it's Maltinoes or Chinese."

Pat, now confident she didn't have to come home to constant abuse, disapproval and rejection, went back to her job. For the first two days she felt very uneasy someone might make remarks about her appearance but she began to relax when she was sure no one noticed any difference. Everybody was too busy talking about Christmas, the presents they received, the parties they attended and she was glad. She knew Mrs. Martin would be just as pleased to hear she was finally settling in and had nothing to fear.

That evening she reported to Mrs. Martin and Phyl that things were going well at school. Then Phyl announced she would be out attending a very important committee meeting. Hoffman summoned the meeting because they were going to be watchful of the government's election strategies and the committee had been formed, especially to keep an eye on things, so nothing would be left to chance.

Phyl arrived at the meeting early, a few minutes before Hoffman, while the other members came at intervals. Hoffman's personal secretary came in accompanied by a man none of the others knew. Hoffman chatted with the newcomer for a while, then the secretary left. By this time Phyl and the others realised he was annoyed. He paced the room constantly checking the clock on the wall, while they waited for the last member to appear. The minute he came Hoffman signalled the chairman, who immediately called the meeting to order.

"My brothers and sisters," he began and nodded at Phyl, "it's 7:30 and we're thirty minutes late." He didn't try to control his temper. "We can't afford to be late. All our plans from here on depend on time. Time is the essence of everything we do. Let me tell you this; one minute lateness could change everything, every event that's carefully planned. We're known for our tardiness and we must do something about it if we're to succeed." He regarded the group with a twisted little smile and sighed.

"I now have great pleasure in presenting Mr. George Steele from New Amsterdam, our friendship goes back a long way. As a member of our committee, he will also be responsible for security and other matters."

"Security! Security?" everyone repeated.

"Look Chief, we don't need any security," the stevedore, who sat to the left of the chairman, said in a casual manner.

"There's an election coming up," Hoffman spoke with emphasis, "And we have important information to protect from the prying eyes of other groups. We can't wait to lock the stable door, after the horse run away." He waved his hands expressively.

"You right Chief," the stevedore admitted and the others murmured, nodding in agreement.

"What's the first item on the agenda?" Hoffman prompted.

"The first item is the plan for joining forces with Mr. Ovanton Lucklow, Union Leader." The chairman, a sugar boiler, spoke with authority, in his comfortable laid back position.

"Look Chief, I don't think that's a good idea atall." Jones, a young civil servant said, looking appealingly to the others. "At this moment, Lucklow is a very popular man with the people too. Remember he faced the police and the authorities. A lot of people thought he would run, but he stood up with the men. So right now the people see him as a bold leader and if you join forces with him, you might be making a big mistake. You could be supporting his following."

"I don't agree with that atall," Rayborn Charles, headmaster, said in his firm, yet tolerant manner of speaking. Everyone knew there was no love lost between the two. "I think it's a good move, to show the people we're all together in the struggle. In this way, we'll be able to combine our following of both middle and working classes and our votes will increase."

"Oh yes! So when the groups come together who will be representing them? Who?" Jones was unimpressed. "The man may well damage the Chief's image. Not may, that's exactly what's going to happen." His chest swelled out with self importance and this always annoyed Charles.

"Youall got to be joking," Clifton Lane, a small dapper man, the last to arrive, spoke with sarcastical emphasis, laughing. "Joining forces with Lucklow! As if the man is any force. That man could barely stand in the Chief's shadow. He isn't polished, he's uneducated like me. So what force and damage a man like that can cause? We don't have to bother about a thing because the people will prove what I'm saying is true."

"That's right." It was Steele the new-comer, happy to voice his opinion. "In this game of politics, you can't match an uneducated man with an educated one. Lucklow doesn't have a leg to stand on the same pedestal with our Chief, it's so obvious." He spoke with an English accent and everyone thought Hoffman had met him in England.

"The problem is, the man's following is growing by leaps and bounds in the working class areas and we have to ensure we get that vote too," Hoffman said, contemplated for while then added, "I have a glimmer of an idea, let me work on it for a while. Now let's move on to the next item on the agenda." He promptly dismissed the matter.

"Right Chief, the next item on the agenda is Operation Mongoose," the chairman said in a lofty manner. "Chief did you get the map as you promise, from one of your friends in high places?" He had a satisfied smirk on his face.

"Oh yes," Hoffman nodded to Phyl who got up and left then returned with the map which she spread open on the highly polished table. "I want you to know the rumour I heard concerning the change in election date, is no more a rumour, it's a fact. It was confirmed today by one of my friends in high places," he stated as he and the chairman exchanged glances.

"Chief, you know you always right about these people," the chairman commented. "You can't trust them in truth. As soon as they realise the impact the people will have, they ready to stall and cheat again. You really can't trust them atall."

"Darn right we can't and we have to force them to keep their promise. That's a gross denial of justice," Jones said savagely.

"That's what I mean," the chairman remarked, "as soon as the people get adult suffrage, these frauds want to change the date and confuse them, so the people won't know what to do."

"That's what the Operation is all about," Hoffman added, pointing to the map, running his finger along the lines. "This is High Street here, running north to south."

"Then this is Government House here," Jones said, marking the spot with his pencil. "Here's the back street, Carmicheal Street and this is the guard house here."

"Where's Hadfield Street?"

"Right here. And that's Parliament Building," the chairman said as he marked the spot.

"You recognise this little square? It's the Law Courts."

"Then the statue of Queen Victoria should be here."

"Yes and right in front as a sign of democracy, eh! We'll show them just what we think of their lying tongues. Deceitful snakes!"

"Where's the Constabulary Outpost?"

"Right here, man."

"This should be the police compound where that bombastic man..."

"Who you talking about, man?"

"Man, I talking about that Charles Batson. That cold-blooded son-of-a-bitch! We got to deal with him first."

"And don't forget the town hall, the constabulary and sanitation buildings. Make sure you mark them all Mr. Chairman."

"Now that we got all the places marked, we got to get down to plan ways and means for Operation Mongoose," the chairman spoke with enthusiasm. "I like the name, Operation Mongoose. We know the mongoose job is to destroy slippery, slimy and deceitful snakes. We'll show them a thing or two," he said with zest.

"I don't like this Batson idea atall." Phyl made her first comment. "I suggest we leave him out and find another way to deal with him. Remember, the intention of this exercise is not to harm any of our people, we all suffer enough as it is. But we want these colonial powers to know we intend to fight for our rights! And if they procrastinate as they did in the past, we going to stir things up plenty. But this Batson idea could lead to injury of many other men and their families."

"But he'd be getting just what he deserves. The son-of-a-cold-blooded-bastard," Jones spoke angrily. "He kicked my brother and smashed his knee cap in the last picketing exercise we carried out. I have no mercy for him and I say strike! We have to teach him and all who want to copy his behaviour a good lesson."

"Man, you're not listening. What about the other men and their families in the same compound?" Charles argued, "You only thinking about yourself. I'm truly sorry your brother got hurt so badly but that's part of the battle we waging, man. It's all a risk, a casualty in the struggle and price we have to pay. Today fo' you, tomorrow fo' me. I sure your brother knew what he was getting into. I think Phyl's reason is sound."

"Sound reason," the dapper stevedore stared at Phyl then at Charles in disbelief. "That man Batson ain't got sound reason for anything when he gone mad. When he say move, you got to move! He loves to rush and trample peaceful picketers. I see that man in action and he get a thrill out of beating up people. The man actually smiling when he doing it, besides look at that man size. He's big crude and ugly to boot. He's trying to impress the white people, everybody could see that. He's..."

"He's ambitious and callous!" Jones cut in, "And if ambition is made of stern stuff, he's well stuffed with it. I... We got to cut that man down to size, he's getting too powerful!"

"Hear, hear! I second the motion," the stevedore said and both men looked at each other intently.

"It seems we're divided on the issue of putting a little pressure on Chief Batson," Hoffman said. "Do you know the man?" He looked straight at Steele, pursing his lips as he tried to appear neutral.

"Naw, I heard people say he's a vicious character and spiteful to ordinary law abiding citizens, but he runs from criminals and bad men."

"If you're with us man, you'll soon get to know him," Jones said with a tight laugh. "Watch out for his brutality, he's a very subtle devil."

"But according to plans here, I won't be given that honour. Though it would give me the greatest pleasure to take him down a peg or two, solo."

"Well... Let's show hands to find out whether we take him down a peg or two," the chairman said, nodding as he made the count.

"I abstain," Hoffman countered. "It's up to you people to carry out these plans, so it's your show."

"Seems we have a tie here Chief. Jones, Clifton and myself, we want immediate action. What do you think about that Chief?" the chairman said.

"What do I think? Isn't this a democratic meeting. The hands told you what to do," Hoffman declared.

"So, that's it then. We save the good Chief Batson for another occassion or he's all yours now, Mr. Steele. Now let's get on with the plans and details of Operation Mongoose," the chairman stated with great ceremony.

They talked for hours.

"You think we should break off now Chief?" the chairman spoke with hesitancy. He was feeling tired and drained, quite ready to pack up and call it a night, but worried what Hoffman might think. He had glanced at the man several times but instead of showing signs of tiring as he and the others did, Hoffman waxed stronger as it got later and he didn't want him to think he couldn't stand up to the strain.

95

"Man, find out what the others think."

"So what you all think? Operation Mongoose won't go into action until the public know the election date change, so we got time to complete our plans."

"I'm tired," Phyl acknowledged boldly. "I could call it quits right now. But before we do, we must decide on a date to complete these plans."

"This is a grave matter as far as I could see. So I vote we sit down and thrash it out to the very end," Jones argued.

"Well, we all know when you're tired you don't do your best, so I agree with Phyl," Rayborn Charles reminded them and the others nodded and murmured in agreement.

"Chief, like you don't sleep much?" the chairman asked as the meeting finally broke up and he was about to leave. "Like you can go on all night," he laughed lightly.

"I get by on five hours at night. But when I'm pressed I make do with three."

"You good, you know Chief. I had a grandfather just like you, you're a born leader. Me now, tomorrow I dead tired and practically got to drag through the rest of the day. I can't survive without me eight hours, not me." He chuckled heartily as he bade them all good night and left.

"Man, you've come at the right time," Hoffman said to Steele after the others left. "I'm more than pleased to have a man of your profession, an expert on our side."

"Chief, you don't have to worry about a thing. I was top demolition expert in my platoon and I'm still the best. So you leave everything to me." Steele beamed at Hoffman, then he went on, "Chief, your members got to smarten up. In this sort of exercise you can't think about sleep."

"The children of Rome," Hoffman replied, "they sleep the sleep of children while Rome burns."

Chapter 10

Phyl seemed a little sober after the committee meeting and Pat wondered what had happened to bring about this change.

"You think we should use force against these colonials to get what we want? After all these British people use all kinds of cruelties against us and we sweating to make them rich."

"You know I hate violence of any kind," Pat, surprised, stated, looking at Phyl inquiringly. She remembered on many occasions Phyl told her in no uncertain terms, she would happily do anything to avenge the horrible crimes the British committed against the people. "Look at my situation. Was it worth all the violence I suffered? I tell you I don't want to be under the same roof with my mother again. Violence begets violence, and don't get me wrong, I won't lift a finger against my mother, but the less I see her the better. Whenever I think of her I turn to stone. She was always hostile to me, always humiliated and beat me for everything, whether I told a lie or the truth or the mistake was slight or serious. I suffered the same fate and lived in constant dread of her, afraid that nothing I did was right."

"Remember all them fights in primary school?" Phyl was introspective, "The one who took the first blow always hit back saying, 'You ain't my mother or father,' then the fighters would clash, hitting, scratching, even biting and rolling on the ground. The fights were mostly to make that point clear."

"Girl, you don't have to remind me," Pat said soberly, "Primary school children are very vicious to one another, but it reminds me about something the principal said to us."

"Trust him to give a long lecture every time something happen. But coming back to what we were saying, I think the majority of children at that age just like to fight and behave like devils. On the other hand, primary schools like Tiger Bay, where you bound to meet all kind of bad people, you have to learn to defend yourself, else you get a good beating every day. "

"It's true. If you can't defend yourself people always take advantage of you. And coming back to the principal."

"Exactly." Phyl cut in, "The people were picketing peacefully when the police rush them and beat them up. Now they ain't taking it, they fighting back. So the only way to stop them is to strike first. When they realise you out to give them the same beating..."

"That's what I mean about violence! People find ways to strike back. My way was to run from my mother, but whether from family or foe, violence is violence. That's what the principal said. You can't remember the time we had the talk about hostility and violence in the home and between the sexes?"

"Hm. Maybe I wasn't at school or the talk just didn't interest me. He always with his 'Things that bother me' column in his weekly paper."

"He was adamant children emulate what they see. So when the husband beat the wife and wife beat the children, then the children fight among themselves. The boys imitate their fathers and beat their sisters, then later on their wives and so the pattern continues."

"Good God! It sounds to me like the women get the worst of it. They get blows as children, sisters, then wives. Don't misunderstand me Pat but your mother make me glad for the parents I have."

"I know what you mean, 'cause I always wished my mother could be like yours. Anyway, the principal said the worst part was when the wife accepts this violence as part of family life. He told us what he witnessed... Coming back from one of his early morning walks, he was just at the head of Vlissengen and D'Anrade Street, when he saw a man beating his wife up. So he went up to the man and said, 'Mister that's no way to treat your wife. You must talk things over and try to come to an understanding.' Then the wife pushed herself in the middle and said 'Look Mister, why the hell you don't mind your own business. If he don't beat me, how I goin' to know he love me?'... Girl, he said he was struck dumb by the woman's attitude. Of course the incident inspired the lecture that morning. He said the only way to stop the spread of family violence is to educate women, who usually shrug it off as a custom."

"You can't stop that man atall. He don't miss a thing. I wonder how come he ain't put that in his papers," Phyl quipped and they laughed.

"Where did all this cruelty start?" Pat asked, perplexed.

"There's only one answer to that as far as I'm concerned. Those cruel Europeans. Those colonials!" Phyl spoke with emphasis.

"Europeans! What they got to do with our people's behaviour?" Pat said in astonishment.

"You mean to tell me you forget already what they did to our ancestors! Don't forget they owned the slaves on the sugar estates and don't forget how those cruel sons of brutes used to beat them just to show them who was boss. Then they beat them for talking in their own language. The poor slaves got a licking every day just to keep them in line and that frighten the hell out of them. And of course this habit was copied by some of the slaves, who had to beat their own children to satisfy the masters or the master would do it himself. You get the picture now?"

"I never thought of it until now... but when you come to think about it you could see how it worked to keep the slaves under their control. Beat them if they resist you in any way."

"But not for long though," Phyl retorted, her eyes sparking with jubilation. "Their own cruelties work against 'cause the slaves hit back and would rather fight to the death. You see, that's the same thing we were talking 'bout just now."

"And that's the crux of everything, 'cause everybody seem to think they're right and violence is the answer to any problem." Pat spoke calmly.

"If it's right for one it's right for the other," Phyl spoke fiercely.

"Well, my mother thinks she right. She never gave me and Ken a chance from the beginning. Then when I got pregnant, as far as she's concerned, if she beat it out of me, she solve the problem. Well she got it wrong. I hope she find that out by now." Pat made a grave little laugh.

"Good Lord!" Phyl cut in, "Talk about the devil, Pat you got visitors." She stared out the window in surprise.

"Is who?" Pat asked, not wanting to get up.

"Girl, it's your sister and brother Ian. "

"Look man, you talk to them and find out what they want to see me about."

"Hello Lillian, Ian... you have a message for Pat?"

"Yes... So what happen now, I can't talk to Pat if I want to?" Lillian spoke bluntly.

"Ehm hm," Phyl muttering, glanced at Pat who was listening.

"You try deal with that." She opened the door for the visitors, while Pat sat waiting calmly.

"Hello Lillian, Ian. How're you?" Pat greeted the visitors as they entered, standing just at the doorway.

"Look don't worry with all of that, yeh! Mom say you must come home right now and she send me and Ian to help you fetch you things."

"I beg your pardon!" Pat stared at Lillian. It was only her tone that betrayed her rising anger. "Look, you go back and tell your mother that I say I'm never going back there. You get that straight... Now good bye dear sister." She regained her calm. "You don't understand me... Go now... and tell her exactly what I say." Pat's face was expressionless as she urged Lillian, who stood rooted in the doorway, puzzled, then suddenly she fled down the steps, Ian following behind.

"Pat!" Phyl screeched, then erupted into laughter, "I can't believe it. Wait, let me control myself." She wiped the tears streaming down her cheeks, "Lillian actually come to march you home!" She guffawed again, "Girl, I was looking to see if she had a whip hiding in her dress. Girl, I was trying hard not to laugh in her presence."

"You ever see anything like that in your life?" Pat broke into laughter as she spoke. "But of course. The little princess now got to do all the housework. She's so lazy already. I bet you all of them now feeling it 'cause Cinderella found a home and while we waiting for the prince they can't stand the thought of you over here, so... "

"My mother out of her wits because I'm alive and strong and she can't control me. So she sends them like Greeks bearing gifts, 'Mom say you must come home now and we come to help you fetch you things.'" Pat mimicked and both girls reeled with laughter.

"Stop Pat, stop. Don't kill me. Cut it out." Phyl was bent over with laughter, "Lillian really looked Greek when you tell her 'You understand me, go now and tell her exactly what I say...'"

"I can't believe... she actually expect me to pack and traipse off behind her."

"Did you see her mouth how it hang open in surprise? She didn't expect you to say that. She thought you're still afraid. Girl, I had A-one

100

entertainment this afternoon... can't wait for Ma to get home to tell her. Girl, my whole body aching from laughing."

"You know they take me for an idiot or something. Go back? Not on your life. Yippee, yippee, yippee, I'm free, free, free." Pat bounced up and down shouting and Phyl joined in her impassioned cry as they hugged each other.

"But mark my word, Cinderella," Phyl spoke soberly, "the old queen in her palace will not give up that easily, she's bound to strike again!"

"And she'll get the same answer every time," Pat reassured her. "I'm free at last to live my own life in peace, and best of all, Ken writes regularly. I have you all and that's all that matters now. But I'm sure Ken and I are destined for a good life together, so I'm willing to wait." She spoke with a far away look in her eyes.

True to Phyl's prediction, Pat's mother paid them a visit a couple of days later. Phyl, her mother, sisters and Pat were sitting around talking and laughing after an early evening meal, when they heard a brisk knock on the door. Phyl looked outside.

"Oh oh." Her utterance alerted the others even before she whispered, "Pat is your mother!" Then she opened the door.

"Do come in and sit down, Mom," Pat greeted her smiling, as did Mrs. Martin and the girls.

"No, no thanks. I'm not coming in. I didn't come to stay long... I only come for Pat." Mrs. Sandiford, smiling, addressed Pat who was amazed by her pleasant attitude.

"Didn't Lillian tell you? I told her the other day I wasn't going back, I've made up my mind permanently... I'm not going with you or anybody you send." Pat was calm.

"Mrs Martin please talk to Pat. You're a mother too." Mrs. Sandiford ignored Pat's remarks. "Tell her to come with me."

"Mrs. Sandiford," Mrs. Martin's tone expressed her amazement, "This matter is between you and Pat and I just hear her tell you she ain't going. I can't force her."

"But if you were a decent mother, long ago you would send her packing, instead of encouraging her in your house even though I send for her."

"Come on girls, you all go outside... Donna, you keep an eye on your sisters and see they don't get into any fighting in the yard. Phyl you stay." Mrs. Martin ushered the girls, who unwillingly obliged towards the door.

"Awright Mrs. Sandiford, let's talk. Explain to me how I encourage Pat, unless you wanted me to leave her out on the street. Madam, you come in here for the first time and you never ask this child how she feel. When was the last time you see Pat?" She waited, but got no reply so she went on, "Me and these girls never miss a day when Pat was in hospital and I never see you nor Lillian and the boys... not even one day!"

"Oh, I now understand why you setting my daughter against me," Mrs. Sandiford spoke angrily.

"What? Setting your daughter against you? Pat is your daughter, so you beat her till she fall down unconscious and loss..."

"Mind your own business!" Mrs. Sandiford said in a rage.

"Your business. Well let me tell you. If any one of my girls, from the baby up, frighten of me I would be ashamed and know I fail them. That's my business, to take care of them and don't abandon them. So Pat was my business when you abandon her at the foot of the steps and in the hospital."

"I'm going for the police to get my daughter back. I'm her mother I mind her all the time without..."

"Look lady, go and bring the police, I will tell them the truth."

"Pat is my child and for all these years I didn't see anybody around when I was struggling to bring her up and send her to high school." Mrs Sandiford's voice rose angrily, "And you got no right to jump in the middle!"

"Listen Madam," Mrs. Martin spoke coolly, "I'll ask you not to raise your voice in my house. We wasting time arguing. Pat is the one to decide and she did. It's up to her to change her mind." She glanced at Pat.

"I'm not going back ever!" Pat upset and embarrassed spoke firmly.

"Well we just wasting time," Mrs. Martin insisted, and opened the door.

"I ain't taking it, it ain't ending so. And you all goin' to hear from me." Mrs. Sandiford, consumed with wrath, stormed through the door.

"Thank God she's gone. Peace blessed peace," Mrs. Martin said, shaking her head as she closed the door.

"This is terrible. I'm sorry for all the commotion my mother cause," Pat said, fighting back tears. "I can't understand. She called me all kind of names, slut, tramp, ungrateful. She beat me up. What she want with me? I'm not going back!"

"Look Pat, sit down here an' relax." Mrs Martin guided her to a chair, "Don't worry with your mother. You don't have any problem, she's the one with the problem. She doesn't feel good unless she got somebody to abuse for her sufferings. As if she's the only woman in this country to struggle to bring up a child. But she don't dare beat and threaten Roy Sandiford children. She don't dare."

"But..."

"No buts Pat. You got to be strong no matter how much she threaten you, and you're old enough to make up your own mind. Coming back with police indeed," Mrs. Martin scoffed at the idea. "I can handle her. But all she want to do is strike fear in you, so you frightened and worried and trot back there."

"But I'm worrying... 'cause I know she's not going to stop...and you've been so good to me."

"Coming here. She's no fool... and she's not going to come back here, you mark my word."

"Where will it end Mom... There's got to be an answer to this situation."

"Time is the answer child, just give yourself time," Mrs. Martin said, placing a comforting hand on her shoulder.

Chapter 11

Hoffman had had many meetings with Lucklow, the fearless union leader. Lucklow spoke on his platform, supported his policies — lauded his tenacity as he faced the enemy, colonial agents bent on enslavement or destruction of the people. He argued against the divisive consequences of fragmentation, earnestly pleading a case for unity.

Lucklow's advisors and advocates listened grudgingly, but gradually they began to thaw. Then suddenly caught up in the spirit of the times, they in turn bestowed lavish praise on Hoffman for his singlemindedness and selfless efforts to unite the middle and working classes into a strong political force. An action they deemed a master stroke.

It was on the first Sunday afternoon in April that the public was invited to a special meeting to validate and pledge their solidarity. The Sunday afternoon sky was heavy and overcast with the threat of seasonal showers, but undaunted thousands and thousands of inhabitants from in and out of the city made their way to the meeting. They filled the Green, they packed into the opposite square extending the Bourda market now empty of scores of sellers from the country who provide the city with fresh greens, vegetables, ground provision and fruit. They swelled into every side street, expectations running high as they waited for the proceedings to begin.

The chairman called the meeting to order, made a witty welcoming comment after which he spared a few remarks of his own.

"Look around you my brothers and sisters, I tell you I've never seen such a coming together. And you take it from me, this country has never before experienced such a spectacle! Look around you." He surveyed the multitude, "Can you count the numbers?" he asked.

"No, no!" The crowds chorused.

"I beg you count the numbers!"

"No-o-o-oh," some chanted while others chuckled at his request.

"Neither can I. But my heart is filled with joy to see so many, many of you here this afternoon and in such overwhelming numbers. Let the powers that be take note. We are no longer dormant and we will not take matters lying down. They know that victory's in our reach." He paused. "The mills of God grind slowly but they grind exceeding fine!" He spoke in an ominous voice.

"Hear, hear! Amen amen." The huge crowd roared.

"I am no speaker... so without much ado... I must say it gives me the greatest pleasure to introduce the greatest of all greats, the eminent Brother Hoffman."

As Hoffman moved forward, the crowd began with a slow hand clap which erupted into a thunderous applause as he stood before the loud speaker. He raised his hand and immediately, the gathering was as quiet as a cemetery.

"My brothers and sisters!" he began, "It gives me the greatest pleasure to speak to you on this most propitious occasion!" And the crowds roared.

"Hear dem words boy!" some cried out, while others raved. "Jesus! Who can beat that!... O rant, o rant!"

Hoffman, taking no notice went on, "I am greatly overwhelmed, seeing you here in such vast numbers on this particular Sunday afternoon, when we'll most certainly receive showers of blessings!" He looked upwards and the crowds grinned.

"Your presence here assures me that not only are you in favour of this marriage, but it also assures me of your loyalty and support, the support my Brother Lucklow and I need to continue in this struggle for justice and social equality!" He paused a while, then began again, "There is an old saying, 'Too many cooks spoil the broth' but, I say 'In unity there's strength!'" He spoke with emphasis and the crowds cheered. "How long will they continue to harass us? I tell you my brothers and sisters, it's only a matter of time, because they will not be able to stem the flowing tide." His voice gained momentum, "For we will move on and on and on and we will not allow the enemy to rest until we have driven them into the sea." The crowd went wild.

"My brothers and sisters," Hoffman continued, when the noise finally died down, but this time he spoke so softly into the loudspeaker, everyone strained forward to hear, "I repeat in unity there's strength and I will now present the man who made this union possible. He's no less a speaker, for he has spoken well for you, in all your struggles against exploitation and oppression! Yes, he fought long and fearlessly and walked side by side with you. In times of troubles he has been your mentor, during all manner of provocation. He's upright and honourable. I now present to you one of our lowly sons of Guiana, Brother Lucklow!" The crowd responded with a deafening applause as Lucklow came forward.

"My brothers and sisters, thank you, thank you from the bottom of my heart!" Lucklow said, when the applause died down. "Your applause is gratefully acknowledged! I must say I'm no orator like the eminent Brother Hoffman here, but I'm greatly encouraged by your approval." He spoke in a quiet, simple manner. "We have been together for a long long time, we stood together side by side through many bitter battles. You were there.... those of you who know me well... when we suffered beatings, many injuries, harassment and we went to jail together. We have given the powers that be cause to worry and now this alliance will give them greater cause to worry. So we must continue the fight. My Brother Hoffman just said that in unity there's strength. I will add the more we stand together as one band, the stronger we will be! Let the powers that be watch us grow. And we will continue to grow from strength to strength, in spite of their harassment and continue to struggle for betterment for ourselves, our children and all the generations to come." He paused, thoughtful, then began again, "But I must let you know that victory isn't easy. This is just the beginning, and the battle will be long and hard, nevertheless as long as we sticks together, with confidence and patience, we will be victorious." The crowd applauded.

"My brothers and sisters, your happy faces tell me this marriage is a good thing, so I'm with you as long as you need me. Now let us give three cheers for the alliance, Hip, hip..." He shouted again and again while the crowds responding, hands in the air, stamped, shouted and screamed.

"Thank you! Thank you!" he acknowledged, then moved to a seat on the platform. Hoffman moved closer and he and Lucklow went into a huddle.

During this interval the chairman made much of the alliance, "My brothers and sisters!" He directed the crowds attention to Lucklow and Hoffman. "Just look at the married couple, what a beautiful sight! See how they consult with each other. Isn't this the way all marriages should be?"

At this point, Lucklow, who had been standing with Hoffman, suddenly sat down, then immediately got up, paced a while before he returned and continued the discussion.

"It is written 'What God has joined together let no man put asunder!'" The chairman spoke as though divinely inspired and the gathering roared their approval.

"My brothers and sisters," Lucklow now came forward with hand raised and the utterances died down. "You know the reason for our alliance. For sometime we have been meeting and discussing our situation. But now the time has come for the alliance to decide on a leader. My friends you cannot serve two masters. I have represented you to the best of my ability but the decision rests with you. If you feel I've served you faithfully and honestly, or if you think I have not served you well, the decision still rests with you, you must choose as you see fit. My brothers and sisters, it's now up to you!" He stood hesitating, thoughtful, uncertain and the crowds grew restless as he stared ahead, saying nothing.

"Let's move on man! Let's move on!" some started shouting.

"Br... Br... Brother Hoffman will now address you." He stammered, unnerved by the shouting as he moved towards his seat, pensive. Hoffman had sprung something on him that wasn't in the plans for the afternoon and he had committed himself. He knew his honesty always paid off. Looking back at his past, he could never in his wildest dreams believe his simplicity and openness would be instrumental to his present position. Hoffman did hint the matter could be settled at another meeting but that could lead to division and disunity. They had come this far. He had faith in his fellow men and was confident his past actions would see him through. He agreed wholeheartedly with Hoffman's philosophy about unity of purpose and democracy. Whatever his doubts, he must cast them aside in the interest of the people.

The crowd now sensed a dramatic change in events. They too were taken by surprise especially by what they were asked to do. So, they began talking and as they talked opinions collided, sometimes violently as they compared each man's popularity, skill and power as a public speaker. They recounted as far as memory would allow, demonstrations and protests against the government. Some swore on oaths while others were willing and ready to come to blows as they wagered how each leader displayed acts of courage and endurance when confronted by the police, riot squads, big business bosses and landowners.

"My brothers and sisters," Hoffman spoke softly as he came forward and all the arguments were suspended. "You just heard the eminent Brother Lucklow and I'm sure you understand what he said! Now, I view our organisation like one big family." He laughed lightly and the crowd nodded in agreement.

"You also know.... that in any family there must be a head!" The crowd continued nodding and murmuring in agreement. "A ship can't have two captains or else the ship will travel in all directions. If we want to travel in one direction, there can only be one leader!" He glanced from face to face as he spoke, "It is for you to decide by your voices and show of hands whom that captain will be. There were many times when you walked with Brother Lucklow against great odds. You stood the test of time against all kinds of brutality and harassment, you name them. I know you suffered them and I praise you for your outstanding courage and vigour. But I too have walked with you when you carried pickets protesting this barbaric system. I was there when they rushed, harassed, beat, kicked and trampled us all! And they had to let us go too." He paused, gazing at the multitude in the surroundings. "All the world's a stage, and all the men and women merely players. They have their exits and their entrances and one man in his time plays many parts." He paused, then in the stillness cried out loudly, "I ask you... is valour all you ask of a leader? If valour is all that is needed I tell you Robin Hood would be king." The crowd chuckled heartily.

At this moment Lucklow hurried forward, bowed to Hoffman, raising his hand in protest. "My brothers and sisters, please have me excused! We need not go into all of this. I am willing to stand by your decision... whatever..."

"Wait man, wait, wait!" some chorused.

"You can't butt in like that when the man speaking," someone shouted.

"Let the man speak! Let the man speak," others said.

It began to rain, yet the crowd stood their ground, drawn by the tense drama.

"This is a democratic meeting, let Hoffman speak yeh!"

More shouts followed. Lucklow's hands fell by his side as he backed away. He realised he had made a great blunder by interrupting, even though he had hoped to prevent any discord.

"You all see how uneducated people don't knows how to act in these things!" someone shouted brazenly, this was followed by more shouts. All of this happened in the space of a couple of minutes then Hoffman rushed forward with his hands raised and silenced the crowd.

"My friends, the honourable Brother Lucklow means no harm. You know it as I know it. However, let me say this to you. I have worked hard, struggled long and I'm not willing to give up easily, so remember, I'll leave this saying with you, 'There is a tide in the affairs of men which, taken at the flood, leads on to fortune. Omitted, all the voyage of their life is bound in shadows and in miseries. On such a full sea are we now afloat and we must take the current when it serves...'" He paused, noting how the crowd hung on to every word he spoke, they stood transported. "'... or lose our ventures'" he said with great emphasis.

Suddenly the silence was shattered as the crowd came to life hissing, shouting and whistling, "We want Hoffman, We want Hoffman!" And no one felt the rain though they were well soaked by this time.

"My friends... I encourage you..." Lucklow said, stepping forward, "I encourage you..." He got no further.

Plat! plat plat! He was hit on his chest with ripe tomatoes. "Enough is enough! We want Hoffman. We want Hoffman!" they chorused. Plat.. plat.. plusk...plusk plusk! Lucklow was covered with eggs and tomatoes, missiles of degradation. Now Hoffman rushed forward with hands outstretched, too late. Lucklow as usual stood his ground, fearless in the face of danger. So I have come to this! he thought, but cried out boldly, "You have made your choice, my brothers and sisters!" He bowed to Hoffman, left the platform, head held high and the gathering broke up in an uproar as the rain poured down.

Immediately, some of Lucklow's followers rushed to his side, the expression on their faces grave and militant while the majority of the gathering began making tracks for home. Still a number stood around, looking lost, confused by the turn of events, speechless in the face of the excitement and jubilance displayed by others.

"Hoffman is our leader! The winner and champion of all of them. It is written. He shall lead us!" they shouted and sang as they danced in the rain, quoting prophesies from the Bible.

"My brothers and sisters, it is with regret..." Hoffman's voice cracked over the loud speaker, the thunder drowning out his voice, so he gave up. Secretly, he was elated. Lucklow had been his own undoing, all he did was to help fate on a little and achieve his aim, public affirmation of his political role as leader.

Phyl was depressed by the incident. She knew people threw rotten eggs at faltering, boring speakers, as well as those who in the public estimation had dubious reputations. But Lucklow had been greatly admired by everyone. He was simple, without flowery phrases, but everyone saw him as a fighter and a leader. She tried to recall what triggered the crowd into such reckless behaviour but things happened so quickly it wasn't too clear. One moment the crowds were applauding him then in another she saw them pelt him.

She reached home subdued and thoroughly wet.

"Girl, why you so quiet tonight?" Mrs. Martin asked, she had grown accustomed to her lively reports. "You catch a chill or something? Look how you wet to the bone. You ain't say one word since you come in."

"I alright Ma, just thinking." She responded without enthusiasm.

"The meeting come off alright? The rain keep falling so."

"Well Ma, the honeymoon over."

"What you mean?"

"Well some people pelt Lucklow with rotten eggs and tomatoes." Her voice was breaking.

"Let me help you get off these wet things, and get a towel to help dry out your hair. You so wet," Mrs. Martin fussed. "My God chile, is now what you tell me sink in!" She returned with the towel looking puzzled, "You don't mean that after all that man did for them same people they pelt him down? They goin' mad or something. Don't tell me they forget already!"

"I don't know Ma. It was all so sudden. The same time I thinking about leaving, the rain coming down harder. He come forward and start to talk. Then some people start shouting and the next thing was the eggs and tomatoes flying at he. It was terrible Ma, tears was running down his face when he come down off the platform."

"That's more than terrible. That man lead those brutes who was so frightened to stand up to the white people and demand more money. He lead them in front of the police and the riot squad. That man get thrown

110

in jail for them. He stand up to the white people and wouldn't bow down! The brutes get what they want and they ain't care one thing 'bout he now. That's wicked. If they don't want he, they still got no right to pelt the man."

"Where's Pat?" Phyl asked anxiously, despondent, noting Pat's absence, remembering Mrs. Sandiford's threats.

"Eh? Pat alright. She lef' before the rain come down hard to get her lesson book... something like that, from a teacher friend. She got to prepare her work for tomorrow."

"Oh, I thought..."

"Ah ha!... You think Mrs. Sandiford come and carry on with the police and Pat gone with her. Set you mind at ease. But if I was in that Bourda Green this afternoon I would still be in a big argument. Is a good thing I had my ironing to do. People too fickle minded," she said sagely. "I guess the Green was in a big uproar."

"Well, some people were going on, but most people was caught offguard." Phyl reflected, "I remember a group of people shouting he wasn't educated... that tell you how they thinking. I just wanted to get home."

"Look don't worry yourself too much. I think I hear..." she said listening. "Finish drying your hair I sure sure I hearing footsteps like Pat." She hurried to the window. "I know it was Pat," she remarked, opening the door. "Thank God at least you dry. See what you can do to cheer your friend up 'cause her spirits low tonight." She took the umbrella from Pat as she entered. "An' I always feel Lucklow should never get mixed up with them slippery-tongued politician. A union leader is a different kind of fighter. He just too honest for them rogues and was bound to get in a tangle, but 'boat gone ah fall an' it can't turn back."

"Is what happen, what happen?" Pat looked at Phyl's sombre countenance then at her mother for enlightenment.

"Phyl's goin' to tell you," Mrs. Martin replied, "Politics is a game you got to be very tough to get involved." She then left them.

Chapter 12

Phyl told herself the people were responsible for Lucklow's demise from politics and Hoffman had nothing to do with it. After a while she pushed the incident away in the furthest recess of her mind and refused to think about it. The work helped. She kept herself very busy with the secret proxy lists. Over the past year, Hoffman had gradually collected the information and there was a tremendous amount of work to complete before the election date was announced. Her responsibility was to get the work done and Hoffman would put his plans into action.

During the first week in May, they heard that the new date of the election would be announced in the official Gazette, by order of the Election Commission. A few days later, there followed another announcement in the daily papers that an eminent lawyer would be making a hurried visit to Great Britain invited by Lord Carbury, great nephew of the late John Halpenny who left his entire estate, monies and jewellery to his old and trusted retainers, Josiah Brown and Beatrice Bishop. When questioned, Mr. Hoffman made no comment. It was believed that one of the benefactors was seriously ill in hospital.

Phyl, Mrs. Martin and Pat listened to the news with great interest.

"Mr. Hoffman said he was glad to meet this Lord Carbury and talk with him privately, on behalf of his clients." Phyl smiling, explained after the news, "You know he's paying all Mr. Hoffman's expenses in the bargain. I think Mr. Hoffman is very smart."

"That don't sound right to me," Pat commented. "Why can't Lord whoever he is come here? After all, he's the one contesting the will. And what was that we heard about one of the old people sick in hospital."

"That's the first time I hear about it, Hoffman didn't tell me that. The reporter probably making up the whole thing you know how they love to make a big sensation out of everything," Phyl spoke acidly.

"Why should they do that?" Mrs Martin asked in surprise.

"Youall know they would do anything especially when Hoffman's involved as long as it suit their purpose." Phyl said in a huff, her annoyance escalating, "They didn't even say which one of the benefactors in hospital. That alone tell you if they know the truth we won't have to wonder is which one."

"Don't get excited," Mrs. Martin said.

"I'm not getting excited!" Phyl snapped, "It just gets me mad when they talking wildly, without facts to substantiate their claims."

"Well me child, let me tell you, where smoke there's fire, an' all kinds of things happen in this world. Don't forget Hoffman is a lawyer and a man just like any other man. So he got bad ways too. It's the same thing I was trying to tell you when the rumour was flying around about his behaviour. Anything could happen, so keep an open mind. I know you admire him and he got some good points, but there's always temptation. Remember the people say he doesn't handle any case 'til you pay him every cent. And he does make sure he get payment."

A week later, Pat and the younger Martin girls were home on the school holiday. The girls were skipping in the yard while she and Mrs. Martin were seated at the windows. Their attention was drawn to a woman surrounded by a group of excited children entering the yard.

"Good morning, Phyl mother," the children called out, "this lady got something to tell you." Mrs. Martin signalled to Pat to open the door. She didn't know the woman climbing the stairs wearily while the children sat on the steps or joined in the skipping.

"Lady come in an' sit down. What can I do for you?" Mrs. Martin greeted the stranger as she entered.

"Good morning. I know you wondering who I am, but the children tell me you're a good lady, so they bring me straight to you first. My name is Beatrice Bishop," the woman explained, smiling bashfully as she sat down.

"I hear that name somewhere before," Mrs. Martin remarked, knitting her brow, trying to remember.

"I'm sure you hear it over the air in the news." The woman spoke in a soft, meek voice, "I'm one of the two people Mr. Halpenny leave his estate for." She didn't smile nor show any enthusiasm or excitement.

"Oh my God!" Mrs. Martin and Pat chorused, gazing at the woman in astonishment.

"But lady I can't understand..." Mrs. Martin faltered. She had been looking the woman over carefully. Beatrice Bishop was wearing an ill-fitting flowered patterned dress and a pair of run-down brown shoes, badly in need of repair. On her head was a broad brimmed straw hat which needed a band around the crown, the brim was a disaster with straw sticking out in all directions. The woman looked sick too!

"Please read this," Beatrice Bishop said in her meek voice, as she gave Mrs. Martin a sheet of paper. "I can't read and write, but I get the lady I'm staying at to write it and read it back to me, she did her best."

Mrs. Martin took the letter, studied it shaking her head. "Everything written there is true," Beatrice Bishop assured her.

"Come Pat. You read this for me. My eyes ain't so good already an' the person who... I mean it giving me hell to read!" She passed the letter to Pat.

Pat gazed at the letter. "I'll try," she said as she appraised the difficulties, understanding what Mrs. Martin meant, the spelling, the writing, she'd have to decipher as she went along.

"'Please help,'" she read, hesitantly, "'The lady with the letter is truly Beatrice Bishop that the white man dead an leave all his estate, money and jewellery for her and the other man. The lawyer that looking after the will take all their own money an' jewellery that they work for, then tell them he got to get more to fight the nephew in England. He take every last penny an' it break the old man's heart, so he dying in the hospital. She can't live at the estate 'til the will prove so she living at me. I willing to help, but I very poor an' my old husband ain't workin'. She's a nice lady, but some time she get sick 'cause the trouble resting on her mind. But when she feeling good, she help me in the house. She is begging any help you can give, food or money, but she must get money or she lose everything. Please help.' It's signed Elizabeth Ambrose," Pat said as she came to the end.

"Lady, I ain't hearing right," Mrs Martin said, exchanging glances with Pat. "Lady who's your lawyer?"

114

"Is Mr. Hoffman," Beatrice Bishop replied.

"Hoffman, Lucius Hoffman," Mrs. Martin repeated and the woman nodded her reply.

"You mean that man tek youall savings and jewellery that you buy with your own money you work for?" Mrs. Martin pressed and Beatrice Bishop continued nodding.

"Look at this," Beatrice Bishop said, she leaned back in the chair as if she was exhausted, reached into the bag she carried and took out some clothing. "A kind lady give me this... but I would rather money, so I could give the lady I staying with something. You know she's really nice to me. She's no relation to me yet she invite me when I was looking for a place to come and stay with her. I would give her some money and save up the rest to give Mr. Hoffman. I got to get enough even if I have to walk the whole city." She spoke with determination.

Mrs. Martin signalled Pat to get her handbag, shaking her head sadly. What a tragedy, the woman look exhausted already. How was she going to travel around the city in the state she was in. When Pat brought the bag, she pressed a note in the woman's hand. She wanted to ask her how much money Hoffman wanted but decided not to tire her further.

"Whenever you pass this side again, you must drop in," she added.

"You're a kind lady and thank you very much," Beatrice Bishop said.

"I only wish I had more to give you now. Hold on a while, Pat goin' to give you a few cups of rice," Mrs. Martin said.

"Thanks for everything," Beatrice Bishop said as she took the brown paper bag and stood up to leave. "Goodbye." She went out the door and down the steps.

"Walk good, Miss Beatrice an' may God see you through your troubles. An' don't forget to drop in another time!" Mrs. Martin declared sighing. Beatrice Bishop nodded her head as she carefully picked her way down the steps to meet her patient guides, who immediately took charge, escorting her to another household.

"Ah feel sick," Mrs. Martin said as she and Pat watched the group from their window. "The woman is destitute... beggin' her bread from door to door... a pauper! After inheriting all that money."

"But the man Brown like he can't take it either," Pat replied, "like he ready to crop out. Miss Beatrice is stronger."

"Stronger! Pat, to me that woman look like she goin' to fall down any minute. I feel for her... but I was praying she didn't."

"You're right she look sick to me too and I was worried. But she got to be strong to be making all these rounds."

"I think is the spirit not the body; that goin' slowly. So is something inside that keep her goin'." Mrs. Martin left the window and sat down in her rocking chair, still shaking her head sadly, "Pat, I tell you if that man bleeding dem people the hands of the Lord is goin' to be on him an' his generation." She sighed heavily, "The mills of God grind slowly but they grind exceedingly fine... an' he goin' to meet it if it takes a hundred years."

"But he'll be dead then," Pat said, trying not to laugh.

"Well then, his generation goin' to meet it." Mrs. Martin closed her eyes deep in thought. "I wonder what Phyl goin' to say. You know when she's fo' you she stick by you to the end."

"You can say that again." Pat agreed. "Phyl's very loyal to her friends. But don't worry Mom. She's got a sound head on her shoulders, even my mother used to say so and sooner or later she'll see things differently. You can count on it."

Phyl went shopping downtown the day after Hoffman left for Britain. She walked along High Street on her way back home, then turned into Regent, when it occurred to her she was in the area marked for assault in Operation Mongoose. She walked past the town hall towards the law courts where the statue stood tall and buxom in the centre of well kept lawns.

Pensive, she stood on the opposite side of the street under a shady flamboyant tree close by, gazing at the statue. Soon it would be flat on it's face, where it ought to be, a heap of stones. A tremendous blow to those deceitful colonials who stretch out one hand in friendship, while in the other hidden behind their backs was some weapon ready to kill or cripple. Hoffman knew them well indeed! He understood all their subtleties.

She surveyed the area, looking at every detail. Then, satisfied the cause was just and their plans thorough, she made a short-cut through well-trimmed cherry trees that fenced the town hall. When she reached the street she saw a small store on the lot nearby, just several feet away from the building marked for destruction. She stared at the store in alarm. She had forgotten it and no one in the committee could have remembered it was so near. They all knew the other building would be empty when the time came to strike, but the shop would surely be destroyed.

116

"Hello Miss! Looking for something? Can I help you?" A young man came out the doorway.

"Ah... yes!... No... I mean I'm waiting for somebody and was admiring the display," she said then regretted it. She wasn't interested in the store window until the fellow spoke, but now that she looked at it, it wasn't attractive at all. "Well to be honest, I wasn't paying too much attention until you spoke to me. But if it was my job... sorry for being so presumptuous..."

"No, no that's okay. I like that. I would appreciate your ideas. I'm Thomas Barnes." The young man hesitated, "And this is my store."

"Oh my God I didn't know. I thought... Sorry."

"No please go on. I'd really like to hear what you were going to say." Thomas Barnes spoke warmly, "You could be doing me a service."

"Well, I would put some of those items in the corner more to the centre so people could see them. Then I'd put the ribbons over this way." She indicated the position, "Then you could drape some of the ribbons like a water fall and the window would look brighter, more attractive. I didn't know the store belonged to you or else I wouldn't shoot off my mouth like that."

"It was my grandfather's and he left it for me. He was a porkknocker, so he bought it as insurance for his old age. But he really left it for my parents."

"So your grandfather was a golddigger. He probably used to tell you all a lot of stories about the bush!"

"Oh yes, but he died. Then my parents died, so it's just me alone fighting it out. I have a sister in England."

"I'm sorry to hear you've lost your parents and grandfather."

"Pardon me Miss... I really don't know what got into me." Thomas Barnes made a little embarrassed laugh, "Here I am running my mouth off to a perfect stranger."

"Don't worry about it, it was nice talking to you. But I have to go now."

"Give me a look up anytime you pass here again."

"Goodbye and thanks for the chat," Phyl said and departed.

Life's full of surprises. She reflected as she hurried along. Thomas Barnes was an even bigger surprise than his store, a real nice fellow, with an athletic build. His teeth are so white she thought. He's neat and polished, and he looks only a few years older than me. Hmmm. What am I thinking at all. I just met the fellow by accident yet here I am listing his

117

special features. But he's warm and friendly, somebody I could feel at ease with. There I go again. She laughed to herself and looked back only to see Thomas Barnes gazing after her, waving.

Thomas Barnes stood outside his store thinking about the encounter. He had come out of the store on impulse, only to see this very attractive girl gazing into his shop window. He was not one to talk much and couldn't understand what happened to him, but he'd shot off his mouth to a complete stranger and scared her off. The more he thought about it, he was sure he made her leave. She had been waiting for someone she had said, and he was glad, hoping to get more time to talk to her, but no one came. Anyhow, he was going to be on the lookout in case she passed his way again. He went back into the store only when she was lost from his view.

When Phyl reached the office she couldn't settle down to do work. The store and her encounter with Thomas Barnes remained on her mind. She kept looking anxiously towards the entrance and was relieved when George Steele finally came through the door.

George Steele, in his mid-thirties, was still unmarried and attracted to Phyl. She was just the type of girl he would like to marry: independent and self assured. He made many attempts to win her affection, offering to take her out and walk her home. But she continually rejected his advances, telling him bluntly she wasn't interested. But this only kindled his ardour. The more she brushed him off the more he persisted, positive he could make her change her mind.

"Hello George," Phyl greeted him, "I'd like to talk to you for a moment, something important."

"Okay dream boat, your word is my command," he said in a flash of excitement, smiling with joy, advancing closer. He had been waiting patiently for such an opportunity and now he thought his luck was about to change.

"Let's go into the inner office where we can talk privately," Phyl added and he rushed to open the door smiling in anticipation, thinking she didn't have to be so grave about it.

"Well," he whispered triumphantly, quickly closing the distance between them, "you finally came to your senses eh."

"Look George. I thought we solved that matter already. I want to talk to you about Operation Mongoose."

"What do you mean? What about it?" he demanded, surprised. "You know it's planned for tomorrow, the day before Hoffman returns," his face set as resentment stirred in him.

"I know that," Phyl spoke curtly.

"Then why are you wasting my time?"

"If you listen, you'll find out! I was out today, there's something we didn't see on the map. You can't do it!"

"I don't know what you're rambling on about. A job has to be done... It just has to be done." He stared at her, sighed and controlled his frustration.

"When we checked the map and pin-pointed all the places, I don't think anyone remembered the small store. It's just a few feet away from the building used by inspectors and personnel. When that building's hit the store is bound to be destroyed. I was downtown today and I saw it. It's too close," she anxiously explained.

"Look, simmer down girl. What's the fuss over an old store anyway? That's one of the hazards of this operation. What's it got to do with you?"

"I told you I was downtown today and passing there. I actually talked to the fellow who owns the business. He inherited it from his parents and both of them are dead."

"That's just too bad," Steele taunted, feeling he had her right where he wanted her. "If the store is hit he'd just have to start all over again. And I must add, if..."

"What you mean by if?" She stormed, "It's as clear as day when the other building is hit the store will be destroyed! Don't tell me you're quite satisfied to see our own people struggle and end up with nothing. For God's sake George Steele, this is not a World War and we're not fighting to destroy German soldiers! These are our own people struggling like hell to survive."

"Okay, okay. It doesn't call for that." Steele surrendered. He was embarrassed. "According to plans, that area is the first to be hit but I'll go and take a look myself. That's all I can promise, then I'll decide."

"When're you going," Phyl urged.

"Tonight. Tomorrow night we strike. Hoffman returns the day after. Ah ha..." Hesitant, he coughed slightly, "How about accompanying me? I have two tickets to the concert at the Empire to see that Baritone singer. What about me and you..."

"What about me and you?"

"You know what I mean. I'd like to take you to the concert. So what do you say to a night out with me?"

"I have other plans." Phyl's face was expressionless as she spoke, but she felt warm inside as she watched his smile suddenly wiped off his face. That should fix him. Trying to manoeuvre her to go out with him. She made a vow she wouldn't be seen with him. His constant boasting and arrogance annoyed her. The lousy worm!

"Okay Miss High and Mighty. If that's the way you want it." He stalked out of the room, slamming the door behind him.

After he left, Phyl felt uneasy. Then, shrugging her shoulders as if to throw off his ill-manner, she went back to her desk.

"I tried my best, but it didn't work," she thought, sucking her teeth in annoyance.

The store and it's impending destruction, plagued her for the rest of the day, no matter how she tried to convince herself it didn't bother her one way or another. She left work and went home too preoccupied to engage in the usual exchanges. She snapped at and scolded her sisters. Mrs. Martin and Pat knew she was worried about something and it was no use trying to pry it out of her. They had to be patient.

Phyl tossed and turned all night and didn't fall asleep until the early hours of the morning. Then she dreamed the city was in flames and there was no water. She saw people running around with large buckets in search of water. Thomas Barnes' store was in flames, but the man stood in the midst of the fire and wouldn't get out, though he wasn't trapped. People shouted and screamed at him to get out, but he acted as if he didn't hear or care. She too stood in the crowd, watching the flames devour the store and she cried out to him the door was clear, he could get out safely, hurry, hurry! But he stood firm and unflinching, while sweat and blood streamed through his pores. Then as the flames burned closer, he began to fade away.

"Good Lord," she awoke with a start, "I hope I didn't cry out in my sleep." She waited to see if any one had heard, but no one came and she was relieved.

"Ma, you know I'm going to be late for work," she said as she prepared for work. "I thought you would wake me up."

"Well, Pat tell me you sleeping and I know you don't sleep late, so I peep in an' I meself decide to let you sleep a li'l bit longer 'cause the first time I look in you was just tossing and turning."

"I hate going to work late."

"And I know that one day late never kill anybody yet."

"Gees Ma, you don't know how much..." She started to complain, paused and said amicably, "You know what? I won't come home until after eight o'clock tonight. So don't worry about me and dinner, I'll get something to eat at Brown Betty."

"Well if you goin' to work late, see, is a good thing I let you sleep some more. You so moody these days. Now what you so pleased about? Just let me get you some tea before you up and lef' without putting anything in your stomach."

"Just thinking Ma," she said as her mother hurried off.

As soon as she left, Phyl quickly folded a pair of black slacks, a faded brown cotton blouse and a stole, pushing them into a carry-all bag with the usual paraphernalia she took to work. She had been thinking about Steele when her mother's words gave her an idea. How she resisted the temptation to hug her when she said, 'one day late never kill anybody yet'. She knew he didn't care a thing about Thomas Barnes and she didn't trust him. But she had a conscience, so it was up to her to do something. She couldn't sit idly by. The more she thought about what she had in mind to do, the more excited she became and her heart beat fast. She could barely wait to put her idea into action. It was going to be a long day.

Steele was not around when she arrived at work. She saw the bags that belonged to the other typist and the girl who worked on the copying machine. She knew they were out on errands for Hoffman and would be back soon. Their absence would give her and Steele a good opportunity to thrash the matter out. She wished he would hurry up and get there before they got back. Half an hour later Steele breezed in and she was furious.

"Hello beautiful," he spoke with brassy assurance as he sauntered over to her desk. "From the look on your face I know you're thinking about me. You're lucky I came in this early, but I'm a man to my word."

"Early. You're late... and you always come as you like when you know Mr. Hoffman won't be around." Phyl spoke coldly.

"Ah come off it girl... I'm in charge here when Mr. Hoffman is away."

"In charge!" Phyl snorted, beginning to lose her patience.

"Girl, you don't seem to understand my position here. The organisation needs my talents... so quit spying on me."

"Spying on you!" Phyl's nostrils flared, she was ready to do battle, "It's your job to do the spying."

"Look girl!" he cut her off, "I know why you're always so mad at me. There's an old saying that opposites attract. A strong-headed woman like you need time, so I'll be patient. Let's go into the office now you've blown off some of that steam. It's safer."

He glanced around them, "Where are the other girls? You're talking about me... where're they... it's nearly ten o'clock."

"You're in charge... so you ought to know." Phyl rose with a cynical laugh and went ahead into the office.

"Did you look over the area you promised?" she asked as soon as the door was closed.

"What's the rush. You didn't even give me a chance to sit down before you pounce on me." Steele retorted, offered her the chair while he sat down on a wooden box, legs crossed.

"For heaven's sake," she replied, waving away the chair, she knew he wanted to toy with the situation. She moved backwards to the door.

"Do you think I have time to sit here admiring you, while you glare at me. Come on. What is it you want to know?" He smiled at her slyly.

"I wish you would behave like an adult sometimes!" She reached the door, put her hand on the knob, ready to open it.

"I've never met a girl like you! You want something and now you're acting as if you don't care. I'm the expert and I'm telling you nothing can go wrong. The store's 'bout twenty feet away from that building." He was emphatic.

"Twenty feet! It doesn't look like all that distance to me," she said in disdain, hit by the seriousness of the situation.

"Look girl, you're so head-strong and won't listen. Those buildings are situated in such a way, there will be little wind between them, then the type of charges used will reduce any chance of fire. So rest your pretty head tonight with the knowledge nothing will go wrong. You'll see and Hoffman will be impressed with my performance. Orders are orders."

"You don't seem to understand. That building's old and too close... then you're forgetting there's paint, oil, putty, threads, lace ribbon, twine and all the things that could ignite easily."

"And I'm telling you nothing can go wrong. Your friend is in good hands."

"I don't know the chap. I told you I saw him only yesterday when I was downtown shopping. But remember the aim of this operation is not to hurt our people. I got nothing more to say. The others should be back soon, so let me go." She opened the door and went back to her desk. She knew it was no use arguing, he was never going to miss this chance to show off his talents. It was up to her to make sure no harm would be done. Her mind was moving quickly to the things she had to do later that night. She really wasn't at all surprised by his decision. It's a good thing I came prepared she said to herself.

She worked a bit later than usual that evening, lingering until dark. As soon as Steele made his first rounds outside the building, she hurriedly slipped into the slacks and the blouse, covering with the stole. She waited until she heard his footsteps at the back, opened the jalousie, called out she was leaving and sped through the door. She knew he had to make two more rounds outside to provide himself with an alibi, so she had an hour at the least and there was no need to hurry. She stopped at Brown Betty for a patty and a cup of coffee, afterwards she looked at the displays in a few store windows as she gradually made her way to Barnes' store.

She had just arrived at the store and settled in the dark passageway, when the Stabroek Market clock chimed eight. The night was dark and windy. She was pleased about the former, but the latter she knew could be the cause of destruction. He knows the wind would be right, she muttered to herself, peeved, as she stood in the shadow, deep in the dark passageway, leaning on the wall of the store. She was there for about ten minutes, her ears tuned in to all the sounds around her, when she thought she heard a movement inside the store and instantly crouched nearer the fence. Good Lord! It can't be! No one's supposed to be in there at this time of night she muttered in alarm. There was a scraping sound as if something was being moved from one place to another. She sensed someone standing in the same position she had been a moment ago. A bolt was shot and a door tried. Only then she realized she was standing smack outside the doorway. If she were discovered, how was she going to explain her presence there! What on earth could she say. She tensed, waiting anxiously, but relaxed when the footsteps died away. She remained crouching in the shadows, blending with the darkness, alert, waiting for any sound or movement.

She pondered the reasons for her involvement with Hoffman, his plans for the election and felt these were nothing to lose sleep over, compared with the plan for tonight. Her dream worried her a great deal and she was certain Barnes' store would be destroyed. Worse than that, there could be loss of life or limb. She was scared, but was glad she had come.

She did not hear the stealthy footsteps until someone stumbled over her stooping form.

"What the hell!" She recognised Steele's voice as he quickly grabbed her by the shoulders.

"It's me, Phyl," she said weakly.

"Girl, what in the bloody hell're you doing here?" Steele's tone was savage.

"Shh, shh lower your voice," Phyl warned, her courage returning.

"What the hell're you doing here!" He snarled.

"You still don't understand? Well let me spell it out... Waiting for you and when you climb over that fence... I'm going with you. You stick that in your pipe!"

"What? Girl, you're crazy or what! What the hell is this happening to me at all tonight? What kind ah crosses is dis 'pon me atall." Steele lapsed into creolese, a grave transgression for him and she giggled.

"Crosses 'pon you!" she retorted, "We both fighting for the same cause... So I'm just making sure things don't get out of hand here, tonight."

"I have an urgent matter to attend and you're wasting my time!" he said with passion.

"Carry on. But remember is you and me, wherever you go I'm going too." Phyl was determined.

"What's going on out there? Is who out there?" a voice shouted from inside the store.

"Jesus! Somebody's in there!" Steele said alarmed. "That man will be out here in a flash. Now the whole bloody job's botched."

"Amen. Ah told you to keep your voice down," she taunted.

"You're a treacherous girl! I must talk to Hoffman..."

"What's going on out here?" Thomas Barnes spoke harshly. He appeared suddenly in the passageway, torch in one hand and a crow bar in the other. He shone the light in Phyl's face, "What's going..." His voice trailed off as he recognised Phyl, then he flashed the light on Steele. "Having trouble with your boyfriend?" he asked. Steele still held her by the shoulder.

"Boyfriend," she repeated. "I know him but he's not my boyfriend. I ran into him and he tried to get fresh... blocked me in here. I was just about to scream when you..."

124

"Listen chap!" Barnes shone the light in Steele's face again and held the crow-bar raised and ready for action. "So you're one o' them chaps who can't keep their hands off women eh! Take off before I wrap this crow bar round you neck!" Barnes tone was ugly as he stood relaxed coolly appraising Steele. But Steele could feel his antagonism and knew he was at a disadvantage. A confrontation at this time was out of the question.

"I'm going to get you for this," Steele hissed at Phyl, "if it's the last..." The words died on his lips as he stomped passed Barnes. Phyl smiled to herself, she knew he was no match for the well-built and armed Barnes. He didn't dare make a scene. Always bragging about his combat or survival techniques, but in a real tight corner it's a battle of wits.

"Sorry, Miss," Barnes turned his attention to Phyl. "It's a good thing I recognised you instantly. You could've been hurt..."

"But I wasn't and thanks for rescuing me."

"Miss... You shouldn't be alone in this part of town and at this time of night." His tone was unmistakably disapproving.

"I'd better be on my way then and thanks again for helping me." She moved off, somewhat embarrassed.

"No, no. You mustn't do that. I would like to see you safely home, if you don't mind."

"But I don't want to put you to any more trouble."

"No trouble atall. I was just locking up to leave when I heard the noise. It would only take me a minute to get my things, but come inside it's safer." He moved aside to allow her to enter and she hesitated only for a moment. "That fellow might come back. He really looked vexed." He went in locking the door behind them. "Be back in a minute," he added going through another door into an inner room.

You won't have to worry about him coming back now or later. You scared the hell out of him, Phyl thought, smiling to herself. God or fate took the situation right out of her hands and the store was saved. Actually Barnes saved his own shop. He appeared at the right moment and pulled her out of a tough spot, while she was racking her brains, thinking of a way to manage the situation. Then he protected her, causing Steele to flee, 'cause he didn't want to be recognised by anyone in the area; time to think about his threats later. Barnes whistling suddenly penetrated her thoughts, he seemed pleased even though he disapproved of her late night excursion. She identified the tune and chuckled. It was Nat King Cole's "Unforgettable". It seemed they shared the same sentiments.

After a couple of minutes Barnes came back. "Let's go, sorry to keep you waiting," he said, eagerness written all over his face. They went outside and he carefully barred, bolted and tested the door, "I put on an extra lock. After what happen here tonight I can't take any chances."

"I must apologise for upsetting your plans for tonight, Mr. Barnes," Phyl said as they moved along.

"No... You didn't upset anything. I usually stay in the evenings to get a few things done that I couldn't find the time to do during the day. I'll feel better if you call me Tom." He looked at her intently, he didn't know how he was going to do it but this might be his only chance.

"I didn't even introduce myself. I'm Phyllis Martin, call me Phyl, all my friends call me Phyl."

"The truth is," he took the plunge, "since yesterday, I've been thinking about you. I think somebody up there likes me." He looked upwards, nodding his head.

"I feel I owe you an explanation," Phyl began to say.

"You don't owe me anything. You don't know how glad I was to see you again. So, you said that fellow wasn't your boyfriend?" he asked and she shook her head slowly.

"I wouldn't give him the time of day," she laughed. "He's got an oversized ego."

So the man meant nothing to her. He just wanted to clear the air. He knew instinctively she would be right for him but when he saw her in the chap's embrace, he thought it was hopeless. She's very attractive and he could understand the fellow's feelings, despite his crudity, but he had no right to behave as he did. She shouldn't be on her own in this part of town so late at night. She so serious now and he at wit's end... but he could not turn back.

"He was no gentleman as far as I could see. That idea you gave me yesterday," he changed the subject, "about the store." He explained, noting her puzzled expression, "I..."

"You're going to make the change?"

"I changed it already," he said, smiling widely, exposing his beautiful teeth which she regarded with pleasure.

"You're joking. Why didn't you show me?" She was quietly astonished, he had actually gone along with the idea.

"Well for one thing, I didn't expect to see you tonight, then everything happened so suddenly. Afterwards it was more important to see you safely home, and I only just remembered."

126

"I'm flattered. I really didn't expect you to do anything."

"Why not? It made sense. You'd be surprised at the change it made... even added a few more customers to my list. A lady told me she was looking for some edging and it was by chance she saw it in my window, after she couldn't find it in any of the other stores. So you see? I'll use the same idea a little different in the other window." He continued to talk about his plans for the store as they went along.

She found him easy to talk with and soon told him about her parents and her job. He understood why she seemed so different from the other girls he had met. She was independent and polished. She was a challenge. He was not going to let her slip out of his reach.

"It's hard to understand why such a pretty girl like you don't have a special boy friend. But I'm not complaining... that's good news for me." He hesitated a moment, "I don't want you to think I'm forward, but I'd really like us to be friends. Better still I'd like to meet your parents. I hope Saturday isn't too soon?" He couldn't suppress his eagerness once he let go, "That's if you don't have other plans."

"I won't mind atall," she replied. By this time they reached Phyl's gate so they chatted for a while. "I'm glad you took the time to see me home." She extended her hand and he held it, "It was a real pleasure and it gave me the opportunity to see you again."

"What time will you come?"

"I hope eight o'clock isn't too early?" he asked and she agreed thinking how uncomplicated he was.

"See you on Saturday then," she said and he let go of her hand and stood watching as she went into the yard, tripping up the stairs. Light-hearted, she waved good bye, feeling pleased and peaceful.

"Girl, I was getting worried after eight strike and you didn't come home," Mrs. Martin said, opening the door before Phyl knocked, "I keep looking out for you all the time."

"Ma you like to worry yourself too much... look," Phyl pointed to the clock on the shelf. "Is barely eight-thirty... sorry I'm late old girl."

"The last time I look out I saw you and the young man walking slow, taking you all time. So I say he must be one of the fellas from your work place bringing you home an' I feel pleased you with somebody."

"He's not from my work place. He's Thomas Barnes. I saw him yesterday and then just by chance tonight. His parents are dead and he's got his own little store. Ah... he's coming to see me on Saturday night."

"Hm," Mrs. Martin responded, thinking about Phyl's moodiness over the past weeks. She was praying something like this would happen. Phyl's growing older day by day and even though she happy an' involved in this politicking with Hoffman, it's time she settle down, while she's still young and shape her own life, raise her own family. Maybe this young man is a start in that direction. She was pleased. "Hope is a son-in-law ah getting," she added playfully.

"Oh Ma! That's all you waiting to see," Phyl replied, giggling, hugging her, mother and daughter regarding each other with mutual understanding. "Is nothing like that atall. We just meet... we're only friends."

"Well, let's wait an' see," Mrs. Martin patted her on the shoulder and followed her to her room, "Sleep good chile." She spoke gently.

"G'nite Ma," Phyl spoke softly, "We'll talk more tomorrow. Don't want to wake up Pat."

As soon as Mrs. Martin left the room Pat sat up, pulling off her covers. "Who's sleeping? Mom was worrying. I didn't want to encourage her so I came in after telling her you'll be here soon. What happen girl?" Pat stared in surprise at Phyl, Phyl seemed very pleased. She didn't have to insist. Phyl her eyes shining, barely suppressing her emotions revealed her meeting with Thomas Barnes, the day before but neglected to mention how they encountered each other that night.

When they had exhausted all probabilities and possibilities of the relationship, they fell asleep.

They were sound asleep, like most of the city's inhabitants, when a loud explosion shattered the air, followed by another, startling everyone.

Then realization hit Phyl.

"Girls, you all hear that?" Mrs. Martin, anxious, rushed to the girls' rooms, "You see! Your father 'pon night shift again... an' I always tell he... he never at home when anything happen!"

Everybody began talking altogether as they tried to place the explosions.

"That sound like two explosions to me. They hit bam bam, quick, one after the other," Mrs. Martin said.

"It sound like is right here in the city," Pat suggested,

"Where Ma, where you think?" the younger girls asked.

"Ma, you sure sure is two?" Phyl asked yawning.

"Of course is two. You know, I can't sleep when you' father ain't at home!"

128

"Ah thought was more," Phyl exclaimed, her face expressionless. "Ma, look, let's go to bed... is not here... we safe! Besides me and Pat got to go to work tomorrow; and Mr. Hoffman will be back too." Phyl went back to her room followed by Pat. She climbed into bed thinking it had happened at last and she couldn't wait for the morning paper to read all about the statue lying flat on the grass, broken into a million tiny pieces and a big hole in the House of Assembly. Barnes store was safe.

When she finally fell asleep, she dreamed she saw the statue falling unceremoniously to the ground. There was marble lying everywhere and people were flocking around, gazing at the scene, their faces showing no expression at all. Then she dreamed she was trapped inside a burning building, smoke and fire were everywhere, she couldn't get out. Suddenly a fireman appeared with his helmet pulled down, shading his eyes from the smoke and heat. He held a hose in his right hand as he ran to rescue her. He got her out safely and promised to take her home if she would wait, he had to put the hose away. As he spoke he pushed his helmet back, wiping away the sweat from his face and she stared in surprise at Thomas Barnes. The hose in his hand was not a hose at all... it was a crowbar.

Chapter 13

Phyl spent a restless night, but somehow she awoke feeling better than she had in the past few days. She thought about Thomas Barnes and the anxious moments she had spent. He was the cause of her worry and the source of her peace. Unknowingly he had averted his own catastrophe. He had sallied forth like a true warrior, well armed, protected her and routed Steele. She smiled when she thought about Steeles' vow to get even. His threat was proof of how demoralized he was. She remembered the bitterness and resentment she saw in his eyes, as he gazed hard at her. She knew antagonism had taken the place of his precarious affection for her and he would stop at nothing to destroy Hoffman's confidence in her.

She glanced at the old grandfather clock, it was nearly ten-thirty and Steele hadn't shown up. It would serve him right if Mr. Hoffman suddenly appeared, discovered his arrogance and laid down the law. She fumed. Everybody knew how much Hoffman detested tardiness; but this never seemed to bother Mr. Steele. It would be just good for him if Hoffman cut him down to size. She studied the situation. There was no other alternative than to tell Hoffman the truth. She believed in him and what he was doing but was sure he wouldn't want innocent people to be hurt nor their means of livelihood destroyed.

It was nearly lunch time and Steele still hadn't put in an appearance. The typist and the other office help left early for lunch, still no Steele. She, engrossed in thought, bent over to retrieve an eraser off the floor, didn't hear footsteps, but felt someone standing very close to her desk.

"Only a dummy like you would creep up on me," she said, straightening up and was shocked to see Hoffman. Undaunted she went on, "Bad joke. I took you for Steele." She laughed outright.

"So I gathered from your description," he said laughing.

"Nobody expected you until later his evening," she explained

"That too I gathered! When the cat's away the mice will play." He gestured at the empty places, "If people don't think this job's important enough to warrant their presence here, they'd better start looking for something else!" He shot out angrily "The minute my back is turned..."

"Look I'm sorry about it," she interrupted his tirade, "but it's no use telling me... How was your trip?" She attempted to steer the conversation into safer channels, "Did everything turn out right? Those poor people are depending on you... you know that," was all she dared say at the moment, fully aware of Beatrice Bishop's plight.

"To the latter question, I should say things are going just the way I expected. You're right girl, I have no right bawling you out."

"I'm glad to hear things will work out well for them," she responded, feeling soothed.

"There's no doubt everything will eventually turn out well for them. But these matters take a lot of time. So patience is the essence of success," he added, and Phyl saw the far away look in his eyes which appeared whenever he spoke about the future.

"However, we got to act more responsibly!" He was back to the topic which had occasioned his anger. "If we want to run this country, these absent people got to understand what responsibility means." He looked at the empty places, shaking his head. "These same people are the ones who will to teach their children and their children's children to be responsible or else, I'm certain as I'm standing here, we are doomed to failure." He nodded his head as one fully accepting the challenge, "Girl we got foh wo'k hard 'pon dem foh get dem foh change dere ways," he stressed.

"I... Ah..." she began and Hoffman interrupted, "What happened to the things we planned? I found out there were two instead of three. What went wrong?"

It's now or never! Phyl thought, "How did you find out, you read the papers?"

"You know I rarely read the papers. When I arrived at the airport, I was met by a group of reporters. I don't know how they got wind I was on that plane, that was a last minute decision on my part. However, they literally bombarded me with questions about my visits and the bomb-ings."

"And what did you say?" she asked eagerly.

"Now... what could I say? I was astounded such a thing could happen here," he chuckled heartily. "You'll be able to read my nicely worded comments about colonial skulduggery." They both smiled, thinking the trip was a clever alibi. He went on. "There was one reporter who wasn't satisfied with my answers, so he tried to press me for more information about the will and the other party in England. But I repeated what I told them before... My trip proved to be amicable and successful for all parties concerned. Then the fellow threw this one at me: he wanted to know what will happen now that one of the beneficiaries is dead. I didn't know that! Do you know the man is dead?"

"Dead!" She repeated as though struck by lightning, "I know he was sick... but dead... will that alter the will, I mean?"

"Don't look so worried," he said, laughing at the expression on her face. "Whoever his next of kin are, his relatives, they will benefit same as he, when the will becomes probate. Rather, whomsoever he named as next of kin... so put your mind at rest." His tone indicated his past annoyance was over.

"I have something to tell you. I'm responsible for the operation not coming off as planned," she explained.

"You responsible! How?" he asked, amazed. She calmly explained.

"He's right Phyl, orders are orders!" His tone was subdued and controlled as he glanced curiously at her, "We can't have too much sentiment in this thing." His countenance suddenly changed and he laughed heartily, still observing her closely. "Good Lord girl! You mean to say you went downtown and actually told Steele you going with him. You tried to get Steele to retract. Steele of all people. You're one hell of a girl." He clasped her hand, shaking it all the while, "You deserve a medal for that! You're the kind of girl a man should be proud to marry; Steele should marry." He winked at her and she guessed he and Steele had a man to man chat about her. "Anyhow this is no game for the squeamish," he wagged a finger at her. "How's our special project coming along?" he asked and she was glad he changed the subject. She led him to the inner office. There she unlocked the large antique cabinet and he checked the contents with satisfaction.

"How's the remainder?"

"Should be finished in the next few days," she said, relaxed.

"Let's hope there's no other changes in the voters list." He studied the lists she held for him. "We got to play it safe now. We got to take some and leave some for another time." He looked at her knowingly and they chuckled together.

They returned to the outer office, after locking away their secret resources. Just then Steele came breezing in. He stalled, surprised to see Hoffman. But he rebounded courageously.

"Hello Chief!... Had a good trip?" he asked with an air of confidence but Hoffman observed him casually, saying nothing.

"Didn't expect to see you back soon. Oh... I, ah... the job came off in grand style." He addressed Hoffman in a lively manner, but the other remained silent. "Listen Chief... I've got something important to discuss with you privately. If you could spare the time. This girl... "

"On my time. If it's so important why weren't you here all along?" Hoffman spoke coldly and turned to leave. "Phyl already told me enough." When he reached the door he said to Phyl, "I hope that thing will be finished by weekend... I'm going home to get a couple of hours sleep." Then he went through the door without even glancing at Steele.

The stillness in the room was shattered as soon as Hoffman drove away.

"You poisoned Hoffman's mind against me as soon as you got the chance," Steele stormed at her.

"You're crazy or what? I don't have time to talk about you," Phyl protested.

"So that's what you meant to do to me." She ignored him and went on with her work. "You're a dangerous girl! You told him a pack of lies," Steele raged.

"I think you're suffering from shell shock or delusions of your importance," she shot back.

"I'm going to see to it that he hears the truth, if it's the last thing I do." He stormed through the back door and she heard him banging and throwing things around in a rage. But she felt no sympathy for him, he had allowed his conceit to cloud his reason. She prayed the afternoon would end quickly, so she could go home and forget Hoffman and Steele existed. She kept thinking about Thomas Barnes all the time. She was attracted to him from the very first moment they met. He seemed to have a very sobering affect on her. She couldn't help remembering the ease and confidence with which he tackled Steele. Then once the incident was over, he never mentioned it again. She was really looking forward to his visit on Saturday night.

Phyl left work on Saturday around noon after putting away the last of her project. She stepped out in the bright noonday sun feeling as if a heavy load was lifted off her mind. She surveyed the hustle and bustle around her as she made her way home, marvelling at the scene as though she was seeing it for the first time. The streets seemed so alive with women. Proud working girls with heads held high, dressed in tailored skirts, sedate blouses and high heels, stepped daintily among the throng of housewives and aged grandmothers in colourful dresses and headties carrying huge baskets to market. Others, laden with the spoils of success-ful bartering, sweated with their burden, pleased with their purchases. She turned a corner, then waited for a crowd of cyclists to pass. They moved at a slow, idle pace crashing into each other as they rode along, creating a fount of amusement for themselves, but irritation for un-suspecting cyclists who hurried by.

Phyl suddenly felt tired. She could barely drag herself along and had just decided when she got home to fall into bed and take a long nap. She was a couple of blocks from home, when a violent explosion shattered the air. Every pedestrian stood still and cyclists ground to a premature halt. Then another followed by a third and final blast.

"Sound like the electric company to me."

"That done with boy."

"But is what's wrong with these people atall."

"That got to be the water works, that sound close by!"

"You all deaf or what? That got to be downtown!"

"Well that sound like is Booker's to me... an' I got family wo'king downtown. Leh we go boys!" Crowding together spontaneously, pedestrians babbled and argued excitedly. Then cyclists in the lead, they took off in one direction or another.

As the jostling crowds raced by, Phyl, and several other women stood aside on the parapet. After they swept past, she hurried onwards with a vigour to match theirs. She reflected on the explosion: at the moment, their committee had nothing planned. Therefore other groups were also taking things in their own hands. Hoffman started the fire, now others would also add fuel to keep it going, an object lesson for those cunning and brutish colonials. Serve them right.

"Chile, I was worried about you after I hear dem explosion!" Mrs. Martin declared when Phyl entered the house. She and Pat stood in the doorway anxious, while the girls clustered around wanting to know if Phyl had any news for them. "I okay Ma. I wasn't far from home when the bombs went off. I feeling tired, tired," she informed them, flopping into a chair.

"Like people gone crazy or something," Mrs. Martin said in disgust.

"You right Ma. I had to jump in the grass before the crowds crush me to death. You should see how they rushing to get to the scene of the bombings." Phyl yawned wearily as she spoke.

"But all this bombing and destroying can't be right!" Mrs. Martin protested. "Some say is because the government pushing de people dem around, changing the election date. But I don't think this bombing an' bombing that going on can a make any difference, 'cause we goin' to suffer for it, an' that's why I worry when you all 'pon de road."

"Ma, you don't have to worry about us."

"Why? We don't know where these people goin' to strike next... an' the police ain't even got a clue! You can't get a word out o' dem. As for the Batson, he's just a big blow hard. He ain't got a scrap ah brains."

"Ma, if these bombing got anything to do with the election I sure none of us will come to any harm. Whoever doing it know very well what they doing." Phyl pointed out, "They're right to strike back to show these colonials they aren't docile and mean to fight... they can't continue to keep this country back by denying people their right to vote."

"But the Bible say violence will lead to violence! Why can't people find other ways to get their rights? Is intelligent people involved."

"You forgetting is the government first use violence against the people. All they were doing was marching and picketing peacefully for their rights. Don't forget they brutalise and abuse the slaves and the estate workers who was just asking for better treatment and fair wages. They start it first." Phyl was relentless.

"Chile you full o' fire, back to your old self again but I still don't agree."

"Well they start it and now they getting it back in fine style. Only the other day me and Pat been talking about the same thing, remember Pat?" Phyl glanced at Pat who nodded her head, "They been doing it for years

135

and getting away with it, so the people got to retaliate or they take advantage of them."

"They got to be other ways and means of settling these problems."

"What other ways Ma? The other ways will work only after we show them you just as strong." Phyl paused a moment then went on, "Ma you remember Boy Boy and Sago?"

"God! I can never forget dem two boys." Mrs. Martin assured her nodding her head. "I used to be afraid, that one day Boy Boy would kill Sago with blows; an' fancy it, now the two o' dem is good friends."

"That's because Sago fight back. He stand up for his rights and Boy Boy so shock at the blows he get, he had to give in and be friends."

"That was two boys fighting 'gainst each other, this situation different different." Mrs. Martin refused to accept Phyl's logic.

"Is the same thing Ma," Phyl said forcefully. "One think he superior and the other one fight back to show he got the same rights and power. I feel if you want rights and power in this world, you got to fight for it... you got to!"

"Come chile, in this house we don't have to fight for power and rights. We got understanding."

"Ow Ma, that's not fair. You're my mother and..."

"Don't forget my mother," Pat said, breaking her silence, her manner calm and sober. "I think we getting things mixed up. We talked about violence... now we're talking about destruction! Mom's right... this thing could lead to a lot of senseless destruction. Then you have to rebuild, wasting time and money which could be spent improving on what you have. Maybe I'm not political, I'm just too sensitive."

"You got to do something bold, rash! You got to dare them or they ignore you as they been doing all the time. Violence, destruction, it doesn't matter what you use against them. They're cruel and think they got all the power on their side." She paused thinking about Thomas Barnes store, shrugged her shoulders. "Look, I'm so tired now." She got up yawning, "I could sleep right here."

"Girl, since you come in, we arguing away, let me get you something hot." Mrs. Martin moved towards the kitchen.

"Don't worry yourself Ma. I more tired than hungry," Phyl said moving to her room. Mrs. Martin, following her a few minutes later, found her fast asleep in her working clothes.

In the weeks that followed, loud explosions rocked the city and in the country, the damage was massive. Irrigation dams, kokers, private property and machinery belonging to sugar estates were sabotaged. Government buildings, schools, businesses and homes of private citizens were fire bombed and lives were lost. The situation was dangerous. When the announcement came that the new election date was set for the first Monday in July the people concluded that the destruction was directly responsible.

Soon after, official notices were posted in an earnest attempt to put the election machinery into gear. During the unrest, the challenge of deciding on candidates for the election was merely suspended. Now election moved into full swing.

Every night, hundreds again began their tramp around the city, seeking out meetings, gossiping about prospective candidates, criticising, praising, ridiculing, arguing about their motives, character and ability.

The very first evening Thomas Barnes visited Phyl, he made a favourable impression on the Martins.

"Don't talk all the time an' forget to give your friend something to eat," Mrs. Martin whispered quietly to Phyl, reminding her about the refreshment she had specially prepared for them. Aloud she said, "Son, I'm glad to meet you, but I'm sure you won't want old people like me around." She motioned the others to follow her inside.

"I hope you don't mind if I call you Mom," Barnes said, "I'm sure Phyl told you I lost both parents, so please stay. I'd like you to." Barnes would not let her leave, and Mrs. Martin accepted his invitation. She seemed pleased.

"I told Ma your grandfather was a porkknocker," Phyl began.

"Yes, he was a real old time golddigger," Barnes eagerly agreed and everyone, realizing he enjoyed talking about his grandfather, looked at him expectantly. "He worked mostly around the Venezuelan border. It was through him we got the store. He bought it and a small cottage on a half acre of land in Campbelville. My parents are dead and that's why the property now belong to me and my sister in England."

"But that's unusual!" Mrs. Martin exclaimed, "I don't mean buying the property is unusual, I mean about your grandfather putting his money into something..."

"I know exactly what you mean," Barnes said chuckling. "A lot of porkknokers used to put their money into something else. Of course we all know the old story about them feeding horses with hundred dollar notes."

So they all talked, swapping stories about people they knew, whose relatives were porkknockers, who went on spending sprees as soon as they came out of the bush, wasting their new found wealth on 'bad' women and drink.

"He was one in a thousand to put his money to good use," Mrs Martin remarked. "Mr. Barnes, I tell you, your grandfather was one hell of a man."

"Call me Tom, Mom," Barnes said and Mrs. Martin happily obliged.

"Well Tom, I could tell you, in dem days those men were reckless."

"Mom, those were reckless days too. You got to remember men went into the bush with nothing, just they two long hands. Then after suffering all kind of privation and starvation, they came out with pockets full of gold. I think is that cause them to do foolish things."

"That's right. And everyone of them went back to the bush with not a penny to their name. Some families I know actually had to borrow money for their passage an' ration just to get dem out of their hair," Mrs. Martin said jovially and everyone laughed heartily.

"It's no laughing matter," she declared. "Is serious business, We could laugh, but there're many families broke an' living in poverty, whose fathers, brothers or close, close relatives is golddiggers an' if they don't grab dem just as they land from the bush, ah tell you is hell to pay. Your grandfather must ah signed a pact with your grandmother." She spoke seriously, curious to find out the reason the man showed such strength of character.

"Well, according to my mother, it was really my grandmother's doing. You see my grandfather was a real lady's man, but my grandmother was a woman with a hell of a temper. So when she caught him red-handed and vowed to put the akia stick on him asleep or awake, he didn't stick around to find out whether she was joking or not. He abandon ship and head straight for the bush and stayed for a couple of years. By that time he got tired of the bush life, and my grandmother too cooled down especially after he showed her all the gold he brought back. That's how they bought the house and the business. But he never trusted himself to stick around Town too long 'cause..."

"I bet he didn't!" Phyl cut in, "Not with his tastes and I'm sure he had a whale of a time in the bush too."

"That's exactly how the story went. There was no stopping that man." He winked at Phyl as they all chuckled good naturedly. "But he made sure he was out of my grandmother's reach," he added.

Phyl was pleased Tom fitted in so well with the family and the evening was a success. She knew her mother liked him. Tom told her when they alone, "I know some fellows when they go to a girl's home for the very first time the girl's mother usually give them a hard time." Finally he took his leave promising he would call soon.

Phyl thought about Tom often. The truth was, he was never out of her mind. There was a simplicity about him which touched her. He was easy to get along with, courteous, honest, sincere and sensitive. But there was nothing delicate about his powerful arms, sleek body and graceful movements. She looked forward eagerly to his next visit.

Tom too, was thoroughly pleased with his first visit. He hadn't been around much with girls. He knew he was simple and straight-forward and not given to many fancies. He was the kind of person, who when he fixed his eyes on something, instinctively knew whether it was right for him or not. Now his attention was on Phyl, he sensed a warmth heighten in him that he had never experienced before. As the days slowly dragged by, whenever he thought of her, a powerful emotion gripped him and he knew that he wanted to be with her for keeps. But he didn't want to push his luck. He might wear out his welcome. With these thoughts in mind, he decided to be cautious.

A week went by and he missed her, and the friendly family atmosphere. Phyl had introduced him to everyone except her father who hadn't been at home. He was very lonely these days and though he was no stranger to loneliness he realized he had made a stupid decision to let the whole week pass by without going to see her. Saturday night was the worst night of his life. It was unbearable, he didn't think he could wait until the following Saturday to pay her a visit.

"I hope you're not busy," Tom cautiously asked a very surprised Phyl, when she opened the door to his knock. "I hope I'm not disturbing the family?"

"Oh no! Just me alone. The others are out."

"Well in that case I'll come back another time when..."

"Don't be silly! Come on in." she said, holding his hand. "I can't say I'm not surprised to see you, especially in the middle of the week. But you don't have to go. I'm very glad you came."

"You know how it would look if nobody else is round." He appeared uncertain, "Though I'd really like to stay."

"Don't worry. Ma and the others will be back anytime. Relax. Ma said you were going to come." She made a little nervous laugh, feeling suddenly alive and light hearted.

"The truth is, I wanted to come," he admitted, when he finally went in and sat down, "but I thought you might be busy or get bored with me hanging around."

They went on talking about things young people talk about when they are reaching out and getting to know each other, until the others arrived.

"You see my words come to pass!" Mrs. Martin greeted them smiling. "Boy, she was moping 'round this house with a long face I couldn't tek it anymore. I went out for some fresh air," Mrs. Martin said jocularly and Phyl flushed with embarrassment.

"Ow Ma, Ma that one hit hard. You know that's not true! I was just feeling bored."

"Is the same thing," Mrs. Martin insisted.

"I was bored too and decided to pass around," Tom chimed in. "And I hope you don't mind."

"Not me son, come whenever you want. Is up to this lady and you, not me."

It was a week of surprises. The next day, as soon as Pat entered the house Mrs. Martin knew from the look on her face that something was very wrong.

"My mother was at school today," Pat told her as she slumped into a chair looking defeated.

"What!... Your mother actually went to your school! What's the matter with that woman? Why she have to go there atall."

Mrs. Martin was momentarily stunned, then she added "You know I shouldn't ask such a stupid question... It was only a matter of time before the idea get in her head."

"But, it wasn't the first time." Pat controlling her emotions, explained that her mother had been there before and she had hurried through the side door to avoid her. "But today she actually got hold of a teacher and told her after all she did for me, as soon as I get job, I move out and wouldn't even give her a cent, after all the trouble she had bringing me up without a father and all the sacrifices she made to send me to high school and she went on and on." Pat's face showed her outrage and she trembled as she spoke.

"Lord, that woman ain't got no shame. She making her business an open book for everybody. I know how you feel. I would feel the same if was me. That woman got some kind ah devil in her!" Mrs. Martin declared. "But what you going to do child? We got to think of something an' move fast because she going to strike again an' shame you 'til you fed up an' go back."

"I'm never never never going back, I suffer enough!" Pat spoke with feeling. "I was going to visit her at one time, but when I reach the corner, everything, everything come right back to me and no matter how I tried, it was just as if a weight was pulling me back. And whenever I think about her... the hair raise on my body. She wanted to kill me because I was pregnant!"

"Come on Pat! Pull yourself together!" Mrs. Martin said firmly. "Don't let her get you down. You're a strong young woman an' you got to think. Let's go into the kitchen." Mrs. Martin took her by the arm and led the way, then put on the kettle to boil. She was worried. She knew Pat was still afraid of her mother. She quickly made two cups of tea, then, placing one in Pat's hand, she guided her back to the sitting room, insisting she drink it immediately.

"You can't fall to pieces every time your mother appear. If she only realise that, you right back in the palm of her hand again an' she'll hound you down," Mrs. Martin warned. "You got nothing to be frightened about any more, the worse pass already. Is up to you now. However you make your bed you lie on it, whether you make it hard or soft."

"But all those things she told the teacher and whoever else she care to tell, soon the whole school will hear about all my ungratefulness from the time I was born, how my father abandon me, all the lies and the gossiping I have to live through."

"You can't worry with that now. We got to find a solution to this problem. Isn't there somebody at the school, the headmaster or somebody you can trust, who can talk to her an' prevent her from worrying you during working hours?"

141

"I think I can talk to the headmaster," Pat said considering. "He's a pleasant man, the fatherly type, but," she hesitated, "it's just the thought of telling a complete stranger."

"But you need somebody there to stand up for you! And you won't have to tell him every detail, just tell him enough so he could get that lady to stop persecuting you; besides he can handle the teachers and the gossiping. I know your mother well, once she feel the coast clear and she can go to your school anytime, you goin' to be in hell."

They went on discussing the situation. Finally both sat quietly absorbed in thought.

"You're right Mom," Pat acknowledged after a while, "the headmaster is just the person. So I'll hurry to school early tomorrow morning, before the gossiping break out and talk to him."

Mrs. Martin looked at her, sensing her determination and was pleased she was able to convince her to take a stand for her own piece of mind. "Child, I glad we could talk things over. All I want is fo' you to get some peace...is up to you to do the rest." That woman mean not to give this child one moment peace, under her roof or anybody else, she reflected.

"Thank God, I got you to talk to Mom... or I don't know what I'll do!" Pat hugged her, "I don't even feel so upset now."

Pat knocked on the headmaster's door around seven-thirty the next morning. She had no doubt about him being there, because he lived across the river on the West Coast and always took the first ferry boat to the city. She knocked on his half-opened door and he welcomed her in. She was very nervous, even though she rehearsed what she was going to say. She found it difficult and embarrassing to talk to a complete stranger about her mother. She remembered when all the girls at school talked excitedly about their mothers and the special way they were treated, the special little plans they made for them, she never risked joining in. She couldn't forget the very first time, they were all talking about the things they got for their birthdays and she quite innocently remarked her mother didn't remember, causing all the girls to laugh and snigger, all except Phyl. Since then she learnt to be silent and indifferent. But when she was forced to talk, the words always stuck in her throat and there was a tight feeling in her stomach which moved to her throat, making her feel sick, same as she was experiencing now.

"Well, Miss Sandiford, you're very early this morning." The headmaster greeted her with a smile. "Problem with your charges?" he asked and waited. He was a very perceptive man. At the moment Pat was tense and nervous, so he knew he must be patient.

"It's a private and personal matter, sir." Pat tried to control her nervousness.

"Well I'm sure it's not very easy for you then." His voice had a soothing effect and suddenly Pat felt safe and found it easy to explain about her mother's visit the day before and her present situation.

"I know how distressing this problem could be," he responded, after thinking the matter over carefully. He didn't press her with too many questions and Pat was relieved and grateful. It was awful talking about her mother's cruelty, and now her constant harassment. She was glad he didn't have to go into details.

"I understand how you feel," his voice penetrated her thoughts, "but I hope you don't mind me discussing the matter with my deputy. You know I'm not always around,"

Pat nodded. She saw the wisdom in what he said, and she trusted the deputy. She was fed up and knew that alone, she was no match for her mother.

Mrs. Sandiford didn't show up for a while, then one afternoon as Pat turned the corner and she was confronted by her.

"You avoiding me! Your own mother who bring you in this world and struggle and sacrifice to mind you without a father," Mrs. Sandiford's voice rose spitefully. Pat stopped dead in her tracks. She had left school with a few of her devoted admirers in tow. She was completely confounded by the attack.

"So this is the thanks I getting? You now become a big woman since you get a job and move out!"

Fear gnawed at Pat's stomach. She could feel the squeezing, choking sensation, rising in her throat. Her knees felt weak, but she remembered Phyl's mother's words and stood her ground. "Come! You all run along home without me," she called each child by name, hoping she sounded bolder than she felt. But some lingered, refusing to be shooed away, their curiosity roused. They had a ring side position and were not about to miss the excitement.

143

"I didn't know you wanted to see me," Pat spoke thoughtlessly. "Why didn't you come over to Phyl's house?"

"Your friend house?" Mrs. Sandiford was irate at the memory of the heated dispute with Phyl's mother. She had made up her mind she was never going back there again. "You left my house and now you got the presumption to tell me I must go running behind you! You got a home and I expect you there!" she blazed out.

"I have a home right where I am, and I have no intention of moving. Why can't you leave me alone?" Pat said.

"You offering me words after all I go through for you?" Mrs. Sandiford said at the top of her voice. People attracted by her loudness, gaped and stopped to listen. She knew she was in control. "Is me!" she thumped her chest, "bring you in this world and struggle to bring you up without a father!"

Pat felt lost, she could not avoid a scene.

"You see what I tell you, Joyce! You here how the children nowadays ungrateful!" A woman said loud enough for Pat to hear, "That's why I don't want any children... 'cause after all you go through with them they does just up an' walk out an' lef' you high an' dry."

"Aye!... And you hear how she answering back the poor woman after all she suffer." Her companion replied, "This one look like she's a teacher... so she's a big shot now! You self hear how she showing off with she big English 'pon the poor woman, she own mother."

Pat felt stripped by the remarks. Angry and distressed at her mother's display, she was on the verge of tears.

"What's going on here?" A voice said with authority, "Get on home you children." The children, recognising the voice and the speaker, fled without a second command. It was the headmaster.

"Miss, this is your mother eh?" he enquired, looking at Pat intently. She nodded and she knew he understood. "This is a family matter." He spoke to the crowd around as if they were delinquents. "I trust you wives and mothers have more important things to do with your time." He stood erect, staring at the offenders unblinking, communicating his disgust, waiting until the sting shot home and they left.

"Miss Sandiford, you go on home. Everything will be okay," he said, when the last bystander grudgingly left, "I'll have a chat with your mother."

Pat could barely acknowledge his willingness to help, everything was swimming before her.

"Hello Mrs. Sandiford. I'm Pat's headmaster." He introduced himself. "I hope you don't mind if I walk along with you. We can chat as we go along." He smiled at her, Mrs. Sandiford returning his smile, said nothing but walked along with him.

"Such a fine young woman, a conscientious worker too. I trust you are proud of her." The Headmaster continued talking about Pat, praising her but Mrs. Sandiford made no remarks.

"We can't be too careful about providing gossip for idlers," he said with emphasis, paused, waited, still no response. "Today the world is quite different," he continued, "and we parents must realise our children are our greatest gifts. So we have to do something more than feed and clothe them. We must show then how much we appreciate them in the same way they strive to show us how they appreciate us. If not we'd have no future with them."

Mrs. Sandiford kept nodding but remained silent. He wondered if she understood what he was getting at. He wanted to elicit some kind of response from her just so he'd know how she was thinking. He tried another tactic. He talked about the school, the teachers and the pleasure he got from observing the children's progress. Then he talked about his son and his wish for a daughter.

"Try to think kindly of your daughter and things will work out right for both of you," he said as they parted, then stood, looking at her receding figure, thoughtful. He had protested, probed, persuaded, confessed, advised and he had made no progress with Mrs. Sandiford. She put up a block which was difficult to penetrate.

Alone, on her way home, Mrs. Sandiford's thoughts were bitter. She persuaded herself she wasn't wrong. That girl was a heartache to her even before she was born. She hadn't wanted a child and didn't know what to do. So she had to give up everything and live a life of suffering and sacrifice. Now it was Pat's duty as a child to pay her back for what she went through. Pat, strong and healthy, was living at other people and leave her with everything on her hands, she thought. The days ended with her being tired and exhausted. Lillian's forgetful and slow and everything's in confusion.

Now Roy Sandiford up an announce he's going to live at the estate till the house running smooth, 'cause he fed up leaving every morning without breakfast. At least he could help out till Pat come back, instead he means to cut my allowance. If only Pat listen to me, she won't get into trouble in the first place. Since she living at the Martins she get bumptious. But I'm not giving up. She's got to come back!

Waves of anxiety washed over Pat as she made her way home. Her mother had established one kind of relationship with her, no wonder she always felt she was a burden, a nuisance and unloved. When she ran into her unexpectedly and looked at her harsh, unfriendly lips and unsmiling face, she reacted to all she had grown up to expect, abuse and hostility. She had made a mistake when she mentioned the Martins, that only incensed her already hostile nature. But that didn't lessen the fact that her behaviour was downright obnoxious, bordering on lawless. Her sole aim was to shame her publicly, just to get the better of her. But she was more determined now, more than before, to stand up to her. If the headmaster hadn't intervened she didn't know how the situation would have ended. She knew her mother well. She hadn't seen the last of her.

Pat waited until after dinner to tell Mrs. Martin and Phyl about the incident, to get it off her chest.

"Pat, I was thinking the other day. Why not send a small piece for your mother?" Mrs. Martin said, she was sitting in her rocking chair, eyes closed, thinking she could see no end to the situation. So the money might keep her cool. Pat's salary was small, but she insisted on paying for her board and lodgings. It wasn't going to be easy.

"I know it goin' to be hard, especially now you trying to save for when you get into Training College... But see what you can do."

"The other day I was thinking the same thing. But you know is not money my mother after. She wants me back because she can't control me now and she miss the drudge. She never one day showed she cared for me a tiny drop. She wants me back to take the hard work off she and Lillian backs. But I'm going to send that money even if I have to do without! And I know it won't come to that. I have you and I'm at peace here."

"You see what I tell you Pat? The old queen won't ever give up!" Phyl tried to make light of the situation. "But seriously Pat, what you plan to do?"

"I'm racking my brains all the time trying to find the answer. I tell you this world really got some problems and trials. If I wasn't so close, it would be difficult for her to get to my school."

"That's it! Get a transfer!" Phyl said excitedly. "And for a long time she won't know where you are."

"You're right Phyl! To tell the truth the idea never crossed my mind. I feel so at home there."

"It's a good idea. It will keep her guessing," Mrs. Martin added. "Until she ketch up with you again." And they all laughed.

"I'm going to see the Headmaster tomorrow about it. Lord! Please help me to get a transfer!" Pat said looking upwards.

Part Two
Chapter 14
July 1952

The night before election the populace turned up en masse to hear what Hoffman had to say. Dense crowds jammed the Green, the deserted square outside Bourda Market and all neighbouring roads. Rumours had spread around like wild fire that if the people exercised their right to vote this would not bring about any significant improvement in economic and social life. Consumed with doubts, they became anxious about the future, afraid that if they voted, they might be trapped into a situation which could deprive them of their livelihood, which depended on the patronage and capriciousness of the system. Voting could be a change for the worse, not better.

"My brothers and sisters," Hoffman spoke into the loud speaker, "I'm extremely happy to see you here tonight in such vast numbers. I hope you will be at the polls tomorrow in the same vast numbers." He laid emphasis on the last two words. "My friends lest you forget, I want you to tell me what day is tomorrow?"

"Polling day, polling day," some shouted.

"I can't hear you!" he cried out, "I can't hear you!"

"Polling day, polling day." They shouted in one accord.

"Ahh, you call tomorrow polling day. The day you go out to vote, to exercise your franchise, your right to choose whomsoever you want to run this country, to ensure you and your children go to bed with full bellies, a roof over you heads and clothes on your backs." The crowd grinned feebly, unnaturally.

"Ha!" Hoffman said gravely, "You laugh eh... there's an old saying, 'what sweeten goat does hu't he belly.' Then there's another, 'not every cack' cack' is a laugh.' I think the second one expresses your feelings here tonight."

The crowds hmmed and murmured, but he continued, "It's good to laugh though the truth hurts... and I'm glad you can laugh at your problems! You and I know it hurts like hell when your children hungry. And it hurts like hell when you can't put a proper roof over their heads, much less pay for their education." His tone was grave. "But isn't that what you want for your children? Full bellies and a roof over your heads?" he cried out loudly.

"Yes... Yes!" some shouted back.

"Well, my brothers and sisters, let us return to what I was saying. You call tomorrow polling day but I call it the Ides of March." He bellowed, "Tomorrow is the Ides of March! And from tomorrow onwards we sink or we swim." The crowd groaned.

"I know there have been some, who have been spreading fear among you, telling you that if you vote for me, you will surely lose your job, your one and only means of livelihood. It's a pack of lies, nothing but a pack of lies!" He shouted angrily, "Lies! Pure propaganda spread by their lackey's and hirelings. I don't have to tell you who they are. You know them well. No names! No warrant!"

The crowds groaned again.

"Yes, they are paid to tell you lies. These knaves pay their lackeys to frighten you, so you stay home. Then what? You're right back in their cruel grasp. Then they will laugh behind your backs and say; 'Look at the poor wretches, they're fighting for freedom, now that they have it, they're afraid to exercise it, the fools!' So when their lackeys, who can't help themselves out of a shower of rain, come to you, you show them your mettle. Show them your mettle," he repeated, intent to spur them on.

"As one great writer aptly puts it, 'Men are sometimes masters of their fate, the fault is not in our stars but in ourselves, that we are underlings.' I plead and command you tonight to show them your mettle. Resolve to leave your homes early in the morning, be at the polling station at six o'clock, make no fuss, get into no arguments, just cast your votes! Think of your hungry children and stand firm; but most of all do not be intimidated by the powers that be! Put your ex's where it matters and don't be frightened."

"No, no!" was the response.

"Are we going to sit cowardly by and continue to be their pawns? Why man, they doth bestride our narrow world like a colossus, and we petty men walk under their huge legs and peep about to find ourselves dishonourable graves! These barbarians have trod on us!" He was now fully roused, "They have exploited your ancestors and mine. They have treated them and us, less than human. Stand up, I say to you, stand up!"

"Right! No more, no more. We ain't taking it so." The crowd shouted, now fired with enthusiasm.

"Stand up and be counted," he shouted back, "Let your votes be counted to right the ills and evils of the past."

"Aye, aye!" was the solemn response.

The meeting was grave, the people were no longer jubilant and light-hearted, as in the past. Hoffman's entreaties were met with nods, murmurs and gloomy enthusiasm. The air was heavy with uncertainty and tension. Now that the dawn of the long awaited day was about to break, in the great contest for rights and social justice, the participants appeared to be as temperamental and as tense as thoroughbreds at the starting gate. But Hoffman, aware of the position, continued to urge them on.

"I charge you as the day breaks tomorrow, go forth and continue the fight of our forefathers. Let them be proud to know they were not beaten, flayed, quartered and beheaded in vain! Let them know, their blood was shed to give you courage to continue the battle, so let us continue the battle! My friends, brothers and sisters, we must continue the fight or it is better we had not been born. Therefore, I urge you in the words of that heroic English character, before he and his soldiers went into battle, 'Once more unto the breach, dear friends, once more'." Hoffman's voice rose to command, "'Or close the wall up with our people dead. In peace there's nothing so becomes a man as modest stillness and humility,'" he said calmly. "'But when the blast of war blows in our ears,'" his voice now quickened with vitality, "'then imitate the action of the tiger. Stiffen the sinews, summon up the blood, disguise fair nature with hard favour'd rage; then lend the eye a terrible aspect; let it pry through the portage of the head like the brass cannon! Let the brow o'erwhelm, as fearful as doth a galled rock o'erhang and jutty his confounded base, swilled with the wild and wasteful ocean.'"

He paused to take a breath, then continued with passion while the crowds stood in silence, eyes riveted on him. "'Now set the teeth and stretch the nostril wide; hold hard the breath, and bend up every spirit to his full height! On, on, you noble people whose blood is fet from fathers, who know to war! Forefathers that, like so many Alexanders, have in these parts from time to time, fought and shed their blood for lack of argument _ dishonour not your mothers.'"

He made a warning gesture as he slowly took the crowd in, in a sweeping glance.

"'Now attest that those whom you call'd fathers did beget you! Be copy now to men of grosser blood and teach them how to war! You men and women, show us here the mettle of your pasture, let us swear that you are worth your breeding which I doubt not: for there is none of you so mean and base, that hath not noble lustre in your eyes.'"

Intense emotion had transformed his features as he charged, "'I see you stand like greyhounds in the slips, straining upon the start. The game's afoot. Follow your spirit; and upon this I charge you, pray to God, and be at the polls tomorrow!' Goodnight my brothers and sisters," he whispered as if he was drained, mentally and physically.

Phyl was up, long before five o'clock. She and Pat breakfasted then were ready to begin, what they later declared, was one of the most gruelling days of their lives. Pat's school was used as a polling station, and she was on holiday, she agreed to help Phyl, whose task was to escort and prod voters to their polling stations.

At five o'clock, the girls were already on their way to old Mother Barton, already past her eightieth birthday and confined to a rocking chair, with a lame knee. Mentally alert she had kept abreast of all the changes taking place. Phyl had met her earlier, while distributing pamphlets and had continued the visits. Mother Barton had an insatiable appetite for news and Phyl took a liking to the old woman. When at last polling day was announced, she vowed to Phyl, God willing, she would be the first to vote and insisted Phyl take her to the polling station. Even though she lived with her daughter, Phyl was pleased to oblige.

"Children, I walking this walk today for my mother, grandmother and all my generation! Even if it kill me!" Mother Barton said leaning on

151

the arms of Phyl and Pat as they moved along. The girls laughed outright at her determination. Phyl had insisted they use the taxi service set up by Hoffman, but Mother Barton was determined to go only on her terms.

"I wish they could see me now, wid mi chest in the air, I going to vote." She said with emphasis, "You think I goin' to miss this? Not me, I ain't missing it at all!" She was a lively old soul. She had told Phyl a lot of stories about slavery she had heard from her grandmother and Phyl had passed them on to the others; she was always an eager listener, encouraging Mother Barton with her recitals, though she knew there was no stopping her once she got started.

"Chile, I walking to that polling station and when I done vote, I could drop down dead." The girls giggled again but inwardly prayed nothing of the sort would happen.

"Me fall down! Me! I only joking girls, we is a strong generation and we don't fall down so. You know you got to put li'l humour in the thing. And I means to walk back when the morning brighten up and tek a li'l rest. I want everybody to see me, an old woman goin' to vote, proud to do it too. I doin' my part and they must do theirs." She stopped for a moment, "Ah got to rest the old foot you know." Then they moved on.

"We got to thank God for sending Mr. Hoffman or I would dead and never know 'bout voting, ain't that is true girls?" she asked, but didn't wait for an answer.

"Hey, I tell you, things really change in this country and Mr. Hoffman is goin' to fight for more things to happen! He is goin' to lead this nation, God bless he," she said sagely. She kept up a lively chattering, until they reached the polling station then immediately cast her ballot.

"My girl," she said to Pat, "if you could take me home now, I'll be very glad. I feel exhausted." It was a long, slow trek for her but she had accomplished what she had set to do.

"Awright Mother Barton. Don't worry. The taxi coming in five minutes, and I goin' to take you home," Pat said. She knew the trip was a great strain on the old lady, even though she lived only a few blocks way. Pat helped Mother Barton to a seat outside. "Thank you mi girl," Mother Barton said, as she sat down, "You know was only big talk ah was makin'. The journey got me so tired, ah longing fo' meh rocking chair, but you can't let yourself down at all."

It was a hectic day for Phyl. Apart from assisting the handicapped to the polling station, she had a long list of doubtfuls, who needed encouragement or prodding. The morning moved slowly and many times she was exasperated at the poor show of voters. But from lunchtime onwards, the situation changed dramatically. There was a continuous stream of voters and this went on until polling closed.

Though she and Pat were all but done in, their spirits rose as they continued with their tasks until the very end.

Although practically exhausted when they reached home, neither could relax. They flopped into morris chairs near the radio, shooing the others into silence. Very tense they listened to every scrap of news, claiming they were too tired, even to lift a spoon.

"Come on girls. I know youall tired," Mrs. Martin said good naturedly, "but you got to put something in you all stomach. Youall ain't come home whole day, so I prepare dinner early so you can eat as soon as you come in."

"Ma, I think my stomach close right up. I don't even think I have one, all I want to do is rest right here so I could hear the news," Phyl said.

"I sure you got a couple hours more before any results start coming over. So you all go in an' lie down an as soon as I hear anything, ah will wake you up," Mrs. Martin said.

"Eh eh Ma! I staying right here!" Phyl insisted. Neither she nor Pat made any effort to budge from their curled-up position. "The thing is, while you waking we up, we missing out, we want to hear every word, right now, sleep out of the question."

"I think I know the best thing for the two of you," Mrs. Martin said, she had no intention of giving in. "Is just the thing to pep youall up, I just can't stand the sight of the two of you, looking like two tired old dogs!" She hurried into the kitchen and the girls couldn't help laughing as they said, "We okay, we okay!" But she ignored them, "Youall stay quiet an' just let me follow my own mind, yeh."

"Pat, we getting her potion, mint and toyo," Phyl whispered and both laughed quietly.

She was back a few minutes later, "I was prepared fo' you all, so sit up now and drink this." She handed them cups of steaming tea, which they took without a murmur, both knew when she meant business.

The Martin's household, like many others, remained awake all night. They listened, to the election results, sometimes with suppressed excitement, sometimes cheers and shouts could be heard echoing all the way through neighbourhoods. Phyl and Pat were foot-sore and tired, but not too tired to jump up and cheer or dance as the reports were announced. Excitement reached a fevered pitch, when it appeared Hoffman was a winner all the way. He had won a seat for himself and some members of his party. He had made some inroads in the city. Then the results from the country areas were reported and it was clear he had lost to the opposition. He had failed to win the confidence of residents outside the city. His struggle for leadership had been challenged and he was not as popular as he thought.

"Something gone wrong. It can't be right after all the work and planning," Phyl said, stunned, dragging herself to her room. "I can't believe it!" She flung herself into bed and fell fast asleep. Pat too, following in her wake, did the same thing.

The people had exercised their franchise.

Then they came. They came from the furthest trails between the Pakaraime and the Akari mountain chains. They came from as far north up the Waini Point to the Rupununi Savannah in the south. They sailed down the Orinoco and the Essequibo Rivers and tributaries in the west, and as far east as the Corentyne River.

They travelled in canoes, balahoos, launches and steamboats, trains, trucks, jeeps, cars, dray and donkey carts and overwhelmed the city like the tidal Atlantic.

They came to see their "own boys", the men they had elected to represent them, formally installed in the Legislative Assembly. They had come into their own. The voices of the Africans, Indians, Portuguese, Chinese, Amerindian and Mixed Races had been heard.

It would be a sight to remember; a more spectacular event than a cricket test match between the West Indies and England with it's promised pomp and splendour, colour and glitter. The buglers and the horseguards in full dress; the militia band in formal white tops and serge bottoms, adorned with shiny brass buttons and lily-white gloves to complete the effect. Girl guides in cool blue and scouts in crisp khaki, marching smartly along to take the salute, from the governor in his plumed helmet.

They filled the square around the Public Building, which housed the past but would now house the newly elected members of the assembly. They lined nearby street and roadway, stood on balconies, verandas, steps, climbed on gate posts, fences, roofs and perched on every available branch of nearby trees, in order to get a good view.

They stood waiting, expectant, waving the Union Jack, wearing rosettes, buttons and other tokens of loyalty, while the sun beat down on the hundreds of thousands of spectators, jammed together, to watch the proceedings. They craned their necks and strained on tip-toes, in order to establish the identity of guests and participants as they arrived.

The bugles began.

"Look, look, that's the governor car, right? The governor come already?" said a man in a white long-sleeved shirt, buttoned up to the neck.

"No man. That's the Chief Inspector of Police," corrected a middle-aged man, who was dressed smartly for the occasion, in his pin-striped suit, vest, collar and tie.

"Oh, oh oh! He is the man who does send we policemen foh beat up we people, when they picketing. Oh oh!" The man in the white shirt spoke as though he had made a discovery.

The bugles continued and cheers from the gallery trickled down to the spectators.

"Ah ha! That's the governor and he wife now," Whiteshirt spoke with assurance.

"No man! That's the A.D.C. and his wife," Pinstripe said, annoyed. "Look man, why you talking so loud if you don't know anything."

"Look lady," Whiteshirt, now feeling somewhat ruffled, scolded a woman standing in front of him, with a child in her arms, "how you can put the child in front o' me? Is how you expect I goin' to see."

"Mister, what you want me to do? He got to see too! You want to lif' 'e up foh me?" she asked rudely.

"I don't know why allyou women likes to come to these things and drag along all these children. These places ain't foh children," he said annoyed. "I don't know why you didn't stay home an look after the child."

Whiteshirt was peeved, the child's head as well as the flag he carried, kept bobbing up and down, blocking his view.

"Yeah! Yeah!" Wild yells went up from the crowd.

"Is who? Is who?" Whiteshirt asked, straining on tip-toes peering between the woman in front and the flag in her child's hand.

"That is we boy from Buxton! I know he good good! Nobody can't tell me I wrong now!" he hinted broadly, then joined in the yells. "Yeah, yeah, yeah, yeah!" he shouted at the top of his lungs.

155

"Christ man, Christ! You don't have to make all that noise man. You nearly deafen me." Pinstripe said gruffly, "Like I find the wrong spot to stand up."

"Yeah yeah! Yeah yeah yeah yeah!" The crowd shouted as one newly elected member after the other arrived, walking proudly waving to their ecstatic supporters.

"Yeah yeah! Yeah yeah yeah yeah!... yeah" The din drowned out every other sound, then, suddenly died down only to rise again.

"Who? Is who is that white man down there with glasses, that all we people waving and shouting to? Look, look 'e waving back to them!" Whiteshirt asked puzzled.

"That's not any white man!" the woman with the child said. "That's the man who own the drinks company," she said. "You ain't know one thing!" she sneered.

The yells and cheers, now rose louder than before, it was earsplitting in intensity.

"Yeah yeah yeah!" Whiteshirt joined in "Is we boys! Oh God, is we boys." He bounced up and down in excitement, "That's Hoffman and we boy, Chandra, the doctor from the Corentyne and the other fella is... man, all ah them is we boys walking together and nobody can tell me I wrong now! Eh heh!" He said vehemently, bouncing up and down with increased vigour, supporting the unceasing noise, which drowned out any chance of arguments. Meanwhile, the new arrivals reached the public gallery and stood waving to their supporters, who by then, were uncontrollable. It was only when they were spent and weary, the noise died down.

"Nobody can't tell you, you wrong Mr. Knowall?" The woman with the child said scornfully, "The man is not a doctor, he's a dentist!"

Then the trumpets sounded and the bugles played the fanfare, which announced the arrival of the governor. A lively cheering burst forth from the gallery down to the spectators, the governor had arrived! The ceremony that would mark the turning point in social events was about to begin. Everyone stood erect and still to the strains of "God Save The Queen."

"Is what was that brass thing that man was walking around...?" whispered Whiteshirt.

"Shut up," hissed Pinstripe with venom.

When the anthem was completed they were at ease again, Pinstripe was disgusted, "Man, you talk so much, you don't even know when you mustn't talk! You don't talk when the anthem playing, you stand still without making a sound," he said crossly.

"Man, is who I goin' to ask? You like you know everybody an' everything." Whiteshirt said sheepishly, "Besides, that is the white people anthem!"

"Look man, any anthem playing you stand to attention. But when you get your own, you could do what you like. There is a time and place for everything," Pinstripe scolded.

"Look man, don't worry with all them long talk." Whiteshirt interrupted, "Tell me what the long brass thing..."

"It is a mace!" Pinstripe cut in, the situation was becoming unbearable. "Is not a long thing and the person carrying it is the Speaker of the Assembly and before you ask me anything else," he laid emphasis on the last two words, "the mace is a symbol of authority, the Speaker always has it, once the assembly is in session, like today. He carries it to remind people to be orderly, like you man, you need some orderliness," he said, stressing every word.

"Okay, okay, mi brother, I learn something here today. If I didn't come and stand up here near to you, I won't know that. And if I di' hear anybody talk about the Speaker carrying the mace in he hand, I would be thinking mace is spice! Why a Speaker in the House of Assembly carrying..."

"Awright, awright, okay man," cut in Pinstripe, "Just forget the explanation. I had enough."

The ceremony had begun, that would proclaim the newly elected as legal representatives of the people. The people had come a long way in their struggles and the future was no longer an illusion, it looked bright and tangible. They had made their choice and got what they wanted.

"I don't know what to do now," Pat said to Mrs Martin, one day nearing the end of the school term.

"What happen Pat, is your mother again?" Mrs. Martin asked, noting her serious expression.

"No, thank God I haven't seen her. I've been sending the money like you and the headmaster suggest through the post office, cause I can't take her sour disposition," Pat said.

"Chile, life is not without problems, when you solve one set an' think everything alright, another set waiting round the corner, ready to butt you down, an' you ain't get half the problems yet."

"It's a joke, not a real joke, if you know what I mean. Remember I asked the headmaster for a transfer and he patiently helped me to get one, but now that I get it, I don't know what to do."

"That's good, you lucky. Thank God you get through." Mrs. Martin said pleased, but puzzled by her seriousness, "It far from your old school, nuh?"

"Far, it couldn't be further. It all the way up the Demerara River," she said, "and I was hoping I'd get another one right here in town."

"Well you can hold on 'till you get another one," Mrs. Martin said, trying to cheer her up.

"That won't be till next year April or September, because all transfers are made before the beginning of the new term. I don't want to have another run in with my mother, so I just have to take it or leave, besides..."

"You got to take it then," Mrs. Martin cut in.

"You're forgetting something very important," Pat said.

"Oh my goodness!" Mrs. Martin said remembering, "Phyl wedding! It completely slip my mind for the moment." She understood why Pat didn't want to take the transfer into the river area at this time. "Well Pat, you see what I always tell youall. You can't get 'two sweet out o' one joint of cane! You can stay an' help prepare for Phyl wedding an' go to the 'queh queh' her aunt keeping in the country or go up the river an' come down in time fo' be the first bridesmaid. We all goin' to miss you, especially Phyl an' she would dead if you not at her wedding. But is not 'till Christmas she an' Tom getting married, so you an' she got time to discuss it."

Chapter 15
1953

Phyl's heart beat fast with excitement as she neared the shop. She couldn't keep her secret any longer, she had to let Tom know. He had been such a devoted husband, since they were married six months ago. Though he hadn't wanted her to go back to work, after they got the loan from the bank, he had finally agreed that she'd be happier there, than alone at home. Home! She remembered the look of sheer joy that transformed his face when she, Pat and Ma had hung up new curtains in the redecorated house in Campbelville. Then his excitement when the carpenters started working on the store. She knew when he heard her news he'd be walking on air.

She reached the store and saw the painters working on the outer walls.

"Hello Mistress. How you keeping?" The foreman called out and she quickly pressed a finger to her lips, indicating she didn't want Tom to know she was there. She peeped through the half opened doorway and saw Tom, engrossed, with his back to the door, surveying the scene before him. She crept quietly in. She gazed at the brightly painted shelves counter tops, newly purchased bins and trays in wonder, she felt a great sense of pride of ownership for herself and especially for Tom. He won't have to worry about her leaving Hoffman at all she thought. She was prepared to leave the minute the painters left.

"A penny for your thoughts," she whispered and Tom, startled swung around.

"What you doing here Phyl? Girl you make me jump. I didn't expect you down here this afternoon."

"Well I thought you would be glad to see me."

"Course I glad to see you," he said embracing her, "but it was you who tell me this morning, you don't want to see the store 'till it finish. Something wrong?" He observed her closely.

"No man I just decide to come so we could go home together, is nearly five o'clock you know."

"Girl, not this afternoon. After you said you wasn't coming, I promised the painters to help them shift somethings around at the back so they could come in and finish up the back room."

"Awright, that's okay. But I remember one night when somebody was working late, that person drop everything he was doing to take me home," she said, trying to keep a straight face.

"My wife blackmailing me! Lord help this poor man," he said laughing. "But seriously Phyl, you know..."

"And that same person said a pretty girl like you shouldn't be downtown alone. So when I said I didn't want to give him anymore trouble if you see how his face fall. He insist..."

"You win, you win!" he said, hugging her. "I knew from that first day I spot you, you're a darn smart woman. Just let me talk to the painters, then wash up."

She followed him to the back room, where the paint was stored and mixed, she smiled to herself remembering it was the smell that nauseated her, making her suspect she was pregnant, now it didn't bother her anymore.

"Look at this place Tom, what a mess!" she said looking around. "It really needs a woman's touch to put things in order." She viewed the disarray of boxes, paint pots, drums, sacks and canvas. "We could put a fridge in that corner and a small stove over there. I will fix it up and make it into a nice kitchenette."

"That's my girl talking," Tom said pleased.

"Then we can bring down your grandfather couch and I'll put that here," she indicated the spot. "We can make this back room comfortable. So whenever we're ready we can rest or take a nap especially now I'm going to be a mother and you a father."

"Phyl! You sure?" He looked at her as if he couldn't believe his ears. "You sure? I know was something on your mind when I see you come in," he said, embracing and kissing her. "I'm going to be a father," he said proudly.

"Sh, shsh," she tried to still his outburst.

"A son! Phyl, I don't care, I want everybody to hear, you are carrying my son, my son!"

"Our son, our child. But I sure by now everybody hear already."

"Girl, we have to go home to celebrate, then I have to write and tell my sister! Yes girl, home is the best place when I in this mood," he said, thinking how he had waited for something like this to make his dreams come true and his life complete.

Phyl was thrilled by Tom's excitement. How he rejoiced to know he was going to be a father. That was the easy part. She knew he was going to object, when she told him she wanted to keep on working and it wasn't going to be easy.

All the way home Tom talked about the baby, which he was certain would be a boy. His plan for the store to belong to his son, his eldest, whom he was sure would follow in his footsteps. Then, filled with pride, he told Phyl he had long ago selected a special name for his son, his grandfather's name.

"Alexander," Phyl said with disappointment. "It's so ancient, so old fashion, you know what I mean," she hurried on when she saw the look in his eyes. "Man. I sure we could find a more modern name."

"Phyl, I made a promise to myself, I'd name my first son after him! After all he was a man with a lot of guts and if it wasn't for him we wouldn't have the store, so it's Alexander or nothing," he insisted. She had made no reply.

"Come on Phyl, we got to agree now. If it's a boy, my first son will be Alexander! If it's a girl she's your choice; but I just know... its going to be a boy."

"Okay," she said, "Let's not make an issue of it now. We still have a lot of time to talk about names."

After they got home, Tom said, "Girl, we forget completely to stop by Mom and tell her the news!"

"We could tell her later, but right now I don't feel like sharing it with anyone else. I know it sound selfish, but that's how I feel. So tomorrow morning when you going down, you pass and tell Ma, if you still want to. I writing to Pat as soon as possible to tell her we want her to be godmother. What you think about that?"

"Suit yourself, Mrs. Barnes. Now you sit right here." He guided her to the settee. "Come on girl, put your feet up so you can take the weight off them." He took off her shoes and she enjoyed his pamperings, "Tonight I'm going to cook you the best dinner you ever had in your life."

"No Tom, I want to help, I don't want you to treat me as if I'm an invalid."

"Not a word out of you, I'm not going to listen to any argument," he said in mock seriousness.

"Tom, you make things so easy for me." She kissed his hand and squeezed it.

"Ha, we're going to have more of that later," he said pleased, "I'll be back in a minute." He returned with two glasses and a bottle of wine left over from the wedding celebrations. He poured the wine, "To us Phyl, may we always have the same contentment and peace we have right now. To the mother of my son."

"To us, Tom. To the proud father of my child, I hope he never changes!"

"Well girl, tomorrow is a new day for you," Tom said, later on that night, as they lay cuddled happily in each other's arms. "I know it's hard, but you know you can't go back to work."

"How you mean, Tom?" she asked, glad he was the one to bring it up. "Why, I'm not even showing."

"You can't go back to work in your condition. You know it's not safe. The last time I didn't want you to be lonely and unhappy, but now this is different. Your sister can come and stay with you during the day," he hastened to add before she interrupted.

"But man, I'm not sick. And don't forget we agreed that as soon as the painters finish I'd be leaving Hoffman."

"But girl, I don't want you to work any more. I want you at home where it's safe," he insisted.

"Come on, Tom. There's no heavy weight for me to carry around. I'm as strong as an ox. I stopped at the doctor and he said I was as fit as a fiddle and I feel so too."

"Did he actually say you can go back to work?"

"Of course he did, 'cause I ask him outright and he said he saw no reason why I shouldn't as long as I'm not lifting things around. Then he said the more women who see pregnancy as a healthy happy period and not as a sickness, doing what they normally do, they will be happier and have easier labour. Don't forget there're lots of women who have to work hard to make a living, 'cause they have nobody to depend on, their children father abandon them."

Tom remained silent and Phyl said, "I promise I not going to lift anything nor overdo, and as soon as the painters finish I leaving Hoffman immediately..."

"What about Hoffman? When you planning to tell him you leaving?"

"As soon as he come in tomorrow, but I'll have to give him a little time to get somebody to take my place. I just can't leave him abruptly. You never know when we may need his help."

"Alright, but make it soon, cause you know I'll be worrying and I'll be very glad when you leave Hoffman for good."

"You're a darling Tom," she said smiling, satisfied that he took it so well. It wasn't so bad after all. She had worried for a while that he was going to force her to stay home but her mother had never forced her to do anything. She thought about the argument she avoided over the name he chose for the baby and was pleased about the way things had turned out so far.

Tom too was pleased. So far they avoided any bickering, no clash of wills between them. Secretly, his one thought was for the day when Phyl left Hoffman never to go back. She had formed her own political views long before she had met him. Though he never said it in so many words, he viewed Hoffman's brand of politics with disfavour. As far as he was concerned, he was a small businessman and voting in the interest of business was the best thing for the country. His sole aim was to make the business successful and take care of his family.

Everyday the city was in an uproar with picketing and protest. Phyl regarded the disturbances with indifference. She couldn't explain whether her attitude was due to her marriage, Tom's lack of interest or her pregnancy. But she was aware her former zeal was gone.

Hoffman was the first to inform her trouble was brewing.

"What're your new plans to press on for the leadership role?" she asked him one day when they were alone.

"Girl, the first thing we got to do, now our people have a chance to hold the reigns of this government, is to break the back of colonialism before it strangle all of us to death!" She saw his eyes sharpen. "You see right now, we're at the wicket. We got to make as many runs as possible and quick! Then we have to turn and bowl them down fast. Timing is the important factor, as always. So for a while, I have to put my own personal goals aside, because in the final analysis, it will more than pay off."

"Ah, well," she said nodding her head, as she pondered his statement, but later forgot everything about it.

But when the gossip started, followed by news on the radio and in the daily papers, she remembered the conversation. At first, there were accusations and cross charges of election malpractices and this set in motion a police investigation into the allegations. Then there were regular "walkouts" by the newly-elected members of the Assembly who refused to honour the oaths of allegiance or the Speaker of the House. The new members swore and made unseemly gestures at each other across the floor. They even challenged one another to fistic battles. Parliament was always in an uproar, every session was a fiasco.

The public curiosity was deeply roused. Staunch supporters, took up regular positions outside parliament so they could see and hear "foh demself". Naturally, there were heated arguments about who upstaged whom, resulting in altercations and arrests by the police who were never far away from these gatherings.

But a more sinister aspect was developing, seriously threatening the very fibre of tolerance which had existed. This was the intrusion of a philosophy and conspiracy of a catch phrase, "race for race" or "apan jaat".

Phyl was disgusted by these events. She thought that with the solid establishment of the elected, a new parliament would remove the imbalance, the negligence and sluggishness which characterised colonial rule. She had believed the new parliament would make decisive changes in order to improve the way of life of the people, but every day she was becoming more disillusioned, more anxious about the future.

She had already given her resignation to Hoffman explaining she was leaving to work with her husband.

"I wish more of our people would get involved in business." He congratulated her, "The more we own, the better off we are!"

Now, on her last day on the job, she was making sure everything was in order before she left. She was thinking of the plans she and Tom made for the grand opening on Monday. They were going to be very busy over the weekend getting the place in ready for business, with the whole family excited about helping them.

Her mother was having the time of her life talking about her grandchild and telling the girls about taking their nephew or niece for early morning walks on the sea wall or afternoon strolls in the big gardens or the little gardens. She smiled to herself as she remembered the regular Sunday feast her mother prepared for her and Tom, from the time she was told the news about the baby. Every Sunday her sister religiously brought a basket filled with home made treats, delicious, heavy homemade bread with its nutty aroma, pine and coconut tarts, sweet bread or pumpkin pone and the never to be forgotten tureen of creole soup, with instructions to drink it right away. She and Tom made intimate little jokes, about the miracles her mother later told her the soup would perform, especially in her condition. Thus happily absorbed she heard mild taps on the door and wondered who it was. She knew Steele was outside, but he wouldn't knock, he knew the door was open. She moved towards the door, but it was pushed open before she got there.

"Is my brother Hoffman here yet?" one of the men asked, while she stared in surprise at the Premier Dr. Chandra Ram Jattan, shirt tail hanging over his pants as usual. Immediately behind him was his body guard, Son Son Sookdeo, with a face like a huge breadfruit jammed into his solid torso, supported with arms and legs as robust and hard as greenheart planks. Real tough looking for an Indian, Phyl thought. Everybody knows Son Son Sookdeo used to hang out with prostitutes, big-timers, drunks and thiefmen down Lombard Street. Now he's decked out in a shark-skin suit, Clark's shoes, catching swank, mopping his forehead with a big white handkerchief, trying to look important, his stetson raked back on an angle. Bringing up the rear, was the Finance Minister Sri Paul Debiden, short, wiry, handsome, always tossing his long black curly hair; arrogant and a wiz with figures. People say his mother is a black woman, she recalled. Of course, his hair is a dead give away.

"Mind if we come in? I know he's never late," Dr. Chettie said, glancing at his watch and Phyl, overcome with shock, stammered her welcome.

She couldn't believe her eyes. She had heard a rumour Hoffman met secretly with the opposition at a prominent hotel downtown but had dismissed it as idle talk. "What time is Mr. Hoffman expecting you?" Phyl asked and Sri Paul responded. "Well you know he's never late, so make yourself at home," she added, attempting to hide her awkwardness.

She observed the body guard had already made himself at home. He checked the windows, secured the locks and was giving the office a general going over, before he sat down, directly across from the doctor.

"I should have left already, but I'm just straightening up a few things," she explained: she had a funny feeling she wasn't supposed to be there. She quickly closed drawers, glanced swiftly around, picked up her bag and was about to leave when Hoffman came through the door.

"We met your secretary and she welcomed us," the doctor said before she could make any comment and she wasn't sure whether his comment was straightforward or a hint.

"I thought you had left already, Phyl," Hoffman said surprised. "I'd asked Steele to leave the door unlocked, not expecting you'd be around."

"That much I gathered," she said, glancing at the visitors. "Good evening." She nodded as she moved towards the door.

"You know, I trust what you have seen here tonight is taken in the strictest confidence," Hoffman said and she stopped. "The English say 'sealed lips save ships', and we say, 'eyes nah see, ears nah hear, heart nah leap' another one is, 'when mouth open 'tory jump out.'"

"You have always trusted me in the past, so I see no reason for you to feel you can't trust me now!" she said, deeply offended. "As for what you said, my headmaster would say, 'Mischief thou art afoot, take thou what course thou wilt.'" She delivered her parting shot and went out the door, with Hoffman's merry laughter ringing in her ears.

Then she too began to laugh at her own daring as she quickened her pace to get to the store. She was glad it was finally over, she had severed the ties. She felt no guilt. She had been deceived and so had the people. She had not believed the rumours. Now tonight her last few moments on the job, she had a classic revelation. Mischief was indeed afoot! It was unbelievable that he had questioned her; maybe he did so for the benefit of the visitors. What hurt her most was the fact that the men back there allowed their followers to believe they were dead rivals. And it wasn't the kind of rivalry which stemmed from differences of political opinion and conflicts of interests. It was the type of deep rooted hostility they exhibited in the House and at public meetings which now appeared to her to be nothing more than a front, aimed at encouraging strife among their supporters while they met secretly. She wished she could hear what they were discussing. She felt very uneasy. People were fighting against each other everyday and it was growing worse while they sat back calling each other brother and talking to each other with such sweetness and respect. Who would believe it! Ha, she made a grave little laugh, then recalled what her mother said years ago, about the rumours concerning Hoffman's behaviour.

"Girl, I been 'pon this earth long before you. You remember the story about the little piggy an' his mother, piggy ask Momma why she mouth so long an' Momma tell piggy, you ah come chile, you ah come!" She laughed out suddenly.

"Miss you okay, you feeling awright?" a middle-aged man walking along side her asked, gazing at her, puzzled.

"I okay mister, quite okay. I never felt better in my life," she said and somehow managed to hold back although she had a strong desire to laugh hysterically. It's over and I don't have to go back anymore. Thank God! she said to herself. Me and Tom are set to fight it out on our own.

Chapter 16

"W̲e're going to make it girl," Tom said to Phyl during one of their slack periods as they stood in the centre of the store.

"The opening sale did it," Phyl spoke confidently. "When people come in and see everything bright and new with fresh lines of stock, they had to come back, bringing a friend or two."

"Well, my mind now at ease 'cause the things moving off the shelves and we're always busy," Tom acknowledged. "That means regular payments back to the bank and we could still put something away for a rainy day."

"So why you worrying if everything going alright?" she challenged him affectionately, went behind the counter, pulled out a stool and sat down.

"Well," he hesitated, his manner half confident, he walked around the counter and stood beside her, "I'm still thinking about all the money we got tied up in stock for the Christmas season."

"Man, you're a real worrier." She patted his hand fondly.

"No, no, it's not that. I agree with your idea that people buy more clothes and things for their children for the season and women buy more for themselves. But I keep thinking about putting all that money on a new cash register. It was a mistake. We shouldn't."

"Of course we should." She asserted her position, "It cost a bit, but I know it will add a touch of prosperity to the business. These things matter

168

to a lot of customers who come in. Man you forget the old one always jamming and giving us a hard time to open every morning."

"Girl, you're right, the whole place now look posh," Tom conceded a few weeks later, at the end of January, when the register arrived. "Every customer I serve make a remark about it!"

"I expected that, but you like to worry," she reproached him gently.

"Girl, you're my good luck. I know nothing can go wrong as long as we're together. Is only one thing..."

"Here we go again," Phyl cut in, laughing. "Tom, we talk about that over and over and like everything else, that too will work out well."

"Girl, I would feel helpless and frighten if anything go wrong. The hospital is the best place."

"What could go wrong? Old nurse Phillips delivered me and all my sisters in that same house besides delivering thousands of other babies. The truth is, I scared of the hospital cause I hear they leave you all to yourself, whether is your first or fifteenth. I want you and my mother around. So how you going to hold my hand when the pains come, if I'm in hospital?"

"I don't know anything about these kinds of things, is my first time too and I'm worried for your safety."

"Look stop worrying 'cause you could start me thinking all kind of things could go wrong and I want to keep a positive mind about the whole thing, so promise you won't bring it up."

"Girl, you brave more than me." Tom reached out to embrace her. "Girl, you getting so large I can't even get my arms around you like before." She wriggled out of his grasp playfully, tripped, but Tom caught her in time.

"You okay girl?" Tom looked at her anxiously, holding her firmly.

"Sure, is just a little shake up," Phyl said, as she tried to catch her breath.

"Come, lie down here." He carried her to the couch. "Sure you didn't hurt yourself or strain something?"

"No, I'm okay. I'll just sit down and catch my breath. I know what's going through your mind, but I'm okay Tom, seriously. Now Mr. Barnes, please get on with what you were doing." She attempted to divert Tom's attention, "Don't stand there staring at me as if I'm going to disappear any moment into thin air, like a genie." They laughed as she gave him a slight push.

They chatted while he tagged and arranged items on shelves. But she was certain the trip began the first stage of labour her mother and the doctor had told her to expect. She knew Tom was a worrier and he was already alert, anxiously watching her every move. She wanted to explain to him what had happened. But to tell Tom would only excite him further and there was no telling what he'd do.

"I'm going to see Ma," she said after fixing his lunch.

"Something wrong?" he probed.

"No man. I just want to talk to Ma and remind her about preparing lunch for us on Saturday. Remember we opening late and we'll be very busy. Ah got this calling for something different I want to ask her to make some black pudding for me, with a lot of pepper."

"Look Phyl," Tom cut in, "I locking up this place and coming with you."

"What for Tom? Anyhow, if it will make you feel better, I'll wait for you at Ma. Okay? So pass around and pick me up,." she said giving him a quick smack on the lips. He stood at the entrance watching as she waved good-bye.

Tom closed the store half an hour earlier that afternoon and rushed to his mother-in-law's house, to find Phyl in the advanced stage of labour. "Girl, why didn't you tell me?" he said as he sat near her, holding her hand, looking at her anxiously.

"Sorry man. I know if I did, you would go crazy with worrying what to do and just panic; I didn't want you to get excited and close the store because I know I had a lot of time." She smiled weakly, "I wanted to surprise you with your son when you came."

"Girl, at least I could have called a taxi. Anyhow, how you feeling now, you getting any pains?"

"It coming again." She gripped his hand tightly and he held his firm, unwavering, supporting her grasp.

Later that evening, Tom stared at the tiny six pound bundle and thought his chest would burst as he gazed at his daughter. He and Phyl had performed the miracle of life, they were actually parents. It didn't matter that he had a daughter instead of a son, he could wait. But no matter how he tried, he couldn't hold the tiny baby the midwife tried to place in his arms. He was too nervous and afraid that he would hurt the fragile body or it would slip from his grasp. He could not explain, why his arms and fingers felt weak, lifeless, everytime he tried to take his daughter. But he was certain that in a few more days he could hold her.

Chapter 17
1954

"Gosh Phyl, you look great!" Pat said, appraising her, "Look how you blooming girl!"

"You too Pat, you're still very beautiful. Stunning. Ma always said so; like the river area really agree with you," Phyl said as they hugged each other, "It's as if we ain't see each other for years."

"That's why when I got your letter, I decide to take the urgent and private leave I was saving up."

"Pat, ah hope you plan to stay for the weekend, cause we have a lot to catch up with." Phyl spoke with girlish enthusiasm.

"Girl, you know I would be glad to stay, but the steamer travels back on Saturday, so I'll stay today and tomorrow, but I have to leave early Saturday morning; I'll make it up when I come down for the christening."

"As for that, Tom and me decide from the very beginning, that you, his sister in England and his good friend from school days, remember the best-man?" Phyl said, "will be Daphne's godparents."

"Well I'm glad that's settled," Pat said, nodding.

"Not quite, girl. We still have to think of another name for her and I leaving that up to you, 'cause I tired racking my brains to find one that's suitable. Tom won't help, he says it's our problem. Whatever we choose is fine with him."

"We'll find something fast, don't worry... How's Tom taking to his daughter?" Pat asked. "He always wanted a boy."

"You won't believe it, but right now he's walking on air! He dotes on Daphne and forget he wanted a son; he even had the name ready. If I don't keep an eye out for him he would spoil her. He picks her up every minute."

"I'd love to see them together!" Pat said, amused.

"Oh you will, cause that's the first thing that man does as soon as he get in the house. Sometimes I think he deliberately wake her up, just to hold her, that's the same man I write and tell you was afraid to hold her when she was born! Lord girl, when we get together we talk so much that I forget. Come an' see Daphne."

They drifted into the bedroom and leaned over the cradle, admiring the sleeping infant.

"She look so big. Did you get a lot of trouble? How much she weighed when she was born? I can't remember. Phyl, she looks just like you!" Pat spoke all in one breath.

"She weighed six pounds, is just that she put on weight fast. You want to hold her? I don't think I had too much trouble."

"She has beautiful tapered fingers, look at them. She's going to play the piano. No man, let the child sleep. I'll get my chance after Tom come home."

"... must repeat that bit about her fingers when Tom come home, he would second the motion 'cause as far as he's concerned she's the most, everything, including beauty and talent, which of course, is at the top of the list."

"And you just as proud Phyl."

"Don't ask! But I just want to watch her grow and be there when she needs me, just like Ma." Phyl spoke with ease and earnestness.

"Girl, how I envy you. You know what I mean?" Pat's voice shook, tears welled up in her eyes. "I'm so happy for you, but watching Daphne makes me think of... of the past."

"Come on Pat, I know how you feel, but right now let's forget about the past and think of the future. Can't have you sad in this house." Phyl led the way and they sat down on the bed. "When last you hear from Ken?"

"Girl, I haven't heard from that man since Christmas," Pat said, trying to overcome her emotion.

"Girl, I sure sure is his studies preventing him from writing and no matter what you think, Ken loves you, keep that in your head. I never saw a man so smitten. I know things will turn out right for the two of you. Ken told me he would never marry anybody..."

"When did he tell you this?" Pat asked surprised. "You never told me."

"Man, I wanted to tell you, but after what you were going through in the hospital and asked me not to tell Ken, I didn't dare tell you. I said I'd wait 'till you were strong, then your mother started to pester you and..."

"I don' t understand. What you trying to tell me? You heard from Ken?"

"Well, I might as well tell you the truth, I had written to Ken."

"But I begged you not to tell."

"Okay, shsh, let me explain," Phyl interrupted, "please hear me out. I was only thinking of you, I know I made a promise when you had the miscarriage, but I was very angry and hurt at the way your mother treated you..."

"But I begged you not to, for Ken's sake I didn't..."

"What about you, Pat. Let me get it off my chest once and for all. Girl, I couldn't sit there and watch you willing yourself to die. If it wasn't for Ma, I don't know what I'd do. It was hell watching you drifting. You were at death's door, the doctor and the nurses everybody had given you up! Did you expect me to sit there and do nothing? I'm your friend remember. What would Ken think of me if I didn't tell him? He was the father. And I feel he should share the burden as well as some grief too." Phyl's explanation was followed by silence.

"And Ken kept the secret all this time too," Pat broke the heavy stillness.

"That's how it looked on the surface, but he was anxious and very worried about you, he wanted to write and tell you he knew what you went through, but I told him what you said, he didn't want to add more worries, especially because of your condition. Pat relax, I didn't tell him you wanted to die and had all of us terribly upset. I just told him you were in hospital and how that happened. Girl, I'm sorry I kept it all these years, but life is so complicated, so many things keep happening, mostly

I was thinking of you and the best time to tell you. Well it out now. Thank God!" She sighed as if a weight was removed.

"I'm sorry I doubted you had my interest at heart, even though you broke your promise. So, Ken knew. I used to think he took me for granted and never asked whether I got pregnant or what. So I started to doubt he really cared."

"Don't you worry on that score," Phyl said reprovingly.

"Anyway, I'm not even going to tell him I know, I don't want him ever to feel obligated to me. Like the old people say: 'let sleeping dogs lie.'"

"Obligated my foot! That man loves you. It's going to take some time, but I'm sure it's going to work out right for the two of you."

"Girl, you're a real sister. I'm never going to doubt you again," Pat said, squeezing Phyl's hand, "but I worry about him not writing. Any way, let's talk about the christening."

"Well, let's check the calender to see what dates available to you in about a month or so from now, I could go and talk to the minister immediately."

Afterwards, they spent an enjoyable time, reminiscing.

"Well of course this is the end for me and Hoffman," Phyl said, explaining her disillusionment at the way things were going politically. "I think I leave at the right time 'cause I was just getting frustrated." But she didn't fully explain what annoyed her most about Hoffman.

"Girl, I know no matter how much you try to avoid it, you had to break with him for good," Pat said then went on to talk about her experiences.

"Girl, I was shocked the first day when I see these little tiny Amerindian children, travelling, paddling their own canoes, coming from as far as ten miles up river!"

"I never knew they travelled so far, I always thought the school was in their community."

"Not always, but they're so accustomed travelling long distances on the river, that to them it's like walking down the street."

"Just thinking about little children in those canoes, with water threatening to swamp it any minute scares me," Phyl said shivering. "I won't like to be one of those mothers, waiting for my child to come home in the afternoons, I don't know that I'll send my child to school at all."

"It's their way of life," Pat said smiling. "There is a saying that Amerindian children live like fish in water, most of the children in the area can swim. At first I used to be afraid, but now I wave them good-bye just like anyone going down the streets, now I'm learning to swim too! With all that river and creek water around me, girl I think it's for my own safety."

"Is only Amerindians living in the area?" Phyl asked.

"Some farmers, who plant cassava and other ground provisions, golddiggers, a shop keeper and a group of Jordanites living in a community by themselves, not too far away."

"Jordanites! I didn't know they lived up the river too. Do they sing and shout and carry on like these in town?"

"The same same way!" Pat said with emphasis and both laughed merrily. "But let me tell you girl, they are self-reliant and strong. They grow their own food. You know the etay and the coria palms? They use the nuts to make oil for cooking and claim the fat is richer in protein, so they have no use for fish nor meat. Then they use the palm leaves to make baskets, hats, mats, pallet beds and utensils for storing their food. They're really strong and hardy."

"You know Pat, when I was a child even when I was a teenager, I loved to stand up and watch them when they carrying on their service at the street corners, especially 'round Bourda Market on Sunday mornings. But the best thing I liked was when they beating that tambourine, shaking and chanting, I tell you, I use to watch them spellbound."

"What I liked was to watch the elder, when he giving the sermon and calling on the sister to quote passages from the Bible. It was always fascinating to see the woman find the chapter and verse so quick, then the elder repeating word for word after her: just pausing to make his own interpretations. But girl, it was his antics that use to make me laugh. Then when he was satisfied that he said all that he had to say, he would tell the sister, 'Go on sister you read that next line' or 'sister you repeat that line again, let me get it straight, 'cause this Holy Word could cause a lot of contention, when you don't get it in the right context.'"

They chuckled as they reminisced and Pat went on, "But I admire them, because no matter what others think, they carry on with their way of life regardless and I admire them more, now I see how they live. It's a miracle to see how white they continue to keep those long, flowing robes and proudly tell you, they don't use soap."

"How they manage that girl, with all that black river water 'round them?" Phyl asked, surprised.

"They never tell anybody and nobody could guess their secret."

176

"Well I guess when you're living in those isolated areas, you use whatever you can get, but I tell you, every housewife in Town would like to know. So how you getting on at the school now?" They continued to fill each other in and the days moved quickly. Then Tom took Pat to see the store before she left.

"You did an excellent job with this place, Tom," Pat said, amazed by the changes, she had known the drab little store.

"I couldn't do it without Phyl," Tom said as he proudly showed her around, "Phyl's the one with the ideas, I could never bring it off like this, every bit of success we've had is all due to her. I don't know what I'd do without her."

"Phyl feels the same way about you and you make a fine couple," Pat declared, and wished Tom good-bye.

Later that Saturday morning, Phyl went down to the church to talk to the minister about christening the baby. She was in the vestry when she heard voices coming from behind the screen, which divided the large hall into an office and waiting room, so she sat down to wait her turn.

"Ah, the poor soul has passed away, may God rest his servant." She recognised the minister's voice.

"You're right Father, God knows best. That poor woman died a beggar and grieved to know she would never inherit what was rightfully hers," a woman said, and Phyl, now alert, decided that as much as she disliked doing it, she had no choice but to eavesdrop.

"My dear Mrs. Forde, it's too late to think about inheritance and it's earthly problems, may her soul rest in peace. I know she in the arms of Our Saviour at last. It was a very christian act you and the other ladies did and may God bless you too."

"Father it was the only thing we could do, especially in the circumstances, myself and a few other members of the Bible class lived in the same area with her and we knew about the terrible plight she was in; so we couldn't let her bury like a pauper, after Mr. Hoffman refused to give any help. The woman hadn't a soul in the world, no family. So we put the situation to the bible class and that was it," Mrs. Forde explained.

"Well, we're all servants of the Lord, and you and the other members are serving God in your own way. I am also willing to do my part, so tomorrow, I will perform the last rites and I can assure you that Beatrice Bishop's soul is at peace."

177

"Oh God!" Phyl cried out and the minister and Mrs. Forde rushed out from behind the screen.

"Mrs. Barnes!" The minister said, recognising Phyl, he had performed the marriage ceremony. "I didn't know anyone was out here. Waiting to see me?"

"Thanks for everything," Mrs. Forde cut in, before Phyl could reply, "I have to run now, see you tomorrow then." Looking at Phyl intently she said, "Chile is what wrong, something happen? You know the lady? Father tell her is the living we got to fear not the dead, the dead gone already. This flesh aye! This flesh!" She moaned and shook her head as she went out the door and down the steps.

As soon as Mrs Forde left Phyl asked the question which was foremost on her mind.

"Father Adams, please don't think that I'm rude, but I couldn't help overhearing what you said just now, did I hear you say Beatrice Bishop?"

"Yes, my child. The poor woman is dead and I'll be performing the last rites at her funeral service tomorrow. Do you know her?" he asked.

"I don't know her personally, but I know about her and the inheritance, it's unbelievable," Phyl said.

"My child we have to pray in these matters and ask God for His guidance." He saw how disturbed she was by the news. "God takes care of things in his own way." Then he added cheerfully, "I trust everything is fine with you, how is your family? Your mother told me about the baby, a boy eh?"

"It's a girl, that's what I came to see you about. I got a shock just now. We would like to christen her."

"Good!" Father Adams said pleased, "I'll be delighted to do the honours."

After she left the church, Phyl paid her mother a visit.

"Ma, thanks for sending one of the girls to keep Daphne," she began, "I was looking out for Donna..."

"One of them. I had trouble, 'cause all three of them wanted to go an' that would cause a problem, so I put my foot down an' send Elaine; she not forgetful like the Donna, then Babs burst into tears, so I had to tell her next time she will go. You know the two o' them together is like thunder an' lightening. Girl, you putting me in big story with these girls." Mrs. Martin said, smiling, pleased that she could help.

"Ma, I arrange the christening with Father Adams, but something happen. I had to come as soon as I leave the church and tell you," she said and paused, "Ah, is bad news..."

"Look girl, don't keep me stalling, you got me in suspense already," Mrs. Martin said anxiously.

"Well, Beatrice Bishop is dead," Phyl said as if she still couldn't believe what she heard.

"I know that was going to happen!" Mrs. Martin burst out. "I always felt it in my bones" she declared. "How you know?" she asked and Phyl explained.

"Girl, I very glad you come to tell me, I got to go 'round to the church tomorrow afternoon an' see her fo' the last. The poor woman is finally at peace, no more worries 'bout inheritance, she is finally at rest." She paused. "Hay yah, that man Hoffman got a lot to answer for! I tell you 'moon ah run til day catch um,'" she spoke solemnly and waited for Phyl to defend him. However, Phyl made no attempt to reply, the news had disturbed her, more than any other.

"Limey go home"; "Ban the British"; "Britannia rules the waves not Guyana"; "Slavery is dead"; "Massa day dun"; "Plantation wages is starvation wages"; "Give us our daily bread and a li'l' dab o' butter"; "Free our People"; "My wife and I are savages"; were slogans paraded by activists protesting the plight of the people, strongly advancing the cause for a break with colonial rule. The pace of protests had stepped up, as every day the numbers of and reasons for pickets increased.

They picketed the public buildings, offices, the homes of colonial representatives, and foreign companies. They were present at each and every public function: screaming, hurling insults or chanting slogans. However, demonstrations of hostility were not only directed at colonials; as emotions ran high, activists crossed picketed opposition strongholds, meetings and homes whenever possible.

"Imperialist stooges"; "Capitalist cowards"; "Big business stinks"; "Bourgeois mentality"; "Marxist mules"; "Kremlin tools"; "Dr. Take a slow boat to Russia"; "Keep Stalin in the rice fields"; "Who went to school in August?"; "Larn to speak a prapa"; "We 'pon top"; "Apan Jaat".

Sometimes the picketers hurled insults and cursed each other and since they had long ago lost the taste for argument, fighting and violence broke out among them.

179

Then the riot squad came, closed in deep rank and file, with helmet, baton, hose and tear gas; wreaking vengeance, leaving in it's wake drenched bodies, burning eyes, runny noses, sore and broken limbs.

In the beginning some of the participants were scared and scampered at the awesome sight of such heavily armed guards, for fear of the punishment they inflicted; but the wounds quickly turned to scars of triumph, to be worn like medals of honour and became the incentive to be bold and daring.

Then the crowds grew larger and larger, as these intrepids, now sought ingenious ways to protect themselves, padding bodies against crunching blows, covering their faces with wet handkerchiefs to dull the sting of the gas. They stood their ground and did battle with their persecutors. However, not to be outdone, the star performers, the newly elected in the House of Assembly, continually pursued acts that were labeled: gross misconduct, disloyalty, slander and sedition. With the Assembly disintegrating into disorder the Governor called for the English troops and closed the doors of Parliament.

Chapter 18
1959

"Come on Alexander! Come my little man." Tom said, "Come hold your baby brother, see daddy holding him too."

"Tom, maybe he doesn't want to hold him today," Phyl said.

"Today. No day, he won't even play with Eric. Look how Daphne ready to take him, see." He placed the tiny, month old infant, in Daphne's readily outstretched arms.

"I like baby, I hold baby," Daphne crooned.

Barely allowing the infant to rest, Tom took him back.

"Alexander is just one year younger than Daphne and if she can hold him, he can do it too. After all he's a boy," Tom said, annoyed.

"Ain't you stronger than this girl? Show her your muscle how they big, do it just like I teach you. Ha, see. He loves to do that." Tom smiled as Alexander slowly flexed his right arm.

"Well, come on now and take your brother," Tom persisted.

"No!" Alexander said, shaking his head furiously, "Don't want no baby. Baby bad!" He kept his hands stiff and straight by his sides.

"Take him whether he's bad or not," Tom said, pulling Alexander's arm out.

"Don't Tom! You heard what the child said, besides he still a baby too, he's only four years old, so don't force him if he doesn't want to hold him," Phyl said.

"I just can't understand this boy atall," Tom said crossly.

"Please give me my son. It's time to nurse him." Phyl took the baby, sat down to breast feed him. "Come Alex, come watch the baby nurse." She called, "Come you sweet li'l devil," she urged Alex, who stood watching his father. "Okay then, come let me give you a big kiss." Alex moved slowly towards his mother. She held out her hand and he ran to her. "Want to go an' play with Daphne?" she asked when she kissed him soundly. Alex nodded his head. "Okay, run along now, but come back an keep an eye on Eric an tell me what he's doing," she whispered as he tripped lightly out of the room.

"Phyl, you got to stop spoiling that boy." Tom said angrily, "I can't understand him, at all, one minute he's crying, sulky and the next he's so full of life."

"Ah, come on Tom," she scolded, "You heard him say the baby is bad. I think we put off getting another child for too long and now Eric is here, Alex jealous."

"Jealous of what! Look how you spoil and pamper him. I play with him when I have the time and that is most of the time I'm home. He just want to have his own way and to be petted. See the minute you called him, he rushed over so you can make a big fuss of him."

"But he flexed his arm, when you ask him to." Phyl's tone was clearly reproving. "And look how his little eyes light up, when he did it for you."

"But that's the same thing I'm talking about, he always wants to be the center of attention," Tom said.

"And that's what I mean! He was the center before Eric came. It was Alex this and Alex that, now that the baby's here, he's hurt."

"Stop siding with him, he's a boy, not a girl and even Daphne doesn't behave like him."

"I'm not siding with... Yes, I'm siding with him, 'cause I'd feel the same if I was in his shoes. One minute everybody falling over me, then the next minute they falling all over the baby and completely forget me."

"Well, he's got to learn that he's not the only fish in the sea," Tom said.

"Give him time and he will," Phyl advised.

"But is time he change."

"You know when he thinks no one looking, he goes into the bedroom and watch Eric, he holds his hands and play with his fingers. He does that over and over," she said.

"You allow him? Suppose he hurt that child? I don't want to hear a word when it happen."

"Alex would never do such a thing. He likes Eric too much, but he doesn't like the fuss we make over him, that's why he won't hold him no matter how you force him. Tom man, try to understand him," she pleaded.

"You maybe right," Tom said grudgingly. "After all, I didn't have a brother, there was nobody after me, so who am I to talk."

"We got to trust him. Don't force him Tom," she encouraged. They said nothing for a while, then Phyl remarked, "Tom, something bothering you? You on edge these past days and I know when something worrying you, we've been married long enough. I know you well. Is something to do with the store."

"Well..." Tom said.

"Business can't be that bad since I left a couple weeks ago, but if it is it will pick up for July, for August holidays and outings. Getting trouble with the shipping people to uplift the rugs and the china that come in?" she probed.

"That's what worrying me." Tom said, "I can't move from the store. Like you can't trust people nowadays atall. I got to send your little cousin away. I didn't want to bother you so soon after you left, but since you ask, I got to tell you."

"Frank! What that boy do now. If that is what he deserves well, fire him."

"I don't want to cause any family rows, that's why I hesitate to tell you about him," Tom went on, "One week after that boy started and that was before you even know you had to come home. I notice he used to help himself out of the cash register, that's why I insisted either one of us handle the cash."

"Why didn't you tell me this before?" Phyl asked.

"Well, when I spoke to him he said it was just a small piece to buy lunch, he show it to me, so I shrug it off, although I put a stop to it. I mean, what is twenty-five cents to row about? But the thing that madden me, is that I use to hear the register ring when I go to the back room and if I ask him if it's a customer — that boy is a good liar — he'd say yes, is just school children buying a pencil or eraser. Then it click to me that school children noisy and these children so quiet, I get suspicious. So one day I wait behind the door and caught the boy red-handed, look I was so mad, I tell him to leave right away; but that boy cried like a child and tell me things bad and he don't get anything where he's living with another cousin of yours."

"That boy is a good liar!" Phyl said with disgust. "He was the only one in the house not working and that's why Aunt May ask me to help just to keep him out of trouble. That's why she sent him down to Town in the first place! He and another friend, Narine, was leading a rice farmer ploughing bull down the back dam; they were going to sell it to a man who offer them a couple hundred dollars."

"That's it, is the same thing he wanted to do. Yesterday, I decide to check up on that boy to find out what he doing outside so often. I found that boy hiding brand new tools in those empty crates outside."

"What!" Phyl said in alarm. "The tools we buy to sell."

"Yes, and he had the face to tell me, he was just borrowing them to do some work at home, so I ask why he didn't take the old ones. That boy got to go, 'cause I can't trust him no more atall," Tom said.

"I know Tom," Phyl agreed, "but I can't let him loose before I write and tell his mother..."

"But that won't solve my problems! I got so much to do in the next few days and he got my hands tied. I want to send him packing right away. Girl, if you been down there this could never happen." Tom was perplexed.

"Ha, glad you miss me, but you said he was stealing even while I was there, so he was just waiting for a better opportunity. Man we got to think of somebody right away, then with all these strikes and labour unrest in the city, we really need a watchman cause things going from bad to worse."

"That's another big thing, you see what I tell you. These people don't have a clue how to run this country." Tom didn't disguise his disgust. "Since they back in Parliament is talk, talk, talk, wasting precious time."

"But they have to talk, Tom! That's how they'll understand each other and plan where they're going."

"Where they going! As far as I'm concerned they don't know where they going. They wasting time and money taxpayers paying them to talk about Russia. What the devil, they think Russia care about you and me! Then this slavery talk drives me wild! We can't waste time living in the past forever, we got to move ahead like other nations and make sure these white people don't exploit us again. But all the while they wasting time, the people situation remain the same. No jobs! Why the hell they don't talk and argue how they can create more jobs: then look at all the strikes going on, Lord, I never thought this country would come to this, and all of this bad for business!"

"We get into this situation because everybody want a raise at the same time," Phyl argued, "Is everybody on strike, transport workers, teachers, civil servants, everything is at a standstill. Everybody is in for a hard time. The government got a problem now to get the people back to work."

"Ha, ha!" Tom laughed, scornfully, "Problem! Man, they could solve all the problems! Remember those political meetings, it was them who make all those glorious promises to the people, put us in, vote for us, we will wipe out poverty with increased wages and more jobs, no more starvation for you and your children. As for Hoffman, remember, 'I promise that your children will not go to bed with hungry bellies,'" Tom mimicked. "They promised and now it's their problem to make those promises real."

"But Hoffman is only part of the government," Phyl quickly pointed out. "He's just the opposition, he's not the party in power."

"And he's surely doing his part. I understand he's the man behind all these strikes. With the help of the CIA, he's backing the majority of the unions to keep the country in a state of unrest. Meanwhile the people suffering. Now tell me, why they can't put heads together to improve this society? The only thing they agree on, is to further race hatred and to break up business. This country is at the mercy of the two of them, each one would stop at nothing to get his way."

"You sure right about that, there will always be a tug-o-war and we'll have no peace," Phyl said, thoughtfully.

"That's why I never wasted my vote on none of them," said Tom. "I vote for business. I was never taken in by Hoffman's big talk. Long ago I know where he was going to lead this country. Business is what makes a country prosperous and we have the resources to create business, to create jobs so people can work and get what they want to improve their own standard of living. The government job is to keep an eye on business, make sure they don't rob workers and see them put some of the profits back into the system by helping to build roads and other facilities for the people and the country."

"So we're right back to the reason the people're striking," Phyl reminded him.

"And we're right back to why a government of the people, they claim they're for the people, can't afford this waste!" Tom said heatedly, "Why encourage the destruction of machinery, equipment, buildings and raw material? That won't raise wages, that would put people out of work! How would you like somebody we employ to destroy our goods and set fire to the building because we didn't give them a raise? I tell you Phyl, I'll..." Tom hesitated to say what was in his mind, but Phyl knew the store was the centre of his life and from the expression in his eyes, somebody was going to get hurt if such a thing happened. Then her thoughts flashed back to the dream she had years ago, and she knew that Tom would give his life for the store, if it came to that.

"I understand how you feel and people have no right to destroy people's property but you agree they have to do something in protest," she said, soberly.

"Not if their way to protest is to burn and destroy the same businesses they depend on to make a living, that can't be reasoning," Tom said, still angry. "It's sickening, we got the greatest potential in the whole West Indies and we can't progress. That is because, in the first place, these men who running this country don't know one blasted thing. As leaders they too damn selfish and the final thing is that we'll all be in goddamn ruin in the process."

He spoke with such intensity that Phyl became alarmed. She had never heard him make such utterances and she worried. He was on edge about everything. She had to think of something.

"What happening man? Cheer up. Things ain't all that bad. We still got our store and we got to fight to hold on to it. Thank God we not on strike! Wait!" She silenced Tom who was about to interrupt, "Don't think I'm not concerned about the store and how all these strikes will affect us," she said frowning, "But we got to hope that things change soon."

"Sorry girl," he said, regretting his outburst, "Everything getting so out of hand all around and nothing seems to go right with me. I was just blowing off steam."

"Well, at least I find out what's worrying you. But it's no use worrying over what we can't change. As for Frank, we got to get somebody to take his place and get that watchman, 'cause there's bound to be a lot of break and enter now that people ain't working. Meanwhile, keep Frank busy all the time."

"That boy is in a class by himself and I surely ain't looking forward to another day with him."

186

"You go and lie down and take a good rest, after all today is Wednesday and that's why you take the half day."

"I had to run from that boy. I couldn't stay in the shop as usual. Anyhow, I'm at peace here."

"I'm going to get you something to make you relax better." She went into the kitchen returning a few minutes later with steaming cups of tea for herself and Tom.

They were sipping, quiet, thinking their own thoughts when there was a loud knocking at the front door.

"You expect somebody?" Tom asked.

"No, I wonder who that is at this time of the day," she said, getting up quickly. "Let me hurry and see is who, before the noise wake up Eric."

She was gone for a while and Tom wondered what was keeping her so long. He was just about to drift off to sleep, when he heard the front door close and Phyl say, "Sit here, I'll be back in a minute."

"Tom!" she called out as she came into the room, "Boy, I think we solve one problem."

"Solve, which...?" Tom asked sleepily.

"This young man is a godsend. He asked if you want anybody to weed the yard, you know you didn't have time to do it lately. He's out of work now, so I agree to let him do it; he's the only one in the family that was working. He look neat and tidy and said he got a good primary school education. His mother died and left he and some smaller brothers and sisters. Then his father move out leaving all of them, gone with another woman. Come take a look at him I didn't tell him anything, but I think he's just right for the job."

"Girl, I think it hard to get up. Once he okay with you, you know is okay for me," Tom said.

"Come on man," she urged. "You talk to him and let's get it over with now. I won't have to worry about you and Frank, when you leave in the morning. Then with your mind at rest you going to come back and have a good rest." Tom got up reluctantly.

"This is my husband," she introduced Tom.

"Good afternoon Mr. Barnes. Your wife hire me to weed the yard and I'll do a good job, but if I finish half this afternoon, you'll pay me? I need the money."

"Sure and what's your name?" Tom asked.

"Paul, Paul Ben," he said. "I live just around the corner and that's how I know the yard need weeding," he explained.

187

"So you out of work eh?" Tom said.

"Yes ah..." Paul Ben said, somewhat embarrassed.

"That's nothing to be ashamed of," Tom said, trying to put him at ease, "The way these politicians running this country, we all would be out of work soon. How'd you like to come and work for us?"

"Work, work here and look after the yard?" Paul Ben asked surprised.

"No man, we have a small business downtown and now Phyl's home with the baby, we need a reliable person."

"Mr. Barnes you making jokes," Paul Ben said, more surprised.

"Man, you want the job or not. You look honest and straightforward to me, unless you don't want a steady job," Tom said.

"Is just that I can't believe it! Thanks, thanks."

"You good with figures?" Tom asked.

"Oh very good. If my mother didn't dead and leave us, I was going to study accountancy," Paul said and added, "Please excuse my behaviour just now, it was so sudden, I thought you was making fun."

"Man, I too tired to make fun, and remember, you still got that chance to make that accountant, we all get chances to make something good, whatever we want to be. Look, you say you're just around the corner. Well tomorrow morning, pass and pick me up by a quarter to seven we'll go down together. I'll explain everything to you on the way, and don't worry about wages. I'll pay you better than the big store. So it's all agreed then."

"Yes Mr. Barnes and thanks again," Paul Ben said.

"Well see you tomorrow morning" Tom said anxious to get back to rest. "You finish the weeding and the mistress going to pay you. If you want you can bring another brother on Sunday and the two of you can knock off the rest of the weeding quickly." He left then, with Paul Ben still mumbling his thanks. He went back to the old settee and threw himself down, chuckling, thinking about the look on Paul Ben's face. Paul had saved him from having to deal with Frank, but he had to thank Phyl, he didn't know what he'd do without her. She always could find a solution, he'd let her know as soon as she came back. However, when she returned to tell him Paul was doing a good job, he was fast asleep. She kissed him on the forehead then tiptoed out of the room.

The country was at boiling point. Tension seemed to be part of the life style of the people, especially those who lived in the city. Strikes, go-slows and walk-outs were the order of the day as well as a spate of political meetings, which kept them well charged.

Government, opposition and independent members of the cabinet, conducted meeting after meeting, with the fervour of an election campaign. This time, however, there was a noticeable difference in the subject of attack. The common enemy, the colonials, had gradually, but finally departed from the House of Assembly, leaving the august and honourable members of the local cabinet in the firing line. So while the major opposition forces continued to lambaste the erstwhile and departed, ascribing to them an immortality as "villains of the piece", they were now propelled to the front lines, tangible, obnoxious and ripe for scorching.

Sometimes these meetings were located only a short distance from each other. In some instances, they were barely separated, a block or two apart, so traffic at a common point was only possible, through the generous disposition of followers and listeners. Loudspeakers blared, driving neighbourhoods to distraction. Would-be followers suffered the same consequences and in no doubt about the real purpose behind these plans.

During these meetings, audiences were restless, some roamed from one gathering to another searching for excitement and entertainment. It was the beginning of viciousness, terror and what was later called a legacy of unspeakable evil.

"Hey Stella an' Charlie.. is where you all goin'" Cynthy asked.

"Hey Cynthy an' Georgie!" Stella responded, "You all walkin' out chile!"

"Actually, we goin' down to this meeting an' stretch we foot li'l," Cynthy announced.

"Is which meeting you goin' to eh? We goin' round by Hoffman side an' hear what he got to say 'bout the strikes," Stella explained.

"Look Stella! Look quick man," Cynthy spoke excitedly, "Don't stare an' leh the girl see I pointing she out."

"Is who man? I ain't see is who you showing me yet." Stella glanced around awkwardly.

"Because you looking in the wrong direction, look over so," Cynthy said in exasperation, indicating the position with her finger, "Is Doris an' dat new man she runnin' 'round with."

"Is he?" Stella said with scorn, "Is he she lef' me good good step-brother for? Call she, call she quick let she know I see she," she said to Cynthy.

"Dor-is, Dor-is," Cynthy bawled out, clapping her hands, "Is me, Cynthy!"

"Good Christ!" Stella hissed as Doris stopped, looked across the road and reluctantly began to cross over, "Is he is the man I hear she an' he 'pon the poodle bike all over the Town. You mean is he, she lef' me good good..."

"Good good what," Cynthy cut in, "You know that Clarence hand fast and he like to beat up women. The girl right to lef' he," she stated flatly.

"Eh eh, chile!" Stella spoke scornfully "Watch the two o' them holding hands! The girl now in love, he look like real mook man to me!" She and Cynthy chuckled in derision.

"Good fo' you, take that fo' you fastness," Cynthy added. "Is you tell me to call she, she right to show off 'pon you now!"

"Eh eh, chile, is where you an' Sam goin' in such a hurry?" Cynthy asked Doris and her partner, who had reached the small group. "Look is your old friend Stella, your sister-in-law," Cynthy said to Doris smiling slyly.

"I know it had to be somebody like you!" Doris said, in a brittle voice to Stella, "And when you see that fast-hand brother of you tell he to read the papers, especially the divorce section and look fo' he name, it goin' to be there, for all the world to see."

This information was met with stony silence from Stella.

"Look man, doan worry wid that now, tell people is where you all goin'." Cynthy tried to steer the conversation into safer channels.

"We goin' down by Hoffman meeting, but we hear they got another one just by Haley and Hadfield Street, so we goin' to pass an get some fun. Is all in the way," Doris said.

"Eh eh, me ain't know they got another one there too."

"You din't know that?" Stella said. "If you ask I could've tell you." She had found her voice.

"You always know, Stella!" Charlie countered, "You goin' to always get yourself in trouble, I don't know why you don't shut your mouth li'l bit!"

Stella ignored him.

"Look, you all come along leh we go yeah," she said and they moved off.

"Doris, is true you an' Hoffman is family?" Cynthy asked as the party moved along.

"You mean you din't know that!" Stella said in a superior air.

"Christ Stella, ah just talk to you, woman. You like to run you mouth so?ø Charlie said.

"Look, you try with that poodle bike an doan worry let it scrape me foot, yeah," Stella hissed at Sam, who was trying to manipulate the bicycle so as not to touch her.

"So, is Hoffman doing the divorce fo' you? So we hear girl." Cynthy said, "And you know Clarence frighten that man like six months in jail, is just good fo' he. He like to beat up women well he now meet he meter!" She laughed scornfully, "Hoffman now goin' to shit he up."

"Christ, is wha' wrong with these women tonight! All yuh lay off the blasted man name, you all goin' to talk 'bout he whole night?" Georgie cried out in disgust. "Look Cynthy, if you can't find nothin' else to talk 'bout, I goin' back home," he warned.

A silence followed which no one tried to break, only the sound of a loudspeaker, some distance away.

"My friends, my friends, fellow citizens," a voice said.

"Listen, listen, leh we listen!" Stella, true to form, directed the group.

"Are you satisfied with the way things are heading in this country?" the voice exploded over the loudspeaker. "I know many of you standing here tonight are concerned about the state of things in this country. What is happening in this country today? Let's face facts. What are the elected doing to this country? When the British were here, they fought to get rid of them and what do we have now? I tell you, we have nothing but strikes, walk-outs and disorder! We cannot progress with disorder, we must have discipline."

At that moment, the blast of another loudspeaker a couple blocks away filled the void, "You got to stand up and fight, you got to stand up and fight to the last drop of blood!" It echoed clearly.

"Ha, you see what I mean!" The first loud speaker echoed, "That proves my point. Those words are dangerous words, besides, I applied for a permit to hold this meeting at that point, but when I arrived there about two hours ago, some hooligans made it impossible for me to remain there. I came here and the police tried to harass me. I promise you, it certainly will not end here, my friends." He was indignant. "Now you

191

tell me, how can we hold another meeting in this small area? Ha, my friends, I don't scare easily, but I wanted to bring these facts to your attention and to show you that these things lead to disorderliness."

At this point the other loudspeaker interrupted again, "Youall got to be militant and watchful at your work place! You can't sit down like cowards."

The first speaker glowered at the intrusion, "We need discipline in order to survive!" he shouted defiantly. "We need discipline to develop this country, today things have gone to such a point, that an employer is virtually afraid to have a civil conversation with an employee about his work, lest the employer is deemed as insulting and harassing the worker."

"Is what he talking atall?" Cynthy said in a loud voice for all around to hear. The party had reached the gathering and pushed their way into the crowd. "Only yesterday, Georgie tell me he an' he supervisor had it out, down at the water works! He was goin' to the to the W.C. and the man up an'ask he where he think he goin' so early. When Georgie tell he, this man start getting on bad an' tell he if he sick, why he din't stay home so he could be near the toilet," she said in a huff, then added, "Like you can't even go to the toilet, when you want to nowadays. Is what this country comin' to atall?"

"Girl, well Charlie working with a man they does call he The Colonel. When he givin' you orders an' you ask he questions, he does insult you an' ask you if you hard of hearing, you din't go to school or if you went to school in August!" said Stella. "Like you ain't got no rights when these big shots insulting you. Look, Charlie just set he friends fo' cuss he up, yea!" she declared.

"You talk too damn..." Charlie's voice trailed off, as Cynthy called urgently to them, "Listen, listen, he saying something 'bout Hoffman."

"His sole aim is to cause unrest in this country," the speaker said, "His game is to destroy, not..."

"Ring that bicycle bell, Sam," Cynthy ordered. "Is you cousin he talking about Doris. You ain't hear wha' he say." Sam ignored her, but she reached over and rang the bell.

"Ow man, ow! You all talking so much already, people could barely hear what the man saying. Now you ain't satisfy, you goin to make more noise?" a listener spoke out boldly.

192

"Is who is she atall? Is who is she now!" Stella asked, only too glad to join in. "Lady, you ain't know this is a free country an' we do what we likes!"

Cynthy continued ringing the bell.

"You all ain't got no manners, no training nor discipline! Is the same thing the man just talking about!" the woman said sternly.

"Run the bicycle 'pon she," Doris said to Sam, "since she know we ain't got no training nor discipline!" Sam ignored the instructions but Doris grabbed the bike and pushed it against the woman.

"Ow me foot, me foot! You all see my story here tonight?" the woman appealed to the other listeners. "I come here to listen peacefully to what this gentleman have to say, and these hooligans push the bike on my foot because I talk about..."

The gathering was in an uproar. The speaker aware of the disturbance, called out, "Please, we must have discipline, I'd like to carry on please. As I was saying, Hoffman..."

"Is wha' he talking 'bout Hoffman atall! Who the hell is he atall? Look pass me a handful of them li'l bricks, yeah! I goin' to show he something," Doris fumed, but did not wait for her request to be fulfilled. She bent and picked up handful after handful of gravel, which she showered towards the platform.

The crowds were already scattering. They ducked and ran in all directions.

"Oh God! Come leh we go home sister, this meeting got trouble," a woman urged her companion, who didn't need a second urging.

"Fireworks here tonight," a teenaged boy said, gleefully. "Man come leh we stand up this side and watch them parade."

"You could stay if you want," said the lad next to him.

"Not me, 'cause I ain't able let nobody blind me! I gone yeah." He took off.

"Leh we hurry and go yeah, before these hooligans hit we or blind we," said another to her companion.

"Is wha' wrong with you? Mind what you saying yeah. Leh we go quick, before they start 'pon we now!"

When the offenders were quite satisfied they had broken up the meeting they too took off.

"Leh we go before the police come!" Doris said. She didn't have to insist. "Ah had a good laugh tonight." She was pleased.

"We goin' now and hear what we boy got to say."

"My dear brothers and sisters," Hoffman's voice boomed over the loudspeaker, "I know how you feel or else you would be somewhere else tonight." He hinted broadly, and the crowds joined in uproariously.

"Your numbers alone tell me how you feel and that's why you're here. I know how a mother feels, when her child can't get enough to eat. I know how a father feels when his child don't have enough to eat and nothing much to wear. I know how a man feels when he can't give his wife or child mother enough money to buy food and clothes and pay the rent. What these people want you to do?" he bellowed, outraged, "They want you to remain quiet and watch your family starve while their tables are filled with delicacies. Even their dogs are eating better than you!"

"You know the thing Hoffman," someone shouted.

"Is true, is true," some women chorused.

"You know them well, 'specially the women who work in their houses, No names!" he hailed out.

"No warrant, no warrant!" the women chanted.

"Yes, even the scraps the dogs eat from their masters tables, far better than the food you and your family partake of. What is it they want you to do? I will tell you what you have to do. You have to force them to give you good wages, you got to fight for it and as I stand here tonight, I tell you, you got to help yourself. A poor man got to help heself," he stressed the local vernacular and the crowd roared. "I tell you, you got every right to help yourself, whatever you can put your hands on, man. Help youself." The crowds yelled and cheered, they understood the full meaning and were beside themselves in applauding the suggestion.

When the noise died down he continued "If they don't want you to help yourself, let them agree to give you respectable wages, so that you and your families can live like decent human beings."

And the crowd again went wild to his entreaties.

Chapter 19
1962

"Ha! So you finally managed to tear yourself away from your precious charges, eh!" Dr. Godfrey Khan chuckling, said in his crisp, borrowed English accent. "Do you think your little patients will survive the rest of the evening, without your devotion?" he teased.

"Quit that Godfrey. You make me sound like a latter day saint." Dr. Ken Masterson said in protest. "I'm no more obsessed about my work than you are."

The two colleagues met on the main thoroughfare, in the Public Hospital compound.

"How are things today?" Ken asked, attempting to shift the conversation away from himself, but Dr. Khan was not easily discouraged.

"Don't give me that Ken," he said. "You know how news travels around this institution. Man, everywhere I go, the nurses are talking about the new, handsome and devoted Dr. Masterson, your word is their command. See what I mean." He thrust his chin forward, directing Ken's gaze to the nurses, strolling briskly past them on the opposite side of the narrow road.

"Good Lord man! Look at their eyes, all dripping with admiration. How do you like that? Not one of these Florence Nightingales looking at me. I'm putting on my best and sexiest smile and what the heck, I get ignored anyway," he laughed merrily, then added, "'The handsomest doctor in the place', that's what I heard them saying the other day at Surgical. Christ man, some people got all the luck," he said in a mournful tone.

"Look who's talking," was Ken's swift rejoinder. "See what I mean? Now what do you say to that? That little Douglah nurse, nearly tripped over, trying to slow down and preen herself to sashay pass us, just to get your attention." Ken averted his face from the embarrassed nurse-trainee as he chuckled.

Dr. Khan swore and said, "She's not looking at me, she's looking at you!"

"That's because she's probably embarrassed," Ken cut in, trying to sound grave.

Dr. Khan repeated his favourite swear word and Ken lost control, laughed and said, "I'm sure she heard you this time, the poor thing is disconcerted. That's another thing that gets around this institution, your swearing and those bawdy jokes you keep throwing around. You scare the hell out of them, because they don't know when you're going to spring one in their midst."

"Naw! They love it," Dr. Khan assured Ken. "The other morning I went into the ward and the charge was holding forth with the nurses about one of my jokes and they were all having a good ole time, laughing, until they noticed me. Boy! That shook them, you should have seen them hurry away with faces like martyred saints. Don't worry man, they love it."

"How did things go today?" Ken asked, "I hope that now these politicians see it fit to declare a coalition government, that would stop the brutality and savagery we're witnessing."

Dr. Khan registered his contempt by erupting with such venom, that Ken was startled. He was aware his colleague had a gift for adorning every discussion with expletives and not even the most sober professional discussion escaped his spirited decoration. Even so, Ken was always caught off guard. He glanced around, looking bewildered by the onslaught and said gravely, "Not so loudly, man. Visitors are within earshot."

Dr. Khan swore again, amused by Ken's expression, "You buy that! Stop what? The people got to come to their senses by themselves; the politicians encouraged the blood letting, now they can't stop it! Besides, they don't care a rot, why should they? They're achieving their aims. They have learnt well from the British to divide and rule. They have been their most apt pupils. I don't see why they should care about the people, since they don't have to clean up the mess, the human debris, we have to face daily. They don't have to face a man with his guts or stomach hanging out or his bloody ----------- torn off! They don't care a damn!" he said bitterly.

"Were they around a few hours ago when the nurse wheeled that man in the theatre? The man was strong and I did my best, but it was too much to ask. He was a healthy, middle-aged man but his chest was split right open and by the time we put him back together, he died." Khan said intensely, "But I tell you, the poor man was better off dead anyway, what's the use of being alive without his vital organs. Man, if I could get the whole bunch of politicians together, I would cut theirs off and see how they like it. I'd really like to chop their bloody..."

"Okay, okay, alright." It was Ken's turn to cut in, "I understand very well how you feel. How do you think I feel?" he said, annoyed.

"Don't really know," Dr. Khan said impolitely. "I face it every day, when I try to patch, sew, and stitch those terrible gouges and slashes, severed limbs and lashed faces and the worst thing for me to face is castration. It's barbarous and unpardonable."

"It isn't easy for anyone," Ken said frowning. "Where are your nerves, man? Do you think it's easier for me? And don't pride yourself that your blitz experiences, make you a better judge. Or that I'm unscathed because I'm not a surgeon. Don't forget about my precious patients, as you call them. Some have suffered their share of assaults and rapes, then the trauma from being witnesses to the savagery you describe as well as the trauma from losing parents or close relatives."

"Apart from that, I too have my personal griefs. I have lost an aunt and a cousin, in one of the train incidents on the West Coast and another cousin in the Sun Tarpon explosion. My aunt was hysterical; I went out there hoping at least to identify the body. I was out there man! It was a terrible scene which I'll always remember, a horrible wreckage of wood, strewn luggage, arms, legs, heads without torsos — torsos without heads or limbs. It was a gruesome sight, absolutely impossible to identify anybody. It was a river of blood and human debris. So don't try to be arrogant with me, we both have our cause celebre and crosses. But, I can never understand the men who incite such savagery." Ken shook his head and outwardly bristled at the memory that was provoked. "Let's change the subject," he suggested. "I try to keep my mind submerged in work, that way it's easier to bear."

"Yeah, I forget Ken. Keep a stiff upper lip, in the spirit of the good, old British tradition and training. One must never forget one's position," he mimicked, but his anger and bitterness had subsided.

"I hope when this episode of our lives passes," Ken said, still shaken, "people will remember the cost and the consequences and never, never again want to repeat these animal acts."

"I hope so too," Dr. Khan agreed. "I hope it wasn't for nothing," he said calmly. "Hey Ken," he said surprised, "I thought you were on your way to your quarters and we could have a game of cards or chess. Man, I don't feel like tennis this afternoon."

"Ha, wasted thoughts, I don't feel like it either. I promised Frank Harvey in Casualty I'd see him, see you later. That's if you're not deep in one of your arrangements," Ken laughed.

"With an unfortunate chap like me, I have to catch whatever crumbs I could get, whenever you're not around," Godfrey Khan replied.

"That's highly debatable," Ken said and left him.

As Ken made his way to casualty at the entrance of the hospital compound, his smile faded as he reflected on their conversation. He had had his share of grief and no one could know that better than he! God knows, he had come home hoping for peace and quiet; his own experiences had been sufficiently shattering. Mind you, he knew his work would be well cut out for him. He had been aware of the demands; but the race riots and their savage acts, upset his private as well as his professional affairs. He had bragged so much about his country while in England, so sure it was one of the few places on earth, where people of mixed races lived in peace and harmony. He was appalled to come home to find the country torn apart by civic strife, shattering his hopes.

He understood Godfrey's outburst a while ago. Every nerve was on edge, everyone was tense, praying, hoping they would not be the next victim. At the moment even his private life looked desolate. He had made every possible effort and so far, he was no nearer his goal. Maybe it was the price he had to pay for his past stupidity and bunglings! It's always easier to say we have learnt our lesson after experiencing the terrible pain of emotional suffering. He didn't doubt he was wiser now! That was why he wouldn't give up his search for Pat. Although, presently it seemed he had reached a dead end, be would never stop trying. It was just as if she had vanished. No one around where she lived knew her, nor her family.

It seemed all the old tenants had moved out. There was only one old lady around who had a dim recollection of Phyl. She had rambled on about a store and about other people he didn't know. Nevertheless, if he had to visit every store downtown, he wouldn't rest until he got some trace of Phyl and she of course would know where Pat was, he hoped! He reached Casualty and went into the inner office.

"Very serious Doc. What's up?" Dr. Harvey greeted Ken, "Something on your mind?"

"Everything and nothing in particular," Ken answered, brightening. "Seems pretty quiet around here to me. Where's the action you assured me I'd see? Where's the action man," he teased.

"Don't push, give it time, so when it strikes don't tell me I didn't warn you," Dr. Harvey declared.

"What strike? You were just exaggerating." Ken said, "Everybody knows that Casualty is touch an' go, but you insist it's the worst place in the whole world." Ken grinned, "You said patients stood in long lines reaching around the corner outside the compound and the line in the compound doubled up, reaching as far as the laundry. Where are these lines? There's not a soul in sight, not one prospective patient, this place is as quiet as intensive care," Ken joked, while his colleague listened, unruffled.

"Laugh all you want Ken," he said, "But stick around. It won't be long before you get a load of it for yourself. This time yesterday things were humming already, it was children's day. I suspect we have an epidemic of whooping cough on our hands, you stick around my brother, just stick around and I'm not exaggerating. Last week, it was diarrhoea and vomiting. You couldn't find a place in here to stick a pin. And don't forget the cases of racial violence, they all pass through here. Then there're the regular cases of wife beating, injuries from street fights, neighbour-hood altercations, accidents, children with second, and third degree burns, those who swallow small objects and worst of all the unusually high number of children who drink kerosene oil; now that takes the cake! I don't think there is another place in the world, where there are so many kerosene drinkers."

"Sometimes I lecture the parent or whoever comes with the infant; but what I really want to do, most times, is belt them a couple across their derrieres and not delicately, either. These people are absolutely careless!" Harvey's eyes gleamed with annoyance. "Could you believe parents actually leave bottles with kerosene oil, cups and pots of boiling water within reach of small children? Then, blame the children for the accidents! I'm mad as hell these children are seriously injured because of their parents' carelessness, I can't endure such crass ignorance!"

"We need to educate them," Ken said. "I have a case now, where a mother pushed her eight year old son's hand in the coal fire, because he stole some sugar. Sugar I tell you, and this little tyke's hand, his right hand at that, is so badly burnt that it will take a long time to heal. Then a longer time before it's restored to it's full use... all for a little bit of sugar!"

"They need the law on them," Dr. Harvey said, "only the law could force these parents to stop their cruelties. Lord man, you'd think when slavery was abolished, the cruelties of that era were dead and gone. The injuries I attend here, get me boiling mad, because it's the parents who're inflicting these terrible punishments on their own children."

"We've got to force them to act responsibly," Ken declared as they moved around the empty room.

"Ah ha!" Dr. Harvey said, "Here comes our first case Dr. Masterson. This is how it usually begins," he winked at Ken, "and then... Okay Irving," he said to the nurse who accompanied the stretcher, then wheeled it near the examination table. "Strip her blouse off quickly," he spoke crisply, "then take care of those shoes and stockings. That's a compound fracture with serious tissue damage."

Ken stood back observing their quick-studied actions. Dr Harvey had already flipped back the eyelids of the inert patient, then held the left wrist.

"Diminishing pulse," he stated, "How's the pressure Irving? This one is a real bleeder!" He was examining the wound at the back of the head, which seemed to be the reason for the blood soaked blouse.

"Nasty gouge," he informed his associates. "How's the pressure Irving?" he said to the nurse as they ministered to the patient. "She's a real looker."

Ken drew nearer, there was something about the inert form that alerted him, then as Dr. Harvey raised the left hand and the nurse shifted, he saw the ring and thought the probability that there could be two was remote. He sprung into action.

"I'll take over now," he spoke crisply to nurse.

"Dr. Masterson, I..I... " Nurse Irving, started to protest, but training made her give way. She had heard about the tireless and devoted Dr. Masterson. But he had no right to barge into casualty and...

"You may step outside nurse," he said and she went out. He recognised that girl, she thought, I wonder who she is? Nurse Irving hurried off to Nurse Carr in Admission, thinking she might know the girl's name or something about her. She smiled in anticipation.

"What's going on man?" Harvey asked, observing Ken with a puzzled expression. "What got into you?"

"A friend of mine," Ken admitted.

"Well, you know what's going to happen now that Irving is out of this room," Dr. Harvey warned.

"I couldn't help that," Ken said. "I had to do something. Anything!"

"When you put it like that, what could I say? This thing is serious. Come on man, admit it." He urged Ken.

"Yes, it's serious, very serious," Ken said after a moment. "I hate to think what would have happened, if I hadn't come here this afternoon. Let's hurry up here and get her into the ward."

"Okay old chap, we're nearly through. Is there anything else?" Dr. Harvey asked as he gazed at the patient.

"Let's see how things go," Ken said, deep in thought.

"Ken, she's going to be okay, don't worry too much." Harvey offered friendly advice, "The darn thing is, we can't do anything about the leg until after the x-rays, and that's the unfortunate thing about this hospital. It may take a couple of days to get the x-rays done and that's going to be very painful. Hope she comes out soon," he comforted.

"I'm sure she'll be okay," Ken agreed and mumbled his thanks. "See you later." Then he and the orderly wheeled Pat through the side door as Dr. Harvey rushed to take charge of another emergency.

Ken could not remember how he got through the rest of the evening. From the minute it dawned on him Pat was the unconscious patient he wasn't himself. Since his return six months before he had spent all his spare time making inquiries. Now the unexpected had occured. Had fate brought them together? There had to be some great hand, behind their present encounter, because it was a decision he made on the spur of the moment to visit Harvey. Yes, it was Godfrey and his arrogance that pushed him towards Casualty. Was it? Or was it that great hand which made it appear like Godfrey's doing. He mused. He and Harvey had worked swiftly, suturing the terrible wound on Pat's head. She was a bleeder indeed and she remained unconscious throughout all the doctoring and stitching. He was worried about the concussion.

"Doc, the lady is one of your family, nuh," the orderly asked Ken as they wheeled the stretcher quickly, but skilfully across the hospital compound. "Don't worry, I know them nurses in that Accident Ward, so she in good hands," he assured Ken. Ken half listening still deep in thought, nodded his head.

"So if you on duty, me and nursie here goin' to see the lady comfortable. Everything goin' to be awright!" the orderly insisted.

"Are you on night duty nurse?" They had reached the ward. Ken assisted in transfering Pat to a waiting bed.

"Has the nurse come in?" he asked.

"Yes Doctor, I'm on night duty," the nurse eagerly replied. "The Charge will be here in a few minutes, but if you're on call, I may be able to help. "

"That's okay nurse, I'm off duty tonight, I was caught by surprise I didn't get a chance to change," he said almost cheerfully.

"Doc, I know how you feel, especially when one of your own family got to come to this place," the orderly said as he hurried off.

Ken remained with Pat for a while. Then he told the nurse where he would be, if there were any changes in the patient's condition. He had finally found Pat. He willed himself not to think of any complications which could arise from the concussion she suffered. She was going to be okay, he said to himself. He knew the leg was badly fractured and there was serious tissue damage; he was sure she was hit by a car! The leg would take time to heal. He cursed the ineptness of the x-ray system, but his main concern was for the blow and the gash on the head. He wondered where she had been and how it happened. He remembered that awful night years ago, when she was viciously attacked by her mother and quickly pushed the incident from his mind.

He thought about the promise he had made that same night, which he meant to keep but he had betrayed her. He swore that from now on things were going to be alright for him and Pat, he knew his true feelings for her had never changed. Just seeing her again, after such a long separation, had roused his emotions. It was a terrible struggle for him to control himself and the days ahead were going to test his strengths as well as his weaknesses. More a test of his weakness! He smiled to himself. He had paid the price and he meant to make a clean breast of the matter, there would be no more deception. As soon as she was well enough, he was going to tell her the truth. Things people thought were buried in the past, usually had a way of surfacing and quite unexpectedly. He was taking no chances. The only way to start was to begin with a clean slate. He was on his way to tell his mother he had found Pat. Rather Pat found him. He would need her help to see Pat through her convalescence. But did he dare tell Pat the truth? Surely she would understand, but it could also be the end for them. Ken wrestled with these thoughts as he drove quickly through the streets of the uneasy city, to his old home in Charlestown.

"Tom, something happen! Is not like Pat to say she's coming to spend the weekend and stay so late to turn up. It's nine o'clock already and she never come so late yet," Phyl said.

"Maybe something make her change her mind. She'd probably come in the morning," Tom said. "You quite certain she said tonight?"

"Yes man, she said Friday night! She wanted to have a longer weekend, because she got to go back to Training College Sunday night, so she could prepare for classes for Monday morning," Phyl explained.

"I can't think what would keep her so late, unless," Tom said amused, "unless she decided at last to get a boyfriend or find some old cracker and stop hanging on, waiting for that chap in England," he grinned.

"Okay, okay, forget I said that," he added, seeing the cold stare he got from her. "I know how you feel about Pat, but you got to face facts. I think it's stupid to wait for a man who's scarcely written to her in the past few years and lately not at all. Phyl, it doesn't make sense, a beautiful girl like that got no right wasting her life away for a man who's probably happily married and with a family of his own."

"I thought about it myself, over and over. But I can't bring myself to accept it as a fact. Ken Masterson dump Pat like that and without a word. I'm not going to believe that, I won't." Her expression was grave.

"Try to be practical," Tom said. "Even in your own mind you feel he dumped her, it was you who use the word dump." He tried to soothe her as she glared at him, "So you suspect he would. Man, there's a limit to loyalty: the man is a big shot Doctor by now, he's probably found some English woman and married her and he's living comfortably. He's human too, 'cause it's a lonely world out there. My sister use to write and tell me, loneliess is sheer hell out there. Christ! I know, cause it was hell for me, right here, but thank God I was patient, 'til you come along. So if he get's a woman to suit him, who're we to judge. I feel she's wasting her life foolishly."

Phyl did not reply, she sat thoughtful, reflecting on the situation.

"Alexander, Alexander!" Tom called out, "I sure that boy hearing me and just won't answer. Alexander! Come here at once!" he bellowed. "Where is Eric?"

"Gees Tom. You don't have to shout like that," she reproached him. "I sure he could hear you. You have no patience with Alex at all. It gets on my nerves how you stretch and strain that name. Why you have to call out that whole long name. What's wrong with saying Alex? Everybody calls him Alex. Then you always bawling him out."

"Don't start on me again with that, Phyl! You see clearly that boy want to have his own way. You didn't see what happen a little while back? Daphne brought her school work to show me and ask me to help her with some sums. Eric wanted me to read a story for him, but that boy Alexander is a horse of another colour. I had to insist he bring his books and show me what he did in school today. Then he took his own time coming," Tom said angrily.

"But that's because you're always criticising everything the child do. You criticise the way he writes and you criticise his work. You criticise his books and tell him there're fit for the rubbish. Then you turn around and tell him, he's the untidiest boy in the whole school, his clothes always filthy. You tell him in the morning he's clean, but when you see him at the shop in the afternoon you're ashamed of him. Now you tell me how you'd feel, if your father's always ripping you apart?" Phyl's tone was cutting.

"Look Phyl! Isn't he always dirty? Look at his books. If he can't get things right now, when is he ever going to get them right? Man, I worry if he's ever going to be responsible, 'cause in a few more mornings, I'm depending on him to take over this store," Tom expressed his real worry.

"Look, give him a break man. Ease him and give him a chance to grow up and be his age," she said angrily.

"That's it, see. You always defending him, always running to his rescue and that's why he will continue to behave the way he does. He only got to look around and watch your face and he know you on his side. You see up to now, he can't come since I call."

The air was electric with tension.

"Daphne, see where Alexander is and call him for me," Tom called out.

204

"Yes daddy! I think Alex in the storeroom downstairs searching for something," Daphne said. "He's coming now," she added. Alex walked into the room.

"You call me Dad?"

"Christ boy, where you been atall. Look at your clothes."

"I was down in the store room searching..."

"What you searching in that room for? Boy, look at you," Tom said crossly, avoiding any eye contact with Phyl.

"Dad I was, I..."

"Look boy, get in that bathroom immediately, before I lose my temper," he ordered Alex, who stood uncertain, glancing from one parent to the other.

"Dad the door fasten an' I couldn't get..."

"The bathroom," Tom shouted to Alex, who did not move.

"What is it Alex?" Phyl asked.

"I ah, find that box with with the padlocks Dad was searching for, it was under the big box with the coloured paper."

"Eh eh, boy how you find that. Go bring the padlocks, they're rusty eh?" Phyl asked.

"No Ma, they look new. You still want to see them?" Alex asked hesitating, looking at his father.

"Sure, I know Tom glad you find them, so run along and bring them; then hop in the bathroom and get rid of some of that dust off you skin."

"Well, he found the padlocks you thought you lost," Phyl said when Alex left the room. "Look when he come back with them, try to make him feel good; loosen up with him a little bit."

For a while they had forgotten about Pat, until they were about to turn in for the night.

"This is not like Pat at all," Phyl voiced her concern again. "Something wrong. But what got me more worried, is that she said she was going to give a friend who live in Plaisance a lift home, then she was going to ride through a short cut from there to get to our place quickly and it's the short cut she want to take that got me worried. It will be late and that country road is usually deserted. It's not a safe place for Pat with all this racial tension going on. She could be raped and lying dead or injured by the road side or some trench corner!" she expressed her fears.

"Stop worrying. Plaisance and these areas near town didn't have one report of racial violence, so you have no cause to be worrying. She could get in an accident, but by now she would tell the police or somebody where to find us. We're going to see her tomorrow and her explanation is going to be so simple, you'll wonder what you were worrying about. Is only one thing," he said after a short silence, "I don't think that motor bike was a good idea atall! She shouldn't buy it, that thing is too fast for a woman."

"Tom, we have to put in a telephone," she said, thinking her own thoughts. "We're too far away from the police station, the hospital and everything. We need one in the store too. It will save you a lot of useless running around. I sure something happen," she added with emphasis.

"Stop exciting yourself, things always look worse in the night. Try to relax and get some sleep. Better still, let me help." He drew her closer.

They still had no word about Pat the next day, which was Saturday. Saturday was a very busy day for them, so the whole family worked in the store. Tom and Phyl were kept on their toes, while the children pitched in, doing small tasks, all except Alex.

"Come and see your son," Tom called Phyl. "Everybody else doing something except Alex. Eric is happy to be the lookout for the children, who like to pick up small things, Daphne busy tidying that corner, but Alexander is no where in sight. I had to search for him, come and see for yourself." He beckoned and Phyl followed, "Don't make too much noise," he cautioned, as they moved towards the storeroom, which they had renovated and expanded. There, boxed in behind some crates and boxes stacked to the ceiling, was Alex. He had found a place to be by himself and with chalk in hand, he was busily and contentedly writing and drawing over the surface of the boxes.

Tom was about to bawl him out, but Phyl gestured to him, and she led him away.

"Phyl, we can't let that boy always get his own way," Tom said, when they got back to the front of the store.

"Let's leave him for a while Tom, he looks so happy. I can't stand anger in here today, my nerves already on edge. We'll talk to him tonight. Did he clean out the trays with the hinges and screws?" she asked.

"Yes, but he had other work to do. He was to let me know when he was finished but he didn't even bother to tell me." Tom was exasperated.

"Well at least he did the job. Let him be Tom."

"Okay," Tom said grudgingly, sighing. "Only for your sake." He was anxious about her. He had noticed her staring at the entrance, several times. She even made trips to the door, where she stood looking up and down the streets. She had kept a lively pace, walking backwards and forwards, staring out into the distance, shaking her head, murmuring. He knew Pat was on her mind. She was eager to get home and when they did, he was dismayed to see her continue her restless march from window to window.

"It's times like these I so glad we were able to help Ma to get the place near us here, so I don't have to worry they're far away, and even though Donna and her husband living with his family, I worry when I don't hear from her. Nowadays, life isn't predictable, anything could happen," she remarked to Tom as she moved restlessly around.

"Now you worrying about everybody," he said. "Please come and sit down near to me, you got to relax."

"Don't tell me you forget already. Remember, it was the same day Ma moved up here, it was the same day she would have been on the launch with Aunt Bertha and her grandchildren going to McKenzie; Ma would be dead by now, not one of them was found! I can always sense when something wrong. You know, I think I going down in the village, I don't mind it far, but I'm going to get to a telephone and call the college. I'm sure they could tell me something about Pat. You think if she was in an accident, we'd hear by now?"

"I'm sure if she was in an accident, we'd hear by now. Besides if you call the college, nobody's there, only the watchman and he don't know anything. I sure Pat going to turn up this same day. Man come and give me a hand with these invoices," Tom coaxed her.

"I don't even know if I could concentrate on that now," said Phyl, "But I'll try." She sighed and sat down. He was glad because he felt it might take her mind off Pat for a while.

Twenty-four hours had passed, since Pat was admitted to the Georgetown Hospital. Ken visited her that evening. He was standing near her bed, watchful, waiting, worrying, admiring the beautiful, but unconscious patient, thinking about the arrangements he had made for her to be transferred to a private room. He had made sure her leg would be x-rayed and set soon. Suddenly he heard her moan lightly. "I must get to Phyl," she mumbled. "Somebody help. Oh my head." She tried to focus and her vision settled on Ken.

"Lie still, you're okay," he tried to be calm, but couldn't control his racing heart, the moment he had waited for had arrived. He stared at her diligently.

"Who is it? I'm dreaming," she said. Ken wanted to bridge the gap quickly and tell her his name, but he dared not. He thought the shock might be too much for her. He wanted to make sure she was back to normal. So, he stood silent, waiting to be recognised, agonizing as the moments dragged by.

"Ken, is you? I'm dreaming." She focused and attempted to sit up. "It couldn't be, Ken's in England." She spoke slowly but clearly.

"No, I'm right here," he said, he couldn't let it go on any longer. "It's really me, feel." He placed his hands in hers. "How are you feeling now?" he asked. "Try not to get excited," he spoke calmly.

"It's really you! I can't believe it's you here in Guiana." She struggled to sit up, "Oh my head," she winced.

"Yes, but don't try to move. It's really me. You've had a bad accident, your leg is broken and you have a nasty wound in your head."

She began to examine herself, carefully, "God, my foot really hurts and my head feels as if it would burst. Oh my God!" she cried out suddenly, "Phyl, Phyl, I was going to spend the weekend with her and I got hit by a car, she's looking out for me. I know she's going to be very worried, when I don't turn up, she has to know. Now just look at me, teaching practice begins on Monday and I'm a mess. I must get a message to Cooky." She was now fully agitated.

"It's not such a bad mess Pat. I'm relieved you're okay and I finally found you. Let's leave things as they are now. Later you and I have quite a lot to talk about. Just tell me where to find Phyl and this Cooky person. I'll get everything settled, you've had enough exertion, so let's call it a day."

"What day is it? How long was I out? Ah... Phyl's got to get the message tonight, I mean as soon as possible," she said and he answered as calmly as he could.

"Ken I can't believe it's you after all these years. I didn't hear from you since '58, so I still can't believe my eyes. Is something wrong?" she asked, noticing a change in his expression.

"No, nothing is wrong, I just want you to get well as fast as possible. I'll call the nurse to give you a sedative. I'm going to see Phyl now then I'll be back soon." He signalled the nurse.

"I don't want to sleep right now. Everything's happening too fast, I want to think. Didn't you say you were coming back?"

"Look Pat, I should give you a sedative. Doctors orders. The strain of thinking is just going to make your headache worse and I'm concerned for you," he said, with more than doctorly concern.

"I want to be awake when you return. I promise to take the sedative then." She gazed at him, he at her, both remembering the past then he gave in.

"Promise to close your eyes then." His voice choked with emotion. The nurse arrived and took Pat's pressure and pulse, whispering the results to Ken who nodded with satisfaction. He wasn't worried anymore, he knew she was going to be alright.

After his departure, everything came back to her in a rush, the accident, her complete surprise at seeing Ken face to face, the flood of memories he brought back as he held her hand and in the presence of the nurse! She couldn't stop herself from thinking. Ken was right, she should have taken the sedative, but she had to sort things out.

The accident was bad enough, but to be confronted by Ken after regaining consciousness, would have been a challenge even in a healthy condition. When did he arrive home and why didn't he write to her all those years? What caused the gradual decline before he stopped writing completely? Why hadn't he tried to contact her since he came home? Something he said could be part of the answer and the reason he didn't contact her. He had said it really wasn't such a mess because he found her. But why didn't he write her for four whole years? Why didn't he?

The strain of thinking was too much, she felt as if her head would split. She was going to call the nurse, she didn't want to think anymore. Then she remembered his hesitation, when she reminded him how long it had been since he'd written. She felt his hesitation. Yes, she was sure he was holding something back. She was going to lie there and wait for his return, even if her head split. Yes, she would close her eyes that might ease the pain. Ah, it helped when she closed her eyes. Yes, she would ask him directly if he was married. Now that she let the fear out, her head didn't feel so tight anymore. But he had held her hand. Tonight he held her hand and looked at her the way he used to and she remembered the first time she was attracted to him by those same penetrating eyes. She never stopped loving him and thought he felt the same way; although, she sensed something was different. Life could be so promising and yet, full of pain. She remembered while on her way to Phyl, she had made up her mind to erase Ken out of her mind and life, once and for all. She was going to tell Phyl about her decision. Then she had the accident. Now she must wait for Ken to return and put her mind at rest.

"Tom, did you hear a car drive up?" Phyl asked.

"No Phyl," Tom said patiently, "You hearing things 'cause your mind on Pat."

"Now I sure I hear footsteps and don't bother tell me I hearing things, 'cause if you can't, you got to be deaf or you playing tricks on me," Phyl said, listening attentively.

"Hm, eh heh. You're right, it sound like somebody coming up the steps," Tom admitted, then they heard quick taps on the door.

"Sit down, Phyl," Tom said, while his hands restrained her movements as she jumped up to go. "You don't even know who it is, let me check first. You can't trust people nowadays." He went to open the door.

He was worried about her. She was nearly a nervous wreck worrying about Pat. If it was the police or the dead runner from the hospital, who reported family deaths, it would be better if he took the news, because he would soften the blow, she was very jumpy and at the point of panic.

He opened the door with trepidation and saw a tall, dark, well groomed man in his late thirties.

"Good evening. Does Phyl Martin live here?" the man asked. Tom stared at the stranger appraising him. He couldn't be a policeman, thought Tom, unless he wasn't in uniform or he's a detective. He's even too polished for that; the dead runner is out of the question.

"Phyl Martin," Tom repeated, pleased by his own expectations.

"Yes, Phyl Martin," the stranger repeated clearly, nodding his head and Phyl rushed to the door.

"Ken! Ken Masterson!" She spoke with disbelief, "I would know that voice anywhere. Tom, this is Ken man, Ken and Pat." She tried to explain to Tom who stood aside speechless, "Come in Ken, come in," She held Ken by the hand, then they were shaking hands and hugging each other.

"This is my husband Tom. When you said Martin, I'm sure Tom was wondering who on earth is this man asking for me as Phyl Martin. My God, Ken is only one thing could bring you here," she said pleased, "Pat! You're looking for her." Then her expression changed.

"Well no, I saw Pat," he hurriedly explained, "I was with her tonight. She's in hospital, she had an accident and I was lucky to be at Casualty when she was admitted. So after she regained consciousness, she asked me to get in touch with you. She was worried you would be worrying too. You're still great friends, eh?"

"Oh God, she's hurt bad, dying?" Phyl asked anxiously.

"She was critical for awhile, she has a serious gash in the head and lost a lot of blood, then she has a fractured right leg, but she's going to be okay now," he said with relief. "Though it will take some time before she's on her feet again; I think she's going to be okay, once there's no other complication."

"Tom, I knew it, I knew something was wrong, the moment she didn't turn up. It wasn't like her at all and with all this violence, I was thinking the worse. But thank God she's alive," she said, relieved. "You had trouble finding the place?"

"Not at all. Kitty and Campbellville used to be my romping ground as a boy. You know I went to your old place a couple times asking about you. It was surprising no one there remembered you. I've been searching for Pat, since I came home at Christmas, I even went around to her old home but drew a blank."

"Boy, we moved up here years ago, when Tom and I got married, Ma's living up here too, just around the corner, that's why no one remembered any of us. I think all the people who lived in that yard moved out."

"So that's why no one remembered the family except one old lady but she rambled on about a store."

"Yes, we have a store. I remember the old lady. She outlived all her children and refused to go to the Palms, says she prefers to die first. So all the people in the neighbourhood chip in and look after her. You look great, Ken. I'm really happy you decided to come back home. If you know how relieved I am about Pat. I thought she was dead," she said soberly. "But I tell you, you give me one hell of a surprise. I could guess what happen to Pat when she saw you." Phyl and Ken continued chatting for a while.

"Well, I must go now. Pat's waiting." Ken shook hands, "I didn't even ask... any children?"

"Sure... three, two boys and a girl," Phyl stated proudly.

"And you're attractive as ever. See you another time."

"Tell Pat she'll see me first visit in the morning," Phyl said, trying to suppress her excitement. "It was really good of you to come and tell us, Ken. It feel so good, like old times. Hope we see you again."

211

"It sure feels good seeing you again," Ken replied.

"Did you study medicine, you're a doctor?" Phyl asked as Ken was about to leave.

"Yes, thank God," Ken acknowledged, laughing lightly. "This is one of those times I'm grateful I studied medicine, truly grateful." He bade them goodnight as Tom and Phyl accompanied him to the door, then waved to him as he drove off.

"Tom, Tom!" Phyl shrieked in delight as soon as Tom closed the door. She hugged him, kissed him, twirled in a dance around the speechless Tom. She was delirious with joy, "It's going to work out after all for Pat and Ken, I was right! Did you see his eyes when he talked about her. You could see clearly he still loves her. I knew it, I knew it!"

"You're right," Tom admitted, "he really cares for her and don't ask how relieved I am that you're happy. At one time I thought you were going to have a breakdown, but I can't help saying that it's very unusual for a man in his profession to come back to his old girl friend."

"Well Tom, I'm so happy for them. I want to shout."

"Woman, you crazy or what? Come let's go to bed."

"Man, I really don't think I could sleep now at all! I'm just too excited at the thought they're going to get married, after all these years."

"Come on Phyl it's late, lets go to bed," Tom coaxed. "Come and share some of that happiness with me." They embraced and he guided her towards the bedroom.

"Is that you Ken?" Pat whispered, Ken was just about to turn away, thinking she was asleep.

"How are you feeling, is your head still throbbing?" Ken asked, observing her closely. "You've got to take that sedative now," he spoke firmly.

"Okay, but not before you tell me if you found Phyl and gave her my message."

"I found her alright. I didn't know she was married. I knocked at the door and this guy whom I later found out was her husband, opened it and gave me a good going over with his eyes. Then she came to the door and was she shocked! Just as I was when I realized it was you. I guess we were all shocked to see each other. I'm very happy I found you, Pat." His voice was gentle, "I've never stopped loving you. I want you to know how I feel. However, you must rest now."

"Ken you make it more difficult for me to say... I just can't find the right words," Pat said, thinking how much her future depended on his answer.

"What is it Pat?" Ken asked, "Please tell me, I don't want you worrying."

"Are you married?" she spoke without hesitation.

"No, I'm not," he said eagerly, noting she was visibly relieved.

"Are you engaged, dating?" he asked, although he knew what the answer would be.

"Ha!" she laughed, "There's a nice old guy but I haven't yet decided," and they chuckled together, but he knew she was teasing him. She had been faithful to him all these years. He reproached himself for asking, thought about the past and felt terrible.

"By the way, I've lost your ring," she admitted, bringing him out of his reverie. "Probably came off when I had the accident."

"No... I have it right here in my pocket." He patted his breast pocket. "I'll keep it for you... My God Pat," he said, regarding her with deep admiration, "Even ill you're beautiful, you haven't changed atall!"

"Look who's talking. You haven't changed, then there's that added professional charm."

They talked for a while, until Ken said, "I'll call the nurse to give you a sedative, you need a good night's sleep. I'll see you tomorrow morning before I go on duty." He called the nurse, then waited for the medication to take effect before he left.

As he went about his duty, Dr. Ken Masterson thought that since his return, it was the first time he felt cheerful and light-hearted. He was actually walking on air and Pat was the reason. She was the centre of his thoughts, night and day. His greatest desire was to see her strong and well so he could put into action plans which he had kept to himself. Bit by bit, Pat had explained the situation between herself and her mother, who now lived at Diamond estate with her husband.

She and Pat must patch things up. After all she was still Pat's mother and he would try to help them to heal the breach. At least, Pat should keep in touch with her, do a bit more than send a registered envelope at the end of the month. If it wasn't for him, Pat might not have had cause to leave home but he was doubtful about this. He felt the woman had been the genesis of all the problems between himself and Pat. She had been stupid and intolerant. It was difficult to predict people's behaviour, he mused, considering his own. He still had to let Pat know the truth. He was uncertain Mrs. Sandiford would change but that was irrelevant to him and Pat, who was long ago out of her domination, so it didn't really matter. What was important to him presently, was his secret. As he thought about it and the time drew nearer when Pat would be discharged from the hospital he was even more excited. He wanted to surprise her and knew nothing else would give her as much pleasure as his surprise.

In his search for her he often followed the routes they had traversed in their careless fashion to keep their meetings secret. The thought she might be married had entered his mind, but seeing her again would be enough. He knew he had no right to expect more than he was capable of doing.

It was then he saw the house and the memories flooded back. He felt Pat was very close, she had always loved the house. It was a neat bungalow which stood in Anira Street, half a block away from First Street, a beautiful old house in a quiet area, standing well back from the road with enough space for a kitchen garden, flower bed and could support the needs of an army of children. His thoughts raced ahead into the future as soon as he saw the empty house and made the decision it would be Pat's. It would be the most telling expression of his love for her. It embodied all their past hopes and dreams. It was the bridge that would extend far into their future. His reward would be the look on her face when he gave her his present.

As Pat got better she was eager to get out of the hospital. Then as the day of her departure drew nearer, she became anxious. Would she be able to see Ken as often as she did? Would they have the same intimacy they shared during these past three weeks? It would be quite some time before her leg healed properly, she wouldn't be able to get around without the aid of crutches. She would be thoroughly confined indoors for at least another month or so, she hated the idea and became impatient with her leg. Ken had phoned the Training College and talked with the principal. She remembered Ken's puzzled look when she explained about Cooky, whom he thought was the cook. How she laughed as she told him he was the principal, loved and respected by all the students. Well, she'd have to resign herself to boredom, until she could return to college.

Pat hated her present situation, but reflected that, had it not been for the accident, she and Ken might not have met for a long time. Would the new relationship be lasting? He told her he still loved her. She was almost certain he did from the way he looked at her, but he was different, something was wrong, she could sense it. Why did he take such a special

214

interest in her? Was he humouring her? Then she berated herself for doubting him, thinking, if he didn't care he wouldn't spend most of his spare time with her, even the nurses gave her that knowing smile. So she cast her doubts aside.

Then the day of Pat's discharge arrived. Ken, however, asked her to delay her departure for several hours, so he could be on hand to take her to Phyl's. Pat was restless when he arrived around five o'clock in the afternoon. Together they thanked the nurses and left. Armed with crutches and helped by Ken, she carefully negotiated the trial of stairs, a test of her stamina. There was dire need for a lift in that wing of the hospital. She was very much jolted and sore, but she made it safely down the stairs, out the building and into the fresh afternoon breeze blowing from the Altantic, wafting away the strong odor of disinfectant.

As they drove out of the compound into the streets, Pat welcomed the quiet traffic with sighs of gratitude. How easy it was to take simple everyday occurences for granted, she mused, that was until confinement made the pleasure of these experiences impossible! It was pleasant watching people going about their daily business. Children standing at doorways or playing in the yards; boys wrestling and chasing each other around in a wild glee, swimming in trenches, pitching marbles. Women hurrying along to attend to simple everyday tasks: going to market or grocery shopping, taking smaller children to school and bringing them home. Then taking care of hundreds of household tasks and along with that, many held regular jobs to supplement their husband's poor earnings. Even the old woman, who now slowly and cautiously crossed the road, unaided, made her contribution and maybe continued to do so in her role as grandmother. Yet, everyone seemed to take so much for granted and no one seemed to care or remember. She was drawn to a kaleidoscope of activities, acutely aware of all she had missed.

"Why so serious?" Ken asked.

"Oh, I didn't know I looked that serious. I was thinking how we tend to take everything for granted. I was enjoying the bustle, saying to myself, it was just as if I had suddenly come back to life! I felt as if I was shut away for years. I'm glad you were there to make it bearable," she said contentedly.

"It's a fact we tend to take everything for granted," he agreed. "Life is so short, yet we..." he said, when she interrupted, "Why're you going this way? Isn't it longer to get to Phyl?"

"Longer? Look who's talking. This lady is a professional at going the long way home don't you remember?" he said, laughing, while Pat still puzzled, glanced about as they moved along.

"You forgot something?" she asked again. He smiled but said nothing. He had turned through a side street then cut back to the street they were travelling on before and continued onward.

"Remember anything yet," he asked again, smiling, secretly pleased with himself.

"Course I do," she said and they chuckled, "At first it didn't click, but after you turned around I kept thinking, you were up to something, then I remembered. Ha! and you thought I'd forget! I didn't take our walks for granted, especially in this area, there was always the chance somebody would see us. Those were some days." She smiled and he held her hand, content that she was happy.

"Don't tell me that girl, you forget," he teased.

"Only for a moment. I won't forget, ever 'cause that was the only way we could meet and talk," she said soberly. "I'm so glad you remembered." She looked at him intently, "It makes me feel good and it makes the past easier to remember." He drove through Oronoque Street, then turned into Anira. They were quiet saying nothing but Pat was all smiles as she leaned back, relaxed.

"Happy?" Ken asked.

"You bet. I've never been happier in my life," she reassured him. "Broken leg, split head, headaches and all! Why did you stop?" she asked looking out the window, then she noticed the house and cried out, "The house Ken, you remembered the house." Still unsuspecting she said, "Seems like nobody's at home."

"Ah, yes, it's empty. Want to have a look? A friend of mine bought it and I know you always wanted to look inside." He smiled.

"I'd love to, but look at me. That would be too much trouble for you, with me and this leg hobbling in and out," she said, sorely tempted but, didn't move. "Besides it's getting late."

"Oh don't worry about that, I'm sure Phyl will understand." He kept a straight face. "Come on, let me help you out," he said.

"How're we going to get in?"

"I have the key. Ah, here it is." He showed her the key. "Now let me help you with those crutches."

"This is too much, Ken. I'm so excited to see inside," she said, struggling to her feet. "It's like peeping into your own dream, kind of unreal."

"Not this time, it's real," he assured her. They left the car and finally climbed the long flight of steps, Ken supporting her, until they reached the platform, where she leaned on the rails to catch her breath.

"Now you turn the key." He slipped the key into her hand, and she, trembling, placed it in the lock and opened the door.

"Oh, this is just as I dreamed it would be," she said wistfully as they entered. "The curtains are beautiful, all that's needed is a few more pieces of furniture. It would be heaven for me, just as I dreamed."

Her eyes shone with pleasure.

"It's yours to add those pieces of furniture and what ever else you'd like."

"You're pulling my leg, you're joking. Mine! But I thought you said that..."

"That was to get you inside," Ken said laughing. "Would I joke about something as important as this?"

"Then it's true, Ken. It's true," she said, her eyes wide with wonder. She rushed into his arms embracing and kissing him all the while.

He felt his heart would burst with joy.

"Let me sit down and catch my breath, this is really too much," she held his hand tightly as he helped her to the settee. "Ken! When?" she asked, so he told her.

"I kept searching and couldn't find you, then one afternoon I found myself walking past this very house, it was empty and for sale. I felt so close to you then, I knew the reason it was empty and I'd find you. I did Pat, I've never stopped loving you, believe me." He kissed her again and again, whispering, "Everything's going to be alright for us. Are you happy?"

"God know's I haven't felt this happy in years," she said.

Ken was overjoyed, because they had bridged the gap between the past and the present. Yet, he couldn't bring himself to tell her the truth. He knew he loved her as she loved him, with the same intensity and passion as when they parted years ago but she would be hurt by his disclosure. So he prayed, silently, he would find the courage and the right words; he wouldn't tell her today.

Pat rested for a while then he took her on a tour of the other room.

217

"I love this kitchen, it's so spacious, I always wanted a kitchen with lots of elbow room. The bedrooms are cosy. I love this one best, 'cause you can see the sun rise in the morning, there between those mango trees. Who helped you with the furnishings?" she asked, pleased and excited.

"Phyl and Mom." Ken revealed the other conspirators.

"Oh, that Phyl is a real secret agent. She was in on it all the time and never let on. The scamp." She laughed heartily, "Oh please thank your mother for me."

"You're going to have a chance to yourself. I hope you don't mind, but I asked her to come and stay with you during the day. She's glad to help with the cooking and so on, so you could stay off your feet."

"That's okay, but you're sure she wants to? I mean..." Pat hesitated to say what was on her mind, she had not forgotten Violet Masterson's possessiveness.

"Don't worry 'bout a thing," he cut in, "Mom is more than pleased for us and if I'd ask her, she would be here from today."

"I hope you're right Ken," she said thoughtfully.

"Listen Pat, all that sort of thing is over, we're both adults. We'll lead our own lives without unsolicited interference. Will you marry me, Pat?" he said seriously, no smile betrayed his intention, and she could find no words to reply, it was too sudden. "You haven't answered my proposal," he said as they stared at each other.

"If that's what you want." She found her voice.

"No, not that way. What do you want, do you want to marry me?"

"Yes, I do, I do," she said and he kissed her gently on her lips and forehead.

"You don't know how I waited to hear you say that," he whispered.

Later, they sat down to the dinner his mother had prepared and continued to talk about their plans for the wedding and their future. Afterwards they sat cradled in each others arms, talking, until she said her head was aching and he knew she had had enough excitement for the day. As he got her the sedative, once again he wondered where he'd find the courage to tell her the truth.

Pat heard faint taps on the front door, soon after Ken left the next morning. Then she remembered Violet Masterson, the whole thing had completely slipped her mind. She hobbled to the door opened it and Violet Masterson entered, smiling.

"You look well, Pat," Ken's mother greeted her. "Ken told us about your accident, I was going to pay you a visit, but Ken didn't want you to have too many visitors, I guess he wanted to spend all his time alone with you. I was sorry to hear, but thank God you're all right now and you do look well indeed," she remarked admiringly.

"You look very well too, I hope I'm not putting you to a lot of trouble," Pat said and as they talked she appraised Violet Masterson. She was one of those women who looked better as she got older. There was just a line of grey at her temples, but she was still well groomed. She had a trim figure, which she carried with the same air as Ken did. Ken resembled her a lot. You could never be too sure with Violet Masterson! She regarded her coolly.

"You look so happy," Violet said. "You don't even look as sick as Ken said you were."

"Well, it was due to Ken. Oh thanks for helping out with the house, I appreciate all you've done." Then Pat decided to take the plunge, "Ken asked me to marry him and I hope you're happy for him and me."

"I'm glad he did," Violet said. She showed no surprise, "I know both you and Ken are going to be happy at last. Ken, more than ever needs peace, happiness and a calm home life in order to succeed in his practice. I'm glad you understand and you're willing to forget his past mistakes, he's already paid the price."

"Mistakes, paid what price? What do you mean? I thought you were glad that Ken and I..." Pat said alarmed.

"No, I don't mean you child, please don't take me wrong." She began to explain. Then it occurred to her Pat didn't understand. Oh my God, what have I done she said to herself. "Pat, I thought Ken told you, I'm sorry. Please forgive me," she said with regret.

"Please explain to me what you meant?" Pat asked in alarm, feeling suddenly threatened.

"Pat, I only said what I did because I thought Ken told you. He said he would and I trust him. Don't be too harsh with him, it's really my fault." The poor girl looks shocked she said to herself, and I thought everything was settled. She saw a hundred questions in Pat's expression. For the rest of the day, they tried to make light conversation, but it was no use, a gloom had set in. Violet Masterson left with a heavy heart, she had interfered and made a mess of the situation.

Pat, tense, waited, listening for Ken's footstep, when she heard his light quick tread on the steps. He was whistling happily and she tried to compose herself to face him, as he let himself in.

"How's my girl today?" he asked.

"Okay." Pat's attempts to appear light-hearted failed.

"Not a very enthusiastic welcome from the woman I love and who's going to marry me!" He bent over and kissed her, then made a quick professional examination of the wound on her head. "You alright?" he asked. She nodded her head. "Did Mom come? Pat I'm starving! All I had for the day was a couple cups of coffee, if you know how I waited for this moment. What's wrong Pat? You haven't said one sentence since I came home."

He looked her over carefully, considering her expression.

"Let's eat first, then we'll talk later," she said. "No, let's talk now. If what ever it is has that effect on you, let's get it over with. I don't want anything to hang over us and spoil our evening." He spoke firmly.

"Well, I want to know the truth," she said with stony countenance, "Ah... your mother and I were talking and she said something about you, that you had already paid the price, she was glad I was so understanding. At first I thought she was referring to me and..."

"Okay," he cut in, "I know what Mom meant."

"Well, will somebody tell me what this is all about? If it concerns me or you, I don't want to be kept in the dark any longer, I want to know," she said, her anger growing.

"I guess Mom thought I had told you. I told her I would before I asked you to marry me, but I couldn't bear seeing you unhappy yesterday, I..."

"Stop it! Will you please stop trying to spare my feelings!" she said distressed. He knew she was hurt already, "I can take care of myself, after all I went through all those empty years and a lot of pain and suffering." She spoke coldly.

"Very well, Pat. It's not easy for me to tell you. I was married, but I'm divorced."

"Oh my God!" she said stunned, "Ken why didn't you tell me? So you had your fling in London and got married. When it got sour, who else could bring you peace, quiet and calm, but naive and stupid Pat, who's waiting with open arms! Sure, she'd be willing even to be second best. Oh God! I knew something was wrong." She began to cry.

"Pat please, please listen to me," he pleaded and tried to embrace her, but she, with great effort pulled away and made a hobbled, painful rush towards the bedroom. He tried to restrain her, but she went into the room, slamming the door behind her.

He was perplexed. She was crying bitterly. He knew her pride was hurt. Now he had done what he thought was right, he pondered whether he should have done so, but he had to tell her the truth!

"Pat, open the door please!" he called out. She was crying much softer now. "No matter what you think about me, we've got to talk. Please give me a chance to explain."

"Leave me alone. What is there to explain?" she said calmly. "You fell in love with another woman, you married her, then you behaved like a coward. She must have ditched you, then you remembered love sick and loyal Pat."

"It wasn't that way at all, you've got it all wrong. I was not in love with her. Will you please open the door? I can't talk to you this way! Our whole future depends on trust and it's now or never."

"Boy, you got some nerve talking about trust!" she said angrily.

"Yes trust! If you don't believe me it's your choice to do what you want; I won't force you into anything, into making any decision. Will you open the door please!" he pleaded.

She did not comply, but remained quiet, thinking. What did she expect? He had been away so long. They were both adults. He was right. He didn't force her to remain single. But that was so long ago and people change to meet situations and circumstances. He said he was never in love with the woman he married... his wife! Tears came to her eyes as she thought of another woman as his wife. But he asked her to marry him, there was no doubt he still loved her and she could never love another man. She'd have to get used to the idea of his marriage to another woman. She knew her pride was badly hurt. He could still have his pick of other women.

"Pat, are you okay?" he called out. She struggled to the door opened it and he entered quickly, immediately helping her back to the bed.

"Pat, listen carefully, please. I'm sorry I hurt you, but when you love someone as I love you, sometimes the truth is hard to communicate. I thought this matter over and over, I knew the truth would hurt you, but I had to tell you. You see, I couldn't bring myself to live in deceit with you, not ever. It would haunt me. I would always be afraid one day you'd find out and it would be the end of your faith and trust in me. I want our relationship to be built on truth not lies. I want our lives to be happy, not miserable." His voice was firm and passionate.

She looked down at her hands and Ken tilted her head upwards, "Look at me Pat. Do you think I would deliberately set out to hurt you?"

"I've been hurt so often by well-meaning people, do they really care? I carried our child and kept it a secret from you, mostly for your sake, even when I lost it. I never had doubts about you, even when you didn't write often. But I should have put the pieces together when you didn't write at all, you see, I couldn't bring myself to think you'd 'want anyone else. That was girlish, stupid and wrong. I saw the world through rose-coloured glasses. I refused to look at reality."

"Pat, I want to talk about my marriage, so you'll know the truth. I met Edith during my training."

"Are you sure you want to talk about it? I..." she cut in.

"Pat, I want you to understand, so we can begin on the right footing. Edith and I attended the same classes for a while, we did our internship at the same hospital. We seemed to be thrown together a lot of time and it's strange I must admit, but she reminded me of you, there was something which made me notice her at first. I was terribly lonely and we became attracted to each other and we decided to get married. Pat, believe me when I say the marriage was just an arrangement, we had little commitment to each other. Values are quite different in the so-called progressive society. Besides she knew I didn't love her, I used to tell her about my girl back home, but she was just as lonely as I. However, when whatever the attraction we had for each other died, so did everything else and she became careless. The rumours were terrible. You know how gossip spreads, especially when you work at the same institution. But I ignored it until one day the stark reality hit me! Edith took her dates to our apartment. It was all so convenient for her, because when I worked night, she worked days or the other way around, and that's how the truth came to light. There was no doubt in my mind what was going on when I stopped by the apartment to pick up some notes I'd forgotten. They were caught unaware. They were in the bedroom without a stitch on. I was stunned, angry and fought hard to control myself. I told them not to let me disturb them, quickly tossed a few belongings into a bag telling her where to send the rest. That's how my marriage of convenience ended. I swore I'd have no more of that kind of marriage. Do you understand, do you believe me. Say something Pat." He needed her assurance.

"Give me time Ken, please give me time."

"You're right... okay. I'm going to get dinner together. Will you come? Come sit with me. Please."

He left her then and she heard him moving around the kitchen. She could hear the dishes clink as he set them on the table, as she reflected on what he had told her. He couldn't make up such a story. What would he gain? He had more to lose than gain and he needn't have bothered at all if he really didn't care for her. She felt as she did because her pride was hurt, but it wasn't worth losing him for that. But suppose Edith had been in love with him and remained faithful to him, where would she be now? But he did come back to her. It was all in the past. It was no use fighting the way she felt about him. She loved him whether she was his second or first love and he said he loved her too. He was worth waiting for, even fighting for if it came to that.

"I hope you're feeling better now. Come sit with me and try to eat something." He came back to the bedroom and held out his hands, gazing at her, desperately trying to read her expression. He wanted her forgiveness. She grasped his hands tightly and went with him. They sat and ate quietly. He made no conversation. He understood how she felt and thought she needed to come to terms with the situation without his coaxings! She must reach out to him on her own if the situation was to be resolved. He loved and wanted her, therefore he would give her whatever time she needed to think. He knew she was hurt and wished he could wipe out the past, but it was very important to their future.

"I'm sorry I screamed at you. I should be more level-headed, but it was like my whole world was shattered, I mean my girlish dreams of you were shattered and I'm sorry about the way I behaved. Ken, you came back to me and if you had come with half a leg or one eye, I'd still love you."

"I love you too, Pat, I know you were hurt and you hit back at me the only way you could. What matters is that we have a chance again," he said grateful that she was reaching out. They got up and he helped her to the settee.

"I've had my share of hurt," he said, "I guess I should never have gotten into that kind of marriage... Edith was probably paying me back 'cause I used to talk a lot about you in the beginning, and she didn't forget. Then again life is so funny, if you know what I mean, you see, after we split up, I had a lot of thinking to do about what I wanted out of life. It occurred to me, I may have chosen to marry her, because it would be an easy situation to get out of whenever I wanted. There was really nothing binding between us, the only tie we shared was loneliness and that was too flimsy to base a marriage on."

"It doesn't matter any more," she said calmly.

"No, but I wanted to tell you the truth, because somehow things people think are well hidden are usually exposed, when you least expect. I want you to know, finding you restores my faith and gives me a chance to make life meaningful again. Did you know that night, years ago, when your mother beat you so cruelly, because of me..."

"Ken please! I don't want you to bring it up, please," she pleaded, disturbed by the memories.

"I have to now, Pat. Afterwards it will be buried in the past. Yes, that night, I said aloud, dear God let me suffer if I ever forget you. I never told you before, but I was angry, frustrated and hated your mother; I was filled with every devastating emotion. I don't know how I got home that night; I just found myself sitting on the steps and I suffered when Phyl wrote to tell me about your miscarriage. Worse, I couldn't tell you I knew. I've had my private hell Pat, but now I'm glad you still believe in me. I promise you we'll have a good life together. I've never stopped loving you. Never." He put his arms around her, kissed her and was happy when she responded.

"Pat you haven't said much, but I hope you understand and try to forget."

"I'm trying to understand... it will take time, only you can help me forget."

"I'll make you forget, I promise you, my love, believe me I will!"

He embraced her, smothering her with kisses and she didn't pull away. She responded passionately. They were both engulfed in sudden but uncontrollable desire.

Chapter 20

1972

"Ske-ooh! Hel-loo Mrs. Martin!" The woman called out loudly to the hurrying figure ahead.

"Eh eh. Mavis Mother." Mrs. Martin glancing back, recognised the woman and called out, "Hello, what you doing all the way up here?" She waited, then the two walked along together.

"How you do Mrs. Martin?" Mavis Mother said, pleased. "I thought when you look back, you didn't recognise me. I see you pass by me plenty times."

"Pass by you? Where you living?" Mrs. Martin asked, surprised.

"I live in the next street from you, just by the turn," Mavis Mother explained.

"And you never call out to me? Is the first time I see you since I living up here. Man, you should call out to me when you see me," Mrs. Martin said.

"Well, ah know we was not real friends, before I move up here, we was only neighbours, so I was lil' embarrassed to call out to you, anyhow, I decide to do it even if you don't answer," Mavis Mother said shyly.

"You should call me, man," Mrs. Martin insisted. "We ain't close friends, but you self say we was neighbours; and if I see you, I would call out to you 'cause lil' morning an' howdy never kill anybody yet," she chided her gently, trying to put her at ease. "You going downtown too? But tell me girl, what is your real name? Everybody keep calling you Mavis Mother through Mavis; she was a real brazen lil' girl, she used to get we cracking with laugh! How she do?"

"Is true!" Mavis Mother laughed "Everybody down in that yard an' around the neighbourhood call me so through Mavis. And I get so accustom to it, that it never bother me people din't know my right name." She laughed heartily, "Is only my husband an' the family does call me Shirley. But you know, everybody use to call you Phyl Mother, too, but I get to find out your name is Martin." They chuckled.

"You right," Mrs. Martin agreed. "Most parents get to know one another through the children an' that's why we use the children name."

"You goin' down to the meeting too?" Shirley asked, "'Cause is thats where I goin'; you know we election time coming up again — I don't depend 'pon what nobody tell me I like to hear what dem politicians saying wid me own ears. So I tracking me lil' meeting tonight." She spoke with enthusiasm.

"Not me, my dear, I finish with meetings. I going to see Donna. She get a young baby an' I promise her to go down there tonight. Actually, I should o' gone there since early afternoon."

"Hey, fancy lil' baby Donna, married an' getting children already. Is only the other day, she was a lil' thing; the children nowadays does really grow up fast," Shirley said.

"Is true, I see Mavis the other day with her two. The young people nowadays ain't waiting for a thing! But Mavis got two sweet children," Mrs. Martin said.

"But she ain't married! I don't know what she an' the children father waiting for. I thought by now they would do it, at least fo' dem children sake." Shirley's tone reflected her disappointment.

"When they ready, they goin' to get married, don't worry 'bout it too much." Mrs. Martin tried to cheer her up, "I didn't get married until two years after Phyl born an' married ain't everything. Is how they livin' together is more important! And it ain't good to pressure an' force them into it, so everybody can see a big wedding, then next two mornings they at each other throats an' can't live good; that don't make sense. Let them make their own decision, even if they end up fighting, they can't blame you!"

"You know is who keeping the meeting tonight at Lamaha Street?" Shirley said. She had regained her former high spirits, "Is that big scamp Hoffman, that everybody calling 'Big One' nowadays! Damn crook!" She spoke with indignation.

"But Shirley, what you going there for," Mrs. Martin said laughing "if you don't like the man. I know you like to talk an' if that man supporters hear you calling he crook an' scamp, they going to beat you up."

"Beat me up! They can try, but don't forget, I got me own army; all my sons comin' later! Beat me up! I goin' 'cause I want to hear what that barefaced crook got to tell people. Beat me up! Let dem think me two hands paste to me side."

"I know you Shirley," Mrs Martin said, thinking Shirley was always ready and would never back down from a good free for all. "You not going to stand up there quiet an' it goin to be you alone in that big crowd, man," Mrs Martin said gravely.

"Don't worry 'bout me. I must find a couple people there who don't like the rat, just like me an' I goin' to get my chance to spread all I know 'bout he."

"Shirley, is what he do to you this time," Mrs. Martin said laughing.

"Me?.. He ain't do me one thing. Is what he doin' to the people an' they so blind they can't even see. That man they following is a devil an' he goin' to do for all hands o' them! You know he now own the Halpenny Estates. He repair the old mansion an' does run the farm. He live up there sometime. How you like that?" She spoke with great emphasis.

"You got to be joking," Mrs. Martin said, stunned by the news. "Where you get that from Shirley?"

"Eh heh, you don't believe me, eh?" she saw the disbelief in her neighbour's face. "I see it for myself 'cause when I hear I couldn't believe it just like you, so I had to go up there an' find out for myself. So you can go up there an' ask anybody in the village, if they know who own the estate an' they goin' to tell you. He does go up there an' watch the men reaping the harvest. Eh heh!" She laughed without mirth.

"That man stan' by an' wait patiently 'till dem two old people crop off, then he move in. He's a long hearted devil. An' you know, I hear since he own the estate, he paying the men the same starvation wages, he self seh the white people use to pay the workers; but wo'k ain't plenty... people can't get wo'k so they glad to ketch they hand anyplace." Then she added gleefully, "I know that would shock you good an' praper."

"My God, My God! You mean he take them poor people inheritance?"

"Take it, he hoff it!" Shirley said with emphasis. "He's a hoff man by name an' nature. I tell people long ago that man greedy. As soon as he eyes light 'pon anybody thing an' he like it, I tell you is hell to pay, 'cause he got to get it by hook or crook an' hear this one, I hear..."

"Oh my God, don't tell me he take somebody else property!" Mrs. Martin cut in, "Where you does get these things from Shirley?"

"You ain't hearing what going on. You ain't know is he own that gigantic farm just outside town. You know that was government property." She spoke with gusto.

"They can't allow that, the government won't allow that 'cause is a coalition government, girl," Mrs Martin said defensively.

"You livin' in the past, that dead! Anything happening nowadays; this is cooperation government, you cooperate with me, you know, mek a big noise so people think you interested in what the other side doing, but you really giving me a chance to grab whatever I want. So Hoffman grabbing while the other side doing what they likes and we poor people in the middle. This politics is a big grabbing game that's why all these big shots breaking they damn necks to get in." Shirley spoke haughtily.

"Shirley girl, from the look of things, this country in serious trouble."

"You goin' to ask! You ain't see people ain't got wo'k. No wo'k, no money! Food prices skyrocketing an' poor people scrambling same way, yet that man, who is to help the people, getting richer!"

"I know what you mean," Mrs Martin said. "It all around, but this Halfpenny business got me shocked, it serious."

"Is worse than serious, since that man who got no respect for women get into politics," Shirley said passionately. "Fancy, he a big shot lawyer, say he fighting for people's rights an' he got not a pinch o' respect for women at all, always pawing them in public! He ain't even got respect foh the law! And ordinary people like meself laughing an' encouraging he, when he cussing an' behaving so vulgar in public. They forget they got to pay a fine fo' doing the same thing. A man like that can't lead me. He too vile! What he teaching the children and the young generation? You tell me Mrs Martin. Nothing good, nothing good at all."

"But Shirley, I don't blame he, I blame the people, the women. If they would put him in his place, slap his hand, or put a box 'pon he, he would cut out the lawlessness, bet you he don't do it to everybody. But the women he do it to like it yeh," she declared.

"That ain't true, not true!" Shirley firmly asserted. "Not everybody got the spunk to do what you say. Plenty don't like it, but they frighten to tell he not to do it, so they just laugh it off to hide their embarrassment. After all he's a big shot lawyer, he could talk he way out an' make them look stupid don't forget he do the same thing with me an' Mavis. And remember he own family," she stressed the last two words, "say he's a very vindictive man. He got a memory like an elephant. So some o' the poor women at he mercy, they just got to laugh it off."

"I still can't understand why they feel they got to tolerate he disgusting behaviour. But what you tell me 'bout the Halpenny Estates is raw greed, I don't know what that man won't stoop to."

"He would do an' say anything to get what he want 'cause at the last meeting he tell the women, if they support he an' he become leader, he'd bring the price of milk down so cheap, not a child in this country would have to drink anymore sugar water; an' you know these women clap an' cheer an' behave ridiculous, they really believe he."

"Well, that's politics. Tell the people what they want to hear an' shut them up, so they don't ask questions, the man is a schemer."

"Schemer! You ain't see nothing yet; I know he ain't goin to stop, he goin' to scheme an' scheme till he turn king in this country. He leading them down the garden path with a ring in they nose."

By this time, they had reached the main street, only two blocks away from the impending meeting. Huge crowds had already begun to mass, spilling out into all the nearby side streets, halting the regular flow of traffic.

"Come stan' up for a lil' while man, an' listen to what that slippery crook got to say," Shirley said, attempting to get her companion to change her mind.

"Not me girl, I just waiting here 'till the bus come up and I gone. The truth is, I lost the taste for standing up at any political meeting nowadays, after what happening since the hooligans take over. Is too much beatings and throwing poisons on people to to burn them up. Not me. I hear the other night in Big Kitty that an Indian man was the speaker at the meeting, when a van stop an' some men jump out an' tell the black people to go home if they know what good fo' them! Well, the people won't go an' these hooligans warned them again. After the people still won't leave, ah hear these criminals go in the truck for stick an' start beating the people. Then two of them take out kerosene cans from the van an' drench the people with formalin! Man, ah hear it was terrible, men an' women an' children bawling an' screaming they gone blind. I hear is people who passing by in their motor cars help rush them to the hospital. Girl, I want to live to see my grandchildren grow yeh! I don't want this brick, stick an' formalin battalion to cripple nor blind me. I ain't hanging around no meeting."

"And I hear the Indians doing the same thing to they own people," Shirley said. "Eh, look the bus coming." She pointed to the bus in the distance.

"Well girl, I gone an' stand up yonder by the bus stop," Mrs. Martin said, moving off. "An' don't talk too much so they beat you up, take care."

"Beat me up," Shirley said. "Ha ha, if I going down, one goin' with me and if I gon' dead one got to dead with me too." Then remembering her manners, she added, "Take care and tell Donna howdy fo' me."

"Ma, look out quick! Auntie Pat come with lil' Carol Ann and Michael!" Eric called eagerly to his mother, from the yard.

Phyl hurrying to the window called out, "You all help Pat with the children." But Eric was already in charge of Carol Ann whom he hoisted gently on his shoulders and Daphne took Michael while Pat parked the car on the wide wooden bridge leading across the front entrance.

Pat locked the car then followed the children. "Auntie Pat, you know Michael resemble you more and more everyday," Daphne said, covering his head with kisses as she inhaled deeply the fresh baby-like fragrance from the palms of his hands.

The children went up stairs, while Pat stopped to talk with Tom for a while. "Hello Tom, what's up? Got problems with the old bus?" she said, peering into the bonnet of the car.

"Look at you girl! No need to ask how you are at all. The marriage thing really agree with you, you're always in the pink. You know the old saying, if is not the wife is the car." They both laughed and Tom added, "Well, since I got no problem with Phyl this car want to send me crazy everyday if is not one thing is the other."

"What's the problem?" Pat asked, inspecting the engine.

"Starting. It giving me hell to start," Tom said perplexed.

"These look new," she said touching the plugs.

"I buy them only the other day and the battery is fairly new, but this car mean to try my faith."

"Ah... check the oil and water level?" Pat asked.

"Girl, you really knock me out when you ask those questions 'cause very few women pay attention to cars, even Phyl declare, that when anything go wrong, it's the mechanic problem, she's got no time to worry her head with that. But I forget you're used to tinkling with engines, since you had that motorbike. You like the smell of metal, grease and speed." They chuckled merrily. "By the way, still got the old chub chub?" he teased.

"Thomas Barnes don't you dare call my motorbike chub chub! If it wasn't for that same chub chub, I might never have met Ken again," Pat said laughing.

"What you did with it, sell it?"

"No man, I couldn't bring myself to sell it. Not even part with it, even though a friend asked me to sell her. I held on to it for awhile, then I gave it to one of the boys, Ian... he keeps it in good shape."

"How's your mother?" Tom asked, as he pondered the changes Ken Masterson made in her life.

"Same way, same person, sour and rough. She can't change," Pat laughed. "Ken said her disposition is like poison in her system."

"What's the joke Pat?"

"Can't tell you man, eh eh, can only tell Phyl! Ken's too wicked!" She went up the stairs laughing, adding, "Check out the battery cells and the water."

"What you got to tell me?" Phyl said in a conspirational tone, as she met Pat at the door. "What you all laughing at so sweet?"

"Girl, it was all Ken's doing!" Pat said trying to control her mirth. "Tom asked about Mom and I told him she hadn't changed but Ken had a remedy that would straighten her out, but I wasn't going to tell him what Ken prescribed."

"If I know Ken, I know exactly what he'd prescribe," Phyl said grinning. "But girl tell me quick, 'cause I want to know if we got the same idea."

"He said he fix her a strong cathartic!" Pat said and they burst out laughing together.

"Just as I thought. Wicked Ken," Phyl said.

"I don't blame him for thinking as he does," Pat said. "She never got a good word to say to the children, Ken nor me. Then she's always playing tricks that she's sick. Ken's lost patience with her; nowadays he doesn't want to go with me when I take the children. He waits outside in the car. I think he goes with me, just so she knows he's there and we're still together. Then, when I least expect, he appears an' exchange a few words with her and right back to the car he gone girl."

"Pat your mother is something else yeh! After all these years, not even seeing you and Ken married could make her happy. I was telling Tom that your marriage to Ken prove her prediction wrong and she can't accept it. So she trying to make you all miserable, you know she going to continue working on you like she use to do."

"Working on me! Eh eh that dead. I overcome that long ago, so she's wasting her time, Roy Sandiford is the one she should make miserable."

"But you tell me he ain't sticking around long enough."

"Right... he's the biggest sweet boy on the estate now, he's scarcely home, so anybody else especially yours truly is the target. Frankly I've ceased trying to understand my mother."

"Girl, I'm at a loss too," Phyl echoed her sentiments. "I thought, seeing her grand children would make her feel pleased and she would understand life is changing."

"Pleased!" Pat laughed without mirth, "You joking, for that lady such a word never existed or doesn't exist at all. When we visited her a few weeks back, Carol touched one of her old time what-you-may-call-it brass stand. You remember the thing?" she asked and Phyl nodded her head.

"Well, she spoke to Carol so sharply, the poor thing, burst into tears. That day Ken was waiting in the car, so I took Carol to him and went back. Girl, I gave her a good piece of my mind, I told her flat, the forties dead and it would be the last time we grace her door. Girl, by the time I got back to the car the Miss Carol tell Ken everything."

"I didn't know she was so chatty," Phyl said smiling.

"Chatty! You ain't know that girl, however, Ken was so furious, he said the next time I go to see my mother, I better leave his children with him. Girl, I had to laugh 'cause he was the one who said that no matter what, she's my mother and the children's grandmother; he said he would have liked to meet her under different circumstances, he'd refer her to a psychiatrist. He thinks she needs help."

"I don't think that would help her," Phyl responded. "I think a tiny dose of happiness or pleasure would kill her, especially if she was robbed of all her perceived sufferings, and frustrations. So you all try don't kill her by taking her to get help, leave her as she is."

"Girl, I refuse to take her on," Pat declared.

"You know when you mentioned different circumstances, I couldn't help thinking about us. We're both the same age, I got married about ten years earlier than you, then look at our children, Daphne and Michael. She's old enough to be his mother, she's the eldest while your eldest is Carol Anne and she is just five years old. Life is really interesting if you have the time to look at the pattern it makes for people."

"The wonder of it all," Pat said smiling, "is that one time I thought I was the most unfortunate person on the face of the earth with a mother like mine. After Ken and I were married, I couldn't carry a pregnancy full term, I was always frightened when I got pregnant and three miscarriages weren't funny. I'm through all of that now, thanks to Ken; I went to his friend for a complete check up and he found nothing was really wrong with me, but Ken insisted I carried the old fear of my first pregnancy, when my mother was so hostile to me and he said I had to get it out of my system, assert myself. Thank God I'm over all of that now and Carol Ann and Michael prove I got over her, I can go and visit her now without fear."

"Pat, there's no doubt about it, your mother was a cool tyrant. She was always like a tiger ready to spring, you had to be very strong to deal with her," Phyl said.

"It took time and though I'm sorry for her, she's got her own life to live and I have mine." The telephone rang and Daphne answered.

"Ma!" she called. "It's Denise. She and the gang coming to pick me up to go for a ride in the Gardens or the Sea Wall by the Round House. Okay if I go with them?" She waited while Phyl considering, exchanged looks with Pat. Then she nodded her head to Daphne.

"Thing's really change nowadays. I had to give Ma at least two weeks notice before she allow me to go out. I couldn't tell her the same day and expect to go. It was only when I start to work for Hoffman she gave me full independence. Now my daughter and her friends make their plans on the phone and she relay them to me."

"I really admire Daphne though. She's a fine young lady, and she reminds me of her mother. You and she get along just like you and your mother. Girl, I envied the way you and your mother use to get along. She was firm without being hostile and she always threw in her advice, but she was never out to control you. She was a real mother to me."

"Never out to control you nuh," Phyl said grinning. Pat looked at her puzzled. "You're forgetting the tea, man, when Ma said drink, we all had to drink!"

"Man, you know what I mean," Pat said. "But you're right. No one in that house could survive any problem without her mint and toyo."

233

"And nobody could make it as quick as Ma. Girl, I'm sure she had somebody in Bourda market in clover. But when you think about it Ma used to put pressure on you, she made you responsible for your behaviour and the consequences. She always said you couldn't blame anybody for what you did, remember she used to say 'you can't see something staring you in your face in broad daylight, then wait 'till night to take fire stick and search for it.'"

"Is true! She was always telling me I made things worse for myself... my mother was controlling me even though I was out of the house and she always said life's full of problems, but is up to me to solve then the best way I could make it harder or easier on myself."

"How you make your bed... you lie on it!" Phyl added. "How she liked hitting us with that one."

"If you make it soft or hard, is up to you," both women said together.

"Me, I always used to pray to grow up fast, so I won't have any problems. That's what I thought." Pat went on to say, "When I moved out from my mother I could swear that was the end of problems, life was going to be so easy, peaceful and the way I want it. Is then I find out how many problems were just waiting 'round the corner for me. It's not until I married Ken I learned some problems I can't solve atall. Like my mother's attitude, and I won't even try," she admitted. "Some problems take years to solve: me learning to stand up to her. Some I solve as they come along, depending on their importance or priority."

"Ma! Please tell Eric not to trouble my things!" Alex came through the bedroom door shouting.

"Is what now?" Phyl asked, but Alex, face grim, stormed through the house and out the back door. "That's my set of problems," Phyl owned up. She was about to go on when she was interrupted by loud voices and the tramp of footsteps coming up the front stairs. Daphne rushed from the bedroom to open the door and greet her companions.

"Come in a minute, nearly finished," she announced, then hurried back into the bedroom while her friends paid their respects to Phyl and Pat. She was out in a flash with a scarf, bade her mother and Pat goodbye as she followed the noisy group down the stairs.

Pat had slipped into the boy's room to see how the children and Eric were doing. Satisfied they were well occupied with some of Eric's toys she returned to the living room.

"They come and gone like a hurricane!" Pat said coming out of the bedroom.

"Now we can talk in peace and quiet," Phyl replied, relaxed and reclining in a morris chair in her comfortable living room.

"Alex take after his father so much," Pat continued, "he was so quiet in there... I didn't know he was home."

"Quiet, with a big mouth like that? He's always picking a fight with Eric. Ma always say, 'easy snake bite hot!'"

"But you know boys will be boys," Pat reminded Phyl.

"Yeah... Tom saying the same thing... but I think is more than that," Phyl's tone indicated her bewilderment, she frowned.

"Look Mummy, look how nice Eric fix my hair!" Carol Ann called out, sailing gracefully into the room, twirling to the left then right so Pat and Phyl could admire her hair-do.

"Oh my... Eric!" Phyl cried out, she and Pat giggling at Carol Ann's hair, a rumpled, tangled mess. "Bring the ribbons and come, boy. You getting into trouble all around today, first Alex, now look what you do the child's hair. Who ask you to comb it?" she scolded the crest-fallen Eric who appeared, red ribbon in hand.

"Ma..." Eric tried to explain.

"Man, don't worry to fret with the boy," Pat cut in laughing. "If she didn't want him to touch it we'd hear, she would scream the whole place down."

"Ma... is she self lose it and ask me to tie it back!"

"Yes... and you couldn't resist the temptation to put you hand in it!"

"But Ma... I didn't interfere with Alex things at all." Eric protested, "I was just standing near it, watching it and he ups and open his big mouth and say I troubling it!"

"Is his science project?" Phyl pressed on, "Keep far from it 'cause if it only fall down when you around I'm going to blame you. I got to have a serious talk with Alex."

"But Ma... honestly, I didn't touch Alex thing," Eric continued to assert his innocence.

"I understand, but you listen to me and do what I say 'till we and Mr. Alex have a serious talk," Phyl said. Eric nodded, agreeing reluctantly.

"Do me a favour Eric, I forget the bag with Michael food in the car," Pat asked, putting an end to the strained conversation and Eric, eager to oblige, was out the door, down the steps and back in a flash, volunteering to feed Michael.

"He really like small children," Pat informed Phyl after making sure everything was alright with the children. "One of these days Eric's going to be a good father with all the practise he's getting. But coming back to what we were talking about Alex... How's he doing at school?"

"That's another source of my worry," Phyl declared, throwing her hands up in the air in despair. "He failed his exams last year... this year you'd think the boy would buckle down and do his studies. Not he! His exams is only a couple of months away in June. Seriously Pat, I don't know what that boy wants."

"Let's look at it from his point of view," Pat said. "He's probably thinking it's no use studying if he's going to run the store. Then it could be he wants to work somewhere else other than with the family store. You always talking about his lack of interest in the business. Daphne's working somewhere other than the store. He could be frustrated because he doesn't know how to start explaining that to Tom, besides he might not be clear in his mind about what he really wants to do."

"I don't doubt what you're saying. Tom and he don't argue as much now. Tom finally decide to leave him alone, when he found out the continuous pressure was driving he and Alex apart, they were always at loggerheads. But now, things a little better between them. But I know Tom good, he hasn't given up with Alex and his plans for him to run the store. But he doesn't know I heard Alex telling Eric, he could have his place and share in the business, because nobody is going to force him to do what he doesn't want to do and Eric must wait and see."

"You tell Tom?" Pat asked.

"Not yet, girl. The battle between the two of them was long and hard and I don't want to start the tensions again. I'm tired of the tug-o-wars. I think is time Tom find out the truth for himself and face it. I avoiding getting in the middle again."

"You have any idea what Alex want to do? Other than not working in the store."

"Girl, he won't tell me. He thinks I'm siding with his father and in the long run I will force him too. Not me though. I know that will only make him more headstrong."

"Nothing new in that. It runs in the family," Pat said chuckling. "I understand how he feels, although my situation was extreme. But parents should never force children into moulds they set for them, because it will cause the family to break up, I'm an excellent example." She wasn't smiling.

"You're right. Tom had that mould set for Alex long before he was born," Phyl said, reflecting.

"But he's your son more than Tom," Pat said, thoughtful. "He has a mind of his own and he's fighting it, but, you must tell Tom before it's too late. Alex is angry and frustrated and I think you could help him."

"I know what you're saying is true. Daphne is doing what she wants. You know she was good with figures since she was small and the funny thing is, it was Tom who praise and encourage her. Later she helped him with his accounts and stocks, yet she was free to take up her own career, now she's at the bank. With Eric, Tom acted the same way, he wasn't mad when Eric tell him he wanted to be a pharmacist, but where Alex is concerned, he's stubborn."

"I understand how Tom feel. But he got to appreciate the fact that he's doing what he wanted to do. Nobody forced him, he was free to sell the business and do something else. Poor Alex, he wants to assert himself and he doesn't want to hurt his father, that's his growing pains. Sooner or later he got to make an important decision and he needs help from one of you."

"Why so quiet?" Tom asked, he had came into the house, observing the pensive atmosphere. "Just a moment ago I could hear you girls laughing and happy."

"We were talking about the children," Pat ventured, "especially Alex and his moodiness, something might be bothering him."

"Don't worry with Alexander, he's okay. He's going to be alright, is just growing pains." She could sense from his tone he was not duly disturbed.

"What is he going to do when he's finished exams," Pat insisted, "I think you..."

"Don't worry your head with that boy. He's eventually going to see things my way; I just letting him have his own head for awhile, he'll come around in time." Tom was unshakable. "How's Ken?" he asked.

"He's okay," Pat said, then glancing at her watch, cried out, "Oh my God, look at the time, it's nearly two and I got to pick up Ken."

"I thought he was at home, I didn't know he worked on Sunday," Tom said.

"He should be off today, but he said the ratio of doctors to people in this country is an unbelievable one to forty thousand, so that keeps them on their toes. Eric," she called, "bring Michael we're going now." Then bustling the children and their belongings together she started for the door. "See you people another time, right now I got to fly. Eric you go ahead with Carol Ann."

"Look don't bother to go racing down the road and get in any accident," Tom cautioned.

"Boy you joking or what. I won't be able to face Ken Masterson at all, especially where those two are concerned." She motioned to Eric and the children as they went out the door. "And Ken is going to hear every word I said about Ken Masterson's two children, Carol Ann will repeat every last word." They all chuckled.

"Now I know where to drop the hint when I want to see Ken," Phyl said.

"Ken said if she doesn't stop soon, we'll have to work on her to break the habit," Pat added.

"He's right," Phyl said. "Could you imagine the excitement if she repeated something he said about a patient!"

They laughed merrily as Phyl and Tom accompanied Pat to the door, waving as they drove off. Tom stood at the door until the car was out of sight.

"Girl, today is our day for visitors," Tom called out to Phyl. "Come see who coming up the road." She and Eric rushed to the window.

"Is Granny," Eric said, "I going to meet her." He ran out of the house and down the stairs and out into the street.

"You just missed Pat," Phyl said as her mother climbed the stairs.

"So Eric tell me," Mrs. Martin said, "how she and the children?"

"Looking good as usual and confident," Phyl answered.

"Thank God," Mrs. Martin said as she entered the house. "I really pleased for her," she said affectionately. She always thought of Pat as a daughter. "At one time I thought all them baby she keep losing was going to kill her, but she's a strong girl. Thank God she's alive and happy. God bless this house, children." She sat down.

"I can bet my last dollar you only drop in for a few minutes, then you gone to spend the rest of time with Donna again," Phyl said, sitting down next to her.

"How you know that? You're a mind reader," Mrs. Martin asked chuckling.

"Well it's obvious. Since Donna start her family, I can't remember the last time you come and spend more than a few minutes with us," Phyl chided her gently.

"Girl, I treating Donna just like I treat you, look how big your children get now. They busy with their own life, is only Eric home now, and next two mornings he gone too. So I might as well enjoy them when they little."

"Ma, you getting older and you don't have to traipse all the way, downtown to see Donna. She could bring the children up to see you. This last baby is three months old. Strong enough to face the breeze up here and she ain't sick. But you always wearing out yourself, trekking downtown."

"Girl, I come here to give you some news, I didn't come here to be scolded," Mrs. Martin said, smiling. "Then I'm off to catch my bus."

"Ma, you know I worry about you and these long journeys up and down. You know you ain't taking any bus, not one bit. You know Tom will be happy to give you a lift, even if he got to push the car all the way. I hope that car okay now," Phyl said to Tom.

"That car never okay Phyl, but we goin to make it, 'cause I want to check the batteries when I coming back."

"Guess who I saw the other night when I was going down to Donna?" Mrs. Martin asked. "Shirley," she declared.

"Shirley, Shirley," Phyl said thoughtful. "I only know one girl name Shirley, she worked for Hoffman for awhile but I don't think you know her."

"You know this Shirley good good! Is Mavis Mother!"

"I would never associate that lady with that name," Phyl said.

"Me too. And I was surprised when she tell me... brace yourself and prepare for a shock... she tell me Hoffman now own the Halpenny Estates."

"What you got to say to that now," Tom shot back to Phyl. "No wonder everybody calling the man, the Kabaka, he really big now! Ha ha. He's the biggest scamp. He get those two illiterate people to sign everything over to him, after wiping them out clean of every penny they had."

"Don't laugh man," Phyl said tamely. "This is serious."

"I'm not laughing at the people, I'm tickled at the barefacedness of the man. I wonder how he get them to sign away their life. With exs or thumbprints? He probably use the trick I hear some crooked lawyers use, put long sheets of paper with bits of worthless information at the top, then when the client put their thumbprint or ex at the bottom, they type in the rest later. In their case, I don't even think he had to go to all that trouble, cause they couldn't read nor write. Man, they were like putty in his hands."

"Ma, you mean to tell me he really didn't care whether those people lived or died? You mean he sit patiently waiting, knowing they would die sooner or later?" Phyl asked in a strained voice, vividly remembering the time Hoffman returned from the trip abroad to see Halpenny's nephew. He had said, 'Even if Josiah Brown died, his heirs would inherit...' He was so emphatic when he said 'whoever the man named as his heir.' She recalled all the news reports said that neither retainers were married nor had relatives alive and they were both advanced in years. She was upset and felt the need for more air, so she got up and opened all the other front windows. It was unbelievable Hoffman would do such a thing, no matter what else people said about him.

"Ma, they were old people and had no family, nobody to turn to! I still can't believe he'd trick them. If he did, at least somebody would ask questions. Did they make him their heir?"

"Well Phyl, that was a very long time ago. Nearly twenty years, remember? You were young then and people memory short. How many people you think would remember or care? Besides the political upheavals, things ain't change much. The majority of people still 'pon the hustle fo' food and shelter, is the same scraping and struggling to survive. People don't have time to think about anything else. They forget under these kinds of circumstances," Mrs. Martin spoke with the wisdom of her years.

"I always had my doubt about that man's real intention, look at the state this country in," Tom said in disgust. "Look Mom, whenever you ready is okay with me."

Chapter 21
1973

I t was Paul Ben's loyalty as well as his frankness, which made Phyl aware that the situation with Alex had deteriorated. A couple days after her talk with Pat, she arrived at the store early Wednesday morning to be greeted by Paul, who said he had something important to discuss. After Alex was born, she took Mondays off, then with the birth of Eric, she included Tuesdays. So it had become a regular practice for her to take these days especially, whenever she felt the children needed her. Lately, she had become perturbed about Alex's attitude and following her talk with Pat she decided to revert to her old practice.

She observed that Alex was always late in getting home. But when she probed, he claimed he walked home with friends, instead of taking the usual taxi. His explanation seemed plausible, until she mentioned it in a passing remark to Eric. He insisted Alex was never in early, only when he expected her. Now she had cause for misgivings and pondered Alex's explanation. Why did she worry about him so? She remembered the many trivial and harmless escapades she, Pat and other girls got into during high school, so she quickly brushed her misgivings aside. However, she had a serious talk with him. She explained times had changed and what in her day merited a laugh, today the same actions could have far reaching consequences! People had changed and this affected their moods so they behaved differently. She was firm with him insisting he

241

toed the line and he agreed to be home early; but would not tell her who were the friends he walked with. All he would say is they lived in the area. She was puzzled, but pushed the matter from her mind.

"Miss Phyllis!" Paul greeted her as she entered the store, "I very glad you come this morning before Tom."

"Is something wrong?" she asked.

"Miss Phyllis I working with you all a long time now and I don't forget the day you get your husband to take me on when I was down and out. You all treat me well. I get the same wages like the big stores and we work together like family. So if I see you all interest or anything concerning youall go wrong, I got to let you know 'cause if I don't, later on I will I blame meself."

"What really happen Paul? You see somebody lurking 'round the store to break in?"

"No, not that, it worse than that. It worry and vex me, especially when I see you all trying to do the best for your children and some children can't appreciate that. I wish my mother didn't dead and leave me when I was still so young."

"Paul, please tell me a straight story. Which children you taking 'bout?"

"Well it hard and I know it goin' to give you a shock, is Alex!" He finally got it out.

"Alex!" she said, puzzled. "What he got..."

"Wait, let me explain," Paul cut in. "I know how mothers feel about their children."

"Paul..." Phyl was about to interrupt him again, but decided to let him explain in his own time.

"Yesterday, Alex come in the store," he said, and she was surprised because Alex didn't mention it when she talked with him. "And I sure he come in here, because he realize you didn't come, you know he don't like to hang around here fo' long, no matter how you encourage he."

"What he did Paul?"

"He didn't do anything. But is his friends that he bring in the store, that worry me. And is not the first time I see he and dem boys together!"

What friends she thought. Who are these boys that got Paul upset so? "Friends!"

"You right to say, friends! Dem boys ain't friends fo' your son at all. Miss Phyllis, dem boys is bad boys, they always in trouble with the police. The one from Kitty, I know he good. He name 'Cat', he's a up an' coming professional thief, man! The boy so good at the work, you hear the name they does call he. Ah hear he does jobs for a price."

Phyl sat down on a stool. Her knees felt weak and she was sure her stomach did a few somersaults. Alex, with known thieves and criminals?

"What in the name of God is the matter with Alex? Paul, you sure? You know how boys stay. They probably just meet and walk along together. Is not like Alex to have these boys as close friends."

"Miss Phyllis, if I wasn't sure about what I saying, I won't dream to open my mouth. Whenever I see him, he always with Cat and this other youngster, they call him... ah, yes, 'Dealer', he is a card shark. He work with dem men whose job is to fleece innocent people."

"You mean those men who set up card games by the roadside and fool people how much money they could win?" she said, filled with anxiety.

"But that ain't all Miss Phyllis! They walk in here with Alex as if they got a share in the business. The Mr. Cat, he asked Alex, 'Boy you sure this is you fadda place?'" Paul mimicked, "then when Alex tell him yes, he put his hands in his pockets and say, 'Man, Alex you floating in oil, your ole man got a nice spread here an' you keep this thing a big secret!' When Alex laughed, the Mr. Dealer chime in an' say, 'Boy you deh good hey, this is easy street fo' you, 'cause you don't have to sweat, all you have to do is rake in an' enjoy, you fix fo' life, you're a real Mr. Cool!'"

"Then the scamp got the barefacedness to ask me, if what Alex saying is true. Look, I just order dem out the store! Ah tell dem I know dem good. But the presumptuous Mr. Cat, tell me, that Alex know all about dem, 'We is good friends', and is then I get real worried Alex and dem young culprits is good friends. I sure you don't know what going on, so I decide to tell you. Ah can't tell Tom, 'cause he got his mind all set 'pon Alex taking over an' I don't want to upset him but I know mothers understand these things better. You see if he was my son, I'd give him the finest cut tail."

"That won't help, Paul. I don't beat them, my mother never beat none of us and if I beat Alex now, that would only make things worse. Thanks for telling me, I got to think how to handle the situation."

"Maybe is because you all never give the boy a good licking and that's why he trying you all faith."

"I'm glad you didn't tell Tom. I got to talk to Alex. Thanks for coming to me," she said.

She spent the rest of the day thinking about Alex. She was glad Tom took that day to get some business done or he would immediately sense her depression and know something was wrong.

Where had she and Tom gone wrong with Alex? What had they done to cause him to associate with known criminals? She had seen a problem growing way back, when Tom started to press and push about the store. She had been aware of Alex's resentment about anything to do with the store; lately he had completely shunned it. She knew it was his way of rebelling against Tom's water tight plans for him. Now, worse than that, he felt she was on Tom's side and had become reckless. Why else would he be seen with boys who are known criminals. It was nothing but a clear act of defiance.

She reflected on her own attitude, before she married Tom, she had done a few reckless things too. Maybe it was just a passing phase with Alex. But she'd have to watch him closely, and meanwhile think of a way to get Tom to understand the problem he was helping to create; maybe if he hadn't been so critical and demanding, Alex would have willingly approved of Tom's plans for him. Yes, she'd have to think of a way to persuade Tom to understand Alex, but that was a task she didn't savour at all. She knew how strongly he felt about the store and Alex but Alex had a right to choose his own future. She couldn't agree more with Pat when she said Alex was frustrated. Heaven knows since he was born, Tom never gave him a moment of peace to think of anything else but the store. Pat was right, children could be suffocated by the constant pressures of parents to follow their directions. How could I allow Tom to do the same thing to Alex, it's the same thing. I was never suffocated by my mother, yet I allowed Tom to get away with it. I haven't been firm enough with him. She blamed herself for allowing the situation to get so far and hated being caught in the middle. Phyl swore she'd have a very serious talk with Tom. She had to find a way to persuade him.

A couple days later Tom himself provided her with the opportunity. A new consignment of goods they had ordered, arrived and Tom spent another two days trying to get the goods released but made little progress. So he dropped by the store at lunch time to grab a bite and tell her about his progress.

"Girl, I tell you, I don't know what this country coming to at all. Everything is a mess. These past days I up and down at the trade bureau to get this matter settle and all I doing is running around from one person to the other. I ain't get no way yet, but I'm totally fed up already," he said, throwing himself down on the old grandfather couch in disgust. "Is everybody they got running around in their 'send the fool further' game."

"How you mean, send the fool further?" she asked.

"Just that, that's all they doing." He was very irritated.

"But you never had this problem before. I thought the reason they opened this new bureau is to streamline and process things faster and make it easier for people who got their business to run."

"Hm, faster! Since I going there, that office is packed with people and people waiting outside too, but you keep seeing the same faces and new people joining the crowd, faster nuh. Everyday you collect an additional set of papers and all you do is run around and get them stamp and collect more paper. Is stamp, stamp then hand in and collect, collect and hand in. I tell you, it ain't fun. Normally, I'm a quiet man, but you see if this damn collecting and stamping don't stop this afternoon when I go back, I going to blow my cool. These jokers making fun of people! They have people believing that once they get in, things going to be so easy. They could fix everything. Now they making all kinds of nonsensical departments which instead of improving things only making it worse."

"That sound to me, like you got to spend the whole of next week there. Don't forget government places close half day on Saturday so you might as well prepare yourself for another week of running around, collecting more paper and getting them stamp," Phyl said, laughing and Tom couldn't help but join in.

"No way. It goin' to be me and them this same afternoon! I don't know if they think they making you feel important with a big bundle of papers in your hand, some falling all over the place. But I think all these tactics is to give the small businessman such a bad time, they would get fed up, give up and get rid of the business. My grandfather put this business in my hand an' they're not going to force me out!" He spoke with passion. "If this nonsense continue to go on we will run out of stock. These people are jokers, big jokers."

"They can't force us to close," Phyl said, attempting to be optimistic. "We still got stock in our store room."

"But sooner or later we'll run out. And now they start a new thing. A fellow tell me to 'pass me hand' and I'll get through fast. He even tell me the amount of money he pass, because he come from the country and can't waste another week running around. So he show me the son-of-a-gun who to pass the money to. When I tell him that would add to the cost and the selling price of the item, he laughed and said people so glad for he goods, they're willing to pay any price. Christ man, these people don't care about their own, yet they keep shouting, 'the small man is a real man', while they making life real hell for him."

"What time you going back?"

"One o'clock," he said and moaned, "That's another thing they tell you to be there at one, while they strolling in two or even two thirty, but I deciding right now to go in my own time, I ketching a nap right here."

"How long it will take before you get the crates out of the bond? That is on condition you get through by the middle of next week."

"You didn't hear the news? A stevedore fellow tell me, I must try and move fast, because they got a strike or go slow coming up anytime. You know what that means if I get caught in that! He tell me is some country-wide plan to show no confidence in the government and bring it down. You hear about it? I tell he is the first time I hear about it. I so caught up in this business, that I don't even bother to listen to what going on: is all bad news anyway."

"I hear a man talking. But it isn't hard to see they didn't make things better for the people. All you keep hearing is, no money no jobs, more stealing going on, and people not embarrassed like long ago to go to jail for stealing. But the worse thing is a lot of people leaving the country and going to England to get jobs. "

"I think these people gone mad! Strikes! With election not too far off. That's total madness. I sorry for the young people, because the only place they could catch a few dollars is up McKenzie mining bauxite or if they get into teaching and that isn't easy."

"Tom, you never ask Alex what he really wants to do, you just take it for granted that he would run the store. You realize he doesn't like to come near the store, unless we tell him. I think you should talk to him," she said.

"Girl, Alexander isn't ready yet. That's why I'm not bothering him." Tom had his own idea. "You know all young people like to fool around for awhile, before they get serious. Don't worry about me and he." He made light of the situation.

"Tom, Alex never tell me anything, but I'm sure he wants to be a teacher. Remember he was always playing school with Daphne. He and she always falling out because she insisted he was teaching her wrong. Since he was small we use to find him hiding some place playing school, all by himself," she said, now confident she knew exactly what Alex wanted to do.

"I don't know where you get this belief, Alexander want to be a teacher, nearly all children like to play school. He never hinted anything. But who's going to take over when we get tired? Look, don't worry, Alexander will fall in so easy into the business, you too will be surprised."

"You never talk to him so how do you know? I think you don't want to know. You're stubbornly clinging to the idea that he must do what you want him to do. If you don't talk it over with him, you might be the one to get the surprise!"

"Girl, relax and don't worry with me and Alexander. If I doze off, wake me up at one-fifteen." He was quite certain Alex would come around in time.

Paul Ben came in then and that prevented her from pressing on with the issue. She was certain they would have had a very unpleasant argument. It annoyed her he quickly accepted all her suggestions and ideas for the store, but he was so stubborn, unshakable, where Alex was concerned. He was so obsessed with the store, he wasn't thinking about Alex at all. She was furious and decided she was going to have it out with him at home. She had this urge to get the problem out in the open, but she had to tackle Alex about the boys he associated with. She would insist he come to the shop after school in the afternoon, that should keep him out of trouble. She knew he would think she was on Tom's side, but she wasn't going to force him, she had to get him to agree and that would ease the tension which was growing every day between him and the family.

However, when she discussed the matter with Alex, he grudgingly agreed to help, it was a battle of wits and wills. She had to compromise Friday and Monday in order to get him to stay on Saturday but not before he complained he hated the place. She was relieved! She had won a small battle. As for his companions, he said he just met them a couple of times and the boys were showing off the day they went to the store. She let the matter rest.

Things didn't run as smoothly as she expected. For the first week it was touch and go and by Saturday, he was moody and restless.

He mumbled and paced around the store like a chicken caught in a coop seeking a way to get out. Whenever she glanced over to where he should be, it was to meet Paul's knowing stare as he shook his head sadly. Alex was getting under her skin. She changed his tasks and put him in

247

charge of stationery and that didn't work out either. Then she let him decide where he would like to help but that didn't keep him occupied for long. She was slowly losing control. It became more difficult not to lose her temper. By the third Saturday, she knew it was useless, Alex truly wanted nothing to do with the store and she alone was waging a losing battle. Her nerves were on edge and it was time for a showdown with Tom and Alex.

Then fate took a hand in the course of events. Like the day she went downtown to make the deposit at the bank and suddenly came upon Alex and his companions. She was angry, because she had found out the boys had criminal records. She would force Tom to face facts and do something about Alex, she had had enough. But when she was finally able to get him to consider the urgency of the situation, it was during the time he had to move the goods from the wharf, so the discussion was put aside for Sunday. She made up her mind she was not going to spare Tom's feelings, she would tell him about 'Cat' and 'Dealer'. It was up to him to decide, which was more important, Alex or the store! So far it seemed like the store had won.

Then Alex disappeared Friday afternoon.

Phyl and Alex sat looking across at each other in the waiting room at the police station. He sat stony-faced, saying nothing. The thought that Alex would be charged with murder, that he was seen holding the murder weapon, brought tears to her eyes.

She cried quietly and unashamedly. It was unthinkable, no matter whatever else he did, he would never hit anyone to kill them, never! She cried as if her heart would break.

"Alex!" she said. "It's not true! I know it's a mistake. The police can say what they like, I know you didn't do it. I don t know what you were trying to prove, running around with those boys, they older than you and they're criminals." Her tears moved Alex.

"Ma, I didn't do it. I had the wood in my hand, but I didn't do it! I just went in the store behind the boys, when it happen." He started to cry too.

"What criminals you all talking about?" Tom asked, stunned. "Alexander running around with bad boys and you didn't tell me a word." He looked stricken, "Why didn't you tell me before, Phyl, why in the name of God, you didn't tell me."

Then she blew her top.

"Because you won't listen! Everytime I start to tell you something about Alex, you keep putting me off. You always knew he was going to be alright." She stormed at him, "It was always the store. The last time I managed to get you to agree to talk to Alex, the goods for the store was more important, so you left it for Sunday. Tonight is Friday night and Alex in jail. You are always too busy!"

"God Phyl, I didn't know about Alexander and these boys or else I would surely..."

"You mean you don't want to know! How could you know if you don't want to listen." She was so angry, forgetting her reason for being at the police station.

"My God! My own son on a murder charge. I was so blind... Phyl we got to get the best lawyer for Alexander. Alexander!" he spoke to Alex, "You're my son and I know you didn't..."

"Don't call me that name!" Alex said angrily, "I hate it, I hate it! Ma, I didn't do it. You know I wouldn't do it, please get me out of here," he pleaded with her.

"Who did it?" she asked, a bit more composed.

"Ma... I, I... is one of my friends! I mean.."

"Alex!" Phyl spoke gravely, "This is murder! If they were your friends you wouldn't be here 'cause at least one of them would have told the police the truth. This ain't time for petty loyalty. You could be hanged or spend the rest of your life in jail for something you didn't do. I'm sorry, but I have to put it blunt to you. For God sake boy. Think about yourself."

"Ma, the boys say, I'm a first offender and the police can't..."

"Your mother is right," Tom cut in, "If you're innocent, then some or one of the boys is guilty. What happen at the supermarket?" Father and son gazed at each other and suddenly all the past anxiety and anger disappeared.

"We were passing by these stores, the fire and the looting didn't start there yet!" Alex explained, "Then Cat said we could go in Old Choy supermarket and see what he up to. I remain standing in front while they went into the back store, I thought they know the man well. Then I heard fighting and the old man cry out. When I rush in to see what going on, old Choy was lying on the ground and Dealer was just putting a piece of green-heart on a barrel. I don't know why I pick it up. But I was telling them the man look bad and we got to get him to the hospital. Then they arguing that the man old and they can't lift he up. Then I ask Dealer if he know the man so old why he hit him, he could die from the blow and is

249

the same time the police come in and find me with the piece of wood in my hand!"

"Why the police shoot you?" Tom asked.

"They shoot Dealer and me! He tried to get away. They thought I might do the same thing. Is just a slight leg wound I get."

"Alex, they could have killed you!" his mother said. "Those boys are known criminals so the police treat you like one too. Did you tell the police what you told us just now?" she asked.

"I tried to tell them Ma, but they wouldn't listen. They say we went in there with intentions to rob the old man, because of the fire and looting going on. Ma, I didn't even go in the back store, until I hear the man cry out. The police found money hiding in Das and Marshal shirt, but I didn't have any, except the rest of my allowance and car fare to go home."

"Well, I hope you realize how serious the situation is for you especially. The boys don't care a thing about you, you should never have gone into the shop with them at all! But it happen already and I hope you learn a lesson, not one, but many,"Phyl scolded.

"Son, we'll get you the best lawyer," Tom said as they talked awhile longer with him and though he kept a cool appearance, Phyl sensed his effort not to break down again. Her heart ached for him, but she knew there was nothing they could do for him at the moment.

Later, when they got home, they repeated what Alex told them to the rest of the family; her parents, Donna and her husband, Elaine and her child's father and Pat. The sight of everyone together was too much for her and she broke down and cried. So they talked and hashed over all they knew about the best criminal lawyers, but in the back of Phyl's mind there was only one person who could make certain Alex's innocence was proven beyond all doubt. And as much as she nodded her head and agreed with the others that lawyer Baines was the best in the country, she had already made up her mind to see Hoffman.

It was bright morning by the time everyone left and Phyl told Tom about her decision to see Hoffman. "I know him well," she said trying to persuade Tom. "He would be only too pleased to know we go to him, besides he would be the best person to prove Alex is innocent."

"Is up to you, you know," Tom said, feeling guilty about the entire situation.

They went downtown to the store as usual and Tom decided he would go with her, but she pleaded with him to let her go alone, then they would go together the next time. She had never visited Hoffman's downtown office which she remembered he said he would always keep to continue practice, just in case there were a few special cases that were of interest to him.

Three other people were waiting in his office when she arrived and spoke with the secretary. There was a woman a few years older than herself who looked drawn, distraught and very anxious. She sighed and moaned continuously. Then there were two men in their mid-thirties whom she thought looked like hardened criminals but at the moment they appeared quite relaxed, with not a care in the world. One sat cross-legged, while the other leaned forward whispering in his ear. The cross-legged one kept winking at her and made remarks to his companion which she didn't catch, but whatever it was caused his companion to throw her a few kisses while he waited for her to respond. She ignored them thinking they surely didn't look as if they needed Hoffman's services.

It was getting late and Hoffman still hadn't arrived. His secretary had already explained twice to the nervous lady, that on Saturdays, Hoffman came straight to the office, he didn't go to the public buildings.

Phyl too was worried. She was tired of waiting and wanted to leave, but Alex's life was on the line, so she decided to wait. A few minutes later Hoffman came in, walking quickly past them, when he saw her, he paused.

"Well, well! What a very pleasant surprise! Mrs. Phyllis Barnes." He moved a few paces in her direction and taking her hand, holding it in a warm clasp. "And to what do I owe the pleasure of this visit?" He guided her to the door of his inner office.

"Mr. Hoffman!" his secretary said, attempting to control her annoyance. "These people were here long before, especially this lady." She handed him some slips.

"I'll see Mrs. Barnes first." He spoke brusquely as he swept Phyl inside the office and closed the door.

"Make yourself comfortable." He showed her to a chair near his desk, then took off his coat. "It's very comfortable here. There's a cosy divan behind the screen," he gestured towards the screen as he spoke, "that's my little haven, when I want to get away, relax awhile and refresh my thoughts. Girl, you look sweet!" He gazed at her intently. "Hm, you've put on weight nicely, hm hm, that man Barnes picked a winner all right and the sweetest berry." He feasted his eyes on her. "How're things? I won't ask about you, your presence is enough to tickle a man's fancy. I'm sure something serious brought you here." He sat in a swivel chair across from her.

"Yes it's very serious. My son Alex got mixed up with some bad boys and now he's charged with murder," she explained.

"Your son!" he said amazed. "You joking girl! I can't believe your scruples have been lost on your son. I'm very surprised to hear."

"It's no joke," she said. "It's in the papers. But he didn't do it." She went on to tell him what Alex told her and Tom. "I know he's innocent. Will you take the case?"

"Gladly. It would be of special interest to me, I would surely like to find out, how your son got mixed up with criminals. What happened back there between you, your son and his father, to motivate his behaviour?".... Hoffman paused, then continued.

"An interesting experience for me. Have no fear, Alex will be acquitted. But it was a foolish thing he did, when he picked up that piece of wood. Now he must stand trial. However, I'll see what I can do about bail, but this is a very sticky matter. Set your mind at rest, he won't go to jail for a crime he didn't commit."

"My God, thanks! I know I could depend on you to do it, I knew it. I feel good, what will it cost us?" she said, relieved and exceedingly pleased. "We're willing to pay whatever it costs." She saw the glint in his eyes.

"Costs!" he smiled brightly. "Not much really. Very little when you come to think of it." He got up and moved around the desk, put his hands on her shoulder, looked down deep into her eyes and she knew. The blood rushed to her head, her heart thumped quickly. His laughter deep and throaty as he continued, "You know I always had my eyes on you." He spoke in a low whisper, husky and seductive, "And the only reason I let you slip through my fingers, was I didn't want to hinder our purposes at that time. Now, no harm could be done. Well, you've been married for how long, say about twenty years. It's between you and me alone; besides there's so much at stake here."

"You mean... you want me to..." she said stunned. "I can't believe what you're saying, after all these years."

"Come on Phyl. These are modern times and old fashioned virtues are now out of place. Your son's fate hangs in the balance, you don't have too much time to decide. What's it to be? I'm not saying now. Mind you, I could buzz my secretary to get rid of the others. My dear Phyl, don't look so defeated. Everything's going to be okay." He laughed, unabashed, as if they were joking about a mutual acquaintance, his eyes shining brightly as he spoke. But she saw the lust in them and in the way he sucked in his thick upper lip. She was revolted by his wanton desires and his eagerness to satisfy his cravings. She felt numb and didn't realize she had risen from the chair; she was only aware that he held her hand and she tried hard to control herself, as he guided her to the door saying, "Relax outside for awhile, I'll talk to the other clients, then buzz for you."

She sat down in a daze, desperately trying to gather her wits. She heard the buzzer and the nervous lady got up and went in, closing the door behind her. Then she got up quickly and the words kept beating in her head, run, run, run! She didn't know what restrained her from doing just that but she knew when Hoffman buzzed for her she would be long gone.

Ma was right, she said to herself as she hurried back to the store, 'Momma tell piggy you ah come chile, you ah come'. They still had time if she hurried. She rushed through the store and into the back room where Tom was pacing up and down as he waited for the kettle he had put on to boil.

"Tom!" she rushed to him and hugged him, "I'm not going to let Hoffman handle the case anymore, I don't want anything to do with him again. Let's go quickly and see if Baines will take it."

"Phyl, something wrong?" Tom said thunderstruck. "What is it? What happen?"

"Everything, but I can't tell you now, let's hurry to Baines, before he close his office. When I know Alex case in safe hands. I'll tell you everything."

"Alright, we going now," Tom said, turning off the stove. He wanted to ask a hundred questions, but felt the strain of the past sixteen hours was beginning to tell on her and knew that whatever it was could wait.

They reached Baines office in no time and were lucky to see him. He listened to their story and agreed to take the case. This time, the fee was to be settled in dollars, which they were ready to pay.

Afterwards, in the privacy of their home, she told him everything about Hoffman, the time he rescued her from Steele, she left nothing out.

"Girl, why didn't you tell me these things before, especially what happened with you and Steele?" he said, overwhelmed. He couldn't understand politics at all. Why all this plotting and scheming, bombing, planned destruction, treachery and double dealings? What kind of people would deliberately destroy their own country, their own people, just to get what they want. Yet they call themselves intelligent men.

"Tom, I tried to tell you that same night of the story between me and Steele, but you wouldn't listen, so I decided not to bother you."

"My God, Phyl, all these years you have been loyal to a louse, a crooked scheming, double dealing, blackmailing louse, who lusted after you after all that time. I'm just glad it over and you told me everything. I'm relieved you didn't panic and give in for Alex sake."

"It's the first time you said Alex, Tom," she said in surprise.

"Well, I've been a fool in many things and the other night, when Alex tell me bluntly he hated the name, I promise myself to start practising. But I'm waiting 'till this thing is finished and I'll tell him, if he wants to, he could change his name. I won't make the same mistakes again. My family is all I have..."

"Tom, I don't think it's the name that worried Alex so much. He thought you were holding him back in the past and binding him to it, he wanted to be himself and not somebody else," she tried to explain.

"Whatever it is, he's free to change his name anytime he wants to," he said, very seriously. "But coming back to this Hoffman, I'm glad you kept your head and didn't allow that lousy bastard a chance to get at you. The idea! You go to him in trouble and that's the time he take it upon himself to take advantage of you." His temper rose, "Who the hell that son-of-a-bitch think he is atall! He think you don't have a husband who could represent you or I'm afraid of him!"

"Tom let's forget it, it's over." She tried to coax him, "Nothing happened. Forget it, 'cause he's not worth it."

"It ain't over, not by a long shot! That damn man got no conscience! I have to meet that bastard and put my hands on his throat," he vowed as he paced up and down in anger.

"No Tom, no!" She rushed to him and embraced him. "For God sake. Not for my sake or even yours, please, please leave that man alone!" she pleaded, feeling suddenly afraid. "Tom I now believe what people say about his vindictiveness. I didn't like the looks of the two men I told you I saw in his office. I'm sure they wanted to see him for something other than being in trouble with the law."

"Phyl, this is one time I got to fix this particular thing and settle it my way." He was unbending, "I'm not going to pick a fight with him, but he'd better mind, 'cause he might just get his jaws busted. He's a molester of women, hiding under the cloak of his profession. He got no respect for women as far as I'm concerned."

She knew at the moment, his anger made talk useless because he was filled with the desire for revenge. She hoped that by the time the weekend was over, the weight of Alex's predicament would help to thaw his anger and change his mood.

There is a limit to the amount of stress people could tolerate. This depends mainly on the quantity and depths of the experiences to which they're exposed and the intervening periods, during which they will grasp and deal with the situation in hand. For twenty-five years the inhabitants were subjected to uninterrupted periods of unrest of one kind or another. Political and social conditions had stimulated a hot bed of tensions. Each situation followed quickly on the heels of the other, without a break. Any temporary relief the people experienced, was due merely to the nature of the situation and how deeply it affected various groups in differing statas of the society. These periods of change, were perceived as social ills, for one group or another and whether imagined or real, provoked the people to excesses. Now they were satiated by their own actions. They had indulged to a point of over indulgence, they had drunk deep from the fountains of fear and steeped themselves in orgies of hatred. Now, they were repulsed by their own actions and the consequences which they must endure, so a new fear was born. They had experienced and witnessed obscenities and social displacements. It was a nightmare everyone wanted to forget and lived in fear of repetition or revenge. This diminished overt displays or militancy for one cause or another. It was the beginning of a gradual social withdrawal.

The city was in throes of another election. Unlike former campaigns, the rural and urban areas were now conspicuously calm and quiet. Those who had played with fire were seriously burnt and scarred, now everyone wanted peace. Gone were heated arguments, discussions, jeerings and lambastings of prospective candidates. These overenthusiastic shows of support had often led to open abuse, hostility, neighbourhood dissensions, and racial violence. The people had come of age. They had learnt the hard way that a still tongue kept a wise head, kept the head and the body in one piece. They were quiet to the point of being indifferent. Each individual, man, woman, youth or group kept their own counsel, the real drama was soon to unfold.

On polling day, long before the polling stations were opened to the public, people were patiently waiting in long weaving lines, ready to exercise their franchise. When polling began, vast numbers of middle-aged and elderly, stony-faced and serious voters, quickly cast their ballots, then hurried off to the safety of their homes. As the morning developed, there was a marked change in the mood of the voters; sombre faces were replaced by youthful, smiling countenances, the air was filled with suppressed excitement, only the smiling faces seemed privy to the reason for such unspoken delight.

"Mrs. Nelson. You been there already?" Mrs. Christian whispered surreptitiously to her next door neighbour, whom she met in the yard.

"Not yet, Mrs. Christian. And to tell you the truth, I don't feel like goin' either." Mrs. Nelson sounded disgusted.

"You can't do that," Mrs. Christian said. "This is serious business, you ain't see how things goin' in this country? Is now or never fo' we people man! You got to go."

"Look, I fed up. Poor people suffering the same way, no matter who runnin' this country." Mrs. Nelson's tone emphasised her feelings. "They could be white, black, blue, Indian, Portuguese, Chinese, is the same thing goin' to happen! Poor people goin' to get the brunt and suffer."

"You can't say that. Look how thing improve in this country since I was a girl. We got lights in the house and runnin' water. Children, everybody wearing shoes nowadays, long ago is only rich people use to wear shoes. You got to give Jack he jacket man! Things really improve."

"Hmph..." Mrs. Nelson snorted. "Like you ain't understand what really goin' on. You paying through you nose for these things and you still ending up with nothing. 'Cause when these people feel like it, they could ups and raise the prices and you always scrambling to pay bills. I ain't see anybody around here working for a fortune, that they can afford to pay these bills. Look at these light bill people. You can be a good customer fo' donkey years and look how fast they cuts off the lights if you owe them a few months. You ain't see we keeping these people in business, yet they don't care a damn 'bout we!"

"But you got to pay girl, if you want to improve you life, we can't live in darkness," Mrs. Christian said, assured it was it was a case of equal exchange.

"I know you got to pay. But is the pressure to pay out of the little you getting. They say long ago, things was bad, yet we use to pay twenty-four cents for six eggs, now one egg is twenty-four cents. A pint of milk was four cents, now is twenty cents. You tell tell me how poor people goin' to survive?"

"That is why the time is ripe now, for our own people to get a chance to change the situation for poor people," Mrs. Christian insisted.

"And you believe that, "Mrs. Nelson asked, dumbfounded by Mrs. Christian's easy conviction. "That ain't got nothing to do with it. You ain't see we poor people always goin' to be poor and full o' burden."

"But is the same thing I trying to tell you!" Mrs. Christian was becoming irritated by her neighbour's pessimistic views, "You got to trust somebody to do the right thing for you. And the only people you could trust is you own colour. So we got to make sure we put we own colour in and things goin' to be alright in due time, the Indians doin' the same thing!"

"That's a big joke. You never hear when you own bug bite you, it does bite you so hot, it swell up you skin an' give you fever?" Mrs. Nelson let out a sarcastic laugh.

"But who else you can trust, if you can't trust your own people?"

"But I ain't talking 'bout trust. I talking 'bout watching the situation and seeing the trouble we in, is more than trust," Mrs. Nelson persisted.

"Then you got to vote for somebody who you think could right the situation... You can't sit down and take it!" Mrs. Christian advocated.

"Well, we gone right back to square one. All the people I think could do something, one by one, they backing out. Look at that man who own the biggest drinks factory in the country, he paying he workers first-class wages and if he could back out what about me? Something serious had to happen to worry he fo' he to back out. After all, he in politics long and is not that he waiting 'pon the money to lie on or to get rich. Then look at all the independent people who pulling out the country or sitting down and shut they mouth. Something got to be wrong. I tell you, not me, I ain't votin' 'cause is no use and if I was the only person who fed up then I would say something wrong with me. They won't even miss my vote."

"That's the worse thing to do," Mrs. Christian said, shaking her head sadly, "think it over seriously. Whatever we views, we all got to do something, we just can't do nothin."

"Mom! You been an' vote already or you now going," Mrs. Christian's son called out as he came into the yard riding his bicycle, suspending the conversation temporarily.

"I vote already," Mrs. Christian said. "I went since early morning an' hurry back home, 'cause I don't want to be on the road when any story start. But Godfrey, what you doin' back home at this hour? I thought when you lef' work at lunch time, you went to vote and then gone back to work: is two o,clock already. What you doin' out of the people work place at this hour?"

"Gone back to work? I having a ball, but ah come back home to give you the beats. I got one more rounds to make then I goin' back to work." He kept chuckling.

"Well is what happen that got you so pleased with yourself! What's all the excitement about?" his mother asked eagerly.

"Well!" Godfrey said, "When I lef' here after lunch, I went to the polling station. After I vote and went outside, this lady come up to me: she had a set of papers with names and addresses and ask me my name. Ah tell her. This woman find my name on one of the list in a flash, then she asked me if I used to live in Cummingsburg, I nod my head. She even had we old Charlestown address too. Then she tell me I can vote again and I look at she as if she mad or something. So she tell me plenty people doing it and what I must say when I get to the polling station. Well to tell you the truth, I tell she okay, but I wasn't goin' to do nothin' like that, I was frightened! Anyhow, I go along to the polling station and when I get there, I pick up courage and the thing come off right. Well I went to the other polling station. Ah still frighten, but when I land in there, to my surprise, I see a girl that been at the first polling station. She watch me and laugh and I couldn't help laughing either!" Godfrey let go a belly laugh, "Well is now..."

"Godfrey, that is wrong!" Mrs, Nelson cut in, "It ain't no laughing matter! You can't..."

"Is what's wrong with you at all, Mrs Nelson," Godfrey said angrily. "We got to make this our time now. Them others doing it in their areas too. I hear that, besides these people plenty more than we, so we got to do something to help weself, is what wrong with black people atall."

His tone expressed the contempt he felt for Mrs. Nelson's scruples.

"Look, Godfrey boy gimme the joke yeah. You really great," Mrs. Christian said, patting him on the back. "I know you don't like better fun. So you vote three times." She was just as excited as he was.

"Three times! Mom, is what wrong with you at all!" he said with disdain. "Is then the fun begin, I vote four times and I got three more tricks to pull."

"Seven times!" Mrs. Christian said amazed, while Mrs. Nelson's jaws hung open. "You're a real smart man," Mrs. Christian crooned proudly. "You ain't even frighten."

"Frighten! Man when I go to the last polling station another woman ask me my name and we had a little discussion I tell her I did my due already. Then she asked me if I scared. How you like that? A woman asking me if I scared. So when she give me the list with the few names and addresses and the polling station where to vote, the game was on." Godfrey preened; "Then I run into Reggie at one of the polling station... and what you think he doin'? The same thing and is the women doin' it the most. So what. What's all this big fuss about?" he said, mainly to make Mrs. Nelson uncomfortable.

"They goin' to come a time, when you gun sorry you do it," she said shaking her head sadly and moaning.

"Sorry for what? Look rest yourself yeah, that's why we people don't get anywhere. Look Mom," he suddenly dismissed Mrs Nelson, "I ain't comin' home early this afternoon, me an' Reggie meeting after work for a gaff an' a few drinks, to wash the dust out we throat from this mornin' rounds. I gone yeah!" He rode off pedalling furiously, laughing with gusto.

The two women stood staring after Godfrey's diminishing form, deep in thought.

"I can tell you one thing, the young people got more sense than the big people," Mrs. Christian hinted broadly.

As usual, Phyl was at home on Tuesday morning. She felt there were lots of things on her mind which needed sorting out and foremost was Alex. The lawyer was still working to arrange bail for him and she was hopeful. Tom told her he had been to see Hoffman, but refused to tell her what passed between them; but he did remark that he made sure Hoffman would think twice the next time he wanted to put his hands on somebody else's wife. She felt the family was much closer now. She remembered how much Daphne cried for Alex, that fatal night, and for days after, she would burst into tears. She was really disturbed about Alex, so much so, she begged her father not to mention anything about the store to Alex again and he readily agreed.

Around mid-morning she heard a slight tapping coming from the back door.

"Who is it?" she called out, listening intently, she usually had no callers at this time of day.

"Is me," someone said in a small voice, then cleared his throat. "Is me, Mrs. Barnes, please open quick, please." She recognised the voice and was astounded. She opened the door and George Steele rushed in. She couldn't believe what she saw. Steele, usually immaculate, was unkempt, his hair uncombed, he looked a sight.

"Bolt the door quickly," he said, dashing past her. She was speechless, but only for a moment.

"What's the big idea, you barging into my house uninvited and knocking me off my feet, to boot! You're crazy or what? What you doing here? How you know where I'm living?" she asked angrily.

"I know where you living long ago. I pass here lots of times. I even pass by your store," he said and she recognised his bravado, now that he was inside. "You seem very content."

"I can't have you playing tricks and forcing your way into my house," she cut him off. "Get out!" She moved to open the door and he grabbed her hands.

"God girl, you can't do that to me! I'm in big trouble. This is the only place nobody would think to find me. Please Phyl, they're searching for me. I was hiding at my aunt and barely got away in time. You got to help me Phyl, please! I've got no other place to go. If you throw me out I'm a dead man, it's only a couple of days till things cool down. Hoffman's fixing things meanwhile." He hurriedly explained and she bristled at the mention of Hoffman.

"Why didn't he do that in the first place? So you come here to involve me and my family in whatever it is, so we get killed too." She spoke angrily.

"No, no, listen. I can explain." His tone was humble.

"Well, I don't want to know anything. Besides we have no room," she fumed.

"Please Phyl, I'm begging you, I know you have a storeroom downstairs and your husband don't even have to know, nobody must know," he said, reaching for her hands.

"I have no secrets from my husband." She snatched her hands away. "How dare you think I have. So that's why you come to plant yourself here. I'm going to phone him now." She moved towards the phone then to her astonishment, Steele dropped down on his knees. "Phyl believe when I tell you, if those men who're searching for me find me I'm a dead man. Just one more day and I'm safe," he implored.

"Get up off your knees," she said roughly.

But the sight of George Steele on his knees, stirred her. She had been thinking only that morning, she had been able to get rid of the past and wipe Steele and Hoffman out of her life. "You must do something terrible that they would want to kill you. So what's going to happen when they see you afterwards?" she asked.

"Phyl, I did it for our people," he began to explain and she glowered at him.

"Don't give me that," she snapped at him, "you do what you want to do."

"Phyl you got to understand. Our people didn't have a chance against them, so the committee organised another operation and I was in charge. I was able with the help of others to commandeer a few vehicles and like clockwork, we abducted the ballot boxes that were being brought in for the count. Somehow those people got wise. They recognised me so I had to hide, but I gave our people an even break. It was now or never for us."

"Whatever you do is your own problem. You got yours and I got mine. You can stay in the storeroom, until Tom comes," she added grudgingly, "but he decides whether you stay or go. If that doesn't suit you, too bad."

"Oh Phyl! I know you really don't have a hard heart," he said trying hug her. "I really regret not having more time, if I had I'm sure I would have changed your mind about me. But the best man wins for the moment," he added and she couldn't help smiling at how quickly his old arrogance returned. "Thanks a million, I won't forget this."

"Did you have anything to eat?" she asked, noticing the strain under his eyes.

"Girl, the last meal I had was last night. All I had since then was a pepsi," he confessed.

261

"I'll fix you something to eat now, then I'll give you something to take with you downstairs, and you better pray my husband says it's alright."

That evening when Tom arrived home Phyl told him about George Steele. He said he didn't like the idea of him there but agreed as he was there he could stay one more day, then he had to leave.

Conclusion

I t was already two months after the election and Hoffman had not given his customary victory speech. As far back as the people could remember, jubilant supporters rallied round their victorious candidates, who would rehash past ills as well as some of the promises they made to their enthusiastic followers. Now the people were surprised by this strange behaviour. So they gossiped and talked about the voting spree they had been on during the election, as well as the consequences of their actions, with regard to this public slight. However, this grave social disregard was quickly dealt with when, at last, a victory meeting was called.

The crowds poured down from north and south, east and west. They flocked into the city in vast numbers and invaded the Green. Men and women with babies in arms and a massive following of youth, spread out into every side street and avenue, blocking traffic. They had waited long and impatiently for this simple thank you. They had no intention of missing the event now that Hoffman was the indisputed leader of the House.

Everyone was standing in place, long before the scheduled time for the meeting to begin. The gathering was unusually quiet, not a word, not even a gesture would be missed. The chairman began his preamble and in the usual light bantering, the newly appointed ministers came forward, one after the other, made their trite promises, expressed their gratitude and went off stage or stood well back from the centre of the stage. The crowd was growing restless. They had come especially to hear the greatest of all greats and they were already besieged with half a dozen speakers, but Hoffman still hadn't put in his appearance. Their cheers had began to lose that crispness, that resounding quality which made their presence at these functions worthwhile. Then he came on, walking slowly towards them. The crowd, thinking he was now ready to respond, broke into thunderous applause but he completed his discussion with the chairman who introduced another minister, then quickly faded out of sight.

As the minister came forward he was cautiously acknowledged and given an equally cautious send off. Although he was a favourite with the people, they could not help showing their disappointment. They endured two more introductions before Hoffman came on.

As he moved forward the crowds waited, tense, uncertain whether he was ready to speak to them. The applause rained slowly as he came forward, centre stage. Then the cheers erupted with deafening intensity. The crowds roared, they literally went wild as he stood with one hand in his pocket, patiently waiting for the uproar to die down.

"My friends!" he began, his voice resonant and clear, no smile escaped his features, "I know that you have waited long and patiently for this occasion, so let's move on. I must thank you for the enthusiastic welcome you gave your ministers," he laid emphasis on the last two words, "while you awaited my appearance."

The crowd laughed.

"On the serious side however, I must warn you I'm not alone in this undertaking. We, my ministers and I, and you, we are all involved. This is no easy task ahead of us and we have to tighten our belts in order to achieve our goals. Nation building is an uphill task so there's no time for light-hearted banter. Are you with me?" he shouted.

"Yeah, yeah!" the crowd roared.

"Are you with me?" he shouted again.

"Yeah, yeah!" they roared again. "We with you!" they replied in unison.

"Then those who are not with me are against me," he added and the crowd chuckled, as he continued.

"It's a simple matter, simple logic, if you're not for me, then it could only mean that you're against me. Let me tell you here tonight," he said in a conversational tone, "I know all of you who are for me and all those who are against me, great and small."

The crowd chuckled at this revelation and he joined in, but his laugh was without mirth.

"Ah ha! You want to know how I know eh!" he grinned again, still not amused.

"As I stand here tonight, let me tell you I know about all the so-called big ones who are against me. You want to know how I know eh? Let me tell you this secret. They're fighting tooth and nail to hold on to their jobs. That's how I know, yes! I can't rest for the telephone calls early in the morning and late at night. They keep calling to give me the names of their so-called friends, who are against me. Now in their hour of need, they're trying to protect themselves! Yes the Judases of this world are working round the clock to hold on to their jobs, for dear life."

The crowd now sensed he was not amused, although his manner was nonchalant.

"I know a dear arch enemy of mine. This man is one of our top-notch civil servants. I'm not talking about little people like you and me."

The crowd loved this analogy and howled with derision.

"This big shot has openly declared, that the day I run this country, it would be in ruins and he getting out. But let me tell you a secret," he said in a conspirational tone. "Right now he can't keep close enough to the toilet, for the runs he got to make."

The crowd burst into raucous laugher and when the guffaw died down, he continued. "I tell you, he'd better put on his running shoes an' head north, where he's certain things are better." Then he bellowed, "All ye that have ears to hear let them hear! New broom sweep clean. Yes, I can't rest for the number of calls I get, every day and night from patriotic citizens who want favours. They want jobs for their sons or jobs for their daughters. They want scholarships for their nephews and for their nieces. I am hounded night and day. These things take time. And they have to be viewed in their proper perspective." His tone was reprimanding, "These bowings and scrapings go on unchecked around the clock. This nonsense must stop," he said sharply. "I must prevent them. These couchings and these lowly courtesies might fire the blood of ordinary men, and turn pre-ordinance and first decree into the law of children. Be not fond to think that I," he thumped his chest, "bear such rebel blood that will be thawed from the true quality with that which melted fools. I mean, sweet words, low crooked curt'sies and base spaniel fawning. If thou dost bend and pray and fawn I spurn thee like a cur, out of my way," he railed at them and the crowd now sensed his anger, although they chuckled to hide their discomfort. Then he turned on them.

"You laugh! Haw haw..." He glared down at them, "How you laugh... I have also heard your talk! There are many among you who came running pell mell to see me after election, to talk about your petty patriotism and your burning ambitions. One bold fellow had the audacity to ask me, why I'm taking so long to hold the victory meeting? He remarked that afterall, the people were patriotic and thanks wasn't too much to give." He paused looking down into the crowds with a slow, sweeping, penetratingly cold stare, then he let go.

"I see you standing there like Greeks bearing gifts, waiting for your commendations and patriotic pats on the back but whatever I have achieved, it's through my own brains!" he raged. "I repeat and don't ever forget, it's through my own brains!" He tapped his forehead repeatedly as they stood silent, unthinking, unmoving, listening like obedient children and he went on, his face contorted with rage.

"I know all about you. I know exactly who you are. I know your mother, father, sister, brother, uncles, aunts and all the rest. And the time for that is sooner than you think. No name! No warrant! Who the cap fit draw the string," he said with venom.

And a silence fell upon the astonished crowds, broken only by the soulful crying of an infant, perhaps a signal of distress, helplessness, insecurity, a disturbance of the psyche, a plea for protection and comfort, a presentiment of the perversion of social interest. Then, as if in identification and empathy with his plight, others too, instinctively joined in the wailing.

Epilogue 1974

"**M**a, I'm going down to the store tomorrow morning. So if you want you can stay home and relax. You don't have to rush down there on Saturdays anymore, Dad and I could open up for you."

It was Friday night and Daphne was out for the evening, with the gang; Eric was curled up in a chair reading, while the rest of the family were sitting around, relaxed.

"Alex, you're sure that's what you want to do right now?" Phyl asked, surprised.

"Is okay Dad?" he asked his father, smiling at their reactions.

It was only a week since he had been released. He had cried bitterly at that moment and again when he heard the long sentences the others had drawn. They had finally admitted that Alex had remained in the front of the shop, when they had gone into the back room. The family never doubted his innocence. And things had returned to normal in the house.

They talked about the store when he was around, but were careful that none of the talk was directed to him. The constant bickering between Alex and Eric had ceased. Tom had remarked about it, but Phyl felt it was too soon to tell. Right now, they were just getting used to each other again. But the most important thing, was that the crisis was over and whatever else happened to them as a family, it couldn't be worse.

"Look Alex, don't bother yourself with the store." Tom spoke in a friendly manner, "We don't want you to do anything because you feel you owe us anything. You don't."

"Dad, you called me Alex. But I prefer if you call me Alexander," he said in a penitent manner.

"Well, you said you hated the name. So I was practising." Tom glanced at Phyl and they smiled that intimate smile which is shared between husband and wife.

"Dad, I really didn't mean it. I was angry with you and everybody and everything, I'm sorry. I would rather you call me Alexander because nobody else does, that way I know it's my father."

"Well, son," Tom said smiling, "I was thinking, what plans you have for yourself, even if you hang around the store for awhile, what you plan to do about your own career?"

"Well... I... I mean... to tell the truth I always wanted to be a teacher, but now I don't know, well, after what happen, if I stand a chance of being accepted."

"Well you never know. So let's wait and see what happens. Life keep changing all the time and things keep changing too You might be a teacher yet, remember you're still very young; you have lots of time ahead of you. I'm sure you'll complete what I started long before you were born," Phyl remarked, then said to Tom, "George Steele left this with Eric this afternoon." She took a small white envelope from her pocket, which she handed to Tom, he opened it and read the note inside.

"Thanks. Conferred with Steele. Heard the news. Good luck to you and your son. Your husband is one hell of a man, but what was said was done in jest."

Signed L.C.H.

"More likely he meant a dirty joke!" Tom said handing the envelope back to her, while they both laughed.

"Tom, man tell me what you said to him?" she coaxed. "Nah, let's forget that man. Some people got a knack for influencing others, but he," Tom's anger was stirred, "got a capacity for evil, he downright wicked!" His voice cracked like thunder.

"That's putting it mildly," Phyl said. Her thoughts flew back to the first meeting of the Committee, so very long ago, yet the images were clear in her mind as yesterday. How he had tricked and used her for his own ends. Phyl felt bitter and ashamed. Step by step he had spread the net for her and the many angry thousands like her, who were disillusioned by the colonialists. He had enticed them with dangerous promises and they had followed him blindly. He had planned and plotted for his own gain and at the expense of the people. Something in Phyl's stomach began to rise. "Tom, we get rid of the British," Phyl choked, "But we're right in his covetous hands."

Glossary

Bajan - a person born in Barbados.

Dead runner - when there is a death at the hospital, the dead runner runs and carries news to the family.

Douglah - a person of half Indian and half African descent.

Green - a huge open land outside Bourda market used for public meetings.

Jordanites - a religious sect living in Guyana, not affiliated to any of the traditional Christian churches.

Kabaka - an African king of Uganda.

Kokers - Dutch irrigation canals.

L.C.P. Fair - League of Coloured Peoples Fair. An arts and crafts exhibition organized by upper class Black nationalists.

Mazaruni - a tributary in the Essequibo.

Porkknockers - golddiggers.

Sappadilla - a fruit the size of a small apple with a brown skin, the inside of which is a succulent sweet pulp.

Skylark - making fun, wasting time.

Stan' pipe - vertical pipes maintaining running water at a central point.

Trench corner - streets with Dutch canals.

Water works - hydro

Child-father - the father of a child, usually unmarried.